Frances Courtenay Baylor

Behind the blue ridge

A homely narrative

Frances Courtenay Baylor

Behind the blue ridge
A homely narrative

ISBN/EAN: 9783743367661

Manufactured in Europe, USA, Canada, Australia, Japa

Cover: Foto ©Andreas Hilbeck / pixelio.de

Manufactured and distributed by brebook publishing software (www.brebook.com)

Frances Courtenay Baylor

Behind the blue ridge

BEHIND THE BLUE RIDGE.

A HOMELY NARRATIVE.

BY

FRANCES COURTENAY BAYLOR,

AUTHOR OF "ON BOTH SIDES," ETC.

———

PHILADELPHIA:

J. B. LIPPINCOTT COMPANY.

1887.

BEHIND THE BLUE RIDGE.

I.

"Is not the life of every such man a Tragedy made up of Fate and one's own Deservings?"—CARLYLE.

LEADING through a rocky pass in the Blue Ridge—a pass dust-choked in summer, snow-blocked in winter—is a road that seems just the ordinary prosaic highway of the country,—laid out by an engineer, built by a turnpike company, used as a connecting link between the beautiful Valley of Virginia and the world lying on the other side of the mountains. But it is something more. It is wide enough now for two or more carriages to pass each other on it without difficulty. It was originally a faint trail, growing ever more distinct with use, made by the buffalo that went pushing and trampling and trotting along it; by the deer daintily picking their way among some of its obstructions and leaping gracefully over others; by surly, slow-moving bear taking their own time for the journey. Panthers glided swiftly over it, rabbits darted across it, wolves lurked beside it, flocks of wild turkeys flopped or strutted along it morning and evening; the fox, the lynx knew it, as did every bird and beast in the whole country-side. And a creature that added the instinct of all these animals to an acute human intelligence knew it, too, for the Shawnees used it. And so the sun rose and set on it; the anemones and fern-fronds and wind-flowers beside it knew when spring came, although there was not an almanac within hundreds of miles; the sumac and golden-rod proclaimed that it was autumn; the years came and the years went. Over it now came that gallant company of gentlemen-adventurers, the "Knights of the Horseshoe," "in search of the Mississippi and other wonderful and glorious discoveries that shall redound to the glorie of God and the King." They had been sent out by the House of Burgesses, blessed by the chaplain of His Majesty's forces, wept over by the brightest eyes in the colony. They were splendidly equipped, and were ready to do and dare everything that could make the golden horseshoe badge they wore shine in history, and, under the leadership of Governor Spottiswood, they planted the royal standard on the highest peak of the Blue Ridge. "They are looking for *me*," thought the trail. "I knew I shouldn't be buried alive always. Thank Heaven, I am discovered!" This meant civilization, and the Shawnees began to bend and straighten their arrows more carefully than ever. Presently, at long intervals, came pioneers in small companies of two or three, well armed and vigilant, feeling every breeze that stirred to be charged with meaning, hearing a death-knell often in the echoes of the rocks that rang under their horses' hoofs and the branches that cracked beneath their weight, seeing an Indian in every shadow that fell and every leaf that rustled; scenting danger in everything, yet delighting in daring the worst. The buffalo did not like this, and showed it by seeking out other and more circuitous, secluded ways of getting

into the valley. Small trains of pack-mules filed along
it now, bringing a few precious packages and a breath
from the outer world once or twice in the twelvemonth.
The trail knew now that it was a road, grass-grown,
seldom traversed, not always clearly marked out, but
still a road, never again a trail. High-shouldered
wagons were soon pushing aside impeding boughs, laden
with rude household stuff, with children's faces peeping
from under the hood, and a dog trotting alongside and
dashing occasionally into the undergrowth after a rabbit.

"Come one! come all! The more the merrier. It's
a dull life I've been leading," thought the road, and took
the greatest interest in the events of each day, and
looked eagerly at every traveller, and though it was
keenly mortified by their comments on its roughness,
or its length, or the steepness of its declivities, it was
delighted with the improvement in its condition. But,
disgusted by these oft-recurring and unwarrantable in-
trusions, all the animals abandoned their ancient right
of way, and were twitted by the birds (who remained)
with cowardice. The squirrels frisking up into the tops
of the trees saw vehicles a-many roll by now in ever-
increasing variety and numbers. The grass gave up
the battle and retired from the field. The road felt
that it could not be mistaken for anything but a road
again, and that he who ran, or rather drove, must see at
a glance that it was a highway of importance; but it
longed for quiet sometimes. Armies of red-coats came
tramp, tramp, tramping over it after a while, following in
the wake of the knights and carrying the same standard.

A little time passed, and then, to the astonishment
and indignation of the road, wagon-loads of stone were

dumped along its whole length. "Good heavens! what does this mean?" it thought. "I am ruined forever! What on earth do I want with all that abominable stuff when people are always complaining of the few stones that I've always had? What are they going to do with it?" It soon found out; for next day an army of men in masks seated themselves on these heaps, hammer in hand, and having pounded them into bits, spread them evenly across its surface, and then having rolled an enormous iron cylinder across that, went their way, boasting, with the utmost effrontery, of what they had done for "the old road." Crushed to the earth, the road could only submit and rail out its grief to the whole valley. "This is what comes of having anything to do with *man*," it said. "Think of what I have done for him, and look how he has served me,—worse than the very beasts! I might as well have been a rock! I that used to be as green as a May meadow, and that had white violets and wild-roses blooming on both sides of me, and anemones and strawberries and laurel and all kinds of lovely flowers and fruits growing *down the middle!* And now look at me, covered from end to end with this hard stone and filthy dust! Now I am indeed buried alive! I that complained of the buffalo have been trampled to death,—yes, had all the life pressed out of me forever by that hideous mountain on wheels that they passed over me again and again."

The road was now a turnpike, but dead it was not;— more alive than ever, on the contrary, in one way, for all its heart was broken, and it was only the stone effigy of its old self. The ever-changing, ever-moving procession went on over its grave at least, as it does over all graves,

—armies of blue-coats now; other armies of gray-coats; parks of artillery that were almost as bad as the cylinders; regiments of horse thundering forward; regiments of foot falling back; couriers galloping madly hither and thither; trains of wagons a mile long creaking along to camp or capture, with a limping group of stragglers acting as volunteer escort, their fortunate muskets sticking out from the canvas interior where the poor fellows longed to be riding; ambulances carrying the wounded to the rear; general officers, with the staff curveting and caracoling and reconnoitring; guilty citizens on foot flying to the mountains; guiltless citizens hurried off in handcuffs; peaceable farmers in carts getting twice as much as they should for vegetables; frightened women walking away from burning houses, leading little children by the hand.

The road got tired to death of it all as it gleamed white and dusty in the sunshine. It sighed for the days when it was an obscure, dewy, leafy trail, and thought the war would never be over, and looked up at the patient stars in mute despair. But it did come to an end at last, which deceived the road into thinking that peace had come for it as well as for the country. But in this it was mistaken. The procession, somewhat changed in character, went on, only with less demonstration; still goes on, and ever will. Now it is a pair of lovers in a smart gig spinning briskly along to the county fair; the doomed invalid drawn slowly along in an open barouche that he may get a little wan pleasure from country sights and sounds, with his solicitous relatives all about him and Death in the rumble; the farmer perched high on his wood-wagon crawling at a snail's

pace towards the nearest market-town as he lazily cracks
a long whip over horses that go their own sober way,
or returning home, perhaps, singing and shouting,
shaking his head, lashing his horses, his rustic wits and
hard-won wage both gone; the schoolboy whistling
merrily as he whirls down-hill on his new bicycle; the
good doctor's buggy bowling rapidly away in mortal
haste towards this or that neighboring farm-house; the
shackling, heavy-bodied stage-coach which rattles over
its twenty miles or more in a ponderously-lively fashion
that allows the summer tourist to patronize the scenery,
and the South generally, quite at his leisure.

Governor Spottiswood's tramontane expedition had
not long gone its romantic way when there came over
the mountain trail an English sailor-pioneer named
John Shore. He was a large-framed, light-hearted Au-
tolycus of a wanderer, who had left his own country
for the El Dorado that was waiting to be inherited by
the brave and adventurous across the Atlantic. Settling in New England, he tried being everything by
turns and nothing long for some years, and then finding
that it did not differ materially from old England so
far as any improvement in his fortunes was concerned,
and feeling himself decidedly out of sympathy with its
strictly respectable and sternly religious atmosphere,
he " weighed anchor," as he phrased it, and again followed a beckoning Fortune over hill and dale until
she led him into the wilderness. The valley he had
entered was almost an unbroken forest. It had once
been a great lake that increased in volume until it
burst through the encompassing mountains at the
point now called Harper's Ferry, and ran its triumphant

course through the Potomac into the ocean beyond. The whole district of country of which it formed a part was the final expression of King James's liberal sentiments towards the London Company, and extended " westward to the Pacific Ocean and for a hundred miles into the sea beyond." It was so little known that it was not until 1778 that the geographical effort of defining the whole State of Illinois as "a county" was made. It was just the time and place for our pioneer ; this era of large views and hazy proprietorship was the golden age of which he had dreamed, in which everything was to be had for the taking. He had left nothing behind him except the memory of an unhappy home and a succession of experiences which he chose to call failures and misfortunes, but which had more than once brought him to the stocks and the whipping-post, heavy punishments for light offences being the justice of the period. The trouble had been that everything had belonged to somebody else. He saw it clearly now. He had brought with him only a stout heart, a good gun, and a sagacious dog, but he was in a country in which land was held in fee simple. He had only to choose an estate to suit him and keep it as he had won it. He felt the embarrassment of riches, and could not decide for a day or two where to "locate" with all the forest before him to choose from. It hardly seemed worth while to appropriate anything where all was his. He had been long enough in the New World to learn some woodcraft, and he had a fine natural intelligence,—two important possessions when the site of a future home is to be chosen. At last, after prowling about extensively, looking at the sit-

uation, soil, advantages offered by various places (as
determined by certain tests of his own not known to
the modern surveyor, such as examining the bark on
the trees, dipping his fingers in water and holding them
up to see which way the wind blew, and the like), he
fixed upon a certain spot on Little South Mountain
that particularly pleased him.   It was primarily a
splendid grove of oaks.   It commanded an extensive
and beautiful view.   A mountain-stream ran by it as
pure as though its every drop had been filtered, as
cold as though it had been iced, as sparkling as though
it had been just air-bewitched.   It was sheltered from
the prevailing north and northwest winds, as he had
ascertained by the primitive but effective plans already
mentioned.   All these were points so much in its favor
that he eagerly proceeded to mark it for his own.
This he did literally.   He ran as lightly as a squirrel
up a certain fine beech in the grove.   When about
forty feet above the earth he took a hatchet from his
belt and struck several lusty blows that all the listening
forest heard.   They rang out in cheerful defiance on
the still air, and were given back in surprised melody.
The moist chips dropping on the earth sent the scared
lizards like green flashes across the grass into their
hiding-places.   It was the knell of fauns, and dryads,
and elves, if any such were about, and of the Indians
who, all unconscious of their doom, were revelling in
the excitements of their great yearly chase not far
away.   Gone were chiefs, squaws, papooses, wigwams,
moccasins, calumets, tomahawks, from that moment.
The new kingdom had come.

As for John Shore, he dropped to the green sward

below, and when he had marked several other trees in the vicinity in a way that he thought he could not fail to recognize, he took his bearings again carefully, looked about him with an air of satisfied ownership, and departed as he came from the valley, the season being autumn and unfavorable to immediate settlement.

Early in the following spring he was back again, bringing with him a train of heavily-laden pack-horses, and accompanied by three men whose minds he had inflamed by his description of the land he had spied out.

These hardy adventurers, like their brave brother-pioneers all over the country, now set to work courageously to plant the acorn of this our American civilization,—a mighty oak now, which may yet be five hundred years coming to perfection. God save it from decay!

The wolves were soon howling at night around rude log cabins set great distances apart in the valley. The aborigines, who, according to the learned Mr. Nicholas Fuller, are "the posterity of our great-grandfather Japheth," found themselves obliged to tolerate a branch of their family giving good presumptive proof of being relatives in their willingness, even stern determination, to share the family inheritance. John Shore, especially, was soon very widely known among them as "Long Knife," and respected as a brave man and mighty hunter, whom it would be a positive pleasure to scalp. But he, for his part, kept his powder dry, and showed himself a match for them at every point. For three years he played the dangerous game of a life for a life with them, and hunted, and fished, and shot, and

2

rode, and bade fair to become as savage as any Shawnee of them all. And then, yielding to a vagrant impulse, he went off into Pennsylvania for awhile. He was not gone long, and when he returned he went to work in earnest to build a house on the site selected. Being an Englishman, he had his own fixed ideas on most subjects, including house-building, and, being an obstinate man, he was bent on carrying them out. He had no intention of putting up a frail shanty that would "tumble about his ears in a few years; and might blow down any day." If it was a question of that sort of temporary shelter, he preferred a tarpaulin, he said. So he took his axe and hatchet and gun and went off day after day for some months to a neighboring grove, where he propped his gun against a tree and worked with a will, choosing every bit of his wood carefully, and whistling "Bess of Bednall-Green" as he wrought it into the shape and size required. When he had got all the necessary material and had seasoned it, he put up, with a little aid, a well-built, substantial two-roomed cottage of a pattern familiar to him. He had seen such in many an English lane, and when he had put on its steep overhanging roof (which took some time, and kept him "up aloft" much longer than he had expected), and had got a tiny porch in front of it, and a shed at the back, and a rail-fence around it, he was a proud and happy man. Nor was this all. He took incredible pains with his rafters and puncheon floor, and skilfully daubed and chinked the interior. He inserted one precious pane of glass in the stout, cross-barred wooden shutter. He put up some shelves in a way that would not have disgraced a skilled workman. And then, with the "handiness" of the sailor, he set about making some rude furniture, consisting chiefly of a kitchen-dresser, a settee, a table, and some hide-bottomed chairs, and succeeded in that, too. A sociologist would have known what was to come next. Given a man and a house, and what follows? A woman, of course. John Shore swept up his shavings, locked his door, put the key in his pocket, and went off straightway in search of that woman. It was not a search, either, exactly, for he had seen in his previous absence a remarkably pretty Dutch girl, very blue as to the eyes and flaxen as to the tresses, knitting in the court-yard of a certain wayside inn in Pennsylvania; and though he had only exchanged a few words with her, it was she who had inspired his recent labors. The wooing was a remark-ably brief and entirely successful one. In a week he brought the inspiration back, and that with her father's blessing, and mounted on top of her mother's feather-bed, tricked out in all her simple finery and still knit-ting on the particular pair of stockings on which she had been engaged when her impetuous suitor swept down upon her and bore her off. In this way one of the first families of Virginia, in actual practical preced-ence, if not in the aristocratic sense, was founded.

A small stream of new-comers now began to filter family by family over the Ridge, and in a few years the settlement of the country had become an accomplished fact. When the boundary-line between the States of Virginia and Pennsylvania was run after the Revolu-tion, the commissioners so far respected the "tomahawk rights," as they were called, of the early settlers as to allow four hundred acres to every claim of the kind.

This was a respectable property for a small farmer if it had been at all valued or preserved as it should have been. But in the majority of cases it was not. If it was not gambled or raced or thrown away like the large estates of from ten to fifty thousand acres owned by the gentry from the low-country, it was, in its degree, as foolishly managed, or rather mismanaged,—fifty good, broad acres being exchanged freely for a cow and calf, a horse and wagon, or any other possession coveted by the petty proprietors. Gradually the early settler was pushed off by the growth of the new civilization just as the Shawnee had been. The free life (whose worst pains are preferred by some men to the best pleasures that the most sophisticated sybarite could offer) died out,—a mode of existence more congenial to the natural man than any other, having for its gravest duty the cultivation, in odd half-hours, of "a corn-patch" and the garden on which the women-folk insisted, and for its daily compensation getting "to the leeward" of your game and bringing down a wild turkey, bear, three-pronged buck, or Indian chief, as the case might be.

The country filled up with a different class of people altogether: canny Scotch-Irish colonists; Germans from the Middle States, thick-headed, horny of hand; a band of Quakers, involuntary emigrants these, like the babies crowing in cradles hollowed out of large logs,—sly Friends suspected of trading with the enemy, and summarily sent to the rear to meditate on the harshness of "George Washington, that man of war;" a troop of Hessians brought down by that doughty old warrior, General Morgan, who made them turn their swords into trowels and pickaxes and build him a fine house before being disbanded. Dull care had come, and toil, and taxes, and trouble,—in short, civilization. The country was free, but the people were no longer so, and the pioneer, with the Shawnee and the buffalo, vanished forever from Virginia.

* * * * * * * * * *

The valley could not go, and so it stayed at home and got more and more beautiful steadily for a century, more carefully tilled, fertile, gracious of aspect, until it is a wonder its heart was not lifted up as well as its hills as it sat in the sunshine a thousand feet above the sea, girdled by its mountains, glorified by its woods, illuminated by the long-shining curves of the Shenandoah, "daughter of the stars."

And John Shore's house remained. He had builded better than he knew. It looked a weather-beaten structure enough in the brilliant October sunshine; but it had held its own bravely, considering that it was not founded upon a rock and had long been exposed to every wind of heaven. If it spread itself somewhat, somewhere about the time that the last oak of the grove that had screened it fell, it was only to get a better hold on the earth. And it was in making this effort to accommodate itself to its changed circumstances that it lost its compact air and got a loose and irregular expression, which showed that it had entered upon a struggle for existence that made it careless of appearances. It settled down in the rear and hugged the hillside in a way that made the front porch lean in a panic against the wall. The front door, unprepared for and alarmed by such a demonstration, tried to get out of the way, but only succeeded in straining its

b   2*

hinges so that it ever afterwards swung in at a most dissipated angle and outward with great difficulty. The chimney outside went crazy on the spot, and fancied itself a pyramid, and did its best to assume that shape, running up in a wavy line irresolutely for a certain distance, and then stopping and trying to throw stones down on the heads of people passing below. The whole structure was enveloped in a mantle of Time's own weaving,—a sort of atmosphere made visible,—a surtout, pinned on with lichens and fungi that matched so perfectly that they were never noticed by careless observers; marvels of workmanship all the same, olive-green, or gray, for the most part, brown occasionally, and very semi-occasionally crimson, or orange, and fashioned in imitation of other growths, such as a rose, or a miniature forest of firs. But the house was still a good house, and, in its modest way, a comfortable home, which could not be said for the clusters and rows of tumble-down shanties that stretched along the mountain-side, and together made a blur on the fair landscape. No Highland shieling or Russian isba or Colorado "claim shack" could have been more dismally suggestive of wretchedness than those hovels and their outlying "appertainments." Nothing could equal their forlornness unless it was their inhabitants,—that swarm of free-born but fate-fettered American citizens not to be insultingly classified as "peasants," but as poverty-stricken and miserable as the humblest vine-dresser or goat-herd that ever languished under a monarchy, owned allegiance to king or lord, and confessed himself a vassal or serf. A strip of land belonged to each: a few acres of stony ground that a respectable South-

down would have sniffed at contemptuously, running
up towards the crest of the mountain, where a thin
fringe of woods showed against the sunset red,—all
that the axe and the torch had spared of the primeval
forest. If a Shawnee ghost ever left the happy hunting-
grounds to revisit his old home and haunts, it must
have found great difficulty in identifying what it had
left with what it found; and as for John Shore, he never
could have recognized the high-arched, leafy, dewy
covert in which he had set his home in that barren
slope, wind-swept, sun-parched, rock-ribbed. But another spirit from the land of shades might have found
cause for admiration and gratulation in one feature of
the neighborhood,—that governor of Virginia who, in
1651, issued a proclamation commanding that public
thanksgiving should be made for " the increase of children that God Almightie hath vouchsafed to this Colony."
There were children, children, children everywhere,—
little and big, ugly and pretty, sickly and hardy, merry
and melancholy, mischievous and sober, daring and
timid children,—children of all ages, both sexes, and of
every conceivable variety of disposition and looks, oozing
ubiquitously out of every pore of the place, and seeming
as much the prodigal expression of a carelessly-bounti-
ful nature as the ox-eyed daisies and blue thistles of the
meadow-fields at the foot of the mountain. Never did
a blessing so run riot. And, like curses, they invariably
came home to roost under a roof that sheltered so many
other blessings that it was wonderful how they ever
found refuge there, although, like the wild-flowers again,
they did not wait to be set in the carefully-prepared beds
of a nursery, but dropped off for the most part wher-

ever they chanced to be when it was time for lids and petals to close, falling softly down on the hard floor, where they made small heaps of tattered, tanned, bare-footed innocents, and sank into the sleep full "of sweet dreams and health and quiet breathing" denied often to Dives on his bed of down.

"Happy is the man that hath his quiver full," it is written, but plus fourteen arrows and minus as many shekels, and skepticism sifts in sometimes under the door-sills and down the chimneys. Yet it is not in such households that Herodian views of children are held as a rule, and number fifteen is often more cherished and better loved in them than any of its predecessors.

The Shores had not died out of the land, but a super-abundance of olive-branches could not have been said to have caused the decay in the family fortunes which had reduced them to the level of their neighbors. In no generation had there been more than four children in the house that Sailor Jack had built, and the John Shore of 1846 was the only son of an only son. In some respects he might have been pronounced his own ancestor, representing as he did that differentiation of the Shore species which had produced a new variety. As a freak of nature or a scientific result, he might have taken a prize at some botanical show had he been vegetable in origin, so widely did he differ from and so closely resemble the parent-stock. But unfortunately the doctrine of "heredity" was not known on the moun-tain. The most agreeable novelty would have been suspected long and challenged over and over again be-fore being accepted in that conservative community, and with this one the initial shock of surprise was never succeeded by the flush of gratification. The mountain first and last held John Shore strictly responsible for all he was and said and did, which was more than the angels ever thought of doing, and the result was that—well, there were a good many results, as will appear later. As a child, he was not understood or altogether approved of. And then he had grown into a gawky lad who led the horses home from pasture with branches of wild honeysuckle fastened in their bridles,—a lad that made himself a "cornstalk" violin (on which he was forever picking out such melodies as he heard around him or as suggested themselves to him), and liked to repeat such of his mother's hymns as had any imaginative flights in them. "Flowers and fiddlin' and sich ways never come to no good yet," said the elders, and shook their unutterably wise heads, and began to predict the end from the beginning. They continued to shake them when he came to manhood, and developed a passion for shooting and fishing, and spent weeks at a time off by himself in the woods, in harvest season as like as not, and played more than ever on the cheap wooden affair, with a head like a rocking-horse, for which he had paid five dollars, and believed to be the finest instrument in the world. *They* never had any vagrant impulses, and he was as full of them as a swallow; they had no love for music, and he could repeat every strain he heard as easily as a mocking-bird; they saw the sun get up and go down, but never saw it rise or set in fifty years, while he had been gifted with the seeing eye as well as the hearing ear. They never any more thought of gathering a bouquet than of wrapping themselves up in a cloud; he knew the face of every flower for leagues around (and of every tree and shrub and bush for that matter), and was in the habit of going about with a collection of berries and seeds and bulbs in his pockets with which he experimented at home. He had been *seen* to pin a wild rose in the front of his "butternut" coat. But matters did not come to a crisis until somebody told the elders that John Shore could repeat all the psalms of David. That struck them as scandalous. "There's *preachers* as has been preachers for *forty* year that can't do as much, and him not a perfessin' Christian," said one of them, Jake White, in discussing the indecent achievement. "Preachin' is preachin', and perfessin' is perfessin', and ploughin' is ploughin', and fiddlin' is fiddlin'. And, moreover, *my* advice to that there young man is to drop that ere *bow* of his'n and take up that there *hoe* of his'n. And why? Causen he'll never come to a pea's pod ef he don't."

Jake considered himself, and, indeed, was regarded, as the great authority in all religious matters on the mountain, perhaps because of his wide experience in them. Beginning his spiritual career as a "Lutherian," he successively accepted the tenets of a half-dozen sects, so nice was he in the matter of theological tenet, and had been by turns a Methodist, an "Ironside Baptist," a "thin-skin Baptist," a Dunkard, and what he called a "close-communion Christian."

He had been baptized once and "sprinkled" once and "immerged" twice. He had been converted and per-verted, and had reverted over and over again. He had what he called "the searchin's,"—meaning attacks of spiritual uneasiness and doubt to which he was liable.

at any time when the last creed he had "perfessed" began to get too tight for him, and the sap of his soul was rising and burgeoning preparatory to blossoming in a new form. So far from being ashamed of these constant changes in his views, he was proud of being, as he phrased it, "a Seeker," and he declared repeatedly that what he was looking for was *Vital Religion*, and that he never would be satisfied until he got it. He was perfectly stolid under the comments and criticism, kindly or contemptuous, that assailed him. He accepted it openly as part of " what he had to go through with," and what that was he said nobody would ever know. This position was impregnable, and he thought and talked so much about his soul that finally everything was conceded to that remarkably fine, large, sensitive principle that even he could have claimed for it, and he came to be regarded as a most uncompromising and devoted disciple of the highest form of truth, and got no small credit for his inability to be content with the lower ones. When the preliminary pains of the mysterious and mournful malady to which he was subject set in, as was shown by his retirement from the world, and, above all, by the silence that was wont to envelop him while he brooded over the unutterable (a silence all the more impressive because of his habitual loquacity), much sympathy was felt for " Brother White," who, for his part, regretted the sorrowful necessity he was under to question the previously accepted order of things more than anybody, and, try as he would, could give no one the least idea of what he was suffering in his "inside," by which term he meant to indicate the seat of his metaphysical conflicts. And when, after some weeks, "the searchin's" found triumphant, if temporary, expression and profession of some sort, all the mountain crowded to "meetin'" to hear the result of the late engagement between the forces of Vital Religion and this or that "Church." For "Jake," it was agreed, was "a powerful hand at givin' experience." He had had so much of it that he could afford, perhaps, to be more liberal with it than most people, and while some less experienced Christian would get up and shut his eyes and clear his throat, and hem, and haw, and blush, and gasp, and hold convulsively to the last sentence uttered while he felt around in his mind for another, Jake would rise slowly and half closing his eyes let his body sway gently backwards and forwards for a few moments, and then pour out a perfect stream of thoughts, and feelings, and sentiments, and presentiments, and "warnings," and "awakenings," and "gropings," and "groanings" that made him the wonder and admiration of the whole congregation. A long course of sermons from "preachers" of every denomination had given him all the resources that cant or rant, or real, if rough, eloquence could supply, and the phrases he had picked up sounded curiously enough sandwiched in his everyday speech; but when it came to an "experience" they stood him in good stead,—so much so that his friends often urged him to "go on the circuit," to which he would reply by giving his head a mournful shake, and saying, "No, no. I am a *Seeker,—a Seeker,*" as if feeling his liability to be smitten by the sword of speculation at any moment.

Now John Shore, in a community in which children of six were repeatedly "convicted," convinced that is, that they were, as the phrase went, "the vilest of the vile," and, overwhelmed by the blackness of their guilt, retired behind the wood-pile to bewail privately for hours their unutterable wickedness, or asked their relatives to pray for their "poor, lost souls," because they might die that night and go straight to a place which is notoriously full of children—John Shore, I say, living in this atmosphere, never thought about his soul at all, but enjoyed in the body every moment of his existence at this period in a way that could not but have been aggravating to a man of Brother White's spiritual sensibility. And at last he did a thing that made that gifted Christian most uncharitably and finally sure that he "never would come to no good forever and ever, Amen." He married the prettiest girl on the mountain,—a sweet-faced young creature, with unusually long eyelashes shading a fine pair of large, serious gray eyes,—an embodiment of fair and tranquil womanhood, low-voiced as a wood-pigeon and as gentle as a nun. Brother White was thinking of doing the same thing, it is true, *en troisième noces*, and ought not to have regarded it as an unpardonable offence, considering the temptation; but circumstances certainly alter cases. Perhaps he thought that a person of her grave temperament would find a soul more attractive than any mere body could be, and would not be affected by the meretricious charms of a hopelessly frivolous, if handsome, youth. His disappointment made him eloquent in prediction in talking over the affair with a group of his neighbors. "He ain't the man for her," said he. "And wherefore? He ain't suited to her. And therefore. *He'll* be

B   3

a-comin', and a-goin', and a-fiddlin', and a-dancin', and
a-whiskey-drinkin', and a-kyard-playin', and a holler-
baloonin'. And whereas. *She'll* be a-settin' at home,
and a-workin', and a-weepin', and a-prayin', and
a-wishin' she hadn't never to her life's end had nothin'
to say to him and had of married—a wiser, and a
better, and a richer man. And moreover. As I said
before, and as I pinted out, and as I've declared to
you from the beginning, and as I've told you over and
over again, he ain't never been, he ain't never goin' to
be, he ain't got no idea of *seemin'* to be goin' to be, a
perfessor of religion, nor a church member, nor a
backslidin' mourner, nor a miserable sinner!—not him.
For firstly, 't'aint in him to be a-thinkin', and a-feelin',
and a wraslin' child of grace. And secondly, he's so
Pharaoh-stiff he wouldn't let hisself be larnt by them
as is put here to lead, and to teach, and to show forth,
and to be set on a bushel. And thirdly, he wouldn't
be took in, or accepted, or regarded, ef he wuz to
come forrard on probation in any Church *I've* had
nothing to do with, and I've been led, and pushed,
and *driv* to cornsider, and reggard, and study over,
and to look at but not be led by most of 'em, *ornless*
he changed hisself,—changed his heart, and his mind,
and his manners, and his sperrit, and body, and flesh,
and soul. And whereas. She don't know it *now*,
bein' a poor, blind, evil, miserable, mortal woman,
a-reachin' out after, and a-graspin' hold of, and a-seizin'
of, and a-holdin' onter, and a-clutchin' at what she
thinks is worth havin', which it's never been, and ain't
now, and never will be, world without end,—*she's* to be
pitied. For remember. *She'll be a miserable woman,—*

a miserable woman, and a sad woman, and a wretched woman, and an unhappy woman, and an afflicted woman. And then whose fault will it be? It will not be *your* fault, nor *my* fault, nor *anybody's* fault but *her* fault. And she'll have herself to thank for all she's been through, and come through, and has got to go through to the very end of her days in the land which is given her, as sure as my name is White! And lastly. She aint the woman for him. He wants a worldly wife, and a laughin' and prancin' wife, and a singin' and dancin' wife, and a careerin' and cavortin' wife! And she ain't that sort. And so they are just *certain-surely and eternally and everlastingly* BOUND to be miserable, of they don't bust up, and go their mournful ways, unto their life's ends!"

There were other suitors who agreed with Mr. White in his conclusions, although they were not able to express their chagrin with the logical and rhetorical graces that were always at the command of that eloquent speaker,—heavy-broganned, red-faced, rough-handed young men, who had no way of showing regret or sentimental despair except the commonplace one of ceasing to visit the obdurate charmer on Sunday afternoons, clad in slop-shop suits (that effectually disguised such charms of manly bearing and fine proportion as they possessed), lit up by flaming cravats that Cupid, the rogue! had tied about their honest sunburnt necks, assuring them that they were "most becoming," while he held himself ready to tighten the slip-knot if necessary and convert the choking satin of sentiment into the more galling noose matrimonial.

And there were other lions in the path of true love

with a better right to roar than any of these sucking
doves; but, in spite of them all, one morning when the
sun was shining its brightest, and the birds were singing their sweetest, and the clouds of bees swarmed
thickest in other clouds of pink and white bloom in the
orchards, and butterflies floated gayly and lit trem-
blingly here and there, and nature, having unpacked all
the treasures of beauty and perfume that she had cruelly
carried away seven months before, sat down to enjoy
the fair prospect and revel in the novelties of the season
like the veriest woman,—on this lovely spring morning
John Shore opened his gate and led into the old house
a bride as fair as the flaxen-haired girl, its first mistress,
and as sweet as the great whiff that greeted them from
the rain-freshened lilacs along the path, and that was a
breath of heaven! And now it seemed for a time that
destiny was checkmated and the elders but foolish
prophets, for there was not on the mountain a man
more temperate, industrious, and "steady" than John
Shore, or a husband half as devoted. The people who
were determined to find fault with him were driven to
condemn him for being " a poor, foolish creature that
worshipped the ground his wife walked on," for want
of worse to say, while patient, weary women of many
labors and little thanks sighed out a wish that *they* had
somebody "to cut every stick of wood and bring every
drop of water" for them, and Mr. White fell back upon
a formula that had often been useful: " *Wait until the
time of the fulfillin' of purposes has come,* and you'll see
what you'll see." John even became the thing that it
had been said it was impossible for him ever to be,—
" a perfessor," joining his wife's church, known as " the

United Bruthring," in which a flaming "revival" broke out about six months after their marriage,—perhaps because he found it so pleasant to be united with her in anything and everything. Whatever his motives were, his mode of doing this was severely criticised by Mr. White, who took the same step at the same time after an unusually prolonged and acute season of self-communion and metaphysical investigation, in which he had been washed hither and thither by the wild waves of controversy, until, as he said himself, he was "plum beat aout."

"Why, he warn't up at the mourners' bench but one day!" he said, in indignant comment. "He got it that easy! And I was weeks and weeks a-turnin' it over in my mind, and a-lookin' at it this way, and a-lookin' at it that way, and a-lookin' at it the other way; not knowin' half the time what I was thinkin'; a-seein' of the truth now and agin, and a-lettin' it slip, and a-pickin' it up agin red-hot, sufferin' *all* things until grace brought me to yea, verily, Amen! And agin I was *a month* throwed down at the footstool, night and day a-cryin', and a-prayin', and a-beseechin', until the very *children* at the back of the church was almost in fits! That's what *I* had to go through. It all depends on what you've got to go through. When the time for the fulfillin' of purposes comes, it *comes*, and you've got to wait for that time. Searchin' is searchin', and *I* know what that is; and seekin' is seekin', and it's what we are all bound, and obligated, and obleeged, and compelled—which it constraineth—to do, but *findin'* is another matter. No, no, I ain't one to get no sort of religion *cheap*. *It's got to cost like all creation*, and I

ain't a-goin' to stop, nor to pause, nor to halt, nor to
consider nothing until I've got it, if it is to be had in
this here world, or in the heavens above, or in the
waters under the earth." Vital Religion had shown
that it possessed the vital principles of growth and expansion again, and "Brother White" had been talked
of as far up as Timber Ridge as having "give in a powerful experience, and got so happy and so full of glory
that he was carried home for dead." All the other con-
verts suffered by comparison with him, but none more
so than his own brother, Timothy, a solemn, silent man,
who had always been a United Brother at least to the
extent of attending service regularly, paying his dues,
and fulfilling faithfully his duties as steward of the
church, but who had never been known to do two
things,—sing a hymn or give his "experience." His conduct in these two matters gave him a great deal of
trouble, for he was always being reproved for his obstinacy or urged to do his duty. He would have been
expelled if he had not been "a good contributin' member." Such are valuable in all communions, and so at
every service Timothy took his seat and sat out the
exercises like a lay-figure of some sort,—incredibly
stolid, attentive, undemonstrative,—while his brethren
marvelled at his conduct, imagined a hundred theories
by which to explain it, and never hit upon the truth.
It was very simple, and lay on the surface. Timothy
had no experience to give, and he had no voice. One
of the little-great Frederick's giant grenadiers had two
hearts, we are told, and it may be that the elder of the
White brothers owed his abnormal activity in theological matters to the fact that he had been endowed with

two souls, his own and his brother's. It is certain that Timothy was never "awakened," or "convicted," or even "alarmed," in forty years of constant church-going. Yet no one, not the most earnest, the most emotional member of the congregation, ever enjoyed a revival as he did. It was what the opera, and theatre, and balls, and wine, and cards are to other men in other situations, only it was the *one* dissipation of his dull life. It warmed and stimulated his phlegmatic nature as nothing else did,—pierced and roused his sluggish mind, thrilled along his well-muffled nerves, set his slow blood running briskly on its errands,—producing an excitement that was delightful to him, and giving him the most vivid sensations of sympathy, interest, curiosity, of which he was capable. Yet with twenty people shrieking, and shouting, and groaning, and praying before him in various stages of religious frenzy he gave no outward evidence of his inward emotion such as those about him gave. He did not cry out, or weep, or moan, or faint. When he began to be deeply interested he would lean forward in his chair a little, cross his legs, put down his right elbow and support his face in his hand, the better to see and hear. Then, as the demonstrations became more agitating, his pale, deep-set eyes would glow like aqua-marines; he would moisten his lips. When the whole congregation burst into sobs he would run his right hand rapidly through his hair until it stood up around his face in a tragic nimbus in curious contrast with his features, which were those of one of nature's caricatures,—insignificant in size and exaggerated in outline. And when his emotions threatened to get the upper hand of him he would dive suddenly into his pocket

and bring out an enormous bandanna handkerchief,
which he always carried, and firmly bind his legs together
with it just above the knee where they were crossed.
This vigorous measure always had the desired effect of
keeping not only his body in subjection, but of subdu-
ing him into his original state of stolid calm, and of
preventing all flow of feeling and all dangerous consequences. But his brethren were not in the secret of
this bit of moral surgery, and they waxed more and
more indignant as revival followed revival and their
steward still sat a mute and presumably mutinous sinner, so that when his brother in " uniting" himself with
them made such a scene as the oldest members " had
never seen the like of," the contrast was naturally
glaring. It was noticed, too, that Timothy alone had
no praise for the " powerful experience" which has been
mentioned, and this was set down to malice and all un-
charitableness. But the fact was that he had become a
connoisseur in religious emotion, and knew a naked soul
well enough, and preferred it to one clad in the oratori-
cal purple of his brother's weaving.

Unfortunately, John Shore's connection with the
church was of the briefest. There are Pharisees in
every fold, and that ancient element of all the churches
was represented in this one by certain well-to-do farmers'
wives who generally sat together, and somewhat apart
from all the others, in the chief seats. In the course
of the next "protracted meeting" a very poor, and
particularly frowsy, unkempt, but reputable young girl
imprudently took a seat on the end of one of these
benches, tacitly reserved for the elect ladies; and that
from sheer embarrassment and not from any desire to

intrude upon her neighbors. Up rose the leading lady of the party, and, seizing a blue parasol, and a magenta fan, and a gilt-edged hymn-book, she swept ostentatiously across the aisle and took up a fresh position where paupers could not come between the wind and her nobility, bridling haughtily as she did so, and saying, "I can't get religion with no such people." John Shore heard her, and felt as if he had received a blow in the face; but the forlorn girl accepted the insult meekly, and when "the mourners" were invited to go up she rushed forward and fell weeping on her knees beside her fellow-sinners in a tumult of feeling that made her oblivious of the fact that religion was intended exclusively for the rich and respectable. To John Shore's amazement she was not allowed to stay there. Her tattered robe was not the robe of pharisaic righteousness at all, and, unobserved by the preacher, certain of the elders went up to her, said something to her, and then half led, half hustled her to the back of the church, where she was allowed to drop into a seat near the door. On seeing this, John Shore, who was singing a hymn, suddenly closed first his lips and then his book, and, turning, marched fiercely down the main aisle and out of the church, followed by his wife's startled gaze and the eyes of the whole congregation. "Ef *that's* religion, I've got no use for it!" he said, hotly, when explaining his defection to his wife afterwards. "She had as good a right to be there as anybody. I'll not set foot in meetin' agin, and it's no use askin' me."

And so snapped one of the cables that might have held this soul in the storm that was to beat upon his

c

house and make his heart desolate; nor is it only simple and ignorant folk who make the mistake of con-
founding Christianity with Christians—so-called. This
subject was the only one that was never discussed in
the Shore household,—the nearest approach to discord
in a home full of such harmonies as wise thrift, true
and tender love, gentle thoughts, unselfish deeds, to say
nothing of others that were heard evening after evening floating out through the open windows near which
Alice sat and sewed with one foot on a cradle while
John played "Money Musk," and "Watermillion," and
"Zip Coon," and "Miss McLeod," and "Yellow Stockings," and many a tune besides, with a bow that circled
and flourished about him in a perfect ecstasy of motion
that threatened to cut the very ears off his head. No
skies seemed bluer than those that arched clearly above
the old cottage. But suddenly they were overcast and
soon were filled with the very blackness of darkness.
The storm had come. And now the other cable—
which, being made of heart-strings, was so strong that
it might have stood any strain that could have been
put upon it—gave way, too, and John Shore was ship-
wrecked, with nothing saved from the goodly vessel
of all his hopes but a little child and the memory of
a fireside saint.

Three days passed, and then, pale and haggard, he
got up from the bed on which he had been lying silent
and still all day, stung into action by a sound full of
painful suggestion,—the rattle of a milk-pail which one
of the women in the house picked up, the rustle of her
skirts as she left the room, her retreating footsteps. It
was to go on, then, the milking, and baking,—and sweep-

ing, and sewing; work was to go on just as it used to, when she with whom he associated all domestic duties as well as affections would never do any of these things again. His heart swelled to bursting with the thought, so intolerable to all bereaved ones. He staggered a little as he stood on his feet and looked about him with the dazed vision of heavy grief. "I—I am going away, Aunt Martha," he said to the old woman who had taken charge of him and his in the past week, and was sitting before a little smouldering fire of chips nursing the baby. "Take care of that child. I give him to you. And you can live here and take all that there is." He started towards the door as he spoke, caught sight of his wife's shawl and bonnet on the peg where she had hung them, stopped, took down the shawl and walked with it into an inner room, followed by Aunt Martha's anxious eyes and her thoughts of pity for his trouble and wonder at its effects. She could not imagine what he was going to do with the shawl. What he did was to wrap it tenderly about his violin, put both under his arm, and hurry past her out of the house and down the walk. "John! John!" she screamed after him, "where are you going?" "I don't know," came back to her as he passed through the gate.

"When are you comin' back, John?" she persisted, her voice quivering shrilly with age and anxiety.

"I ain't comin' back," he said.

She had taken "John's talk" as merely the wild utterance of affliction; but, seeing this, she hastily put the child down and hobbled after him as fast as she could. She could not overtake him, however, and, after waiting outside a bit, she comfortably concluded that he would "be back to supper" and went in-doors again. Meanwhile, he was making his way rapidly down the Red Lane.

The sun had set behind the mountains, and the pale clear light it had left was rapidly failing. Some little birds were settling down in their nests in the hedgerows for the night with faint, intermittent twitterings of farewell. A light or two gleamed from the windows of a cottage here and there. The cows were walking slowly up the lane with pendulous heads and ears broadflapped, chewing the cud of contentment, swishing with idle stroke the flies from their flanks, lowing occasionally to let impatient calves know that they were coming.

He looked at them as they passed him. They were going home, and he——

A bat dashed past him out into the darkness, going in the same direction. "Ay! that is what I am doing," he thought.

Coming to the mouth of the lane where it debouched into the high-road, he gave one long look back. And then he hurried forward. The shadows closed about him, the road stretched before him in all its lonely length. It seemed to lead to the end of the world.

*   *   *   *   *   *   *   *   *   *

If there was a thing that the mountain hated, it was what it called and esteemed "foolishness." That a man should give up "goin' to meetin'" because a poor girl that he did not so much as know was treated in a way that he did not approve of was "foolishness." That a man should give up his home and friends, and leave a piece of property to be managed by anybody or benefit anybody but himself, merely because he had lost his wife, was double-distilled "foolishness." There were men on the mountain who had lost four wives and had never dreamed of such a thing as letting the light affliction of the moment work permanent injury to such grave interests as pigs, and potatoes, and wheat,—to property, in short,—and who might have lost four hundred (with patriarchal opportunities and advantages in the matter of length of days and number of spouses) without being driven out of the county. And if there was a thing that the Mountain despised it was travellers. It knew that all tramps were travellers, ergo all travellers were tramps. It was true that there was such a thing as authorized vagabonds, who came among them with chromos, and lamps, and cheap flim-flams to sell, in which case their contempt was good-humored and tolerant, and very occasionally they were puzzled by another variety of the genus, the "winged Ishmaelites" of commerce, who drove smart gigs, and were dressed always as for "meetin'," or "courtin'," and stopped only at the large farm-houses, and joked a great deal, and never had anything less than a sewing-machine to "dispose of." But still travelling was travelling. On that point the Mountain was immovable, fixed, firm. There were cases in which travel, as represented by "buggy trips" to regions as remote as the country on the other side of the Ridge, two counties off, had been condoned as a necessary evil, but this had only been when important issues were at stake and hung upon the prodigious effort such as getting a thoroughbred Jersey cow, or selling a horse, or buying seed-corn. As a rule, nobody went twenty miles from home, or ever wished to go that far, or had the least desire, the faintest curiosity, to know

4

what lay beyond the blue heights that stretched along
their horizon, look where they would, and made for them
a compact, complete, and perfectly satisfactory world
with distinctly final, definite limits, such as geography
can never give.

So John Shore was set down as a crack-brained fellow,
—no great loss to anybody,—and the Mountain had
always known how it would be. His return at an early
date was confidently predicted and expected. Good old
Aunt Martha fancied that she heard his step many a
time, and for a year would occasionally set away on
the top shelf of the dresser some dish or other—a pot
of apple-butter, a slice of souse, or a plate of her corn-
muffins—as an *en cas*, should John come back to his
own "clean famished."

Si Hodges, who was the wit of the community,
"reckoned he'd wait till harvest was over." Sister
Parrish, who lived next to the cottage, felt it her duty
to warn Baby Shore, still in short clothes, against
"growin' up to be like his 'Pa-ap,'" who had "gone way
off yonder beyant the Ridge, goodness alive knows
whurabouts, and who warn't no 'count when he was at
home." (In spite of certain obstacles of sex that one
would have supposed insuperable, Sister Parrish was a
United Brother, and as such had a grudge against poor
"Pa-ap.")

Brother White was convinced that "it warn't no use
a-flyin', nor a-fleein', from the wrath of Heaven," which
he charitably assumed to have fallen upon his rival.
"For there's the wind, and the whirlwind, and the
tornadio to overtake," said he. "And there's the thunder
a-rollin' and a-clappin' to warn. And there's the rain

a-downfallin',' and the rivers a-uprisin' to drown. And there's the lightnin' a-dartin' forrards and a-rekiling backards to strike. And there's the hail a-slantin' and a-slitherin' to smite. And there's earthquakes and there's seaquakes to swaller up. And there's wild beasts a-ragin' and a-roarin' and a-gnashin' of teeth to devour. And there's all manner of pesteriferous creatures a-creepin' over, and a-crawlin' under. And there's pits and pitfalls, and traps and trapfalls, and no man maketh a way to escape in that day. And wherefore? Whatever is to be, will be, whether it cometh to pass or doth not attain to it, and when the time for the fulfilment of purposes comes it will not stay its hand for John Shore, nor ten thousand thousand sich, and don't you think it."

On hearing this, the Mountain, already conscious of its vast superiority to every other place, prided itself afresh on its security, serenity, and general stability, and, accepting Mr. White's remarks as a masterly summary of what lay "beyant the Ridge," congratulated itself anew on its enviable character and conditions, and was less inclined than ever to change them for the doubtful good and certain evils of "furrin parts."

II.

" Bedimmed the noon-tide sun, call'd forth the mutinous winds,
and 'twixt the green sea and the azured vault is set roaring war."
—*Tempest.*

MANY a harvest of wheat and corn was planted and
grew into bearded and tasselled luxuriance and golden
perfection and was stored and eaten without any help
from John Shore. The mountain sat high and serene
in idyllic picturesqueness of pose and repose above the
world; it looked down upon all these years, and seen
from a distance by the sentimental observer. seemed a
point in a delectable and delightsome land of agricultural plenty and rural virtue, its every harsh feature of
rocky slope, and brier-set paths, poor soil, and scant
woodland, together with the volcanic fires pent up
perhaps, in its breast, veiled by mist.   And the community collectively known as " the Mountain" presented a
wondrously tranquil exterior, that passed for perfect
contentment and honest toil,—ingenuous preference
for "simplicity" (as expressed by hard labor and scant
rewards) and great uprightness in dealing—with those
of defective sympathy or narrow experience of life,
while in reality there was below the surface the toil
and suffering, the want and ignorance, the tragedies
and griefs, of all the sons of Adam, and as much tendency to drink, and lie, and cheat, and steal, and break
every commandment in the Decalogue as if there had
not been a field, or brook, or flower for miles around to

ask how such things could be in God's sweet world.
Daisies are charming symbols of innocence to the urban
mind, but it is perfectly possible to gaze fixedly at
them from daylight until dark in the revery born of
opium. And young lambs frisking in green meadows
is a pretty sight enough to see, and would be a prettier
if this were not a brutal butchering world, which shows
them to us against a greener background of mint; but
it was while Cain and Abel were "in the field with the
flocks" that the first murder was done. So long as it is
the heart of man that is "deceitful, and desperately
wicked," the most pastoral scenery and sylvan shades
will afford no sort of security that human conduct will
bear any nice relation to bucolic environment, though
we should all go on all-fours like Nebuchadnezzar and
eat grass. Good Friday, 1861, found the Mountain positively agitated, if such a term can be applied to such
an inert mass of disciplined dulness and conservative
custom. A great many startling things had disturbed
the fine equilibrium of its monotony. For a year
vague murmurs from the stormy sea of political difference and strife beyond the mountains had reached even
this remote spot, though small heed was paid to them.
But now Virginia was about to secede. War had come;
and that fact, like a blazing ship, filled the eye and mind
of all who were watching its course, and could be seen
from a great distance, so that the most sluggish souls
were quickened for the time into something like vivid
feeling. The Mountain, ever practical, would have
liked to utilize the heat generated to cook its own
breakfast, and had quite a keen anxiety to know how
far the increased price of pork and wheat would justify

4*

secession, and the overturning of a system that gave
bi-weekly market-days, and regular, if small, profits on
farm produce of every kind. It wished to know, too,
how far it was liable for the promises being made in its
name by ardent orators at the cross-roads, in the matter
of conscription, crops, taxes. In short, it took the natural
and frankly-selfish view of the situation at first and not
the heroic one, and was shrewd enough to see that it
would have to carry its share of the general burden.
And then, too, it was concerned about some other things.
" Bud" Hodges, Si's brother, had been hanged only the
day before for having killed his wife, after being " convicted" almost on the scaffold, and making a long speech
to the assembled crowd, in which he invited them all to
meet him in Heaven, especially his friends and relatives,
apparently with the fullest assurance that he would be
there to welcome them. " A man that can toss more
hay and cut more ice, and plough straighter and longer
than any man 'bout here, and she not fitten to live noway, and the children out-scattered 'mong strangers
they never heerd tell of nor laid eyes on before," complained the party most discontented with the workings
of a law which took no account of temptation, provoca-
tion, nor consequences, led, strange to say, by the victim's
brother.

The preacher who had been with him all through his
trial, like the good shepherd that he was,—a man much
loved by his flock,—had been ordered away after a stay
of eight years among them, which was unsettling.

The crops had failed the summer before, and this, like
all calamities, had fallen heaviest upon those least able
to bear it,—the laborers and owners of small holdings

rather than the large farmers about them,—in the severe winter that had followed.

"Jones's brindle steer" had somehow run a spike through his chest, and had to be shot, valuable as he was. Two sets of double-headed chickens had already been hatched, early as the season was. Altogether it was felt to be a most unusual and troublous time, in which almost anything might happen that was abnormal or painful, such unrest and anxiety was in the air. But, all the same, nobody was in the least prepared for what was coming as fast as—but stop! it is some miles off yet. The day was a busy one. Good Friday always is on the Mountain; not that any part of it is spent in religious observances. Scarcely any one knew what its special significance was to the Christian world. But ignorance is always relative, and they had information of their own about it that they likewise supposed to be as universal as it was important. It was well known among them, for instance, that if flower-seeds were planted on that day they would come up "all colored,"— variegated; that if eggs were set under a hen with no reputation whatever for doing her duty by them, in double the usual numbers, every one of them would turn out a chicken that would live through anything, though it were to thunder during every day of the incubation; that potatoes put in then yielded as well again as those planted at any other season; and that if you wanted to begin any piece of work, from cutting out a dress, if you were a woman, to building a house, if you were a man, Good Friday was the luckiest day in all the year to choose for it.

This being the case, it was not remarkable that in a

region where it was hardly possible for the sheep to cross a meadow without being followed by the slow gaze of four or five rustics, and in which anything like an event or a piece of news lasted for months (with no care at all in economizing expenditure in details), that a man mounted on a large, roan horse rode the whole length of the Red Lane without being observed by a single adult. The children about the houses and in the door-ways, barelegged and tattered, half bold, half shy, peeped at or goggled after him. Eliza Watson, bending over her lettuce-bed, raised her head for a moment as he passed. Jane Woodruff came to the door with her iron in her hand and spat on it before glancing that way. The yellow dog flew out from behind the ash-hopper and barked vague suspicion at the third house. A dirty white kitten was all that was to be seen at the next place, feebly mewing and prowling; at the next, only an absurdly pompous turkey-cock, swelling conceit and defiance with tragic stage-villainous starts and side-swept wings, while his spouses picked their way about in a meek, womanly, or, rather, fine-ladical fashion, as if they were not used to the country and found the walking bad. John Shore—for it was he—turned in his saddle and gazed earnestly at all these familiar sights. The children might have been, and seemed for the moment, just those he had left there; the fowls and animals were of the same breed; the houses were only a shade more dilapidated. Was it really fifteen years since he had rushed away from here with an intolerable sense of loss and desolation that had darkened the very heavens above him and the earth about him? Ever since he had left the high-road and slackened rein he had been looking for startling changes that should in some measure correspond with those he had known; but none were visible. He saw one or two comfortable stone houses on the hills around him that had not been there, a new barn, a few patent gates. He noticed that the land had been divided into smaller fields and seemed better tilled; but this was all. And there was the Ridge as blue as ever; Massanutton mist-veiled, sharp-spurred, distant and beautiful as his lost happiness to his home-sick eyes. There was the Round Meadow greening with wheat as it always was at that season; there were the same sheep, apparently, dotting the same old pastures; there were the rich upland slopes, set in green frames of wood or field, changing color, as he looked, from ochre to dark-purple or velvet-brown, according to the age of the furrows or the blackness of the shadowing clouds, and with a bloom on them like that of the plum. Surely no earth ever looked like this Virginian earth, and no skies could be as ethereal as these Virginian skies, and no mountains so grand and noble as his own Virginian mountains! His eyes filled with tears as he watched the cloud-shadows that swept down them, the sunbursts that illuminated them. Ay! after all wanderings he had got back to *the* land! The land to live in, and to die for! In spite of all sorrows, it was a joy to see it again that pierced his very heart with its sweetness. When he got to his own gate, the great apple-tree near it showered down a lovely welcome upon him. He saw a neat woman's figure in the back-yard; a pink sun-bonnet. The blood rushed to his brain, carrying a wild thought about his dead wife, and then receded again, leaving him very pale. Perceiving that

he was there and that he still halted, the woman approached, crossed her red arms over the fence, pushed
back her bonnet, revealing an ugly face that he easily
recognized, if not the modest beauty of the one he had
thought of, smiled in a way that emphatically illus-
trated the truth that some people gain by being amiable
and others lose (such a toothless waste of gum showed
blankly there), and challenged the stranger to a flirta-
tion or explanation, or both. "What might yer want,
anyways? Won't yer 'light?" she said. "I never
noticed yer at first."

"Do you know me now?" he asked.

She shook her head archly. "No, I ain't never seen
yer before, but I reckon I'll know yer next time."

"I know you. You are Aunt Martha's younger
sister, Jinny Hodges," said he.

"And who are yer, anyways, that knows me?" she
asked, eagerly.

"I'm John Shore."

"Mercy on us! It never ain't! Sakes alive! John
Shore!" she cried. "Whur did yer come from?
Whur've yer been at all this time? Mercy me! Folks
said you was dead. Well! I declare! John Shore!
Al's Pa-ap!"

It was some moments before she composed herself
sufficiently to suggest again that he should "'light and
come in," and then, leading the way, she made a very
pertinent inquiry,—"What did yer come back fur, anyways, John? Walk right in! Al! Al! He ain't here.
He ain't come home yet. My sakes! And yer ain't
dead at all. And what brung yer home? Marthy
always said yer'd come. Set down. I declare to gra-

cious! I can't believe it. Seems like it *couldn't* be.
But yer ain't told yet what brung yer? And yer ain't
never *been* dead, of course. It takes the rag off the
bush! It certainly does." Without waiting for a reply
she clattered on and on, while John Shore looked about
him dreamily, only half catching what was said.

"Yes, me and Al's been livin' on here ever since
Marthy deceased, together, and many's the time Al, he's
said to me, 'I'm master here, Jinny, and you shall stay
here always. I ain't never goin' to turn yer out noways,'" she went on, and, not getting any response from
her companion, she said, tentatively, with raised voice,
"That was when you was dead, John, I mean. Yes,
me and him's always been the best of friends."

John Shore came back to the present, and perfectly
understood the drift of her remarks.

"*I* ain't a-goin' to be the one to turn you out, Jinny,"
he said, kindly. "Don't you be afeard of that,—nor Al,
neither. You've stayed here right straight along and
took care of him, and you've got a better right to be
here than me. And I wouldn't turn out no woman noway. A woman without a roof over her head is like a
turtle without a shell. No, no; I come home because
I heerd they was goin' to jump on old Virginia and
stawmp her, and I couldn't stay 'way after that. I was
gettin' on right well, then, out there,—mighty well fur
me,—but it seemed like I laid on a care-bed after that
news come. I couldn't sleep nor rest; and I hadn't no
peace in my mind, I wuz so oneasy. At last it all come
clear to me. It said plain as I'm speakin' this minute,
'Shame on you; you are a mean-sperrited coward! Ef
your mother was struck, would you stop to think of

houses, and beds, and sich stuff?'   And next day I sold
all I had and started."

"Did you get the wuth of 'em?   Lor' no! of course
not," said she.   "Goin' to the war?   Why, yer
mighty simple.   I don't see as you've got no call to go
to no war, John.   Some sez there ain't goin' to be
none, 'cause the Yankees 'll run away, and some sez it's
goin' to be turrible.   The Ridge has been blue-black
lately, and the sun's set for blood over and over agin.
Pretty nigh twenty men from round 'bout here sez they
are goin' if it comes, and when all twenty gits to fightin'
with maybe twenty or thirty more of *them*, it'll be turrible!   Somebody 'll get hurt with that foolishness yet,
and 'pears to me like they'd all better go to ploughin' and
stop this here talk 'bout fightin'.   If you'll hearken to
me, you'll not go mixin' yourself up with no sich doin's,
no way they fix it, John.   You ain't dead *now*, though
I've been told time and again cornstant that you wuz;
but you'll be *killed* dead before you're done soldierin'—
mark my words, for you'll live to see it,—sure enough
dead and no come back this time.   When they talk to
me 'bout this here scare-all, I sez, 'Stay at home and
mind your own business, all of yer, and there won't *be*
no war.'   So *that's* what brung yer.   Why, yer might
as well have *been* dead as to go get killed, John.   Now
hadn't yer?"

"Tell me 'bout Al," he replied, waiving all argument
on the subject.   "Is he like—her—his mother? and is
he strong and healthy?"

Jinny, still staring at him and nervously swinging
her bonnet by one string now, not only replied to this
question, but talked almost without interruption for

half an hour, and with only such cessation as was
necessary in order to catch a gasping breath. Once
in her voluble flow of narrative she stopped to whip
off a slipper and throw it with a loud "Shoo! shoo!" at
some chickens that were coming in, which caused a
great scramble and flutter among them, a rush of wings,
and one or two loud squawks of alarm; but this was
only a momentary diversion, and she rattled on after it
until her listener's head fairly buzzed with the effort
required to keep up with her. "Jinny always wuz a
talker," thought he, "but when she gets the band on
the wheel now, she goes round like she would set fire
to something or fly all to pieces." When she had said
all there was to say on each subject that crowded into
her mind she ended it with some allusion to his reported
death which had much the effect of selah in the Psalms,
returning to this fixed idea by every conceivable highway and byway. It was too firmly planted among her
convictions to be lightly relinquished. At last, just as
she had opened her mouth wide and secured the essen-
tial condition to further conversation, a side-issue struck
full upon the unexhausted and inexhaustible stores
of her experience, and she jumped up, exclaiming,
"Lor', yer ain't had no supper. Yer'll want something to eat," but even then she she only stopped long
enough to seize the bread-pan and rolling-pin. Making
vigorous use of these, she chattered and clattered away
to John Shore on the hypothesis that he was his own
ghost with the most characteristic perversity of ingenuity until the biscuits were in the stove. "Now, John,
make yerself at home. Do jest as if yer'd *always*
been alive and livin' here," she then said, and dashing

c d   5

into her bonnet, rushed out to disseminate the great news, leaving him very much of a shade, in feeling at least, among the fast-gathering shadows.

She was back again before long; but it was in her absence that father and son met. Hearing the door open, John Shore had risen impulsively and gone towards the figure dimly visible there, saying, "Alfred! Ain't it you, Alfred? My son! My son!" and so had fallen upon the neck of an astonished youth. She found them sitting opposite each other when she came in, and it was but a dissolving view that the elder man got of her when she lit the lamp, which showed him Alfred, his chair tilted back against the wall, his legs twisted awkwardly among the rounds, his hands thrust deep in his pockets, sustaining with round eyes and red cheeks an embarrassing experience. Look as earnestly as he would, John Shore could find no trace of resemblance between the boy and his dead mother, except an occasional transient expression about the eyes; but even that awoke in him so many vivid memories of her that he fell into an absorbed revery in which self-reproach predominated. His wife seemed to be asking in every such glance why he had left her—their son to be reared by strangers. A more stolid, clumsy specimen of the commonplace clod-hopping youth than Alfred could not have been found; for not only had the poetical strain with which his father had been blessed or cursed been left out of his composition entirely, but he was invincibly dull of perception,—a thing-like person who might have raised unpleasant doubts as to the immortality of the soul in some minds, so little sensitive to impressions and sensations was he, so mildly vegetable

rather than animal, as if made to live for to-day, to be
cast in the oven to-morrow. "Slow and fearsome" the
Mountain called him, and added, "but trusty."

Something in him had responded to that cry, "My
son!"—an unsuspected echo such as nature keeps and
reveals in the most unlikely places,—and when he had
recovered from the shock of hearing it he received his
father's deprecating advances with an awkward kindli-
ness that increased his sense of unworthiness, and
aroused a keen feeling of gratitude, though it was a
good-will expressed in no more demonstrative ways or
words than a most protracted, inexpressive stare, an
occasional vacant smile, and a casual "Yer don't say,"
or "That's so," or "Yer right there."

"Yer didn't think yer'd come home and find yer
Pa-ap come to life agin, now did yer?" queried Jinny,
as she moved briskly about the room. "Ef I had of
died *myself* and been buried, I couldn't er been no cer-
tainer of lyin' in my grave forever and ever. And him
settin' there without no windin' sheet nor *nothin'*, as
alive as you or me or the next one, after being dead
nigh on fifteen years, and a sperrit among the sperrits!
It beats all that ever I heerd, and they wouldn't believe
me, and no wonder when I told 'em—(come to supper)
—and I sez, 'Come and see, ef yer don't believe me, and
I don't blame yer for not believin' me, for I didn't believe myself' (the biscuits is getting cold); and that's
the truth, and while I live I'll never say agin that
nobody is dead, nor believe it, *not if I carries the coffin*
(set down, John; take the foot of the table) *and spades
the dirt in on 'em myself!* And they'll all be here pretty
quick, and yer'd better hurry up and git a bite down

(that risin' of Sally's ain't worth shucks) before they gits here to see yer alive and breathin' the breath of life for theirselves, for the news is offsent by this, I can tell yer." The bung once out of the conversational barrel, Jinny's eloquence would have flowed on for the evening, but she had not underrated the reportorial capacity of the female tongue at its best, and it was not long before interruptions came. Before the sun dropped behind the western hills, every family and cottage for miles around had received an electric shock that did as well as a telegraphic despatch, saying, "John Shore has come home."   .

The Mountain for once was completely taken aback. The Mountain masculine got almost excited and said, " Well, I'll be doggoned!"—was even more emphatic. The Mountain feminine grew shrill and voluble with its own exclamations and explanations. The Mountain feminine and masculine trudged off to see if half the wonderful tidings could be true. " John Shore, back," " from Texis," " goin' to the war," " three hundred dollars in his pocket," " ownin' his horse," " all dressed up," was the last figure that could have been expected. The elders were puzzled for a moment, staggered by such evidences of respectability and prosperity. They felt the necessity of investigating these rumors and winnowing the chaff from all this wheat, if it was wheat,—more likely tares. The nearest neighbors got there first, of course, and Jinny, full of the delightful excitement of having a ghost on exhibition, hailed them cheerfully from afar with, " Come in! Come right in! There he sets! Meat and bones, as you see! *Pinch him* ef yer don't believe me! *He* ain't no stiff, nor no sperrit, neither! ha! ha! ha!" A fresh batch of arrivals put an end to the lecture she would fain have delivered on her interesting "subject," and from that moment she was kept so busy welcoming her guests that she could only whisper here and there, "*Warn't* I telling yer the truth, now? *H'ain't* he lively and limber for a stiff? *H'ain't* he, now?" She had to be mistress of ceremonies, for Alfred no sooner saw them beginning to assemble than he picked up a stick, got out his jack-knife, and sought refuge from social duties and domestic complications in whittling. By the time supper was over the whole population of the lane had slouched into and around the old cottage,—"Shore's," as they put it,—down to the babies that could not be left at home for obvious reasons, and Grandma Williams, stone-deaf and frantically curious; down to the very dogs. "Well, ef this ain't as good as a buryin'!" said Jinny, with her most beaming smile, as she gave the old woman a seat as close to the corpse of her simile as possible,—a position which only made Goody Williams more aggravatingly aware of her infirmity than ever, and caused her to cry "Hainh? What's that?" at intervals of about five minutes all during her stay. It was soon impossible to improvise another seat, but still they came. Not vivaciously, or noisily, but slowly, solemnly, greeting John Shore without enthusiasm, very much as though he had left them the day before, regarding him with expressionless eyes in which no beam of humor or friendliness relieved a fixed stare; summoning him, as it were, to give an account of himself, and justify, if he could, conduct so unprecedented. Alfred was chief inquisitor, or seemed so to John Shore, in spite of his youth. Find-

ing himself set before this tribunal, John Shore said
what he could for himself. He could do no less, but it
came to very little. He touched lightly on his reasons
for leaving Virginia, but gave the impression that he
was attempting to gloss over a serious offence. He gave
some account of his travels,—they were not interested
in will-o'-the-wisp chases in the mountains of the moon.
He stated what his circumstances were,—they were
what might have been expected, the elders thought.
Such fruits as insight and experience were but unsubstantial gains in the face of such facts as cropped out,
—the horse he was riding was not his own; he had but
five dollars in his pocket! His patriotism passed for
the windy utterances of a man who had nothing to lose
by commotions and disturbances. His desire to see his
old home even counted against him. He ought not to
have gone away, they argued, but having gone he should
have stayed. The folly of travelling was clearer than
ever. The peace party was strengthened by the fact
that John Shore was going to the war. It showed what
war was.

Brother White (a tottering old man now, as unstable
in body as faith, but still a voice for the community)
expressed the general feeling when he rose from the oak
settee and said, "Well! I never was one to go around,
and about, and above, and below, and hither, and yon,
and thither, and beyant; a-goin' off, and a-returnin' on,
and a-leavin' behind, and a-settlin' around, a-deceivin',
and a-surprisin', and a-piratin', and a-pirootin'. *But* an
if I *had* of been obliged, and obleeged, and obligated,
and bound, and *constrained* to leave my home, and my
friends, and my kin, and my kindred, and my kindred's

kindred, I'd have gone, and have went, and have remained, and *stayed* wherever and whithersoever that
place or places, or person or persons, put me. But it is
for folks to choose or to leave; and to have and to hold;
and to scatter or to gather; and the stony rocks is for
the conies, and the green meadows for them that lies
down. And as for goin' to this here *war*, I'm an old
man, and a weak man, and a lame man, and a bent
man that can't be driv, nor led, nor carried forth, nor
borne along to no war, nor warrings, nor fights, nor
fightings. Whereas. I sez to the young, and the strong,
and the foolish, and the foolhardy—I sez: ' Wait, and
hold on, and pause and consider, and consider agin
when you've paused, and pause agin when you've considered, and reflect when you've paused *and* considered,
before you go to no war.' For what is war? It's *fightin'*,
and you've got to fight or *be* fit. And it's *stabbin'*, and
you've got to stab or *git stabbed*, one. And it's *shootin'*,
and you've got to shoot or to *git shot*, sure. And it's
stealin', and you've got *to steal or git stole from*. And it's
burnin', and you've got *to burn or git burnt out*. It's
hollerin', and hollerbadoin', and hellerbaloonin'. That's
what it is. It's rampagin', and rumpagin'. It's travellin',
and movin'. It's a-handlin' of guns, and turnin' over of
pistols, and a-regyardin' of all kinds of weepons prone
to go off and not to be laid down until the time cometh.
It's death, and destruction, and ruination, and a-gettin'
kilt *or* a-killin',—for whom? and for what? and for
which? And *none* can tell, *nor* discover, *nor* make plain
the end thereof from the beginning, but yet all knoweth
that it overwhelmeth! And what sort of a kind of a
thing is this—to go a-seekin' for, and lookin' after, and

a-searchin' into, and a-stirrin' up, and a meddlin' with,
and a-pesterin' about, anyways—this here *war?* Let
them as arc runagates continuing in scarceness go after,
and pursue, and follow on, and lead forth, and *cause* to
be led forth to the slaughter, a-talkin' of 'South and
North,' and 'East and West,' and 'Union and disunion,'
like as if they *owned* the Mountain. *We'll* stay right
here, whur we've always stayed, and do jes' like we've
always done." He looked frowningly around from his
seat near the door as he concluded at the war-party
represented primarily by John Shore, and then by a
few very young men whose minds had been mildly inflamed by current rumors and speeches, and mopped
his wrinkled face and bald head acrimoniously with
wrathful sweeps of his coat-sleeve.

"Well, now, Jake, I dunno 'bout that," said Bub Williams, upon whom the speaker's eye had last rested,—
Bub Williams, the best shot on the Mountain, and the
hardest drinker, with a finger that seemed to get steady
the moment it touched a trigger, no matter what was
the state of his nerves. "Maybe there's times and
seasons. The case looks to me this way. Ef old Virginny was to say go, I'd go. She knows what's right,
and she'll do what's right every time, en ef she called
I'd have to light out and do the best I could for her.
Fair and square and softly sez I ef you kin, and when
you kain't, give the other side Hail Columbia. The
Yankees ain't done nothin' to me as I knows'on, but ef
they tech Virginny I'm there ! My old rifle ain't wuth
much," he concluded, with a twinkle in his eye that
somehow rippled down all his lazy, good-humored person as he sat half doubled up in the window-seat, " but

I reckon I can give 'em *a salute!*" The young men laughed at this, and John Shore and Bub exchanged a glance of mutual understanding which Brother White caught and resented. He was about to begin an angry remonstrance with " Oh, yes, there's two of you and a pair of you," when Bub's father, Zach, a man of great weight, moral and avoirdupois, picked up his felt hat and running it through his fingers back and forth said gruffly, " I don't want to hear no more talk of goin' to no war, Bub. Leave fightin' to the fools that likes it. You've got something else to do. You've got to plough, and to sow, and to reap, and to harrow, and to stack corn, and to pitch hay, and to cut ice, and to butcher pigs,— that's what *you've* got to do. What's the wages of a soldier, anyways? What's it all about, anyways? I ain't heerd no plain, sensible account of it yet from nobody. I ain't goin' out to fight nobody I ain't got no quarrel with, and ef they comes down here to fight me—well, they ain't come yet. Govermint ain't never put clothes on my back nor my children's, nor food in my stomach nor my children's, and I don't reckon they ever will; so I'll stay where I can do it myself, and let 'em find out what they are fightin' about ef they kin, and fight it out theirselves when they do. What's govermints to me?" Nobody undertook to answer this question, but it was a signal for a general discussion of the issue before them, in which the women joined with much spirit, and when the general fusillade of talk had abated, the elders successively gave their views. The constituent elements of the company were those of all assemblies, as very soon appeared. There was the prophet, who had seen

and known that there would be a war, and that very
war ever since he was born and for ages before,—the
man who predicted ruin for the South and ruin for the
North with the perfect impartiality and the gloomy
satisfaction of the raven; the man who weighed the
probabilities, and announced future results with the
skilled ambiguity of the almanac-seer; the man who
could have averted all such dangers and greater disas-
ters if he had been "govermint," but whose valuable
advice was somehow never taken. And then John
Shore leaned forward and smote his knee with his right
hand, and, with flushed cheek and sparkling eyes, spoke
out all his simple, loyal creed. "It ain't govermint,"
he cried: "it's Virginia!" and went on to declare briefly
his thoughts and intentions. The elders listened frowningly, unconvinced and displeased. Some of the younger
men's faces feebly reflected his ardor, and as he looked
from one to another he felt the chill of the orator who
is not *en rapport* with his audience until he came to
Timothy White. A gleam as of the sun or steel was in
those cold light eyes,—a spark without warmth. As he
caught John's glance, he rose to his feet with sudden
resolution, his face turned crimson. " *I'm* going to this
war for one. I'll be damned if I don't!" he said, and,
throwing his hat down on the floor with a passionate
gesture, he walked out of the room. If Round Hill had
got up and challenged Mars to single combat, the Little
Mountainites could not have been one whit more
amazed. Tim White! the silent, taciturn, undemonstrative Tim White, the most stolid of the stolid, the
quietest of the quiet,—he whom neither love, nor hate,
nor religion had ever moved to open his lips in any

sort of profession or confession, who had never yet given that "experience," to behave as he had done! It deprived the most fluent of speech, and took, as they said, the breath out of their bodies. What a time it must be in which the dumb spoke and the grave gave up its dead! At last, its curiosity slaked, and its work waiting to be done, the company, with scant ceremony and rustic farewells, dispersed as slowly and slouchingly as it had gathered. The women-folk lingered a little with Jinny on the steps, listening to her post-mortem confidences, and they saw Timothy White off under a tree smoking.

"Who'd ha' thought *he'd* spit out like that! Bub's always said he hadn't spunk enough to git married, or set up with a corpse, or do anything," said Mrs. Williams, junior, indicating the distant figure with a wave of her sun-bonnet. "And I never heerd of him being a drinking man."

"They're all drunk. That's about what's the matter," said Mrs. Williams, senior, severely; "though it ain't liquor this time. And if they go on, and go on, till they jaw us into a war, there'll be trouble and to spare for us women, I can tell you. The fools that fights gets killed mostly, but we've got *to live it out.*" With the intuition of her sex, Mrs. Williams had got at the heart of the question so far as it affected the weaker vessel.

When Jinny re-entered the cottage, she said, "Well, Pa-ap, your bed's done made up, and I know you'll say in the morning, 'Jinny, I never slep' no better not in my *grave*,' and when you git up I'm goin' to give you a breakfast that'll make you glad to have rose from the

cold tomb; and I am glad you've come home, even
though being dead, John; and ef you want any water
there's the pump; and ef you holler, Al'll hear you
and come right in; and there's the washin' to-morrow!
So now I am off, and I hope you ain't a sleep-walker
now you've left off bein' a ghost, John, for I always
was scary of nights and thought I seed sperrits round,
and didn't like the looks of sheets on the clothes-line"
(here she briskly closed the shutters, locked the front
door, and resumed from the next room without any
break in her narrative), "and there ain't no grave-yards
'bout here for you to go to and walk about in, so there
ain't no call for you to stir till day breaks" (here she
began mounting the steps). "And, lor! you may be
sure I'll look under my bed this night, for I ain't used
to sleepin' in the house with stiffs, and it sorter makes
me creep and crawl down the back, if you'll excuse me
sayin' so and meanin' no offence to you, seein' you are
alive, as you say, John" (here she got to the head of
the flight and paused on the landing); "and if you
should feel kinder lonesome and *laid out*, John, when
you get in bed, there's a candle stuck in a bottle a-pur-
pose settin' by, and ef you light it maybe you'll feel
easier." Here she closed her bedroom door, but opening
it almost immediately, called out, "John! John! don't
set up late! Don't you, now. It'll jes' give me canip-
tion fits ef I hear yer movin' round about twelve o'clock
in the dark rattlin' your bones like. Do yer hear, John?
Lock yer door. Lock yerself in—ef yer *can*."

"All right, Jinny. What are you afeard of? Go
to bed," he called back, and the door closed again, this
time for the night. "You heerd all that was said 'bout

this war, Al," said his father, after a silence that had lasted some moments. "Are you a-goin' to it?"

Alfred tossed backward the tan-colored locks that were always falling over his placid, moony face.

"No," he said. "I ain't fur gettin' killed. I ain't goin' to budge. I don't want to kill no person. I'm goin' to stay right here."

His father's face flushed. He opened his lips to remonstrate and changed his mind. "I should ha' thought you wouldn't be willin' to do that," he said. "But I ain't been no sort of a father to you, and I can't say no more than I'd ha' thought you couldn't rest at home ef trouble comes."

"I ain't a-goin'," repeated Alfred, placidly, and there was another pause.

"You are glad to see me, ain't you, Al? You don't feel no set aginst me fur goin' away and leavin' you?" the father asked, in a low voice and hesitatingly.

"No," replied Al. "I don't."

"Couldn't you—couldn't you love me a little, don't you think? Not now, but some time?" said the father, with a tremble in his voice. "Say you are glad to see me, Al," he urged, leaning eagerly forward.

"I am glad, Pa-ap. Right down glad," replied Alfred, kindly impelled to satisfy the hunger and thirst that he dimly divined and wondered at.

"Thank you, Al! Thank you, my son!" cried his father, and impulsively seizing one of his hands he kissed it, and then rising walked rapidly into the next room and shut the door.

Left alone, Alfred looked attentively at the large freckled member so passionately saluted, as if to read

6

there the secret of his father's extraordinary conduct. " Well ! I'll be derned !" he said, and re-tilting his chair against the wall sat almost motionless for fully an hour. He often fell into this semi-comatose state. One could not call it a trance, for he was not asleep ; nor a stupor, for he was not stunned ; nor a meditation, for he was not accustomed to think of anything, though on this occasion it had something of all three, so much had happened to daze and confound him. That he had one idea was shown by his yawning prodigiously at last and saying, " Poor Pa-ap," as his eye fell again upon his right hand, after which he, too, betook himself to bed.

The second of July is a noted day in the Mountain calendar always, and was marked by a special event this year, remembered and recalled for many a year after. It is known as " the day the Virgin Mary takes her visit," and if any inquirer, surprised to find this curious bit of Catholic mosaic inserted in a stony and colorless stretch of Protestant pavement, asks anything more about it, he is told that it is " a sign,"— usually, " my father's sign," or " my grandfather's sign," to give it the supreme stamp of authority. It is then explained that if it rains on that day the crops are sure to be as satisfactory as crops ever are to the farmer ; and that if it does not rain on that day a six weeks' drought may be looked for, since not a drop will the heavens vouchsafe until " the Lady returns back to her own home." This being the case, it was natural that in an agricultural community in which this un-poetical version of the Visitation was generally accepted the day that gave good or poor crops was anxiously expected before it arrived and inspected when it came. But this year it was actually a matter of secondary interest, for the axe had fallen, the die had been cast, Virginia had seceded, and this was also the day set for "the soldiers (by brevet) to go to the war." By mid-day the Red Lane was thronged with limp female figures in long sun-bonnets, having baskets on their arms, full of all manner of possible and impossible last things to be offered to or thrust upon the "Shenandoah Scouts," as the company was called, and the fences were lined with children bent since daylight upon "going to see the soldiers go." And in the road were drawn up the husbands and sons and fathers known to the com-munity as "Sal Jones's husband," or "Brown's Jim," or "the Culbert crowd," or "Wilkins's eldest," or "Potter's third," or "old man Sneed,"—an aggregate summed up effectively, if inhumanly, by accomplished political writers as "food for powder." And about these, again, were grouped the elder home-staying men of failing strength, scant breath, and small faith in the success of anything here below.

The scouts had been recruited impartially from the war and peace parties of a few weeks before, for when it came to the point of enlistment it was found that several of the most blatant and bloodthirsty of the former were obliged by a cruel necessity to crush all their military ardor, and discovered daily some fresh and insuperable obstacle in the way of the particular form of patriotism currently spoken of as "'listing for the fight," whereas, on the other hand, a number of men who had been opposed to war in general, and this war in particular, no sooner found it inevitable than they felt impelled, as they put it, to "take a hand and see this thing through."

It was a representative body enough then gathered there, and it must be confessed that in variety of costume and eccentricity of accoutrement it was a remarkable one; so much so, indeed, that it is doubtful whether Alcibiades would have cared to put himself at their head, as John Shore did when the last lingering farewells had been taken, and quite certain that many a European martinet would have disputed their claim to be considered soldiers at all. But brave hearts were beating under those "butternut" coats. Gold lace and broadcloth, pipe-clay and blacking, do not the hero make, and before the war was over, Mars himself would not have been ashamed to own the little cavalcade that now set off of men mounted for the most part on the sorry Rosinantes of the farm, with frying pans tied to their saddle-bows, calico "comforts" strapped behind them with odd bits of rope, and arms that were only equalled by the gun Rip Van Winkle carried on his famous expedition, or that other "queen's arm that Gran'ther Young fetched back from Concord busted."

The children who had swarmed up the clumsy wooden stirrups rode with them as far as the end of the Red Lane,—John Shore had no less than three for his portion,—a girl in front and two boys behind,—and Bub Williams carried his baby daughter that far in his arms, the women trooping along on foot in the rear. The procession halted there; the children were embraced and set down. Then were more last words.

"Be sure and write if yer get killed sure enough, John," called out Jinny.

"You'd better get off, and alight from, and leave that there horse of yours," cried Brother White to Tim. "Yes, all of you, the whole of you. You'll wish you had. Wait till the time for the fulfilment of purposes comes, that's all, and then remember that I said so."

"Go 'long, if you're going," shouted old Williams, gruffly, with a lump in his throat. "Bub, you're all the son I've got; be keerful; but don't you sneak out of nothin', neither, d'ye hear?"

"Oh, Bub! Bub! goo-oo-ood-bye," sobbed Mrs. Williams, junior, who could have better spared a better husband. A loud wail went up from all the women except one brave wife, who called out, "Yer'll all be back home by the time the Lady is."

"Come on!" cried John Shore, and they were off—the Mountain and the United States had gone to war.

If no rain fell that day on the Mountain, there were tears enough shed to make up for it. By the time "the Lady returned back," a third of the scouts, it was known, would never again see the hills and homes they had so recently left, and at the end of four years fifteen tattered, bronzed, indomitable veterans came straggling in, one by one, into the Red Lane, so slow of gait and sore at heart that they would have cried out in biblical speech for the mountains to fall upon them and the hills to cover them if they could have expressed defeat and despair at all adequately. The war was over, and the Mountain had got the worst of it.

John Shore was one of them, and the fact had not the effect of endearing him to the community. In many minds it militated against him distinctly. Who had first brought this war to the Mountain and

e 6*

preached a crusade in favor of it but John Shore? Many women argued that there never would have been a war but for him, and arraigned him as the originator and promoter of the disastrous scheme that had brought them such misery. That he should have come out of it safe and sound when "better men" had perished was a source of irritation to them. But his own estimate of his good fortune was not a high one. "I'd liever have died than to have lived to see this day," he often said, with perfect sincerity, in the first dark days that followed the surrender; and meeting Mrs. Williams, whose husband had been killed in his first engagement, he had quailed almost guiltily before her, and had protested humbly: "I wish it had of been me, Nelly, instead of him, and that's the truth. There don't seem to be no place, leastways no rightmost place, fur me in this world that I can see, noway, and there wouldn't er been nobody to cry fur me." This sad little speech ought to have mollified Mrs. Williams, who had promptly canonized "Bub" as the saintliest of spouses and looked upon herself as a martyr, but it did not. She maintained then and ever after that John Shore had "murdered" her own dear, model husband, and this coming to his ears he was not a little wounded.

There were a good many things to depress John Shore at home and abroad now. One was that he had come back to find Alfred married to, or, rather, married by, a shrewish widow,—a Mrs. Stubbs *née* "Tildy" New-man,—an elderly ugly woman with an uglier temper, and what was more, because incurable, a mean soul. "Tildy" Newman had always been known as "a Screamer," and was often alluded to as "a Captain."

The Mountain had never heard of Woman's Rights, but it had not lacked for strong-minded and self-willed females who held scornful views of men in general, and refused to follow or be led by them in any single particular, and such were called " Captains."

It was by the sheerest exercise of will-power that the Widow Stubbs had first proposed, and then elected, and then installed herself as Alfred's master and the mistress of the cottage, and never was any man more systematically overrun and completely subjugated than her quasi lord and spouse. He may have liked it, and certainly did not attempt to resent or change their relative positions. The very thought of "standing out agin Matildy" appalled him and threw him into greatest possible confusion and distress of mind, so he fell back upon his reserves of constitutional vacuity and phlegm (finding the war from which he had shrunk for four years his portion for life), and cultivated the art of being inoffensive and of diverting the enemy's fire, until he got it down to a remarkably fine point for a dull man. And he solaced himself as he could, chiefly with tobacco and maple-sugar, keeping a supply of the latter constantly on hand, broken up into bits, that he might be ready for any emergency and take one every half-hour until relieved.

If Mrs. Alfred Shore was acutely disagreeable to her father-in-law at this period, though, it must be confessed that it was because she was insufferable, and not because she tried to be. She had never made such efforts to be the woman she ought to have been,—to ingratiate herself with anybody as she did with him,—and this for a good and sufficient reason. The cottage and farm were his. Yet the more she laid herself out to please him, the less she succeeded in doing so. The veneer which calculation and interest lay over a character has the bad fault of peeling off and constantly showing the real grain of the wood beneath; and he knew her better than she thought, and liked her less every day,—a fact of which she was perfectly aware, though she did not seem to be. But it was not alone because the house was not the home that he remembered that John Shore began after a few months to get, as he said himself, " as restless as a panther." The dull, eventless life he was leading seemed more unendurable to him than when he was a young man, even after the excitements and fluctuating fortunes of the past four years, and with his enlarged views and experience of the world he was less tolerant than ever of the intense conservatism, narrow ideas, and invincible prejudices of the Mountain.

It must be confessed, too, that the prospect of set- tling down to regular, hard, and uncongenial work was particularly disagreeable to him, for it was always urged against him, with perfect truth, that he was a lazy man. More than one fault of temperament had developed and crystallized into fixed habit in the long years in which he had roved here and there after the death of the wife he had so tenderly loved. The force of circumstances with him, as with us all, counted for much,—that mighty force pressing every moment and hour and day of our lives upon precisely the points in our natures which are weakest, with a mightier power behind it which only bides its time to seize and sweep one or other of us out beyond the reach of human help and sympathy. The acute misery and its subsequent stupor had passed away; the lack of purpose, the paralysis of will and energy, had remained. The war had healthfully stimulated him in many ways, and while it lasted he had been more like the John Shore of old than he had ever thought he could be.

The incident and variety of the life, its gayety and good-fellowship, even its hardships and trials, had done much to restore his mental balance and natural cheerfulness. And his talents as a raconteur and musician, and a certain peculiar vein of humor, added to his courage and generosity, had made him a favorite among his fellows, which corrected the morbid sense of failure and loneliness he had suffered from. But it had been a reckless and unsettling career on the whole, and now that it was all over, the old despondency settled down upon him more darkly than ever. And so it came about that one evening when supper was over at the Shores' and Matilda had left the room, John Shore said to his son, " Al, I can't stay here no longer. I've sorter got the tramps, I reckon, and there ain't more than work enough for one man here noway. I'm goin' out West, and I don't reckon I'll ever come back agin, dead or alive."

" Peter Robinson!" ejaculated Alfred. " Yer don't say so!" and fell to staring.

" Yes," went on the father, " that's my idee, and so I have went to town and fixed things 'bout this here place. It's all yours, my son, and here's your showin'." Here he laid the deed he had taken from his pocket down on the table, and repeated, " Yes, it's all yours, and I think you kin make a good livin' off it, and I hope you'll prosper right along."

" But what's to become er *you?*" inquired Alfred, still staring.

" Oh, I kin scratch along somehow," his father replied. " Never mind 'bout me, so's you are all right. And Al, I've got one thing to ask er you and I hope you'll do it. Don't let the hogs and cows go trampin' round on your mother's grave. I've done fixed it up good now, and the idee of the fence fallin' down, maybe, sometime, and her bein' run over by stock hurts me powerful, so promise me you'll see that's kep' right. You will now, won't yer?"

" I will, Pa-ap," said Alfred. " But hadn't you better consider on it a while and see what this here projicking is goin' to come to? Hadn't you better stay here with me and Tildy?"

The conjunction of names in this appeal was unfortunate.

" No; my mind's made plum up. I'm goin' to-morrow," said the father, fixing at once the time for his departure. " But, Al, I won't do like I did befo'. I'll write you regular, though I ain't no scholard, and you must write to me."

In this easy way did John Shore deprive himself of everything that he had in the world, and with no other companion than the violin with which he had beguiled the weariness and sadness of his comrades around a thousand camp-fires, prepare to turn his back a second time on the Mountain.

" He only come home to tempt away my husband," said that most illogical of mourners, Mrs. Williams, " and I don't care what becomes of him."

" Cracky! what a fool!" commented Mrs. Alfred Shore,

contemptuously, when her husband explained the situation and gave her the "showin'." "I kain't believe it."

"You ain't oughter to talk like that," he remonstrated, mildly. "Yer ain't oughter, Tildy."

"Oh, kiss the cat!" his wife scornfully replied. "He *is* a fool. A most tremenjus, nateral-born fool. But that's all right. You give *me* that there paper."

"So Johnny Shore's done willed off all he's got, they tell me, and is goin' trapesin' off agin beyant the Ridge," said one of the elders to Jake White when he heard the news. (It was always "Johnny" Shore after this.)

"I've heerd that it's yea and verily," he replied, with unctuous satisfaction. "And who wondereth and is astonished? He always was a no-'count, curous creature, and a mover, and a traveller, and not an abider, and a tiller, and a toiler gathering into barns. And what I've said, and told you, and remarked upon, and showed forth has come true agin and agin in the fulfilment of purposes, and is not to be gainsaid nor denied by them that shoot out the lip, and them that run about and grin like dogs, and *would* go to the war in spite of being held back by the graybeard and the wise ones in the council, which was inspired, and instructed, and filled to overflowing. And observe. They had destruction wrought upon them and was confused, and confounded, and overthrown, and swallowed up! And again. He always was a poor, foolish luniac of a disputer, and perverter, and leader astray, and he goeth to his own and will never be missed here, nor there, nor hither, nor no-whither."

"It's a bad plan, my father usened to say, to take

off your clothes till you're gittin' into bed; and as fur
me——" began the elder. But he was interrupted.
" You don't understand this here case, nor see it, nor
comprehend it. It ain't a thing of clothes nor clothing,
nor beds nor bedding, nor of couches, nor of sofys, nor
of tables, nor of chairs," said Mr. White, turning his
whole long, lank person towards his companion in his
earnestness, and punctuating his remarks by tapping
the palm of his left hand briskly with the fingers of
the right. "It's a question of comin' to the footstool.
It's *Vital Religion.* He ain't never sought fur it, nor
he ain't never got it, nor he ain't never *goin'* to git
it, and it's because he ain't got no single scrap, nor
mite, nor grain, nor speck of real, true, workin', foamin',
fermentin', tearin', *upheavin'* piety in him! He ain't
got, and very few *has* got, any idee what a commo-
tionary, convulsivary, *agitatuating* religion that there
Vital Religion is. Why, *I* ain't never got it yit, and
I've tried the hardest, and laid as close to it as I am
to you. It takes a power of work, and patience, and
time. I don't know as Methusalem could uv done it ef
he'd uv been a Seeker. I've got the searchin's on me
this minute pretty nigh as bad as ever, and me at three-
score and ten! But this I know, and *all* knoweth it,
moreover. Vital Religion is the *only* religion. It can
take you, or me, or even Johnny Shore, like we was an
onion, and strip the devil off, and then pull the sinner
off, and then shuck off the man, and then shake his
miserable soul till the angel that's in him drops out
naked before his eyes clean, and white, and shinin'!
Yes, yes, Brother Williams. It's a wonderful, and an
amazin', and a marvellous thing to them that knows it

at all, or has had any sort, or kind, or description of dealin's with it, is the genuine Vital Religion! And again. The trouble with this here Johnny is, and was, and always has been, that he ain't never climbed up like Zaccheus to see what sort of a religion he was standin' in down below here. He ain't never been a Seeker nor a Searcher. He took the first religion that come along, and it was a cheap religion, and cheap religions ain't goin' to last nor to endure. And now he's a heathen and a Saducer."

"Well, I don't give in to that nor no talk like it," said Jim Wilkins, who was sitting by. "He was as good a soldier as ever shouldered a musket; true grit all through. And but fur him, I wouldn't be a-settin' here, for he was the one that went out at Sharpsburg under cross-fire and brought me back into our lines when I was left out there wounded, and him no great friend of mine, neither. I ain't never goin' to forget that. I sez to him yesterday, 'John, what are you striking tent for now, after marchin' all over creation for four years? Ain't you had enough of it? I wouldn't go straggling off ef I was you.' And he sez to me, 'Jim, don't say nothin' more 'bout it. I'm bound to go.' I reckon he don't like his company *and his captain,* and that's the reason he's goin' to desert. She'll rule or bust" (jerking his pipe towards "Shores')." "I couldn't stand a Captain myself. My old woman's got a temper, but she ain't a Captain. There ain't no better woman than Mandy, and I understand her. It takes an old soldier to be up to 'em. The other night, now, when that big storm come on, Mandy was skeered to death, and every bit of the stiffenin' went right out of her,

D   7

and she got on the feather-bed and screeched like a
wild-cat for me and the children to come on it too. I
was standin' at the door; I warn't skeered,—I'd bin
under fire before; but I seed she was, and I thought to
myself, 'I'll divert the enemy by a flank movement.'
So I steps up to her and sez, 'Mandy, you're behavin'
like a igit. Shet right up now! shet up, or I'll whop
yer!' Yer ought ter seen her! Moses! but she was
mad! She upped and slapped my face fur me, and
called me everything under the sun! But she forgot
all 'bout the thunder and lightnin', and when it was
over she asked me to forgive her, and was as soft as
butter in July fur a week. And I tell you I had a good
supper! That's *tactics*. You can't get on with no
woman long without *tactics* any more'n you can move
a whole army round without 'em. She's infantry, and
cavalry, and artillery, and baggage-wagons, *I tell you*.
And as long as they are only that, I don't mind; but
when it comes to a cornstant guerilla and low bushwhacker like Al Shore's wife, there ain't nothin' fur it
but to desert yourself or to kill her, and you can't kill
nobody now the war's over. It's ridiculous the people
that's let to live and go round loose pisonin' places,
and bullets and powder as plenty as blackberries."

It was Jim Wilkins who slipped a plug of tobacco
into his old comrade's pocket when the morning of his
departure came, saying, "Good-by! Take care uv yourself, you old Johnny Reb, you," and tried to hang a
spruce canteen around his neck.

"Mandy's mother, who's got the cheek uv a govermint mule, confiscated this long ago," he explained,
"and when I know'd you wuz goin', it 'peared to me

liko you'd be certain to want a canteen, no mattor whur you went to; and I knowed that Mandy's mother warn't one to give up nothin' she'd over laid her hands on, and was keepin' tomato catsup in this; and so I sez to her, 'Give mo that canteen, and I'll have it covered agin with leather, and it'll bo splendid to put hot water in and put up noxt agin your side whon you get that bad pain you're subject to,' and I got it away. That's *tactics*, John. And I've done had it fixed up fur you, and I hope you'll take it. It's the one I carried all endurin' the war."

The parting had taken place between John and his family, and it had not boen an emotional one,—Tildy being coolly civil, feeling that she was getting rid of him forever, and Alfrod woodenly undemonstrative, as usual; so it was no wonder that ho was touched by his comrade's kindness, and that his eyes were very moist as he said, "Thank you, Jim. I'm 'bleeged to you; but I don't need it, and ain't likely to. I've got my knapsack and my fiddle, you see. But I'm mightily 'bleeged to you. You are 'bout the only one here that's sorry to see the last of me, I reckon. I ain't complainin', but that's so."

"Wher'll you be to-night?" inquired Mr. Wilkins.

"I dunno; but I'll do very well. Many's the night you and me have slep' in fence-corners and mud-puddles, and under baggage-wagons when we wuz lucky. Ain't it now, Jim?"

"Yes, indeed; but that fiddle uv yourn. How it does remind mo of them old times and all the boys and everything! You couldn't play me 'Zip Coon' once more agin, now, could you, John?"

" No, Jim ; I ain't got the time, and I ain't got the heart, to tell the truth. Good-by, Jim !"

" Good-by, John !" Jim Wilkins walked away slowly and thoughtfully a little distance, and then came back. "John," said he, "I ain't never thanked you for savin' my life, but I feel it *here,*" laying his hand on his heart. "John, I've got a nice tin-cup——"

"I couldn't er done no different, Jim. Never mind 'bout that. Good-by, Jim. Good-by !"

Jim Wilkins walked off again slowly, and again turned back. "John," said he, pulling out a large, dingy, battered old silver watch, "it ain't fit to give you : it don't keep time, and it ain't got no hands, and the works is rusted bad ; but it's a watch, and maybe you could git it fixed up some time." He held it up as he spoke, and it looked like a third-century moon in very reduced circumstances, while his own face was red and eager. " It was give to me by a Yank that I captured once and let go free—just shut my eyes, you know—'cause he hadn't long to live noway, and I couldn't get my consent to 'lowin' him to die in prison. I never thought I'd give it away ; but I'd like *you* to have it, and it's *been* a splendid watch. He give ten dollars for it, he told me. Maybe ef the foraging ain't good whur you're goin' to, you might find it handy. Don't you remember, John, the night me and you got into that store in Frederick and got all them hams together, and wuz goin' fur the sardines and preserves, when the enemy come down on us and run us out without a single derned thing ? Ha ! ha ! ha ! Oh, them was lively times, them was ! Here, John, take it— take it."

"No, no, Jim; keep your watch. I don't want it. Put it up. Good-by, Jim! Take care of yourself."

Again Jim Wilkins started off and got about a hundred yards, when he again returned, running this time, all his thoughts and heart full of "the brave days of old" and the friend who had shared them.

"Here, John. Here, take this. You *shall*, damn you! Good-by!" he called out, hastily thrusting into his comrade's hand something like a bill, if an angry yellow envelope could be trusted, and this time, without waiting for an answer, he went off in earnest. On being opened it disclosed Mr. Wilkins's most precious possession,—which he always carried about with him,—a war photograph of a murderous-looking man in a plain uniform, with no insignia of rank.

John Shore knew it well, and recognized it at once. "Why, ef that there coon ain't give me old Blue Light!" he exclaimed, and felt overpowered, for he had seen that picture before, and knew its history, and how Jim Wilkins valued it. He had heard how he came by it a hundred times, at least, and now he had given it away. "Jim! Jim! you hadn't never ought to have done that," he said, turning to remonstrate with his friend. "Stop! Hold on!" But Mr. Wilkins had cut across a field, and was not to be stopped. On realizing this, John Shore felt very blank for a while. Then he suddenly gave vent to a loud, peculiar cry, which was answered cheerfully from the crest of the hill, after which he felt better satisfied. Jim understood all that he had meant to convey by that "rebel yell," he knew. "Old Blue Light!" thought he, examining the picture critically again before returning it to the envelope.

7*

"Give to Jim by him when he was his orderly. Well, I never dreamed Jim cared that much for anybody. It don't seem right to keep a thing like that," and so thinking, placed it securely in his pocket.

This interview had taken place in the Red Lane; and it was not the only farewell in store for John Shore, for, as he walked along meditatively, he suddenly felt his progress arrested by a soft something clinging about his leg, which, on looking around, he perceived to be a little girl.

"Why, hello! R. Mintah. Is that you? What are you 'bout?" said he, and picked the child up in his arms. John Shore was the friend of every child on the Mountain, but he was in an especial sense the friend of this young person for the reason that it was generally said of her that she "had no friends."

The Mountain had not come to "R. Mintah;" perhaps because she was not a prophet, which was curious, seeing that she came of a sex which foresees everything and is nearly always able to say "I told you so." However, it was "R. Mintah" who had come to the Mountain. She had been found sitting in the Red Lane one morning, a round-eyed innocent, quite absorbed in a lapful of daisies,—the last wavelet of a receding tide of Federal troops,—a little pearl cast up by the storm; in prose, a child wickedly abandoned by its mother,—a camp follower,—grown weary of its accusing innocence and utter helplessness. There she was presently found by Mrs. Newman, who lived opposite,—a slovenly, large-featured, large-hearted woman, who in breadth of beam and mild wholesomeness, in bovine tranquillity, and in the abundance and richness of the milk of human kindness in her, was irresistibly suggestive of one of her own short-horn cows.

And there and then she was clasped to the motherly bosom of a woman who, having nothing, was perfectly willing to divide it, and, possessing already a numerous progeny of her own, whom, with all her exertions, she could not keep other than ill fed and scantily clothed, did not hesitate for one moment to graft this stray bud of humanity on her family tree and give it an equal share of what they all lacked in common, and of the love and care that all alike possessed richly. "Her bite and sup 'll never count, father," she said to her husband. "It might er been one uv ourn lef' to perish." With this she got down a small black Bible which had been left there by a colporteur years before (she kept it on a shelf above her bed, sewed up in an old handkerchief), and not being able to read, had no idea that she was fulfilling at least one of its precepts, when she added, "She's goin' to be one uv ourn from this minit." Not knowing how to write, she took the volume over to one of her neighbors, who was "a scholard," and had the little waif regularly enrolled and incorporated as a member of her family under the name, style, and title of "R. Mintah (Araminta) Newman," to the infinite disgust of her eldest daughter, Mrs. Alfred Shore.

This being R. Mintah's history, John Shore had felt himself more than usually drawn to her, and now he carried her along the lane in his arms, talking to her as he went, until, hearing his own name called, he halted, and looking around and about and finally up, he saw that he had been accosted by Jinny Hodges,—Jinny,

who had been promptly turned out of the cottage long
ago by Alfred's wife, and had gone to live with her
aunt, Mrs. Lem Hodges,—Jinny, who had climbed up
into an apple-tree with the intention of commanding a
view of that lane down which John must pass.

There was a trace of her old coquettishness in the
way she called out "John, John, where are you goin'?
Ain't you got no eyes?" and it sat strangely on her thin
face, wrinkling perpetually into wide smiles. John did
not notice it any more than the fact that she wore her
pink calico, and had on a collar of crochet-lace and a
breastpin, the signs and tokens of a great occasion.
She made a feint of gathering apples for a moment, and
John said, "I went over to see yer yesterday, Jinny,
but you warn't there, and now I'm off."

"Yes, I heerd you was goin'," she replied, looking
down at him, "and I'm sorry you've got that maggot
in yer mind, John. Lor'! nothin' ain't what it was.
I usened to be mighty happy at the cottage with Al,—
that was when you was dead, John,—and ef yer hadn't
uv gone to no war, and had uv—well, anyways, why
can't yer stay along here whur you've been raised,
even ef yer've got to live 'round like me, 'cause that
wildcat Al's married stuck her claws inter yer and
goes on gougin'? You'd get used to it, or perhaps yer
might make another home uv yer own, and live in it;
alone, in course, John, and——"

"No, Jinny," said he, interrupting her. "I can't get
my consent to that, and I'm goin'. That's settled. But
I'd wish to see *you* better fixed; and I wouldn't have
'lowed you to leave Al's house,—it's his house now, but
it was mine then,—only Al thought you two women

couldn't never git on. But you know all about that. And now I must be gittin' on."

On hearing this, Jinny gathered her clothes about her feet, and, slipping down to the ground, came to close quarters.

"John," said she, " are you goin'? Sho 'nough? Yer —yer couldn't take me with yer, John, could yer? If you could, John, I—we—shucks, John! *You* know! I could work 'round, and not cost you nothin'. I'm a powerful hand at washin', and can cook better'n most, and could keep myself. And if you was to get sick and die agin, John, it would be mighty bad to be all alone off there, and I could lay you out just splendid, John! I've got the pattern of them pants you've got on this minnit, and there ain't no shirt or coat that *I* can't make. I'd bury you sho 'nough, and no come back, I can tell you." But even this supreme inducement had no effect upon John Shore, except to make him say hastily and rather harshly, "Hesh, Jinny, hesh! Don't say no more. It's onpossible every way; onpossible, and you ain't ought to er projicked it out, though I know you mean well by me, and right by yourself too. I'll never marry no woman alive," said John Shore, earnestly.

" Well, ef you won't, yer won't," she retorted, cheerfully. " Go yer own ways by yer lone self, and if you come back here agin and tell me you're dead yourself till you're black in the face, I won't believe yer, John; and if I hear you're livin' here and livin' there, I'll think to myself, 'There's no knowin' rightly,' and I never expect to know rightly in this world; for though I've knowed you, livin' and dead, fur thirty years——"

f

"Jinny, shake hands.   Good-by to you!   Take R. Mintah home, and be kind to her when you git a chance.   Go to her, honey" (to the child).   "Good-by, now," said John Shore, hurriedly, and so moved on, as firm as ever in his determination to leave the place, but unconsciously bound to it afresh by the very unexpected evidences he had that morning received that he was not as poor in some respects as he had thought.

III.

"A dog-rose blushing to a brook ain't modester or sweeter."
LOWELL.

THE Mountain had its feet firmly planted in the plain, and could not go straying about the world as some of its children chose to do.   It seemed at first to the little community that the end of the world had come with the end of the war, and that there was nothing more to expect.   It was in a mechanical fashion, at first, that they began to put up their fences, to rebuild and restore, to sow, and reap, and harvest, and take up the old life again, and marks of care and deep-seated despondency were as visible in the faces of the young and middle-aged as they had formerly been in those of the elder folk.   But soon for them all—cruelly soon it seemed to some widows, and mothers, and orphans—the ante-bellum order of things was resumed, with only such individual loss, and pain, and privation as were past mending in this world.   It was as though some rude vehicle had

been roughly jolted out of the deep ruts it had made
for itself and had then slipped back into them again.
No one on the Mountain had ever owned, or so much as
dreamed of owning, a slave, and there was no change in
the conditions of their lives as in those of the class
above them. They had always been poor, they had
always been obliged to work, they had always been
isolated from their fellows; it was only going on with
their accustomed tasks and bearing their accustomed
burdens after a brief, if startling, interruption. Some
of the women whose faces had long borne a pathetic
stamp of conscious or unconscious sadness, born of
the lonely grandeur of their surroundings and the
barrenness of their lives, now sank into a melancholy
that deepened into madness. A few of the old people could no longer bear up under losses and crosses
that their poor old hearts could not sustain. But
new life, new hopes, stirred in the mass of the people,
and in twelve years so peaceful and prosperous was
the country that it seemed incredible that two armies
had ever occupied it for four years and played at
battledore all the while with the Mountain for shuttle-
cock. There had been changes on the Mountain, of
course. " Brother" White had died, for one thing, and
Vital Religion had only abandoned him with the vital
spark, for, falling suddenly ill while away from home
visiting an Irish friend at Harper's Ferry, he had been
converted on his death-bed by a Roman Catholic priest,
and then and there ended his career as a Seeker before
he had time to discover the existence of the Old Catho-
lics or of the Greek and Coptic Churches. The affair
created a great sensation among his friends and rela-

tives, none of whom had the remotest idea what "a Romian Catholic" was, but were impressed the more by his determination to leave no known religion untried. "I see him the night befo' he lef'," said one of them. "And he had the searchin's turrible then, and he sez to me, 'Jo, there ain't no let-up in this here Vital Religion. It's wearin' me plum out. There's pints in the Methodist religion that suited, and pints in the Baptist religion that suited, and pints in the United Bruthring, and the Dunkards, and the Campbellite, and all the others I've tried, that when I stood, and thought of, and reflected about, and meditated on 'em, seemed, and 'peared, and *looked* like they was it. But they warn't. When I come to sift 'em, and to examine 'em, and to weigh 'em, and to balance 'em, and *to live in 'em*, Jo, they warn't it. Not the whole, real true, sho-'nough and no-mistake thing,—no.' Them was his very words."

Five of the "Cross-Roads Wilkins" children had been swept off by diphtheria in a few weeks.

Goody Williams and old Daddy Culbert, at fourscore, had, on the contrary, both got what pugilists would call their second wind, and were trying another round with Time with great spirit. Joe Potter, who had been the poorest of the poor, had set up a "public," and become the richest of the rich, according to the standards of wealth of the community, and had bought a farm in the Valley, and "couldn't see good" when he met his old friends, and attended this or that trial at "the cotehouse" in his own buggy, while his sister had been sent to the county almshouse.

John Culbert, who had been the richest of the rich,

according to the same standards, and the most respectable man on the Mountain, had become both poor and disreputable. "Sal Jones's husband" was dead of consumption, and gone to a world where it is to be hoped he was known as something else than the adjunct of his masterful spouse; and Gus, his brother, had got a place "to stand in a store" in a neighboring town, than which nothing could have been more "genteel." Timothy White had amazed everybody by marrying Jinny Hodges, who got the credit of having "spoke the word." He had long since "taken his name off the books of the church" because they "kep' on pesterin'," and no doubt felt the need of some such stimulating influence as was afforded by his highly loquacious and vivacious spouse. The Newman family had grown steadily larger and poorer. A number of entries had followed in the black Bible, and wonderful characters upon that of little "R. Mintah," as the years went by, ending at last with a pair of "twins,"—"Simon Peter" and "Stonewall Jackson" by name and the scourges of the neighborhood. Yet they were all fed somehow, if but coarsely; and all clothed, though scantily; and Mrs. Newman seemed more profoundly placid than ever, broader and milder, in spite of her increasing cares and the fact that the greatest drain of all upon her motherly sympathies was not made by her children at all, but by her husband, a small man with a waspish temper, a kind heart, and a long-drawn lawsuit with John Culbert about a "yearling" calf.

Little R. Mintah had shared the checkered fortunes of the family, or rather their misfortunes,—for the black squares were out of all proportion to the white,—had been given a child's portion of all they possessed with the other children,. had lacked only what all lacked, and had grown into a slender, round-waisted young girl, small, but perfectly formed, sweet-faced, and ·"tender-eyed" as Leah. Such a shy, quiet little creature was she,—so meekly obedient and tractable, so grateful for kindness, and ready to do or suffer anything for her adopted family,—that it is no wonder that she was liked and kindly treated by them all in the main, and a favorite with Mrs. Newman, who always spoke of her as "a good, willin' child" and loved her for many reasons, but most of all for the benefits she had conferred upon her. Unfortunately, even Juno had her gadfly, and R. Mintah, a poor girl with none of the powers and privileges of a goddess, had a bitter, implacable enemy and sad torment in Matilda Shore. From her very babyhood Matilda had impressed upon her that she was a burden to and a blight upon the family. It was she who set her impossible tasks, and whom, do what she would, she could never please. She dealt her many a blow openly, and more with her tongue that were even more cruel, and made her child's heart bleed inwardly and swell almost to bursting with unutterable grief and despair. She came over every day for the express purpose of sticking a pin of some kind into her, and, finding her digging in the garden, sweeping, cooking, washing industriously, would still bully and browbeat her as harshly as though she had been the idlest, worst girl in the world, which, in fact, was the description she was in the habit of giving of her. When Matilda lived at home, she had rarely lifted a family burden with so much as the tip of one finger, for she was as selfish as imperious; but all the same she invented work continually for R. Mintah, besides seeing that she got a full share of the regular daily duties, and was never so offended as when she discovered that she was pleasantly occupied, if only in shelling peas. "It's scrubbin' you ought to be, down on your hands and knees, Miss," she would say, "and not settin' there playin' lady." But for Matilda's treatment the girl would certainly never have got the peculiarly deprecating look in her eyes that would have disarmed any one less hard and malignant,—a look that had no effect whatever on the enemy, but gave her a friend scarcely less troublesome. Exactly when Jonah, the eldest son (a big, manly, muscular fellow) began to loom up as R. Mintah's champion, and "take her part," is not clear; but it is certain that bit by bit he took upon himself the heaviest of her daily duties, and by gradual, natural transitions became first her friend and then her lover. Great was his mother's astonishment, as she sat one day placidly patching one of about twenty hopeless garments, to have him fling open the back door and call in, angrily, "Mother, mother, did you tell R. Mintah to cut up this here hickory? It's a sin and a shame! She shan't put an axe to it. No; and she ain't goin' to do nothin' like it, neither, while *I'm* here to do it fur her."

Furious beyond precedent was Matilda when Jonah, finding the red mark of her hand on R. Mintah's cheek, and learning that she had been boxed for not finishing a dress of Matilda's in time to wear the preceding Sunday, seized his sister and shook her until she screamed with fright, and threatened worse things if she dared to lay a finger on "his little R. Mintah." It was then that his secret love for the good, gentle, little girl jumped out of his heart and throat, and that for the first time she learned with all the rest what he felt and intended.

"I love her," he said, as bold as a lion, "and I'm goin' to marry her."

"No, no, Jonah! you ain't! You don't!" she cried out, seeing what a tremendous hearth-quake had been created by this announcement, and weeping bitterly she fled to Mrs. Newman, and dropping down by her, would have buried her face in that matron's blue-checked apron, but was repulsed almost as if it had been Matilda instead, and getting up rushed from the room. Mr. Newman was told of it that night by his wife, and the news was so tremendous that it actually drove the law-suit out of his mind for fully an hour; and then it was curious to see how he seemed for the moment to have changed characters with his wife, and to take what had happened in a most amiable and kindly spirit, while she was fretting herself into a fever.

"You must have knowed she'd marry sometime," he said, at first with a masculine irrecognition of the situation that was aggravating beyond description.

"It ain't *her* a-marryin' that I'm a-thinkin' of. It's *Jonah's* the trouble! It's the beatenest thing! How he ever come to think of that ugly little child,—she ain't nothin' but a child,—when he could have any girl on the Mountain, beats all. She's put it in his head. She's a hussy!" declaimed Mrs. Newman, no more just in her anger than the rest of us are. "But she shan't never have my boy,—no! She ought to be ashamed of herself, after all I've done fur her."

"Now, mother, you're gittin' hoppin', and you don't rightly know what you're sayin'. Ain't I heerd you say agin and agin that R. Mintah was the best girl you ever see, and better to you'n any child uv you own, and kind to the children always? and ain't I heerd you wishin' to goodness A. Mander was more like her? And now you're down on her, and givin' her fits. Ef you've got any fuss with her, that's one thing, but don't go on callin' names. It ain't reason. It ain't *law*. Give me the pints of the case, and I'll know what to say. You've lost your temper; that's what, mother. Now git cool, git cool, and give me the *pints* of this here case, and I'll give a *verdick* and stop all this." Mr. Newman's mind was naturally saturated with the legal aspects of things just then, and as he worked away at the huge pair of new brogans that he was greasing he brought his mouth to a focus and listened to what his wife had to say with a highly judicial air of reserve and impartiality. And when she had angrily presented her case, and, with many tears, had sobbed out that she never would "on the face of the yearth" have R. Mintah for a daughter-in-law, and, moreover, threatened a thousand things that she was much too good and kind to carry out, he said, "Mother, you ain't got no argymint at all. Gittin' mad and callin' names ain't argyments. The girl's a good girl and you know it; and ef Jonah's took a likin' to her and set his mind on her he'll carry this thing through ef he's got to git the devil fur his lawyer and pay him with his immortial soul! *You* know what Jonah is. My verdick is, cover down your feelin's, and shet off steam, and stop thrashin' chaff, and tell them two to go 'long and git married together, and

8*

you'll give 'em as good a send-off as you kin. That's
my verdick, and I know what I'm talkin' 'bout. I've
got argymint jes' natchelly. Lawyer Morgan sez
to me to-day when I was goin' over the pints agin and
showin' him how things stood between me and that
damned, lyin', thievin' raskil, Jack Culbert,—he sez to
me, 'Mr. Newman, you ain't had no need to come to
me. You could argy this case at any cote-house in the
country and fetch the jury every time.' And he seed
I was in the right, but said ef I'd take his advice I'd
fix this thing up with Jack Culbert and his lawyer and
stop lawin'. But I told him I'd see Jack Culbert in
hell befo' I'd agree to give him a cent, or one inch of
that yearlin's hoofs, horns, or tail, and so I will."

Mr. Newman was not the only man who heard what
had happened. Timothy White, who was Mrs. Newman's brother, was given a dozen versions of it, and
enjoyed it in his taciturn fashion as another form of
"experience." His advice tallied on the whole with
that of his brother-in-law, but was given far more sen-
tentiously. To Matilda, who came raging and storming
and spitting out all the venom and malice with which
she was bursting, he said, "Let 'em alone. Mind your
own business."

To Mrs. Newman, who wailed out her sorrow and
indignation, he said, "Tilly, you're a fool. Go home
and git back into your right mind agin, and be kind
like you've always been to both them children uv
yourn,"—quite the longest speech of his on record.

To Jonah, who poured out a copious flood of love
and grief and anger, he vouchsafed a curt "Stick to
her."

To R. Mintah, who wept, speechless, and meekly miserable when they met, a mild "Don't cry. Stick to him."

But if Timothy had few words to waste on even such an important matter, it was very different with his wife, who put on her sun-bonnet about twice a day and went to some house where, with the aid of the other women, the whole question was turned over and over, and inside out, and upside down, and "the rights of it," and the wrongs, peculiarities, characters, and circumstances of everybody concerned, were discussed to an unlimited and truly awful extent.

A bad three weeks it was for poor little R. Mintah, who never afterwards forgot the wretchedness of that time. For Mrs. Newman, influenced and inspired by Matilda, took high ground, and sternly forbade the match, and was so unkind and so cold to her little adopted that the girl, who adored her vice-mother, was made miserable. If Mrs. Newman had been Queen of England, and Jonah Prince of Wales, bent upon setting a beggar-maid upon the throne *à la Cophetua,* she could not have been more conscious of the terrible nature and consequences of a *mésalliance,* and more determined to avert the calamity.

As to R. Mintah,—between Jonah, who would not be repulsed, kissed her boldly, night and morning, before the assembled family, and expected her to do exactly what he wished and commanded, and the family, neutral, scornful, talking *at* her, but not *to* her, leaving her severely alone, calling the very children away from her, offering her nothing at table, treating her in everything as a stranger among them, even to the point of doing all her work,—it was no wonder that the loving-hearted child was perfectly miserable. And when Matilda came over with the express intention, avowed before she left home, of "giving that minx a tongue-lashin'," which happened almost daily, the burden of life often seemed to the girl more than she could bear, and she got so pale that Jonah got red with anger every time he looked at her, and so thin that the beautiful red celluloid ring which he had given her (price five cents) rolled off the index-finger of her small, toil-marked hand over and over again. Jonah was tabooed, too, though not boycotted, he being an important member of the family, and his wages more important still; and his mother, after exhausting all her arguments and entreaties, even threatened him one day: "Me and your pap will up and take both uv you down to Mr. Mathers," she said (that gentleman being the Baptist minister, and final referee and chief authority of the neighborhood, combining in his own person as a "preacher" and magistrate all the terrors of the law and Gospel). "We'll see whether you keep on with these here carryin's on."

"Ef all the preachers that ever wuz, and the judges, and the President—ef *General Lee* wuz alive, and wuz to set there and to tell me to give R. Mintah up, I wouldn't do it!" exclaimed Jonah, hotly, while his timid little lady-love sobbed out from behind the apron she had thrown over her head: "Oh! don't take us—don't take us to Mr. Mathers! I ain't never goin' to marry Jo—o—o—nah! Never! Never! Nev—er!"

"She ain't fitten to marry you, and she knows it," said Mrs. Newman.

"No—no! I ain't. I won't!" agreed R. Mintah.

"She's fit to marry anybody!" roared out Jonah, with a stamp of his big boots. "She's worked day and night fur all uv you, she's been driv to death by some uv you, she's the best and the prettiest girl in this whole country, en you might jes' as well try to move Round Hill as me. I'm goin' to marry her."

"You shan't do no sech thing, I say. I'll turn her right out in the Lane ef you say another word!" shrieked Mrs. Newman, quite beside herself, whereupon R. Mintah gave a deep groan of despair, and cried out, as though she had been struck, "Oh,"—and then, catching the expression of Jonah's face,—"I'll go! I'll go!" and actually started to do so, but was seized by Jonah and brought back again bodily.

"Stay still. Stay right here," he said to her, and then to his mother in a voice grown suddenly quiet, "Do you rightly know, mother, what you're sayin'? If R. Mintah is sent out, I'll never darken your door agin, nor she, neither. But I'll marry her all the same. Now, say the word." But Mrs. Newman only burst into tears instead, and would say nothing at all, which under the circumstances was the best thing that could possibly have been said if she had known fifty languages. The truth was that Jonah perfectly well knew the soft and kindly stuff that he had to deal with, and was very sure of getting his way in the end. But he did not get it immediately.

Affairs were in this state of gloom and unrest, when a project was set afoot that created a great stir, and was talked of at "the sto'" (the conversation-haus, club, news-room, exchange, post-office, and grocery of the neighborhood) to the exclusion of every other, almost, for weeks before it became an accomplished fact. It was a proposition of the most novel and startling nature,—of an unparalleled character, indeed. And then the scope of it! It was nothing less than that the Mountain should *amuse* itself! And a picnic at Harper's Ferry, in another State actually, was the mode chosen for doing so! There was no pretence, even, of its being anything but a pleasure-party. It could not be actually traced to anybody, so nobody could be held personally responsible for it. It seemed to be in the air,—a fearful fungus growing out of the decay of all venerable and respectable institutions,— and to combat it was like tackling original sin. The Blue Ridge, Winchell tells us, was once several thousand feet higher than it is now, and has been worn down inch by inch through successive centuries to its present proportions. And in the same way the prejudices of the Mountain were beginning to disappear, and it had become possible for the world to look over its wall and for a winged seed from the flower of a restless and sensuous civilization to drop inside the idea that people could quit work for a whole day, and go "fifty miles" away, for the sole and express purpose of amusing themselves. It was no wonder that the elders denounced it as vicious in conception and ruinous in its consequences,—the beginning of the end of all agricultural righteousness. It was as plain as could be that virtue was staying at home all the year 'round, and working from morning until night, and that pleasure was only another name for vice. Considering the relaxations that human nature had filched from under the nose of the authorities engaged in supporting this impossible code, their view of the case was not unnatural. Pleasure *had* meant vice on the Mountain, as it always must when men who are neither machines nor brutes are expected to live as though they were both; and its votaries were of two classes : the hypocrites, who sinned secretly and sanctimoniously with no loss of caste in the community; and the wilful offenders, who openly abandoned themselves for the time to such gross gratifications as came in their way.

The elders, then, denounced the proposed picnic as the most patent invention of the evil one; but to the young people it opened up irresistible vistas of innocent fun and frolic, and every Jessamy of them all no sooner heard of the plan than he became possessed by the idea of a day spent in feasting and dancing and sweethearting with his Jenny. So that while Daddy Culbert, sitting on a chicken-coop at " the sto'," with his poor old back bent nearly double over his stick, was angrily declaiming in feeble-forcible terms on the puerility and the wickedness of the whole proceeding, saying, " I never heerd nothin' like it in all my born days! No, sir! *I* never heerd of no sich doin's. I'd er got the *cowhide* ef I'd ever talked to *my* father 'bout quittin' my work to go three counties off to a picnic. He'd er picnicked me with fifty on my bare back, and it would er sarved me right, sir,"—at this moment, I say, Daddy Culbert's grandson, who had Montague-Capulet relations of a most tender and complicated character with Miss " A. Mander" Newman, was asking that young lady, with the most unbounded pride and delight, whether he might " 'scort" her to Harper's

Ferry on the following Friday. And even Hi Leathers, proprietor of the "sto'," was so offended by what he felt to be almost a personal attack, since he and his wife and his children seven were all committed to the picnic to the extent of a "snack" (viz., a ham, two cakes, a pot of "apple-butter," a box of sardines) and nine railway tickets, that he first reproved Daddy Culbert sternly for taking and eating an apple off one of the barrels, saying, "Look here! I don't keep a bodin' house. Them apples is set out there to make a showoff, and not for no loafers,"—although apples were as plentiful as blackberries that season,—and five minutes later advised him rather pointedly to "go 'long home, where he belonged,"—conduct that greatly incensed the old man.

Jonah was a great promoter and supporter of the picnic from the first, and worked hard, after hours, for three weeks to get the indispensable requisite for the entertainment. He meant not only to enjoy it, but to make a figure on the occasion. By nice management he engaged a buggy in which to drive R. Mintah into town, having found a man there who for and in consideration of "a likely shoat" agreed to let him have the use of it, and to take charge of that vehicle, so that he could drive home again by moonlight. He bought himself his "weddin' suit." He got a magnificent turkey-red calico for R. Mintah, and told her that it was to be her "frock" on the same occasion. He also laid upon her shrine a yellow parasol, a sailor-hat, a breast-pin, a cake of soap, a dressing-comb, and some other elegant trifles, sentimental in inspiration, but susceptible of practical application. And then he

threw himself down in a split-bottomed chair by her,
put his feet some distance above his head, and, after
haw-hawing in loud satisfaction, said, in his big, boom-
ing, hearty voice, "I tell you, R. Mintah, we're goin'
to *coot* it on Friday!" and abandoned himself to the
most delicious revery. Jonah had reserved the most
impressive details of the scheme to heighten the effect
of the bliss he had planned; but she knew enough to
be dazzled by the prospect unfolded to her, and she
would have revelled in it but for her unhappy position.
She plucked up courage in the course of a week to tell
Mrs. Newman of it, and asked permission to go, with
infinite meekness of mind and manner, but got very
little sympathy, and only such encouragement as could
be found in her cold "Don't come askin' me. You ain't
no child of mine. I ain't got no controlment of you."

Mrs. Newman, for the first time in her life, had
worked herself up into a sore-hearted, wrong-headed
state of resentment and anger that required to be carefully nursed lest it should expend itself, and she took
a perverse satisfaction in the suffering she knew she
was inflicting. So little R. Mintah made herself as
small as possible, and kept as much as possible out of
everybody's way, suing ever by word and look for the
reconciliation her loving heart longed for; and, failing
to get it, she shrunk into a corner, and stitched away,
day by day, sorrowfully, on her raiment, thinking,
thinking, thinking: troubled thoughts of her own un-
happiness and the unkindness she received, but not
bitter, still less revengeful, ones,—tender thoughts of
Jonah's strength and beauty, and wisdom and goodness,
and unbounded generosity and astounding condescen-

sion in caring for a creature so far, far beneath him in
every way,—anxious thoughts of what the end could
be of such a dreadful state of affairs. And night after
night she watered her straw pillow, which was as hard
as fate, with meek tears, quietly shed for fear of waking
the two children that shared her bed. In spite of her
sadness, she could not help delighting in the splendor
that was to be hers. She tried on her new shoes by
moonlight, and had to take them off again almost immediately, so guilty did she feel when she heard their
clamorous dollar-store creak on the bare boards. She
gazed at the dress Jonah had bought, and it seemed
impossible that it could be really hers. People in the
best circles on the Mountain *trimmed* with turkey-red.
But a whole dress of such expensive stuff! What adora-
ble folly and extravagance! And was ever so bright a
sun obscured by such a black cloud? If Mother Newman would only forgive her and love her again, and let
her marry Jonah in ten or twelve years, when she had
learned how to do everything! If she could only put
on that beautiful dress and go off to the picnic with her
full consent and approbation! What perfect bliss!

The great day came, and proved fair, to old Daddy Culbert's disgust, he being anxious for "jest a *leetle* more rain
to round out the corn," but to the entire satisfaction of
everybody else, and by daylight everybody was astir.
Some people, indeed, must have been astir long before,
for R. Mintah, having been kept awake until late by
the feverishness of joyous anticipation, was aroused
while it was still only darkly light by a sound as of
some one moving about the room, and sitting up and
rubbing her eyes, beheld a familiar figure, and would

have exclaimed, "Why, Mandy!" in her amazement,
but that she was met with a "Hesh! Lay still, and
jes' hold your tongue!"

"What are you goin' to do?" she asked.

"I'm goin' to run off to the picnic with Marsh Culbert, that's what!" was whispered back.

"My goodness gracious alive! *You ain't?*" exclaimed
R. Mintah, aghast. "*Mandy!*" But that was exactly
what that rebellious young person meant to do, knowing the utter uselessness of attempting to get leave
from her parents to go anywhere with a Culbert. Accordingly, when fully and festively arrayed, she took
her shoes in her hand, and, with a warning look at R.
Mintah, slipped down-stairs with a heart thumping like
an engine under a full "head" of steam. It was certainly unfortunate that Mr. Newman should at that
very moment have issued from his room and caught
her in the act of leaving the house. The explosion of
wrath that ensued was something tremendous, and soon
brought together every member of the family. Mr.
Newman had long had certain vague suspicions, and in
the torpedo shock of discovery the unfortunate Amanda
had betrayed the rest. There had been rumors of talks
in the orchard and a walk in the woods, too, duly poured
into Mrs. Newman's ears by her female friends and
confirmed by the children. So now Mr. Newman quite
forgot that "argymint" was his peculiar forte, and not
content with "calling names," shook Amanda pretty
roughly and sent her back to her room, and not content with that, even, seized his gun and fairly plunged
down the Lane, where he found exactly the representative of the false brood of Culbert that he thought to

find, and so railed upon and scared that youth that he
was speedily driven from the field, the freckles that had
earned him the sobriquet of "Turkey" Culbert standing
out in unusually high relief from a pallid background,
a fixed conviction in his mind that Mr. Newman had
gone "plum crazy."

The morning having begun thus stormily indoors, R.
Mintah gave up the picnic for lost, and fairly quaked in
her beautiful new boots at the mere thought of ever
having dreamed of such a thing. Amanda's unparalleled audacity, however, had the effect of diverting
attention from her altogether. Such mutiny as hers
was a very minor affair—by contrast almost a righteous
and virtuous outbreak—compared to the infamy of a girl
who could "confound that derned calf!" to her parents'
face and confess openly that she cared for a Culbert.
Mr. Newman could not even pronounce the hated name
without a vicious jerk of the head to the right on the
first syllable, followed by another to the left on the
second, and he stormed about the house so furiously
that Mrs. Newman had, perforce, to take up again her
old *rôle* of soothing and consolatory reflection and comment and amiable impassiveness. It was she, indeed,
who, after watching Jonah fidget about the room for a
while, said, "Go and git ready, R. Mintah, if so be as
you're going to go to that there picnic," and so much
of the harshness was gone from her voice that R. Mintah darted an eager, humble glance at her, and then
Jonah adding, "Hurry up and be smart about it," she
ran off to her room, escaping, as it were, between two
thunderbolts that Mr. Newman was launching at those
"cussed, cattle-thievin', caripterous Culberts." ("Carip-

terous" was a word of Jake White's discovering or invention, and was supposed to convey scorn and contempt
in the superlative degree.) There she lost no time in
putting on her simple finery without any of the fond,
lingering touches and prolonged enjoyment of each of
its delightful details that she would otherwise have indulged in, and going down she ventured to murmur a
very faint good-by to all the family, her eye seeking
Mrs. Newman's the while, and so through the room,
Jonah taking her by the arm and drawing her outside.

"Look-a-here!" said he, indicating with a wave of
his hand that he was a subject to repay critical examination. "Sto' close. Bully, ain't they?"

And R. Mintah, struck almost dumb by what she saw,
could only exclaim at first, "My goodness me!" twice,
and then, "Oh, Jonah, how good-lookin' you are!"

"And look-a-yonder!" he commanded, pointing towards the gate, and R. Mintah looking saw a vehicle as
magnificent as the lord-mayor's coach in an old rattle-
trap drawn by an anatomical study in the shape of a
horse,—a lank, low-spirited white horse with a Roman
nose and a tired tail.

"Oh, Jonah," she exclaimed again, her face flushed
with delight, "it ain't never a *buggy?*"

"Yes, it is, too, as sho' as you are born," he affirmed.
"Come 'long!"

He strode ahead eagerly, and when she came up he
pulled a large basket from under the seat, saying, "And
look-a-there!"

"Oh, Jonah!" cried R. Mintah for the third time.
"*My!* Well, I never did! Pickles! and a coky-nut!

9*

and cakes! and pies! and beer! and I don't know what all!"

"Git in," said he, affecting to ignore her raptures, but really almost bursting with gratified vanity and affection. R. Mintah obeyed. "Put up yer rumberella," he commanded, and the yellow parasol shot up above her head.

"Now, if there's anything mo' that you want, R. Mintah——" he began, feeling perfectly certain that there wasn't.

"There ain't nothin' on the top of the green yearth," she affirmed, earnestly, with a beaming look of tenderness. On hearing this Jonah took his place by her, put his feet on the dashboard, lit a five-cent cigar, pushed his hat well back on his head, and was about to drive off when he remembered that he had forgotten to bring out a whip.

"A *segar!* Oh, Jonah!" said R. Mintah, in a tone of mild reproach, feeling that this *was* giving the reins to reckless expenditure. "A segar! Mercy!"

"Set still and don't you move till I come back," he cautioned fondly. "I don'- know nothin' 'bout that horse, noways, and he may start off and you git hurt. Whoa there!"

He need not have concerned himself about that highly phlegmatic animal if he had only known it. A fire might have been built under "Old Hunderd," as the gray had been christened by his facetious owner, without his moving an inch. But not knowing this, Jonah kept an eye on him while running back to the house. He had disappeared inside, and R. Mintah was swinging her feet in an abandonment of utter content and looking after him with a happy smile, when she heard a harsh, scornful voice behind her say, " Who's that ? R. Mintah ! *You* in a buggy?" It was Matilda *endimanchée* walking down to get in a neighbor's cart, with Alfred by her side taking his pleasure very sadly indeed.

"Jonah he done it," explained R. Mintah. "I didn't know—I hadn't no idee—I never——"

"Git out ! Git right out !" commanded Matilda. "Jonah's my brother, and do you suppose *I'm* goin' to town in a cart and *you* ride in a carriage? No indeed and double deed, Miss ! Ef he's got the money to fool away hirin' round buggies, *I'm* the one to be settin' in 'em. Git right out."

"Sh ! Tildy ! Come on," put in Alfred. "Time's a flyin'. Trains are startin'."

R. Mintah had hesitated for a moment about obeying. Had not Jonah told her to stay there ? · She looked up the path, but not seeing him, she first said,—

"I'm feared to leave this here sperriting horse," and then, scared by the fierceness of Matilda's expression as she advanced a step, saying, "Ef you don't git out this minute I'll *drag* yer out !" she meekly descended to earth again. Matilda immediately took her place, saying, "Come, set here, Alfred," to her husband, who coughed and stroked his chin reflectively, but made no movement.

"Grazin's mighty poor," said he. "I never see it no poorer. Horses is lookin' bad. Rains——"

" Who's talkin' 'bout rains?" shouted Matilda. "Come, git in. There's room fur you and me and Jonah."

Alfred looked at her and then at R. Mintah in a state of dubiety painful to witness. "Ahem ! I dunno, Tildy,

as——" he began, but got no further, for at that moment Jonah ran down the path, whip in hand. Matilda's color, like her temper, flamed high ; but she kept
her seat, and with a sudden inspiration she leaned forward and smote Old Hundred so soundly on the right
flank that, utterly amazed, he was actually startled into
a gallop. Ride to the picnic R. Mintah never should !
But Jonah gave chase, and in a few minutes came up
with her. No power on earth could *keep* the gray in a
gallop. A violent scene ensued between the brother
and sister,—R. Mintah begging and imploring both of
them to stop, and weeping copiously when she found
that neither of them would listen to her; Alfred starting forward and saying, " Tilda ! Look here ! Here
Tilda ! Jonah !" and then turning to R. Mintah with
a helpless roll of the eyes, " 'Pears like they're *bound*
to clinch. Don't it, now ?"

" Clinch" in the bodily sense they did not, though it
was as much as Jonah could do not to lay his whip over
his sister's shoulder. A look came into his eyes, however, that cooled even her fiery blood. Jonah angry was
enough to alarm anybody, for, like the famous Italian
athlete, Milo, of Crotona, he could kill a bullock with a
blow of his fist. Seeing that she quailed before him,
he sternly bade her " 'light." She scrambled out; he
jumped in, called to R. Mintah to join him, and off they
drove, leaving Matilda vilifying and raging with even
greater fury than at first, now that it was entirely safe
to do so, and Alfred doing his best to pacify her with
such obvious truths and aphorisms as occurred to him.

This was not at all the sort of " pleasurin' " that R.
Mintah had counted upon, and for at least a mile she

continued to sob quite hysterically. And of course Jobah had to comfort her, and to do this had to recover his own good-humor first. As soon as he began to make this effort, the situation began to improve, and not long afterwards the sun of their content—the sun that always shone when they were alone together—burst out almost as brightly as though it had never been hidden at all. And presently Jonah might have been observed to be driving with his right hand altogether, finding it absolutely necessary apparently to slip his left arm around R. Mintah's waist, doubtless to keep her from falling out of the buggy,—a shackling affair, certainly, the wheels of which seemed to be trying to run away altogether, curving as they did alarmingly outward as they rattled on, under the peculiar action of Old Hundred, who, head down, was but jogging along in his sleep, with no other incentive to speed than an occasional lazy " Glang !" from Jonah, but jogged so decidedly upward, if not onward, that he threatened momentarily to rend the conveyance at his heels limb from limb. Neither of the young people behind him gave these matters a single thought. Jonah had lit his cigar again. If any tears lingered in R. Mintah's eyes, they were only made the brighter by them. There was no restraint now, she felt,—nothing to be unhappy about,—and she abandoned herself completely to the rare joys of freedom, felicity, and finery. Being only a woman, this last was no inconsiderable item in the delightful total of her satisfaction. Was she not wearing the first dress she had ever had of her very own, bought for her, and nobody else; made for her, and nobody else ? Had she not new *everything !* She had

once in ages known what it was to have new shoes to
wear with an old dress, or a new sun-bonnet with no
shoes at all; but to have dress and shoes and a hat and
"rumberella" all at once, and all given to her by her
dear Jonah, was almost too much, and but for the
sobering effect of the quarrels of the day she could not
have carried them off without being "stuck-up," she
knew. It was not in human nature to stand such
prosperity. It was now that Jonah told her all about
the plans and arrangements he had been making for
the day. What a head for business! What a protector! What a lover! He admired himself unaffect-
edly in these capacities, but he could not do it as
ardently as she did.

"Oh, Jonah, how good you are! And so good-lookin'!"
she cried, in a transport. "Them clothes. You *wouldn't*
steal 'em! Did you borrer 'em?"

"I bought 'em,—every blessed rag," said he, proudly.
"Do I look good in 'em?"

"You are jes' splendid!" said she,—"splendid!" and
worshipped him so openly that he was moved to say,—

"*You* look fine in that red dress. It becomes yer sho'
and certain. You look *powerful* pretty, R. Mintah, in
it, I do declare!"

"Oh, Jonah!" she said again, with no sort of regard
for originality or fear of tautology, and with a deep
blush of gratification. "I *hope* I'm fixed up to suit
you, after all you've went and done. But *I* ain't nothin'.
I never wuz. *You* are the one. You are jes' perfectly
elegunt! I never see nobody like you in all my born
days."

After this it struck them as expedient that the top

of the buggy should be put up and the "rumberella" lowered; and as a veracious chronicler I am obliged to say that in the course of this transaction it somehow happened that the buggy gave out a new and mysterious sound,—was it a creak, or squeak, or shriek? I really can't say. It had not been oiled thoroughly for about ten years, and could not be expected to go on forever without remonstrance. Whatever it was, it must have startled R. Mintah very much, for she cried out "Oh, Jonah!" far louder than she had done at all that day.

He was regarding her fondly with the tender possessive glance of the lover, when quite a string of wagons and carts and "rockaways" passed them. The picnic had swept everything before it, and scarcely at Fair time were more vehicles to be seen. The elect ladies and the Baptist minister even had turned out, and R. Mintah shrank back in her corner under their inquiring gaze, shyly ashamed of her abnormal splendor and her position as "Jonah Newman's sweetheart," glad to screen herself partially from view behind the hood of the buggy.

But Jonah sat up very straight, and, with his hat on one side of his head, and that head set at a determined angle on the other, his feet firmly planted against the dashboard, and his elbows well squared, roared out impudently, "G'lang! g'lang!" and lashed at Old Hundred in a way that made that respectable family horse launch out in a perfectly unprecedented gallop, and commit the indecorum of carrying the laity, as represented by the lovers, far ahead of the church,—indeed, of everything on the road. The minister, who was in the habit of committing dust to dust on the "pike," always, as well as at the funerals of his followers, was naturally indignant at such "impudence," and prophesied darkly of Jonah's future. R. Mintah was quite as much scandalized. She had been obliged to hold her hat on with her hand until the pace slackened, and she then said, "Jonah, you ain't ought to er done that. What got into you, any-ways?" To which he replied, "I ain't goin' to let no livin' creature pass me on the road to day, R. Mintah. No, sir'ee, Bob!"

He forgot all about this resolve, however, as was shown later; at least he got so absorbed in singing with R. Mintah "There was an old man came over the sea," and "My darling Nellie Gray, they have taken you away," and a number of other delightful ballads and hymns, that the whole party he had left behind grad-ually crept up on him again, and finally passed him in their turn with anything but friendly feelings or glances. However, one of the lovers at least was not one whit abashed, and presently both fell to carolling again. How they ever got to the station in time for their train I don't know. They did not arrive until the last mo-ment; and when little R. Mintah, who had never been on a railway journey in her life, saw the bold way in which Jonah went up to the mysterious peep-hole, from which she had supposed that the authorities were recon-noitering the "crowd" to see that they took nothing away as souvenirs of travel,—such as a handsome stove, or an elegant ice-cooler, for instance,—and behaved them-selves generally with propriety,—when, I say, she saw Jonah march up and hail the awful personage there with "Hello, Mister! Give me two showin's fur Harper's

Ferry," and was then guided safely through the awful perils and confusion of the place to a beautiful *red velvet* seat in the car, is it any wonder that he seemed to her as omnipotent and magnificent as Jove? She was lost in admiration of him for some time afterwards. How tall, and big, and strong he was! How "smart" and gifted in every way! What *savoir-faire!* What knowledge of the world! If Jonah had been Captain Cook or Dr. Livingstone, he could not have seemed a greater traveller. Why, he even knew how to manage the springs of the shutter and the window. There wasn't anything that Jonah didn't know. When he put up the window for her, saying, "Set there, honey, where you'll git the wind," and poured three over-ripe bananas and an orange into her lap, and bought a newspaper to read when they should have started, he seemed so positively majestic in his *largesse* and *usage de monde* that she felt for a moment quite mournful over it, and recalled Mother Newman's speech, "She ain't fit fur you, and she knows it," with a sad assent. These doubts assailed her while Jonah was off talking to some of his friends at the other end of the car. When he came back, she had carefully spread a large handkerchief on the seat to protect the red velvet from any possible injury it could receive by coming in contact with her dress,—the very dress she had thought so superb that morning,—and, having settled herself, was toying rather nervously with her "rumberella." "Here! Give me that," he said, in his masterful way, when he came back, and put it in the rack above her head. Good gracious! Who could have ever thought of such a thing as "that there place" being meant for such a purpose?

10

"Will I git yer some water?" he asked, and went off;
and she could see him go to the cooler and turn the
cock, and lo! water in abundance, a glass of which was
brought to her. "Law sakes!" she could but ejaculate,
and then, "Jonah, you're a wonderment!" after which
the train started, and she gave a little scream of terror.
A very little scream; but Jonah said "Hesh up!" in an
agitated, almost cross way; and she was getting more
and more gloomy, not to say decidedly unhappy, when
Jonah repentantly took her hand, put a large fig in his
own mouth and a small one in hers, and whispered,
"Bully, ain't it? Ain't you glad you come?" crossed
his legs, and gave himself up to spelling out a charming
advertisement of St. Jacob's oil. The car was very
crowded, and while Jonah was absorbed in the pursuit
of light literature of a beneficent tendency R. Mintah
looked about her. It was reassuring in the strange,
not to say awful, situation in which she found herself
to see so many neighbors and familiar faces,—friends
she would have called them in the warmth of her own
friendly heart. Belle Poddly and Gus Jones were up
in front holding hands and chewing gum; and how any
girl could marry Gus Jones R. Mintah couldn't see.
And Tim White and Jinny had made themselves comfortable in the next seat. And the Potters were trying
to look as though they didn't belong to the party at all
(for the conductor's benefit); and John Culbert, not getting a seat, had perched on the coal-box and begun on
the hard-boiled eggs already. The minister was reading
a report of a late conference at Zanesville, Ohio, and
looked as though he would give out a text and preach
a sermon then and there for two cents. Jim Wilkins,

who sat just in front and had taken off his coat and hung it up as soon as he entered the car, seemed in excellent spirits, and twinkled all over whenever he looked across at his wife, who sat bolt upright on the other side of the aisle, and wore not only an air of offended dignity, but a bonnet with a huge ram-like front-piece to it which, like the beaked ships of the Greeks, was not without value as showing which way she was moving. Without it, there would have been no saying with any degree of certainty whether one was getting a front or back view of Mrs. Wilkins, so non-committal, limp, and stayless was that admirable woman's figure. With it, society and the family seemed as safe as female virtue and courage could make them; and as she ministered constantly and conscientiously, albeit somewhat sternly, to the wants of her five children, not even the mother of the Gracchi could have presented a finer spectacle of moral excellence and domestic intrepidity. R. Mintah was not sorry that Alfred Shore and Matilda were as far from her as they could get. She wished them farther, indeed; but seeing them reminded her of another member of the Newman family. "Oh, poor Mandy! poor Mandy!" she said to Jonah. "Her heart must be most broke, and no wonder. Never will she see the like of *this* agin. If I'd uv knowed what it would be, it would er jes' *killed* me to be kep' at home, Jonah. It certainly would."

The wonderful journey got more wonderful to R. Mintah with every mile. The way in which everything galloped by the windows, the false starts and backings, the puffings and snortings, the bridges, the towns, the quantities of people everywhere idling and talking,

filled her mind with delightful excitement. The conductor was a great trial and terror to her with his
abrupt demands for "tickets," and his generally authori-
tative air. But what a comfort to see and feel that
Jonah was a match for him. "Will he let us git off
when it's time?" she whispered to Jonah as they rolled
into the Ferry; and she thanked him humbly from her
very heart when he not only permitted her this privilege,
but actually helped her down the steps of the car, saying to him, "I'm mightily 'bleeged to you, sir. I
certainly am." Another train coming from the opposite
direction had just got in, as it happened, and the pas-
sengers, of course, had their heads out of the window
staring at the picnic party, who stared at them in return. Suddenly a lively uproar was heard near one of
the carriages. Cries of "Great Scott!" and "Hello!"
and "Howdy! Howdy!" were repeated in various
voices, variously pitched, and then a loud "Well, I'm
blowed ef it ain't Al Shore's Pa-ap!" followed by "Git
out!—git right out! We are all here. Git out, man,
I say," the last speaker being Jim Wilkins. The
lookers-on within the car, and without on the platform,
all saw a gaunt old man seize his bundle, slowly descend
to earth, and fall feebly on Mr. Wilkins's breast, but
only a few of them heard his "I've come home, Jim,—
come home to stay while I live." John Shore it was,—
"Al's Pa-ap."

"That's right. You done jes' right," said Mr. Wilkins,
affected by the changed appearance of his old friend
and comrade. "You've got tired sharp-shootin' 'round
in the bushes, and you've come back to camp, you
cornfounded old Johnny Reb, you! Whur's Al? Al's

'round here somewhur's. He'll be powerful glad to see you. We are *all* powerful glad to see you." With this he put an arm around his friend, and half guided, half supported him to a seat on a bench near the station, while a rumor sprang up promptly in their wake that " Al Shore's Pa-ap had done come home to die." John Shore had been very ill. He was still miserably weak, and the sight of Jim's familiar face and the sound of his speech was too much for him for the moment. He could not say a word, so Jim talked for both. " Been sick, ain't you?" he said. " Look like you was just out of the horspital, and the doctors had been a-practysin' on yer cornstant. You're powerful weak, ain't you? But you'll git all right, old fellow. Here! you want some Dutch spunk, you do." A flat black bottle was produced from Mr. Wilkins's pocket containing the particular kind of courage that he believed to be needed, a dose of which was immediately administered; and while it is taking effect a question can be answered which is being put on all sides by relatives, friends, and strangers : " What's he doin' here?"

Is every mountain a magnet, I wonder, that collectively they have such strange power to hold and rivet to themselves, as it were, the man born and reared among them, so that he clings to them when he has long ceased to care for anything else, carries them forever in his soul, grieves when separated from them, and is drawn back to them from the ends of the earth? What is the source of that passionate attachment, that mysterious sympathy, which makes a sturdy, hard-fisted Swiss peasant — beer-drinking, kraut-eating, money-loving, unspeakably prosaic—actually die of *heimweh,*

h 10*

while Italians, natives of the enchanting land that "strangers ne'er forget," vend their oranges, grind hand-organs, sell white mice comfortably and contentedly all over the world to the end of the chapter? Whatever the feeling is, it seized upon John Shore when the itching sole had carried him over three States in the various capacities of blacksmith, teamster, and miner; and it was as much as he could do not to jump out of the sick-bed on which he was stretched in Louisiana and plunge through every obstacle of swamp and river and morass that intervened between him and the Blue Ridge when the impulse came, so fresh and powerful was it after an absence of twelve years. Such weary years as they had been of wandering, and hope deferred, and at last of utter defeat! In an unusually pronounced fit of disgust he had left home with the intention of never returning, and had gone out to the Pacific coast, relying confidently, in his usual sanguine fashion, upon that large investment of hopes that yields commonly such small returns of anything except keen disappointment known as "prospectin'." From there he had drifted back again as far as Missouri, and then down the river to Louisiana. But go where he would, good luck had never thrown her old shoe after him, and he had only grown older, and poorer, and feebler, and more discontented with each remove. His discontent was not with his circumstances alone, but with himself. He felt that he had been going steadily from bad to worse in more ways than one; and when he found himself lying in a deserted hut on the borders of Lake Pontchartrain, and heard a mocking-bird singing outside the door like the ghost of the sweet songsters that used to trill about the cottage in the days when he was a better and happier man, he did not think of himself as a martyr at all, but only as a most miserable and wretched old man.

"I ain't fit to live," he groaned to himself; "and ef I was to die here I couldn't even be buried, seeing it ain't a country. It's nothing but a swamp, and you can't dig down two feet without strikin' water. I'll go home as soon as I can crawl. I ain't heerd from Al for three years now,—not sence I asked him to send me a little money. And I ain't wrote. But he'll take me in. Onst I git among the mountains I'll feel different,—I'll *do* different." And so it came about that John Shore coming home, met home, as it were, coming to him, and if he greatly surprised the Mountain he was no less surprised by it in his turn.

It is impossible to give any idea of the extent to which Alfred Shore's eyes extended when he beheld the unlooked-for spectacle of a prodigal parent seated on that bench. He stood stock-still to stare for fully a moment. Then he looked uneasily over his shoulder to see if Matilda was there, his father regarding him the while with a glow at his heart that prevented his feeling the chill of his reception for the time. Alfred, taking in the gaunt and grizzled aspect, and the look of weakness and weariness, hesitated no longer, but advanced. The two men shook hands. "Howdy, Pa-ap; howdy? How do you do?" said Alfred. "Set still where you are. Don't git up." He betrayed his nervousness by the rapidity with which he spoke. His honest, moony face was visibly clouded. He looked behind him again, and added, "Mighty glad to see you." Again he looked behind him and shifted his weight from the right foot

to the left, colored high, put his arms akimbo, and added
another sentence to his speech of welcome: "Folks *is*
a-returnin' back now. Pretty season fur——" Matilda
now joined him. He had seen disgust and amazement
painted so clearly in her face when he had first consulted
it, that he was not prepared to see her step up to his
father, shake hands civilly, and even smile in a cheerless,
constrained fashion as she received him. His face brightened. "That's right, Tildy! That's right," he called
out eagerly from the background in the tone we use
with children, his voice rising on the last syllable of her
name. "Shake hands for Howdy, Tildy. Shake hands
with Pa-ap."

Matilda had taken a little time to consider what she
should do. Was the cottage and farm Alfred's property
now, or his father's? Should it be peace, or war? She
decided that it would be wiser not to commit herself
irrevocably to the latter until she could find out where
she stood.

"Children, your poor old pap's come home never to
go way no more," began John Shore, looking from one to
the other, and feeling that there was something that he
did not understand in both faces. He had no chance to
say more; for Jinny White now bustled up in a state of
the highest excitement, and beginning with a "Well,
John Shore! Fur comin' back alive when you're
knowed to be dead, and fur comin' back most dead
when you're knowed to be alive, you are the beatenest
man or stiff,—call yourself what you're a mind to,—
John, as ever *I've* seed or heerd tell on." On she rattled at a rate of speed that defied competition, or even
interruption, and produced a feeling of desperation in

the course of half an hour in John Shore's mind such as his many misfortunes had very seldom generated. Excessive talkativeness not being recognized in America, as it is in China, as a perfectly legitimate cause for divorce, there would have been nothing for it if Jinny had ever carried out a certain plan of hers, except for John to have gratified both her and himself by sinking finally, definitely, and unmistakably into the silent tomb. He felt this very strongly. He was also grateful for the immense kindness and good-will that she had apparently kept for him. "A good woman,—Jinny," he thought, when she finally left him; "and maybe she suits Tim, who might be took for deef, easy, and pass fur dumb anywheres. She sorter tickles him like, I reckon, and keeps him awake; but she'd harrow any other man up turrible. She makes me feel like my head was a shot-box, and she was doin' the shakin', and doin' it lively! She'd er driv *me* clean, plum, ravin', howlin', tearin', shootin' crazy', *certain*, would Jinny Hodges."

IV.

"You sunburnt sicklemen of August weary,
Come hither from the furrow and be merry.
Make holiday; your rye-straw hats put on,
And these fresh nymphs encounter every one
In country footing."—*Tempest.*

"Acts which Deity supreme doth ease its heart of love in."—
KEATS.

THE picnic had put everybody in such broad holiday
humor that even John Shore was the gainer by it. There
was a general disposition for the time being to let by-
gones be by-gones, and how his heart did warm to find
himself kindly received where he had thought at best
to be only tolerated. He was taken possession of by the
party, went with them to the "pleasurin' ground," and
although not able to take a very active part in the
ensuing festivities, enjoyed his *rôle* of spectator wonderfully. His mercurial temperament responded sensitively to his surroundings, and, shaking off the sadness
that had so oppressed him, he entered, in sympathy at
least, into all that went on, and surprised himself by
the rebound. He had felt humbled to the point of en-
during patiently any slights that might be put upon
him; the relief of feeling that he would not be called
upon to endure them was very great.

When he was comfortably established on the bank
of the river in the shadiest, pleasantest spot that Jim
Wilkins could find, his mind reverted to the expression

on the faces of Alfred and Matilda that had puzzled him. And when Alfred joined him, after a bit, the first thing that Pa-ap, the philosopher, said to him, although he was not "a fool by heavenly compulsion" at all, but a clever and even keen-sighted person enough when his own interests were not at stake, was, "Set down here, Al. I dunno what you are carryin' on your mind. But ef so be as it might happen to be concernin' me, I want to tell you one thing. That paper I give you,— you've got it yet, ain't yer?"

"Yes, Pa-ap—leastways, Matilda, she's got it," said Alfred. His tone was embarrassed, and even slightly aggrieved. He had no more imagination than one of his own turnips, and his father's eccentricities had always annoyed him. Why could he not either go away once for all, or stay at home? A gift was a gift; and his conduct was gratuitous,—as much so as though he had come back from another world, almost. The thought of restitution had been trying to form itself in the dim recesses of his mental apparatus; but as soon as it became visible he felt it and himself taken by the throat, as it were, by Matilda, and not even his favorite "Whur there's a way in, there's a way out" seemed to shed any light on the peculiarly perplexing situation. "What 'll become uv *us* ef Pa-ap takes it back?" was one facet of the problem. "What 'll become uv *him* ef he don't?" was another. "What 'll become uv *me*, no matter which er way they settle it?" was the third, and not the least distressing, so miserably certain was he of the approach of the storm that his soul abhorred. The whole question had been preying upon him ever since he had seen his father on that bench at the station.

But, with the dumb, inexpressive goodness and loyalty
of his nature, he had reached one conclusion and determination to which he could not have been helped by
the most brilliant and logical intellect.   "He's my
father. He's come home. I won't turn agin him, no
way they fix it. Tildy's my wife. I'll do all I kin to
please *her*, and live kind with her, too."

   The expression of his face and the sudden heighten-
ing of its ruddy tints told his father that he had touched
the discordant note.   He looked at him for a moment,
and then said, "I might take back, I reckon——"

   "Don't tell Tildy that," gasped Alfred, turning almost
purple. "I'll—I'll tell her."

   "But I won't," he concluded. "Don't feel bad 'bout
that paper. I don't want nothin' back. I wouldn't
tech it. But I'm broke down. I'm gittin' on fur an
ole man. I reckon you can give me what I want—it's
mighty little—while I'm 'bove ground. No! I don't
want nothin' back."

   Alfred couldn't get any redder than he was already;
but his emotion was violent, and he got pale instead,
at least for him, and said, eagerly, "Don't you tell
Tildy that now. Don't you, Pa-ap. I'll tell her. She'd
—she'd like better to be told by me."

   "All right, Al. Jes' as you're a mind to have it,"
agreed the father. "I thought never to come back——"

   "I wish you hadn't never," thought Alfred, and re-
membering how he was placed, the sentiment as well
as the construction of this sentence may surely be forgiven him.

   "But I had to come. Something drawed me like,"
John Shore went on,—"I couldn't stay 'way. And ef

you'll believe me, my son, I dreamed uv your mother's grave four times runnin' plain as ever I seed it,—plain as I see you settin' there. You ain't—you don't—you wouldn't turn me out?" It was monstrous to a man of his frank and generous character to think such a doubt for a moment, much less express it, and, feeling ashamed of having done so, he added, quickly, "I know you wouldn't;" but to Alfred it seemed a natural enough precaution to take, and, interpreting it as a personal and searching appeal, he first ran his hands wildly through his hair in the energetic intensity of his feelings, and then, ramming them deep in his pockets, affirmed, decidedly, "No, Pa-ap! I sez 'No.' And I sez 'No' agin. And I takes my stand right there." It had been a long while since Alfred had known such exhausting inward and outward experience, and he now relapsed into a serious and semi-comatose state, in which he remained until his services were required to unpack the lunch-baskets,—an occupation to which he betook himself with a heart still burdened by anxieties and misgivings, but no longer in suspense. He was able to give himself up heartily to this important matter. "Good eatin' is a mighty good thing," was a stock sentence of his, and he considered himself a judge of it. He was privately quite of the opinion of one of the Wilkins boys, who wandered about fretfully all morning asking "when the picnic would begin," meaning the great feast of the day. And it was he who labored patiently and untiringly over that feature of the outing without getting the smallest thanks or recognition from anybody, or even a tithe of the delicacies provided, unless certain wings, and drumsticks, and bits

F   11

of broken bread, and odd slices of tart that remained, over and above, when all had eaten, and that had to be disposed of somehow, could be so regarded. On these, at any rate, he dined, and then fell to repacking, and wrapping, and the searching of missing spoons, and washing of plates, as if hired expressly for the purpose; Matilda presiding, but not helping, and taking occasion to ask him whether he had "questioned of Pa-ap yet," to which this Machiavellian Alfred artfully replied, significantly, " We won't say nothin' to him 'less he says somethin' to us, ef we've got a grain of sense, Tildy."

Such a day as it was altogether! For the elect ladies, who sat apart in elegant seclusion some distance from the others, with their huge hampers about them, and indulged in the most "genteel" conversations and occupations imaginable, and were inexpressibly shocked and disgusted by nearly all that they saw, and had the minister to dine with them, and were not at all dull,—oh, no! For Mrs. Wilkins, who positively declined to do anything that anybody else did, and would not eat anything, and steadily refused to be happy or comfortable, and finally strode off into the woods " to look for yarbs," she said, and would not so much as *look* in the direction of Mr. Wilkins all day, but mounted guard sternly over her children. For Zach Hodges, Jinny's brother,—a grave, lantern-jawed, one-suspendered person of settled habits,—who soon despised himself for having supposed that he could "fool around" for a whole day, and finally, in sheer desperation, walked a mile down the river, where he had seen some men cutting and stacking wood for the railroad, and lent a hand, and so killed the only holiday he had ever taken. For Mr. Newman's hated foe, Jack Culbert, who had a passion for fishing, and found a secluded, leaf-shadowed, sun-flecked pool at a bend of the Potomac, and caught bass after bass unvexed of neighbors or lawyers. For Jo Snodgrass, the greatest glutton on the mountain, who fell asleep after making a dinner that ought to have killed him, and waked again only to tackle half a chicken, a pot of quince preserves, and the quarter of a jelly-cake. (Little Wilkins's idea of a picnic seemed practically that of the whole company, and the amount of food consumed by old and young would never be believed; just as an inventory of what was put into the pockets alone of the party to stay the ravages of appetites that seemed absolutely sharpened by such unconsidered trifles as three enormous meals, and course after course of intermediate eggs, figs, raisins, candies, oranges, apples, etc., would never be credited, either.) And what a day—ah, *what* a day for R. Mintah! For did not she and Jonah walk along the tow-path hand in hand for hours, sucking sweetly, and with absolute fairness, at three oranges (one at a time, and turn and turn about), getting more out of them than ever was got out of the golden fruit of Hesperides? And did they not stop at the lock and see a boat glide through? And did they not go on board and explore it, and marvel over it, and talk to the people in charge of it, and find it a thousand times more curious and interesting than some people would the Great Eastern? And did they not talk, talk, talk, and laugh, laugh, laugh? And did they not suddenly remember that they had been gone for hours and hours, and hurry back to join the others? And perhaps they were not hailed from afar with a loud shout, and amiably twitted and joked until R. Mintah, as red as her dress almost, shrank as far into herself as she could possibly get, and Jonah angrily seized the "genteel" Gus Jones by the shoulder and spun him around like a top, saying, "Shet up! Let it drop! Enough's a plenty any time, and I've had enough! D'ye hear?"—a command he was fain to obey sulkily, although he had just been declaring that he would "run Jonah high on that there thing."

They were all soon most amicably and agreeably engaged, however, in eating and swinging, in swinging and eating, in playing games and eating, talking and eating, flirting and eating, singing and eating, while the elder folk sat around on stumps and logs, and looked glumly indifferent, or scornful, or amused, as the case might be.

When it came to "Here we go 'round the mulberry bush," the fun became perfectly uproarious, and as often as Jonah knelt in the middle of the ring he invariably marched over to the spot where R. Mintah stood, took her hand, led her proudly to the centre of the ring, made her kneel down, and with a detonation as of a pocket-pistol "saluted" her,—that is, the tip of her ear, or her hair, or at best her cheek, as she modestly thwarted his purpose by slipping to the right or left, her eyes as bright as stars and her cheeks in a flame. Other swains followed his example, and solemnly and simply led forth other nymphs who did not follow hers, but seemed as stolid under the pocket-pistol process as though it had been an application of court-plaster applied by an elderly physician, and having squarely taken what was squarely offered, returned to their places without a smile. But not so was it with Miss Belle Podley. Anything like the vivacity and coquetry of that young person throughout the whole excursion had never been seen. The pertinence and the impertinence of her lively sallies had kept all the company amused, and more than once won a chastened smile from the minister himself. Her briskness, her good-humor, and her good looks, added to the well-known fact that she was to have a farm of seventy-five acres, made her quite irresistible in some quarters. All the young men were quite wild about her, and if, instead of being what was known as "a bouncer" on the Mountain (*i.e.*, a big, jolly, "peart," handsome girl, with a joke for everybody, equally ready with tongue or fist,—capable, active, saucy, bold, but never bad), she had been a Belgravian or Fifth-Avenue belle, she could not have more perfectly understood the art of drawing them all on and holding them all off. So when it came her turn to take advantage of the mulberry bush, and choose a partner, it was a sight to see her. Rapidly striking the hands of three of her admirers, she dived under the encompassing arms of the circle, and picking up her encumbering skirts, flew, rather than ran, off, and around, and about, and up, and down, and here, and there, the three men in eager but unsuccessful pursuit, until at last she dashed back again, having dodged, eluded, and outrun them all, and, joining the circle, was, according to the rules, safe from further pursuit. Tossing back her magnificent auburn locks, she laughed, and jeered, and pantingly flouted them: "Oh, you can git over the ground as fast as any tarry-pin, can't you? That's right! Hurry up, Gus. You'll

11*

git here after while, like Christmas. There ain't a man on the Mountain as 'll catch *me.*"

She was so impudent and audacious that even Jonah took fire. "I'll show yer 'bout that, Belle, ef I git a chance," he cried, and so a little later she, nothing loath, gave him the chance. But either she was tired from the previous chase or she was not unwilling that it should end differently. She declared that it was the first. R. Mintah was sure that it was the last, for was it not notorious that Belle admired Jonah? It is certain that after a short run Jonah caught her, and, moreover, to R. Mintah's amazement and disgust, he kissed her! Whereupon Belle bridled, and minced, and giggled more than ever, and became so utterly fascinating that the luckless three were reduced to sentimental pulp and darkest despair, while poor little R. Mintah sat apart and suffered the bitter pains and penalties of o'er true and tender love.

It was then that John Shore, looking on, asked Jim Wilkins, "Who is that pretty young thing yonder?"

"Belle Podley?" inquired Jim.

"*No!*" said John, impatiently. "The little one, just beginning to tassel—like." On being told, he called R. Mintah to him, and got no small pleasure from renewing his acquaintance with her. He talked so kindly to her, indeed, that she almost forgot for the moment that Jonah was false and Belle wicked, and life value-less in consequence. Belle had got up a game of blind-man's-buff now, but Jonah had slunk out of it, and would have come straight back to R. Mintah, now that his momentary divertisement was over, had he not seen that she was offended. "To pleasure you, R. Mintah," said John, noticing the young girl's desolate look, "my mocking-bird shall sing," and uncovering a cage he revealed a stout-bodied, sober-plumaged bird, with a calm, intellectual eye and an impudently cocked tail. "Now, Burcegyard," said John, "show 'em what you can do," and began to whistle encouragingly. For some moments the bird eyed the company in general and John in particular with a scornful, imperious air of disapproving scrutiny, and then without warning opened his huge mouth and poured out strains so rich and brilliant and varied that every one was attracted, and Jim Wilkins insisted on knowing "What kind of a sort of a varmint is that varmint er your'n, John, anyways?" A little crowd of people gathered about the cage to see and hear the wonderful songster. "I got him in Loosyana," explained John, "and he's a first-rater, and a tip-topper, Jim, I tell you! The beatenest bird ever *I* heerd, or you either. I'm a-teachin' of him 'Dixie,' and I'm a-teachin' of him 'Yankee Doodle,' to be fair and square all 'round, and when he's a mind ter he can sing 'em both as good as the next one. But ef he ain't, you kain't git a note out of him, not ef you was to roast the gizzard in him by a slow fire. He's game, is Burcegyard, shore, and no mule kain't beat him fur obstinacy ; but I'm bent and determinated on him learnin' them two things, and we are goin' to fight it out on this line, ez Grant said, ef it takes us all summer. He's *dared* me to kill him, with his eye, over and over agin, when he's got tired of bein' learnt, 'n I've been mad enough ter, and I would, too, ef *he'd* of been all. But I couldn't git my consentment to killin' all that music in the cussed little critter's breast."

"Well, hit's the astonishin'est bird ever I see.   I
shouldn't wonder but what you could git five dollars
fur him," said Alfred.

"I wouldn't take five hundred," his father replied.
"Me and him's mighty good company mostly.   Who's
talkin' of sellin'?   No, sir; me and Burcegyard goes
together, and ain't to be bought nor sold seperate.
Curous, ain't it, what a heap uv songs he've got?   I
sets and studies sometimes 'bout the fust bird, and
wonder what he was like, and wish I could er heerd
him."

"Fust bird?   What fust bird's you talkin' 'bout?"
inquired Alfred, thoroughly puzzled.

" Why, there must some time or nuther uv been a fust
bird.   Everything had got to begin at the offstart uv
all, Al.   Don't you see so yourself?" said the father.

"I dunno know nothin' 'bout no fust birds, nor no
fust nothing, Pa-ap," replied Alfred.   " And my advisement to you is not to go talking to nobody 'bout no
sech fiddlesticks 'n foolishments, 'less you want to be
thought simple."

Jonah now came up and would have liked to take advantage of R. Mintah's evident interest in the now silent
songster to make friends again, but she continued to turn
her back on him and affected not to hear any of his remarks, although she had known that he was there, and
why he was there, long before she turned her head and
saw him.   Her Jonah to kiss Belle Podley !   Oh ! it was
shameful, utterly unpardonable, and most miserable!
Even her beautiful red dress looked faded and hideous
in the sickly light of such a sorrow, and she seemed to
stiffen in it until her supple little figure got a look of

positive petrifaction, as outraged love worked griev-
ously within her pure and tender heart and clamored
for expression, only to be rigidly suppressed. Jonah
saw it, and, big as he was, trembled before, or, rather,
behind her,—not that he felt particularly guilty, but
because he saw that he had hurt what he loved,—and
knowing that it was not in her to complain or reproach
him he felt her to be only the more unapproachable in
her gentle dignity.

"'Pears like you ain't enj'yin' yerself, R. Mintah,"
said John Shore, kindly.

"I wish I hadn't never come. I wish I was home.
I *hate* picnics," she replied, passionately.

Was this the day that she had so long looked forward
to,—the day that had been so sweet in the buggy and
along the tow-path when there had been only she and
Jonah, and the rippling river, and the birds, and the
flowers, and no Belle Podley existed at all?

Her eyes were full of tears, which she was determined should not fall, and seeing them, John said,
briskly, "I tell yer, honey, yer sorter moped-like.
Yer want a dance. Whur's everybody? There's a
right smart chance uv boys and girls here, and you shell
all have a dance. Go call 'em,—you tell 'em, Jonah,—
while I chune up. Tell 'em to come here."

In a few minutes the liveliest version of " Miss Mc-
Leod" was ringing out, and such a turf-dance as followed must have surprised even the river, accustomed
as it was to the eccentricities of excursionists. Such
leaping, and bounding, and jigging, and revolving were
never seen there before. The idea had been enthusi-
astically welcomed on all sides, and not only the boys
i

and girls, but many men and matrons, had seized each other and the opportunity to "have a fling," as they phrased it. It was a long dance, and John played his best, for he knew that he could only play that one; and I don't know how it happened, but before the long scrape of the bow which marked "finale," and which John always gave with his head very much on one side and his elbow most impressively squared, Jonah and R. Mintah had "made up." How Jonah managed it I have no idea. The dance did it, perhaps. At least he put his arm around R. Mintah and whirled her off before she could remonstrate, and then homœopathic treatment was tried,—a kiss for a kiss,—and at last explanation.

"I 'lowed to *ketch* her," said Jonah.

"But what made yer *kiss* her?" asked R. Mintah.

"I dunno. I can't rightly say," replied Jonah, not without embarrassment. "She sorter dared me and I upped and done it," he added, using the argument of the soldier, that Jim Wilkins was fond of telling about, who stole a sheep because "it bit him, and he warn't the man to let no sheep that ever was bite him."

"Jonah," said R. Mintah, gravely, "ef you like her more 'n me, say so, and take back your word to me. I ain't never been good enough fur you. Belle——" she choked somehow, and slipped off the dearest and most beautiful ring in the world before he could prevent it and laid it in his enormous palm.

"Hold on! Quit, R. Mintah!" cried Jonah. "What did you do that fur? Don't yer know I wouldn't give your old shoe fur a ten-acre lot er hollerin', bellerin', bouncin' gurls like that there Belle Podley?"

Oh, Jonah, Jonah! Belle had a loud voice, and was standing at that moment with her arms akimbo shrieking and laughing in a way that was not pleasant. But "bellerin'!" She is not without her own saucy charm, and you know it.

"What did yer *kiss* her for then, Jonah?" asked R. Mintab, picking out the weak spot in his defence as well as Ballantyne, Q. C., or Chief-Justice Taney could have done.

"I done told you that I dunno," reiterated Jonah, rather sulkily. "It was all jes' funnin' and foolishness, that's what; I don't care nothin' 'bout her at all. Don't think no more about it. You are the one I want," etc., etc.

After this they had to go for another walk, of course, to say the same thing over and over again in nearly the same words. The dancers went their way also. John Shore was joined by his old friend Jim Wilkins, who was shaking with good-natured laughter: "I ain't shook a foot sence we boys used to cut up didos in camp," he said, "and I thought I'd skirmish 'round a little with Jinny White, but I've got too much to carry. Ouf!"

"Well, set down here by me, Jim, and tell me 'bout yerself,—all yer been doin'," said John Shore, making room for him.

"All right, I will," said Mr. Wilkins. When he had recovered breath, he settled himself comfortably and began: "Well, John, there ain't much happened to call happenin's, skasely, most uv the time sence you went away. I've lived right along here mostly, and been well and done well. I've traded 'round every which er

way, and done mighty well lumpin' this and that. I'm
wuth five thousand dollars this minute. You wouldn't
think it to look at my clothes, now, would you? but I
am. I dunno myself how I got it, but the mill done
most of it."

"I've seed you with a bed-quilt fur a coat, and no
shoes on your feet, and your head plum through your
hat, Jim."

"That's so! You have, John," said Mr. Wilkins,
laughing, and laying his hand on his friend's knee.
"And I've seed you *mighty* ready to creep under that
there bed-quilt at night! and with carpet-rags tied on
your old hoofs; yes, sir, and no hat at all, 'less it was
the skillet you'd stuck on top uv your head. Ha! ha!
ha! We warn't travellin' on our style much them days,
wuz we, John? Great Scott! how you did look the
mornin' we fell back from Second Manassas. You
scared the crows all out the country, John. Ha! ha!
ha! ha! ha! ha!"

"En all the buzzards took after you, Jim, which was
worse."

"Well! ef ever you want a coat or a hat agin, John,
you'll know whur to come," said Jim Wilkins, impressively, when their joint laughter had died away.

"Thanky kindly, Jim. I'd say the same ef I had
anything anybody wanted; which I ain't."

"Well, maybe your reserves 'll come up after while
and you'll win the next fight, John. Don't you go
a-gittin' too down on your luck, and stickin' up no white
flag. The bottom rail gits on top when you least looks
to see it in peace times like in war times. You know
that. You remember that time at Snicker's Gap when

we thought we had the Yankees penned up so's they couldn't git out no way at all, 'less the bottom fell out of the tub, and how they run *us* plum out uv the country and used us up entirely? We didn't feel any too good when we was lyin' flat up agin that fence that night we crope like snakes into the yard of that big white house jes' this side uv Glasstown, and laid in the shadow there listenin' to the Yankee sentinels challengin' each other not twenty feet away. Did we, John?"

"And how we did wriggle out of that when they was changed. That was about the tightest place ever we got in, warn't it, Jim?"

"You made pretty good time considerin' you wuz on all-fours, John. Ha! ha! ha!" (A pause.) "John, ef you ever get in a pinch, and want a little money, do you come right to me. D'ye hear?" (Confidentially. Another pause.) "Yes, that was a mighty nigh thing,— a mighty nigh thing."

"I don't know but what that skirmish on Hog Creek was as bad, Jim. Ef Stuart's men hadn't uv come up jes' when they did, I tell you we'd er been eat right up, —eat right up befo' we know'd what done it."

"That's so. That was the nighest fur me shore and certain, John, fur it was there you——"

"Say no more, Jim; I warn't thinkin' uv that part."

"But *I'm* a thinkin' of it. I ain't never got done thinkin' of it, and ain't never goin' to. No. John, ef ever you want *anything* I can give yer and don't come to me, I'll blow your old brains out fur you, as sure as my name's Jim Wilkins, see ef I don't, you miserable old bushwhacker, you!"

12

" I've got that picter you give me when I went away yet, and many's the time I've looked at it, Jim. Hit was sorter encouragin' 'way off there. And the Lord knows I needed encouragin'."

" Have you? Let's have a look."

John Shore got out his greasy leather case and produced the yellow envelope. His old comrade put an arm around his neck and together they inspected it.

" That's the way he looked when I seed him that day at Port Royal," said Jim.

" Yes, hit's got the look of him 'bout the eyes and forred pretty good. But no picter couldn't be *made* that 'd git all uv *him,* Jim. We'll never see nobody like *him* agin in this world, not ef we wuz to live to be a thousand."

" That's so, John. That's so. We never will. I'd give a good deal to see him come ridin' down the lines in that old uniform of his'n, takin' off that old hat— sorter pulled down over his eyes, it was always—when he heerd the boys cheerin' him! Wouldn't you, John? That uniform wasn't near as good as our quartermaster's,—nothin' like. You couldn't er told him from nobody else,—me or you."

" Yes, you could, Jim, too. Me and *you!* You could er told him from *everybody* else. Picked him out uv a whole army. Well, I reckon he's in heaven now. He 'lowed to go there, and it's none too good fur him."

" Yes, he wanted to go to heaven, and you may jest bet he's gone there, John. And I tell yer ef he'd er wanted to go to *hell,* there ain't sperrits enough there, long as the devil's been enlistin', to keep old Blue Light out!" said Jim, with conviction.

When the pocket-book was about to be replaced, Mr. Wilkins seized it, saying, "Let me fix that." He walked off a short distance, got out his penknife, operated successfully on a certain spot in his coat where he carried his savings (carefully stitched there by himself in consequence of his rooted distrust of all confidants and cashiers), and got out a five-dollar bill, which he put in his friend's book along with the picture, securing the whole with a stout rubber band which he took from his own, and giving it back to John Shore without a word.

"Yes, them was times when you wuz *alive,* ef so be as you *wuz* alive," said Shore, taking the book mechanically and replacing it. "I wish I could live through 'em agin sometimes, hard as some of it was. But it's different with you, Jim. You must have pretty nigh as good a time as can be had. I'm right down glad to hear you've done so well. You was a-tellin' me how it was."

"Yes. As I was a-sayin'. After I got the mill I made money, John. Befo' that it was slow work. I prospered steady, but I never was one to blow 'bout my business. I kep' a still tongue, and done well, and salted down what I made, and done better and better. And I was gittin' ready to fix to build a new house,— sorter settlin' down in my tracks, and takin' things easy, and fixin' to enjoy myself, when, all of a sudden, the old woman took a notion,—the blamedest notion!— and spiled everything. 'Twas to pull up stakes and move out to Californy! You see she had two brothers out there, and they kep' on writin' to her and put it in her head. I thought she'd gone plum crazy when she fust talked 'bout it. It did 'pear like it. ' Break up

here,' I sez to her, 'whur I've got a home, and a good
business, and go balloonin' out yonder the other side er
nowhere?' But Californy was the greatest place that
ever was. Everybody made big fortunes there befo'
they could turn 'round. The grapes there wuz as big
as peaches, and the peaches wuz as big as potatoes,
and the potatoes bigger 'n pumkins, and the pumkins
as big as all out-doors. The very chickens hadn't no
feathers to pick off, and was already cooked when you
was hungry. You couldn't be poor out there ef you
got burnt out twict a week and lost all you had. Every
boy got to be governor of the State, and every girl
married a rich man. Californy was *heaven.* Everything
was better there than nowhere else. You've heerd that
kind er talk, John?"

John Shore nodded, and said, " And I've been fool
enough to believe some of it, too."

" Well, my wife she was full of it. At fust I argyed
the thing with her, like a Jack ; and, of course, the
more I argyed, the more she sot her mind on goin'.
She said it would be the makin' of me and the children, and she wanted to see them dear brothers of
hern. And then I got mad, and I ain't swore sence
Appomattox like I did. I was ashamed uv myself *good*
afterwards, talkin' that way to a woman. And she was
that much more sot, and bent, and determinated. And.
then I sulked like a bear with a sore head for awhile.
And that done no good ; she got *sotter* every day.
You've been a married man, John. You know how it
is. I couldn't bend, and I couldn't break her, and I
wouldn't beat her. I was willin' to do this, and I was
willin' to do that,—anything most to satisfy her ; but

she wouldn't be satisfied no way I fixed it without we broke up and moved to Californy. I begged and prayed of her, even, and her a good woman, too,—says her prayers every night, and reads her Bible on Sundays, and never took off her clothes, but nursed me faithful night and day, when I had the smallpox, and there ain't never been a better mother made,—but she never budged. She said she had the children to consider. *You* remember how it used to was, John, maybe."

"No, I don't, Jim. I hadn't never no disagreements with my wife," said John Shore, his voice softening as he spoke.

"Hum, hum! She died *young*. I reklect 'bout that, —she died *mighty young*," said Mr. Wilkins, reflectively. "Well, John, I seed how 'twould be. I've rode a goverment mule befo' now. So I knowed it warn't no manner nor sort of use, whatsomedever, to try to turn her head 'round, and I'd already tried her with blinkers and 'thout blinkers, tight girth and loose girth, bare-backed and saddled, coaxed and driv, and spurred, and it wouldn't work, seein' she'd got the bit between her teeth, and *wouldn't* go my way ef she died fur it. And I know'd, too—well, you've been married, John! Hum! —I know'd I'd be throwed 'gin the wall and hurt *bad* ef I didn't stop tryin'! So I set and studied and *studied* over that thing till at last I sez to myself, 'You nateral-born pulin' igit! Don't yer *see*! This here thing calls fur *tactics*.' So I studied more 'n ever. And then I goes to Blake,—one-eyed Blake, Fifth Virginia Cavalry, little nubbin of a man with a red head. You must shorely disremember him? Limped a little; warn't nothin' uv a soldier,—wouldn't skeer a rabbit,—but a

12*

square, correct fellow. Yer don't say now that you've forgot *Blake*,—the man that give us a cup of hot coffee the mornin' we started to fall back from Ashby's Gap?"

"Oh, yes! I know *now* who you are talkin' 'bout. It was mighty curous. That fellow had coffee right straight through the war, from fust to last! And him only a private. How he got it the Lord only knows. And it warn't chicory, nor nothin'. It was *coffee*. That there cup of coffee was 'bout the best thing ever I put in my mouth befo' or sence. We'd been on the jump, you remember, fur ten days, and I hadn't had no sleep skasely fur three nights, and it was 'bout all I could do to keep from fallin' off my horse. And when I seed that coffee-pot I thought I seed the New Jerusalem. And Blake he poured me out a big tincupful, and I couldn't stop to drink it, but I warn't goin' to lose nor leave it, not ef I knowed it. So I called to Blake to charge the cup to Uncle Sam and rode off. And my horse would stumble a bit and it was as hot as fire, and between 'em I got scalded right smart, and spilt some which was worse, but what I got was jes' heaven! Oh, yes, I remember Blake."

"I thought you couldn't er forgot him. Well, as I was a-tellin' you, I went to him and give him the wink, and we soon fixed it up between us fust-rate. He was to have the house, and the mill, and the farm fur a year free, and was to make out to ev'ybody like he'd bought it. See? Me a-keepin' of it all the time, of cose. See? And then I sez to the ole woman, I sez, 'I don't want to leave my home, and my friends, and all I've worked so hard fur ever since the war, and go trapesin' off yonder so fur from Virginny, but I see you can't be, and ain't a-goin' to be, happy here no more, so I give in, and you kin pack up and we'll strike camp next week and go to Californy.'

"She hadn't never 'lowed fur me to give in, John, and she looked mighty solemn-like when she heerd me say that,—sorter like she did the day we got married. And then she hugged and kissed me good, and I told her I'd sold off everything and was doin' that thing teetotally and intirely to pleasure her, and I didn't care a red cent fur the resks as long as she was pleased. And she hugged and kissed me agin, and said I was the bes' husband any woman ever had on the face of the yearth; and I felt about as low as they're made,—as mean as a skunk. I couldn't skasely keep from tellin' her the truth. But I know'd I was actin' right, least-ways *meanin'* right, so I never said nothin', and it was settled that er way. Have a chaw, John? This is the 'Farmer's Friend.' I like it better 'n any of 'em. Well, sir, she went 'round the house mighty quiet, packin' and sortin', and didn't talk none hardly. She felt bad, and I seed it, but I never said nothin'. And I went 'round lookin' like 'twas all I could do not to bust out cryin'. *Tactics, John; all tactics!* And when she'd kissed, and cried, and tole good-by all around to the folks, and we'd got on the train, I sez to her, 'Look here, I want to tell you one thing: this here is *your* excursion, Mrs. Wilkins. It ain't *my* excursion. Ef you ain't satisfied in Californy, don't you never say nothin' to me 'bout comin' back,—that's all,—'cause I ain't never comin' back.' She promised she wouldn't, and I seed then she was skeered *bad;* but I never said nothin'. *Tactics,* John. See?" Mr. Wilkins clapped his friend's knee, and, throwing back his head, laughed loud and long, his merry eyes almost disappearing from view. He was obliged to get out a red cotton handkerchief and give vent to a couple of trombone-like snorts before he could resume his story, so great was his own enjoyment of it, and then he wiped his wet eyes and cheeks. "I can't help it, John; I'm jes' obleeged to laugh whenever I think uv that thing. It jes' spurts out. I've done it in church befo' now,—sniggered right out, and caught Hail Columbia fur it afterwards from the ole woman, and laughed wuss 'n ever, tell I wuz as weak as a new-born babe, and she said I wuz gittin' ready fur the 'sylum at Stanton. But as I started to tell you. We travelled, and travelled, and travelled, tell I thought we'd passed all creation. And the country kep' on gittin flatter and flatter. There warn't a mounting to be seen fur hundreds uv miles, ef you'll believe me, and an uglier, and a browner, and a more burnt-up country I never seed, and it jes' did 'pear to me like we wuz gittin' to the mouth of the bad place. Howsomever, we did git to that heaven of a Californy at last, and met up with her brothers, and I bought a little place from the only smart man that had ever been out there, I reckon, for he wuz leavin' it fust chance he got, and we started in. Well! seeh a country as that was! You wouldn't believe it! It was so dry, John, fur months and months that everything turned to powder, and then it turned loose and drownded ev'ything and ev'ybody out, and I don't know which was wust. You couldn't raise a leaf uv tobacco to save your life! And I never eat a beat-biscuit nor had a mint-julip while I wuz there! It was the most God-forsaken place,—the jumpin'-off place, and no mistake. And there warn't no spring-house, nor no ice-house, nor no smoke-house, and nobody to help with the work. And the climate warn't anything to call a climate, and the ole woman got *mighty* sick uv it in a month, but she was 'shamed to say so. I pertended *I* liked it, and we went on. In 'bout three months she couldn't hold in no longer, and she began sayin' she didn't like this thing and that thing. And I didn't take no notice, no more 'n ef I was deef. And when the rainy season come she got droopy and miserable as a wet chicken, and I pertended still I liked it. And she said she never seed nothin' of her brothers 'cause they lived a good piece off, and wuz always too busy to come to see nobody, and she werrited powerful and talked 'bout livin' and dyin' 'mong strangers all the time. And I said, ' Oh, this is Californy ! We ain't goin' to die ; nobody don't die out here ; we are goin' to live here for the next fifty years. I'm 'bout as well contented as I ever 'spect to be,' and she was so furous she wouldn't speak to me fur a week. *Tactics*, John. See ? And we went on fur a while, and the harvest was so poor we didn't make nothin' skasely. But I lived po', and was cheerful all the time, and sez to her, ''Pears to me we ain't comin' out the big end of the horn fur *Californy*, the land of plenty, but we're here now and we've got to stay.' ' Why don't you urrigate, Jim ?' says she to me mad-like, and I tole her I hadn't got the money to fool away on 'bout fifty miles er ditches. I'd heerd rain had been plenty in Virginny, but nothin' couldn't be helped. And, John, what did that woman do ? She got as sweet as molasses-candy that minnit, and sez, ' Ef *you* ain't content here, Jim, I'll go back to Virginny.

I won't stay nowhurs whur my dear husband ain't contented.' *She did!* Women are '*bout* the smartest things
the Lord ever made, John. But I seed things was
workin', and I know'd I had the reins and was set on
drivin' her into a corner, so I sez, 'Thank yer kindly,
mother, but I'm all right. I don't want to go back.
I'm suited out here. I *come* to pleasure you, but I'm
goin' to *stay* to pleasure myself. The crop ain't been
good, but in ten years or so maybe I'll be able to urrigate and we'll do better.' That beat her. She got as
red as fire and wouldn't eat a mite that day. Well, we
went on that way for a while agin, and then all to onst
she broke plum, teetotally down, and caved in, and give
up, and went to bed, and stayed there, and cried herself
into fits 'most. And when I sez to her, 'What in the
name of goodness has got into you? What's the matter
with you anyways, mother?' what do you think she
sez to me, after werritin' and devillin' me cornstant,
and never lettin' me rest tell I give my consent to goin'
out there? She sez, 'What did you ever bring me and
my children out here to starve and die fur? I'll *die* ef
you keep me here.' *She did!* And she meant it, too!
Well, I didn't argy that time, 'n I didn't make no fuss.
I seed she was plum beat out sho' 'nough and had surrendered, and I didn't push things. I jes' said, 'You warn't
satisfied in your Virginny home, and you ain't satisfied
in your Californy heaven, it 'pears. But I'm still willin'
to pleasure you, and do all I can fur to make you happy ;
so stop cryin', and I'll *borrer* the money and take you
back home agin.' And she set up in bed straight and
sez, 'Oh, Jim, Jim, take me home! take me home!' sez
she, 'and I'll break rock on the pike for a livin'. I'll do

anything! I'll thank and bless yer as long as I've got breath in my body! I hate Californy wuss 'n *pison!*' *I* hadn't to borrer no money, and I know'd Blake's time was 'most out, and when it came 'round we lef'. You oughter seed the ole woman! She could have danced a jig fur joy, settled woman that she is. She didn't care no more than nothin' 'bout partin' with them dear brothers of hern. She was crazy-happy ef ever a creature wuz."

" Yer must er been mighty happy, both uv you, comin' back together," said John Shore, who had listened with the greatest interest.

" Well, that's as you may call it, John," replied Mr. Wilkins, dubiously. " I 'lowed it would be. But ef you'll believe me, the ole woman set up as stiff as a ramrod all the way back, and wouldn't have nothin' more to do with me than ef I'd of treated her the wust in the world all through. *She did!* And she's been that way ever sence,—you've noticed her to-day. I darsent run her. *Not fur my life!* But when I look at her I——" Mr. Wilkins here roared afresh, and was obliged to have recourse again to his handkerchief, his friend joining heartily in his outburst, and the pair rocking themselves backward and forward in an ecstasy of amusement for some moments. " Excuse me, John. But I'd *bust* ef I didn't. Ha! ha! ha! ha! ha! I made a big trouble and business 'bout tradin' with Blake to git back my house agin (I let on, now, the mill's his'n), and I tell you she was glad to git back to it! *She'll* never want to do no more movin'. She'll think twict befo' she has any differments with me. She snaps at me like a turtle jes' now. But, Lor! I don't kyer. I've got

the bit in her mouth, and I ain't goin' to do no sawin'
while it's sore. And it's turned out all right. And she's
got all she wants. But, John Shore, I sez now what
I've always said, and there ain't no man that knows
anything 'bout 'em that can say it ain't true, 'Women's
like war. Sometimes they're a scourge, and then agin
they're a blessin'; but with both uv 'em *you've jes' got to
have tactics.*' "

This recital had consumed a good deal of time. The
shadows were getting long on the grass and dark over
the river, and the party began to reassemble. It was
generally conceded that the united forces must march
on the station at once if their train was to be caught.
So a group of men, dimly visible, sitting on logs, smoking and talking, some little distance off, were called, the
baskets were looked to, Miss Belle Podley (with two
young men beside her and a third hanging on at the
back) jumped into a buggy, the omnibus was filled, and
soon nothing but some greasy newspapers and empty
tins remained to tell the woods that they had been
honored by a distinguished company. And I fear that
if the river could have had its way it would have
altered its course and swept away even these traces of
a defiling humanity.

"There's little Stebbins," said Mr. Wilkins. "Howdy,
Stebbins!" as they emerged from the omnibus to find
their train just arrived, and snorting and puffing impatiently to be off again. "You remember little Stebbins of our company,—'Owl Stebbins'" (to John Shore).
"That's him on the ingine. He drives the ingine on
this here night train always. Let's go speak to him."

They did so, and Stebbins was very friendly and invited them to ride with him and have a talk "'bout old times," if they wouldn't find it "oncomfortable."

John Shore had his bird and packages, but he got over this difficulty by giving them to Jonah, who promised to take care of them,—a promise that R. Mintah fulfilled.

This settled, he and Mr. Wilkins joined their friend, who, having wiped away the perspiration that was blinding him with a sweep of his arm, and hitched up his trowsers, and thrown open his flannel shirt at the throat a little, offered each of them in turn a hand hardly to be distinguished from the lumps of coal heaped high in the tender behind him, and, with a hearty grasp, said twice, gravely, "Howdy, howdy! I'm pleased to see you, gentlemen. I certainly am. Git up thar, at the back, whur you'll be out er the way," and would have apologized for the inferior character of the accommodations he was able to offer. Mr. Wilkins, however, cheerfully remarked that he had "rode" in his time "on the roof of the kyars and on the cow-catcher, and warn't partikiler so long as he warn't rid on a rail," and so won upon Mr. Stebbins by his brisk and cheerful demeanor and conversation that, solemn as he was, and the strictest of strict Baptists, in five minutes he had grown convivial and confidential, so moving and search- ing are the effects of old ties and "mountain mist" on the most reserved natures. The train now moved slowly out into the darkness, leaving the station behind it looming large and indistinct, and jewelled about with the lamps of the trainmen. Mr. Stebbins became ab- sorbed again for a time in his professional duties. In the second car Mrs. Wilkins's beaked bonnet brooded

a   k   ·   13

above three children who had fallen asleep. And Mr.
Culbert, also dozing, shuffled his feet about to avoid
coming in contact with the large string of fish that
flopped about them. And Belle Podley giggled, and
shrieked, and bridled, and minced, and arranged her
"beau-catchers," and wetted her red lips, and tossed her
pretty head, and played at being shocked and offended,
or charmed, as the case might be, with her three
admirers. Mrs. Williams, senior, was talking with
Zach Hodges, and agreeing with him that picnics were
failures: "I'd as lieve grabble for taters, and liever,
than to set around and do nothin' all day. It's about
the hardest work ever I tried to do," said she. And R.
Mintah, with her head on Jonah's shoulder, and love
and joy again restored to her heart, was heaving a sigh
of deepest satisfaction that was not satiation, and saying,
"Oh, Jonah, ain't picnics heavenly! Ain't it been beautiful!" The train was running at full speed in a little
while, and John Shore and Jim Wilkins, seated high on
the tender, exchanged remarks with the fireman and
reminiscences with their former comrade and waxed
jovial. The fireman, so Mr. Stebbins said, was an old
soldier, too, and for a long while the talk was altogether
of raids, and battles, and repulses, and victories, with
their attendant features good and bad, harrowing or
amusing.

When it had been going on for some time, Mr. Stebbins took a lantern, and, leaning out, waved it back and
forth six times. "I live up yonder 'bout half a mile
away," he explained. "That's fur my wife. She looks
out regular every night to see me do it. She can see it
plain, and knows I am all right then."

Fate, which had certainly not dowered Mr. Stebbins with the fatal gift of beauty, nor made him very wise nor very great, had made him very rich in a devoted wife, who believed him to be all this and much more, and had then perversely so arranged matters that he was nearly all the time away from her.

"I got a good home, boys," he explained ; "and ef I could jes' stay in it I'd be satisfied. But I'm mostly on the road; and when I'm there I'm beat out, and can't do nothin' but sleep 'n eat. I don't hardly know my own children. But they've got a fust-rate, hard-workin', lovin', pious mother. She's a-bringin' of 'em up correct, I know,—better 'n I could,—and it's mighty lucky, I sez so to myself every day, for I've got to be on the go all the whole blessed time. She sez to me this mornin', 'Father, the baby's had a tooth fur a month and you ain't noticed it.' It sorter cut her, you see, and I sez to her, 'Carrie, I ain't a father at all. I ain't a husband. I ain't a human. I'm nothin' but a steam-ingine; and when I think of the life I've been a-leadin' for fifteen year and better it's a wonder I don't bust my biler all to flinders and jump the track.' 'Well, now, be patient,' sez she to me. 'It 'll all come right, I'm jes' certain. You'll git work in the yard in a year or two, and then you kin stay at home all you want.' Yes, I run this here locomotive by night and I dream uv it by day. I kain't git the blamed concern out 'er my mind a minnit; and some days it 'pears like some-body was lettin' off steam in my head cornstant, and I dunno nothin', and I kain't sleep a wink, and I'm jes' druv plum crazy. And Carrie she makes me lay down, and she sends the children all off, and shets up the house

to make it dark, and jes' sets by me without sayin' a
blessed word tell I feel better. En then she always sez,
'Be patient, father. Keep on fur a while and things
'll git better. They're bound to git better.' She's got
a power er patience, and a power er pra'r; and pra'r and
patience is what the wife uv a railroad man's got to
have, *ornless* she 'lows to go ravin' distracted."

"That's so," said Mr. Wilkins. "And it ain't only
them, neither. It's pretty much all wives and all husbands. It takes a power er patience fur any man to
git on with any woman, and a power er pra'r fur any
woman to stand any man, I do reckon. The best man
that was ever made ain't none so good but what he
might be a sight better; and the best woman that ever
stepped 's got it in her to make Moses rip and snort
round like a bull hornin' one er these here little barkin'
fice dogs. But ef a man's got any *tactics*——"

Mr. Stebbins might possibly have heard something in
this connection of Mrs. Wilkins's famous excursion; but
at this moment he opened a valve, and Mr. Wilkins's
voice was drowned in the terrific blare of sound that
followed.

"There ain't a locomotive on the road like 26," said
Mr. Stebbins, when he had imprisoned the demon again.
"Ef I could take things easy and run her twict in the
week, I'd ruther do it than be President. But I ain't
no owl" (here Mr. Wilkins and John Shore, knowing
that he was ignorant of the sobriquet he had gained in
the army, could not help laughing a little), "and owls
couldn't stand——" Here he found his services required
again, and broke off; then resuming, "Carrie'd feel good
ef she only know'd what our boss said to-day. Sez he to

me, 'Stebbins, you look bad ;' and I sez to him, 'Maybe I do, and I reckon you would, too, ef you'd run a locomotive every night regular as long as I have. Ef I could git that place in the yard I've done spoke about.' En he sez, pleasant-like, 'Well, we'll see. Maybe you will. They're short a hand.' En I sez to him, 'I ain't no owl, but a married man——'' Here he broke off again, and, as he turned around and faced his friends, one could see how in the minds of the frivolous he had come to be associated with the very bird with whom he disclaimed all connection, for his mouth was small, his brows decidedly arched, his nose beaked, and his eyes had deep, dark rings around them,—a natural defect increased by his nocturnal habits. But it was a kind face and a good one in spite of these peculiarities, and, grimy as it was, a light burst from it as if from a dark-lantern when the bright side is turned towards one, when he said again, meditatively, "Carrie 'll feel good and happy when I tell her to-night."

"I'll be bound she will," said John Shore, sympathetically; "and what I sez is you'll git it. That's what I sez."

"Carrie——" began Mr. Stebbins again. He stopped. John Shore, who was looking at him, saw his eyes dilate with horror and his hair literally rise on end. Poor "Owl" Stebbins had heard a sound and seen a sight that made him stone for a second. Then, exclaiming "My God!" he leaped out into darkness,—eternity. The next instant two terrible lights flashed upon each other, two trains rushed together with horrible swiftness and fury. The stars looked down quietly upon the awful sight. The distant mountains faintly echoed the awful "crash." And in a cottage not far away "Carrie" was putting "the children" to bed and thinking of their father.

* * * * * * *

When the men who came to the rescue reached the wreck of locomotive No. 26, they found John Shore held fast indeed by one of his legs, which was caught by the fire-box of the engine, but working frantically with his arms to extricate his unconscious friend, having managed to reach the tool-box. And what was it that John Shore—"worthless" John Shore, "good-for-nothing" John Shore—shouted when he saw them? It was this: "*Thank God! Help Jim. Help poor Jim. Never mind me.*"

This was done as soon as possible, which was not very soon, for he was literally buried under the wreck. And when he had been taken away, and they turned to John Shore, what did they find? Why, simply that all this while the fire-box had been literally burning his leg to a crisp,—roasting it from the knee down.

V.

" What different lots our stars accord !
    This babe to be hailed and wooed as a lord !
    And that to be shunned like a leper !
    One to the world's wine, honey, and corn,
    Another, like Colchester native, born
        To its vinegar only and pepper."

HOOD.

"The Drisdale accident," as it was called by the
papers, was all owing to the mistake of a telegraph op-
erator, but it was as fatal as though it had been planned
by the Nihilists. Zach Hodges was killed outright.
Poor Jim Wilkins died of his injuries, as did Jack
Culbert and Belle Podley. John Shore and Jonah
were among those who were carried to the nearest
house, which was converted into a hospital for the
wounded of both trains. The latter's arm had got an
ugly compound fracture and two of his ribs had been
broken, so that he was not particularly pleased when
he overheard the doctor in charge say that there was
"nothing serious about that case." But with John
Shore it was different, and after a brief examination it
became clear that his leg would have to be amputated.
This was done, and he was no more gratified than
Jonah when he heard the operation spoken of as "a
beautiful thing—about the neatest I ever performed"—
by the enthusiastic surgeon, nor could he feel that he
was "doing splendidly" as the brisk doctor seemed to

expect. It had seemed to him that he had little enough light left in his life when he came home,—only the long, melancholy shafts of the setting sun; but it had been high noon he knew now compared with the blackness that settled down upon him when he knew himself to be a cripple. And, unfortunately, just as he began to convalesce, he heard of the death of the friend for whom he would willingly have made the costly sacrifice, and the result was a backset and a long, long illness of the most weariful, despairing kind. So great was his depression that the brisk doctor was moved to give him a brisk scolding, in which he asserted that he would "never get well" if he persisted in being so gloomy. But finding that this was like telling a clown that he would never make another joke, or an organ-grinder that he would never hear another note of music, he perceived that he had a sick heart to deal with, and, divining his sadness and loneliness, set himself to cheer and comfort this bruised reed, and was so kind and good in a thousand little ways that John Shore ever after loved him for it.

Nothing except an earthquake, resulting in the highest spur of the Mountain developing into an active volcano, could have more disturbed the community than the tragic ending of the long-planned outing. Daddy Culbert's sense of personal loss was sensibly lightened by what he felt to be the righteous retribution incurred by the non-fulfilment of the law written in his own mind and previously very generally proclaimed only to be almost universally scouted: "Thou shalt not waste precious time in play, but shalt work diligently on all the days of thy life without exception." This falling away from primitive ideals, and corruption of the morals and manners of society, he saw had to be stopped at any cost to individuals. Bowed over his stick until he looked like the initial letter of his own name, he shook his head and sorrowed, and said, " This here is what comes of a gallivantin', and picnickering, and the corn not gathered, even much less put up, and shucked, and shelled. Jack, he ought to er know'd better,—done better." Mr. Newman was shocked by this utterly unlooked-for conclusion of the feud that had filled his mind to the exclusion of everything else for so many months, and both seemed and felt perfectly dazed. The yearling calf which had swelled until it had become the world in which he lived and moved and had his being suddenly shrank into its true pilulous proportions, leaving him a prey to vain regrets and a miserable restlessness. As for Mrs. Newman, she was fairly distraught when, after long and anxious waiting, the bad news began to come in, getting worse with every galloping messenger and gossiping idler. And when, at one o'clock that night, poor, pale, chilled little R. Mintah crept out of the covered wagon that had brought most of the sobbing women and sleepy children of the party home again, where had all the coldness, anger, bitterness, of the last three months gone that the two women fell upon each other's necks, weeping, embracing, forgiving, and forgiven ?

R. Mintah spent every spare moment that she could get for the next three days in the exercise of an accomplishment little valued hitherto,—letter-writing; laboriously forming each letter, and blotting it often when made with the big tears that would roll down, splash !

when she was not thinking, on her only sheet of paper, bought, with the envelope, at "the sto'," for five cents. When finally completed, it was addressed to " mistur Jonur Newmen Att the horspitull," and ran as follows: " mi Deere beeloved i didn Wanter leve U.   U no. thay woodn lemmy stay withe U.   Hit pooty near Kild me. en F. U. doant git wel en come Hoam, i'm gonter go ter U. F. i got to Kraul.   ime Desprit wen i think Of U. mi Deere.   mi Hart bleads in Sid.   i cant doe nothin butt Kri All the tim.   in Dever ter rite soon pleas.   mi Deere i hop U wil excuse the Expresure en Badd ritin.   come Hoam Jonur or i Wil Die.   no moar att preasant.   i Liv in the Hopness Of U comin Hoam mi Darrlin Jonur.   mothers lik She Uster was. she Sez We kin git Mairred wen Wee pleas.   o aint Hit joy Full, mi Darrlin.   i seed mizis Jim Willyums yistur Day.   She's moas Kraazy.   her en him warnt Goode frens witches y She's a Takin On soe Orfull.   Rose zis Las kalfs a heffer en Mothers giv herr ter U en mee. but i dont care fur Nuthin Withe out U come Hoam.   i dont tak Noe Pleasure in Nuthin mi Deere. i dont wante Nuthin cep to Have U git Wel en come Hoam. o if i cood see Jonur is wat mi Hart Sez evry minit mi Darrlin.

"Your truely.

"rite soon   r. mintah Newmann."

Over and over did Jonah read this tender and artless production, which had no fault in his eyes, except that it was so very, very short.   And the first thing he did when he was well enough to carry on the correspondence was to answer it in his very best style,—a style altogether superior to hers, as he could not but feel: "My Dear Beloved miss i receive your most kind and efecturely letter and i was more than glad to here from you. it found me recovering Of my helth and i hope these few lines will reich you darling and find you in Joying the best Of helth witch is a grate Blessing. pleas go to town and in quir bout that there Shote i lef there and take it strait back Hoam. if you will excuse me Sayin so feed the heffer a little to gentle it down witch saves Trouble, but don't you git hurted. i aint let to rite more responsably now, and I wood Of ansered befo but i aint been Abel. mother rites me Marsh Culbert's hangin Round—i hop you dont have nothing to say to his foolin or any such expressings while ime gone. he should not take the Hand witch is Belonging to a Nothur. i must bring my letter to a Clous by wishing you good night my Darling

"Yore friend to command

"Jonah Newman."

There was no one to write to John Shore. A little enthusiasm had been aroused by the way in which he had acted, even among people most prejudiced against him, and at first he got some messages of sympathy from old acquaintances and neighbors; but writing was a most serious matter with them all, and with none more than Alfred, and in a little while it was not so clear in some quarters that he had behaved remarkably well at all, while in others the story, like last year's crops, was regarded as disposed of. So the question of getting well, and of his future, was one that he was left to decide for himself without having his judgment biased by outside influences or arguments; and when the brisk doctor rubbed his hands one day, and laughed, and said, "You are all right now, Shore. You'll have to wait a while before you can wear your artificial limb, but when you get that you'll be as much of a man as you ever were, almost. Er—where are you going now?" the blood rushed to his face—indeed, to the very roots of his hair—as he replied, "I reckon I'll have to go to my son's,—a good piece beyond here, up in the mountins."

"Oh, you've a son! That's all right," said the doctor, relieved to find that a patient in whom he had taken an especial interest was provided with a natural protector presumably able to take care of him. "I didn't know how you were situated. When you have made your arrangements, you can leave here any day you like. You can take your leg with you,—the wooden one, I mean,—and I've explained all about that. I think you'll have no further trouble. But if you should, here's my address, and you can come to me or write."

"Excuse me, doctor," said John, "a-mentionin' of it. But what's to pay fur all this here?"

"Pay?" said the doctor, apparently astounded by the question. "Why, nothing at all,—not a cent. The—or —the railroad pays for everything, and it owes you more than it could ever pay for. So make your mind easy. Yes. Of course. Er—who's that calling me out there?"

John Shore had kept his eyes fixed upon his face all the time, and the next time he saw him he began again, "Excuse me a-mentionin' hit, doctor, and excuse me a-sayin' so, but I'm shore as I'm lyin' here there's been somethin' to pay. And I want to know——"

"Oh, there's been something to pay, I grant. There's been the devil to pay, and you have settled the bill, my poor fellow. But there's nothing now, nothing whatever, I assure you," insisted the doctor, who, as a matter of fact, had at that moment a receipted bill (" Dr. Black Dr. to Josiah Turner. To one wooden artificial limb," etc.) in his coat-pocket that it seemed to him was being perused through the intervening folds of cloth by his patient's faded eyes.

"Sir, you're a-deceivin' of me. That there leg, now, must er cost a power of money," said John Shore.

"Oh, no. Legs are very cheap. Almost nothing, I may say. The railroad gets them by the dozen, I daresay. These things are always happening, you know," the doctor replied, with cheerful and unhesitating mendacity.

"How cheap? Would five dollars git one?" persisted John Shore, unconvinced. "I've got five dollars that— that was give to me by a friend, and——"

"Five dollars!" said the doctor, shocked by the extravagance of the estimate. "Not a cent over four fifty, I should say, unless you had a golden leg like Miss—— Well, say five, if you like. I'd let the railroad do it if I were you. 'Who breaks, pays,' you know; but if you are dissatisfied, why I'll hand it over to their agent here for you."

"I'd be obleeged, sir, ef you would,— mightily obleeged," said John Shore, and it was so settled.

It was in the late autumn, on an extraordinarily still and beautiful day, even for the season, that John Shore was brought home like a Spartan on his shield, except that in this unprized hero's veins the blood was still

14

flowing, and his heart, still beating, quickened its action and crimsoned warm as the sumacs by the roadside as each dear, familiar object met his gaze.

All was hushed and husbanded and secure in the lovely valley, which seemed a benediction made visible as it stretched away before him, wide and peaceful, serene and beautiful. Of all the sowing, and growing, and blowing of the past year, nothing remained, except in the stubble-fields, in some of which long ranks of "Cornfederates," as tattered and forlorn as any he had ever seen, still held their own, gallantly upholding a desperate cause; while in others Summer had stacked her arms and surrendered unconditionally to victorious Autumn, whose banners flamed glorious and triumphant everywhere.

Wrapped in the spectral mists of Indian summer, "Burly Blue Ridge" and the distant Alleghanies looked like their own wraiths. The sky was a July sky, deeply, warmly blue and almost cloudless, but the air had the delicious October quality, and felt as though it had been carefully iced to get exactly the right mean between heat and cold.

John Shore's eyes rested now on the old fort redly crowning the crest of a hill; now on Massanutton's spur; now on the Shenandoah, still serenely shining, flowing just as it had done when as a happy boy he had fished and nutted on its banks. And his thoughts were busy,—busy. He got wide views of the country about him through the bare branches, and of the heaven above him, and as he lay there with his own mutilated tree of life stripped bare of the leaves that once clustered so greenly and thickly about it he was getting

wider ones of his own past and future than he had
ever done before, as his childhood, youth, and manhood
passed in review before him. "Oh, ef Alfred will only
be good to me!" he thought, with a hope that was
almost despair. So many things and people had failed
him, one way or other, that he dared count upon nothing, yet could but cling desperately to the bright possi-
bility that his only child would be moved to pity, love,
and cherish him.

He was borne down the Red Lane followed by quite
a procession, composed chiefly of children, past cottage
after cottage, and saw everything as in a dream, and
there was the dear, dear old home again, and there
were the lilac-bushes, and the well, and the orchard.
He could not see them very distinctly for the tears that
filled his eyes. Alfred being hailed, came running out
looking rather scared and decidedly flustered, and
coming up to his father, bent over him, shook his thin
hand and said in a hurried half whisper, "I'm glad to
see you 'bout agin, Pa-ap; I certainly am; powerful
glad. I 'lowed to go and see you. But I hadn't no
money at all, and—Tildy she keeps——" John Shore
threw his arms around his neck and embraced him.
"Hem! It's coolin' fur frost," Alfred concluded. He
had broken off suddenly in the midst of his explanation, and looked wildly about him and up at the sky,
the reason being that Matilda had leisurely walked
down and joined him before he was prepared for the
pleasure.

"Oh, you've done been brought *here*," she said, coldly.
When it was thought that John Shore would die, she
had got the truth about the property out of her hus-

band and had fully decided upon her own course. She would have liked to inaugurate it at once; but the neighbors were there, all kindness and condolence for the time being, and ready, with the fickleness of popular feeling, to make a hero of John Shore, almost, again, seeing him so sorely stricken. So she was obliged to be content for the present with looking on sourly, and saying, when Alfred appealed timidly to her to know where he should put his father, "You can take him in. I'll see 'bout that," to which he replied, coaxingly, "That's right, Tildy; *you'll* do what's right." John Shore, who had been deeply pained by the fact that his son had neither come nor written to him during his illness, no sooner understood or thought he understood why this had been than he promptly and entirely forgave the neglect, only too glad to have a peg on which to hang his forgiveness indeed. His quick ear caught the suppressed tone of Matilda's speech, and he half raised himself on his elbow in his surprise. His cheeks were flushed, and his gray hair, pushed back from his deeply-wrinkled, blue-veined forehead, fell about his neck in pathetic scantiness. "Why, where hadn't I to oughter go?" he said, in tremulous tones of pained astonishment, looking from husband to wife with a troubled glance that said to Alfred as plainly as possible, "Are you going to cast off your poor old father, my son?"

"*Nowhur!*" said Alfred, with a sudden burst of courage, in response to it. "Nowhur at all, Pa-ap, in course, but right here. This here's your home." He spoke with a fire and energy most unusual in him, and Matilda was amazed to hear it. She was still looking at him as he busied himself with the few packages that constituted his father's luggage, when a little boy came limping briskly around the corner of the house and down the path, stopping short at the gate to round his eyes into a tremendous stare at the *cortège.*

It was the queerest little nondescript of a figure imaginable, in a colored shirt of bright calico, a man's waist-coat that came half-way down his bare legs, and trousers of incredible bagginess, as much too large as they were too long, the last defect being remedied by much rolling. The whole costume was rendered harmonious, as it were, by being covered with so many successive layers of what local politicians are fond of calling "the sacred soil of Virginia" as to have fairly entitled him to be regarded as a landed proprietor. Through the torn crown of an enormous straw hat, which had been nibbled by the calves and "worried" by the puppies until it presented in miniature very much the dismembered appearance of a hay-stack in March, protruded a curly flaxen poll. And beneath its ragged brim was a charming little face,—a face full of enchanting baby curves, having baby eyes of clear innocence that seemed surprisingly, vividly blue by contrast with the tanned skin, and cheeks as pink as clover, and a smile, when he did smile, of most peculiar and unusual sweetness. John Shore was won by it at once, and said, cheerfully, "Why, hello! Who's this you've got here, Al?"

"That's Willy. Tildy's cousin. Bob's son. He's livin' with us now."

"Well, Willy boy, howdy," said John Shore, and the child limped down to him and they shook hands, John Shore full of kind interest and Willy all eyes.

l   14*

"Suppose you run in with them things of mine now,
Burygyard, and my fiddle, and bundle. Set 'em
down anywhurs 'most, sonny," suggested John Shore,
presently, and the child seized the cage, in spite of a
vicious peck and squawk from its agitated occupant,
and carried it into the house. John Shore and his at-
tendants followed, Jinny White, who had joined the
party, talking for everybody with all her own fatal
fluency: "I'm glad as though I'd found a gold mind,
John, to see you alive and kickin', fur it's what nobody
hadn't no thought of seeing down here," said she. "And
ef you had uv died, I was goin' down to lay *you* out
shore, John Shore, ef it was the last thing ever I done.
When it comes to buryin's I ain't got my match on the
Mountin', all's agreed, and I know it, and I've been told
so over and over again lately. Fur I laid out every one
of them that was killed when you wuz, John, jes' elegant!
Sairy Dobbin sez to me when she seed 'em all there in a
row, 'Well, fur layin' out straight, and neat, and fixin'
stiffs off *tasty*, you ain't got your ekil, Jinny White, and I
don't kyur who hears me say so.' And, sez she, 'I tell
you what, ef *you* should go befo' I do, I'll take as much
pains to please yer, stiff or no stiff, as I've seed you do
fur other folks, and ef *I* go first I'll be obleeged ef you'll
bar in mind and not disremember that I couldn't never
abide yaller nowhurs 'bout *my face*. I ain't been a com-
plected person to have it livin', and it ain't likely I'm
goin' to be dead.' And that's so, fur even when she
wuz a child she wuz as yaller's her own butter is in
winter, owin' to the stuff she puts in it to the pint of
poisoning; and she *can't* bear no more, 'less it was two,
three yards tucked under her and sorter laid up over

hor feet liko, which need to be kivered every time. Fur
when beauty was shared Sairy Dobbin was behind the
do', as anybody can see fur theirselves. And as I was
sayin', John, I done it all, and it's the wust sort of
shame you warn't here to see the buryin's, fur they wuz
beautiful: two separate sermons to every stiff, and the
biggost crowd come all the way from Millboro', and
the mourners to be heard three fields off! You'll never
see the like in *your* lifetime, John, fur I suppose you
call yourself alive, and air alive, though part buried,
which, I must say, I never will rightly know whether
bein' dead you're alive, or bein' alive you're dead, fur it
beats me to say. And ef you want any custard, or
spoon vittles, or soch, John, made, I'm more 'n willin'
to do it, and I know how ef any woman ever did, fur
my teeth's all gone to snags so's I kin scarcely find one,
hunt around spry as I will with my tongue."

She had scarcely taken breath in the delivery of this
speech, in the course of which John Shore had been
deposited on a cot in the corner of the living-room.
One of the neighbors now broke in with a good-natured
" Well, Jinny, woman, you've got a plenty of *jaw* left."
That made all the others guffaw outright in general
chorus; and, after a lively spar between them, in which
Jinny took the ground that if she had had Samson's
opportunities she would have known who "needed
killin' bad," and he had retorted that "Tim White's
life warn't worth shucks anyways, and charity begins
at home," the little company dispersed much more cheerfully than it had gathered, leaving John Shore much
exhausted in mind and body, but most humbly thankful
that he was "at home."

It was not long before John Shore found out what
sort of home it was that he had come back to, for Matilda waxed daily more disagreeable as he grew better
and it became quite clear that he was a fixture. She
had not meant that he should stay. She had not
thought there would be any great difficulty in getting
rid of him, for when had Alfred ever dared to oppose
her in anything? But, like most autocrats, she had not
known where to stop and when to conciliate, so that
when she began first to suggest that "the old man was
plenty well enough to turn out and root for hisself,"
and then to urge that he should be "told to quit," and
finally to insist that he should "go right off," she was
amazed to find that Alfred had developed a vein of
unobtrusive, non-combative, but perfectly adamantine
"obstinacy," as she called it, that she could never have
foreseen as an even remotely possible contingency. She
could do nothing with him. He simply turned a deaf
ear to all her complaints, arguments, propositions, at
first; and when she finally began to threaten and command, instead of cowering before her and conceding
anything,—everything,—instead of even deprecating
her wrath, or of attempting to persuade her to look
at the matter differently, or using so much as one of the
glittering generalities that he was in the habit of intro-
ducing into such conversations as a sort of lightning-
rod to carry off all dangerous forces, he sat perfectly
still and silent for a moment, with an expression of
abject woe on his honest, vacant face that was enough
to melt a paving-stone; and then, turning about a dozen
colors, he started up from his chair, knocking it over
in the energy of his feelings, and, running his hands

deep in his pockets, shot his protuberant eyes out at
her as if they had been a missile of some sort, and
fairly shouted, " By gosh, Tildy, *never !*" which, coming
from him, was as effective as though he had sworn
fluently in nine languages. The upshot of the matter
was that "Pa-ap" stayed, was begrudged a seat at his
own fireside, fared meagrely at his own table, and was
only welcome to make himself as miserable as he
pleased. Alfred, having gained his point, was content,
and, not being a sensitive-plant by any means, had no
great sympathy for sentimental grievances, and expected his father to be so as well. He treated him with
a kind of gentle indifference that was not unkindness
any more than it was kindness,—the husks of the bread
for which his father's starved heart was hungering,—
his idea being that he was thereby adroitly avoiding
contention by making an unpleasant fact as little prominent as possible. As for Matilda, like Time, she knew
how to take her revenges. She could not drive him out
of the house in one way, but she was not at all sure
that the thing was impossible in another; and if it
were, she meant to indemnify herself for the "plague"
and "pesterment" of the dreadful infliction. All the
odd jobs of the establishment were put off upon him,
in addition to his regular work. It was her delight to
make him fetch and carry for her. She showed a truly
diabolical ingenuity in devising, hatefully, this or that
new device for making him unhappy. She wished to
be unbearable, and nature had eminently fitted her for
the task. And she succeeded in giving as much pain
as it is possible for an enemy to inflict. So systematically was he persecuted, so persistently nagged, so

wholly misunderstood, that, cripple as he was, he would
doubtless have drifted off again for the last time into a
world wide, indeed, and never too kind to him, but
comparatively alluring, had it not been for a new tie,
a fresh interest that had wonderfully sprung up in his
life,—in short, but for Willy, or " Willy boy," as he generally called him. We write " finis" after many a chapter
in the book of life, and feel sure that all is ended for us
and that there is nothing more to suffer or to enjoy or
to hope for practically ; but until the angel of death
traces it with his inverted touch in the sands of time,
the merciful truth is that day will succeed night, and
sunshine storm, and gladness sorrow.

If anybody had told John Shore when Giant Despair
sat by his bedside in the hospital that he would take a
child and set him in the midst of his heart,—that poor,
ruined temple of shattered hopes and faiths and a lost
idol,—he would have said that it was impossible. But
so it was. While he was still unable to get about,
Willy, as he put it, was "detailed for horspitul duty,"
Alfred being away so much, and Matilda determined
not to be troubled with an invalid. It was Willy who
brought all his meals, and sat on the bed near him while
he ate them ; Willy who, with a temper as sweet as his
face, ran all his errands and ministered to all his wants.
In this way an intimacy sprang up between the two
children, for John Shore was as much of a child in some
respects then as on the day he was born, and would
have been if he had lived as long as Thomas Parr.
There was not as much inequality in their friendship as
in that between many men of the same nationality, age,
position, fortune, in spite of appearances, and friends

they became emphatically,—firm friends, and natural allies,—presenting a solid front to society that often baffled even Matilda's spite; and a spite Matilda had against both of them, if ever a woman indulged the noble sentiment. Willy had been "a bequestment," left her by his father, a cousin of hers, who had migrated from the Mountain to the Big Fork neighborhood as a youth, and had carried away an ideal Matilda in his mind whom he believed to be a kind woman,—a conviction always a comfortable one to entertain, but never more so than when he was lying on his death-bed trying to dispose of five orphaned, penniless children. Not that he was harassed particularly by the problem, for with that absolute reliance on his "kin" which Virginians of every class feel, and which is so well founded, it was only a question of judicious choice, selection, arrangement,—the right child in the right place. It was true that he had not been able to take care of them himself; but, as he justly argued, that was no reason why other people should not be more fortunate in that particular form of industry known as "raisin' children." And being a person of confiding character, and rather more than the usual share of parental illusions about the intelligence, beauty, and general worth of his progeny, it was, at last, with a feeling that he was positively endowing certain families, paying them the greatest compliment in his power, and giving them a distinguished and distinguishing proof of his confidence, that Mr. Hardin made the usual provision in such cases for his sons. It was after great deliberation, and with peculiar satisfaction, that he "willed" his last and dearest piece of this kind of property, little Willy, to

Matilda, "seein' she'd none of her own, and knowin'
she'd be glad to have him and would act right by
him." Alfred was quite appalled by this act of testa-
mentary audacity, and gave vent to a shrill "Whew!"
and a "Moses in the bulrushes!" (which was a favorite
form of ejaculation rarely as applicable as in this case)
when he heard of it. He confidently expected to see
his wife fly into a rage and the state that he mentally
characterized as "tantrims and cavort*ments*," but was
as mistaken in his calculations in this matter as she was
about him when the question of John Shore came up
between them later. That capricious matron only
looked angrily at him, and said, "And whysomedever
not, you dumb igiot? Ain't I fitten to raise no childern?" in a way that made him hasten to say in his
"Now-do-be-a-good-little-girl" tone of cajolement, "Of
course, Tildy, and *in* course. I ain't been a-sayin' nor
a-remarkin' no different, is I?" and then later, seeing
how unrelentingly grim her aspect was, "Childern's
mighty handy to have 'round. There ain't nothin' as
I knows on, now, handier. But you'll do well to bar in
mind, Tildy, grown folks will be grown folks, and childern will be——"

"O, shet up! Shet right up!" commanded Matilda,
fiercely, whereupon Alfred finished his sentence *sotto
voce*, disliking of all things to leave an axiom uncom-
pleted and with frayed ends, as it were,—"childern—
specially childern."

The truth was, that in her heart, strangely folded,
like all human hearts, Matilda was pleased and flattered,
as murderers have been known to be, say by the preference of an innocent child. She boasted of the fact

among all her acquaintances, aware that she was not generally regarded in the most amiable light. She announced with a grand air that her "Cousin Bob had knowed what he was about," and that she meant to take the child, though it was "reely no concernment" of hers. She enjoyed for the moment her rôle of benefactress; but it had its drawbacks. There had been a certain dignity in being childless,—it was such an exceptional state of affairs in a community of swarming households,—and she had been vain of the fact as albinos and giants and twelve-fingered folk are vain, and had indulged in much pharasaical comment on the largeness, and helplessness, and hopelessness of this or that neighbor's brood of younglings,—"them Logans," or "Brown's gang," or "Simmons iz iz crowd," or "the Bartlett brats." She had long been in the habit of predicting battle, murder, and sudden death (on the gallows) for them, and boastingly thanked Heaven that she "hadn't never been one of the sort that goes and has a dozen lazy, ugly children a-ramblin', and a-scramblin', and fightin', *and* hollerin' all over the face of the yearth." And now a child had been foisted upon her. The situation was a serious one, looked at from the highest stand-point, and from the mean elevation of Matilda's mind became more than serious for the little creature in question—positively tragic, indeed—as time went on. For Willy came, and proved to be not only very young, helpless, and troublesome, but quite lame,—an after-effect of scarlet fever. He would for these very reasons have appealed irresistibly to the heart of a true woman, but Matilda was not a woman; she was merely a female. So far from

H   15

honoring the incessant drafts made upon the tenderness
and unselfishness that Willy's father had supposed she
possessed, she repudiated them more and more, and,
from being at first coldly indifferent, grew rapidly ne-
glectful, and finally often cruel. There was light
enough left in the dark depths of her soul even to
show her what she was doing, but the only effect that
this ghost of a conscience had was to hurry her into
some aggravated excess of unkindness. The more cor-
dially she detested him, the more comfortable she felt;
and when he was really naughty it was a positive lux-
ury to punish him,—a savage satisfaction, such as only
the hate that ought to be love can give in all its hideous
perfection. Never did John Shore feel so bitterly conscious of his position in his own house, or regret so
deeply that he had put it out of his power to help or
befriend any one under that roof, as when he had to
stand by and see some such scene, and when Willy was
unjustly as well as severely assailed it was almost more
than his generous and affectionate heart could bear. It
was a far more painful ordeal to him than to the child.
He would lie awake and brood unhappily over an outbreak of the kind all night, for instance, while Willy
would be laughing again in a few hours. Alfred, who
longed for nothing so much as peace, and was, besides,
kindly disposed towards the child, was always ready
with excuses for his little peccadilloes, and he had two
forms of appeal which he invariably used on all such
occasions. One was: "Tildy, orphins is orphins, pertikiler when fathers and mothers is dead *and* buried;" the
other was in constant use, being his favorite: " Grown
folks will be grown folks, and children will be children.

—specially children." Neither had the least restraining effect upon the person addressed.

With every hour of every day of that long, gloomy winter in which the icy bondage that held captive the world outside the cottage seemed less harsh and unlovely than the Egyptian rule within it, which seemed to bring his very thoughts into captivity, and often drove John Shore out into the sleet and snow and sent him hobbling up and down the Red Lane for hours until the fever and tumult of his mind and heart had been somewhat stilled by the white silence of his surroundings, the pain of his wound, and the physical discomfort of the exposure,—with every hour of that interminable season the love that John Shore had conceived for the child who had limped straight into his heart on the very first day of his return increased, deepened, strengthened, until it became a passion. While still unable to do so, he had looked forward eagerly, as invalids will, to the time when he should be able to get about and go abroad. And when that time came around he did, with the aid of his crutch, limp over to this or that place, and was civilly enough received, if not precisely with enthusiasm, especially at first. But it was a busy community. No one seemed to have time to talk to him after a bit, and when they did, the talk was chiefly of things that did not interest him. And then he came to feel himself distinctly in the way, except when he wandered over to the sloping, snow-covered church-yard, and sat for an hour gazing at two mounds there,—the graves of his sweet dead wife and his best friend. It was all so strange, so ghostly strange, to him. He was glad to shrink back into the cottage again.

The dreary little room, the black stove, even Matilda's
sharp, sour face, were comparatively cheerful after one
of these expeditions. Coming in profoundly depressed,
he would sink into his chair in the chimney-corner, lay
aside his crutch, and call, "Here, Willy boy, come set
on Pa-ap's knee," and presently would get a sense of
restfulness and warmth and comfort inexpressibly heal-
ing. His life was flowing again in the old, familiar
channel, but oh, the difference! What a strong, free
current it had once been! How richly it had brimmed
over its green banks! How it had rushed with eager
purpose to a desired end! And now there remained
only the rocky bed of the stream, with its tear-worn
channel, dry and dusty, except where one little rill,
Heaven-given, ran crystal clear. Was it any wonder
that he pressed his dear little "Willy boy's" curly head
so fondly against his breast,—"Willy boy," whose smile
and prattle and artless arts had sweetened afresh an existence grown intolerably bitter and desolate?—pressed
it so fondly, indeed, that the child cried out, " Quit,
Pa-ap; you hurted me!" and replied, "Hurted you, honey,
did I? Why, I wouldn't hurt a hair of your head to
save my old skin," and gave him a dozen hungering
kisses in proof thereof. He no more tired of Willy's
voice than of the sound of the brook that rippled out
its rich-throated music all the summer long back of Culbert's meadow. Everything that he said or did, thought
or felt, was of importance to him,—in short, he adored
the child. And Willy loved him, as children commonly
love, selfishly, carelessly it may be, but sincerely, and
how sweetly!

"You and Pa-ap's mighty thick," Alfred would say,

good-naturedly, when some evidence of their mutual affection would strike him. "Yes. Thick as thieves," Matilda would reply. It was a lucky thing for Willy in some ways that he had found a friend in "Pa-ap," as he, too, called John Shore, for like him he needed one sorely. But in others it was unfortunate, for he had not found in that friend a protector. Matilda had done nothing to win the child's affection, it was true, but none the less she resented his having made a free gift of it to her poor, despised, and oppressed dependant of a father-in-law. If Willy had been old enough and wily enough to affect the love and admiration that no one really felt for her, he might have fared differently. But it was not in any child of his tender years and true nature to be attracted by a hard, bitter, ugly face full of fretful puckers, stamped with discontent and dulness in every line; to like to listen to a harsh voice with a most distressing rasp in it; to feel other than repelled by a temper always uncertain and frequently violent; to pretend anything. In the same way if John Shore had been a hypocrite or knave he might have been a match for his son's wife. But as it was, the pair were declared to be "of a feather," were always arraigned at the same time, convicted of every sort of high crime and domestic misdemeanor, and as yoke-fellows were driven by the same harsh mistress, bore the same burden, received the same punishments, and had, like the early Christians, as a compensation for much persecution, "all things in common." This was especially the case when Matilda one day in mid-winter (after John Shore was able to get about) suddenly announced to them that she preferred their "room to
15*

their company," and that they might "git" into the
adjoining shed. Matilda had certainly no idea of con-
ferring a favor upon either of them, and Alfred was
more surprised than pleased when he heard of the proposed change at supper,—remonstrated, even, with a
"Now, Tildy, you haint never a-goin' to do that; no.
It's jest an *idee* uv yourn, that's all," but had the gag
connubial promptly popped into his mouth and was
silenced; but all the same it was the greatest kindness
she could possibly have done them, for it ensured the
peace and privacy they could have got in no other way.

The process of moving into it was one that excited
great interest in the breasts of the banished pair. "We
ain't got but two sound, dependable legs between us,
Willy, and the two of us 'll have to limp about pretty
lively to git ev'ything moved in. When that's done,
I'll take command," said John Shore. This he did, and
set to work at once to make the place not only habit-
able, but as pleasant as his very limited means of producing æsthetic results would permit. He must have
inherited some of Sailor Jack's "handiness," for he succeeded better than the Israelites in making bricks
without straw, and, inspired by love and wit, accomplished the impossible, and turned the dismal little shed
into a fairly comfortable room. The ingenuity and
variety of the. contrivances that he summed up as
"fix*ments*" brought him and them into notice. Matilda
sneered at them, the neighbors ridiculed them in a
kindly fashion, Jinny Hodges came over to see them,
and took up a whole precious afternoon with a "dis-
coursement" upon everything in general and "John's
awful smartness" in particular, and then went home,

and sent back a most welcome contribution to the new establishment in the shape of a box-patterned quilt and two jars of blackberry jam. John whitewashed the walls, put in a window, rehung and listed the door, and put up a rude fireplace to begin with. The lighter and brighter touches were gradually given. "Burygyard" was put well up on the door-post for fear of Matilda's appropriately green-eyed and cruel-minded cat. The photograph of Jackson that Jim Wilkins had given him and another of General Lee were tacked to the wall. (Differently christened they would have passed anywhere for Lafitte and Captain Kidd.) Below them was nailed a picture that had greatly taken his fancy because of some real or fancied resemblance to his wife,—a flaming chromo advertisement of a patent medicine, good-naturedly given him by the druggist of a neighboring town. Alfred, coming in one day and keeping one eye on the door all during his brief stay, made bold to present them with a chair that had once had a cane bottom,—a present that his father received with beaming satisfaction, and skilfully mended and painted that night. He turned an old goods-box up on end as a wash-stand, scoured a rusty tin basin that he had bought for a song at "the sto'," and put it best side out on top of the box with a bit of yellow soap, and, not content with this magnificent provision for his comfort, "rigged up" a roller for a crash towel that he had privately determined to ask for. These with the bed solved the question of furniture for the room most satisfactorily, and only one eyesore remained,—an abandoned stove,—that, think as he would, he could make neither useful nor ornamental. He looked at it many thousands of times with ever in-

creasing disgust, until he at last got an inspiration, some
months later, and forthwith took off the lids, planted
and trained creepers over it far more successfully than
if it had been a majolica jardinière, enlivened it on top
with petunias, geraniums, and one fine calla lily, and
made of it eventually a small terraced garden, of which
he was naturally very proud. He had the growing
touch with flowers, as was shown by the luxuriant way
in which the plants thrived in and overflowed from a
tin bucket with slits cut in the bottom and sides (to en-
sure proper drainage) suspended in his window,—plants
that would have made a point of dying in any drawing-
room, and could scarcely have been kept alive by a
Scotch gardener in a model greenhouse.

The pleasure that he got from doing all this was
only equalled by Willy's delight in seeing him do it.
Half help, half hindrance, the little fellow dogged
his every footstep, prattled without cessation, admired,
wondered, fetched and carried, ran nails in his bare feet,
almost choked himself with a mouthful of tacks, did
everything that ought not to have been done, and left
undone almost everything that he was told to do, not
being able to bear the thought of leaving his gifted
friend for one moment while he was engaged in such
fascinating tasks. And what a moment it was when
they were were " all cleared up," and the room had been
made spotlessly clean, and Jinny Hodge's gorgeous
quilt had been laid over the bed and neatly tucked
in, and John Shore embraced Willy and announced,
" Honey, it's done *done,* and it's fur you I've done it, and
here we'll live together all pleasant and kind always."
It was such a great occasion, indeed, that they were

moved to celebrate it especially, and John Shore, who
had carefully sought in the woods and brought in and
stored quite a little supply of pine-knots and fagots,
went to the place where he had hidden them away out
of Matilda's sight, and soon had a great sheet of flame
crackling and roaring up the chimney. And then he
went out of the room for a few minutes, and came back
wiping his lips, and dropped into his chair, and put
Willy on the stool he had made for him, and buttered a
huge slice of bread with a thick layer of blackberry
jam on top for the child, and they talked and laughed,
and talked again, and then Pap got out his violin and
played until their house-warming was over, which was
only when Matilda rapped sharply on the wall and
bade them go to bed "right straight off." "We've
done got shut uv *her* some, anyways, and this here is
our little home now, Willy boy. Does yer like it?"
whispered Pap, after this noise ceased.

"Mightily, Pa-ap," replied Willy, looking his pleasantest and smiling his sweetest as he glanced about him.
"It's grand!" Willy's age and position and very limited experience precluded his instituting the comparisons
that might have been odious. Anything more splendid
and perfectly satisfactory than this poor place he could
not even have imagined; and from this moment it
became his world, and was set exactly in the centre of
the earth. It was a paradise for him. A bright, loving
little fellow, he had pined under the neglect and harshness, the restraint and dulness, of his environment, and
now here was, all at once, a new heaven and earth only
a few feet away from the old one actually, but morally
on another planet. Such a busy, happy, delightful

m

place as it was, too. It kept him busy and happy and delighted to keep pace with its wonderful life at all, there was so much to see and do and hear and to try to understand. And John Shore was busy and happy, too. There were kites and traps to be made, sleds to mend, walnuts to shell. There were apples and persimmons and nuts to eat. "Pa-ap" would salt rabbit-skins, or clean his gun, or splice his fishing-tackle, or mend his clothes with the aid of a leather thimble of his own construction, a bit of cork, a jack-knife, a cake of wax, stray bits of cord or pack-thread, and a huge needle. Willy would nurse his kitten, or feed his bushy-tailed, alert squirrel, or try to "split up kindlings" with a hatchet on the worst possible terms always with its handle, or roll idly about on the floor watching "Pa-ap's" performances and enlivening the occupation with his clear, treble pipings and prattlings about whatever had happened during the day. And then "Burygyard" had to be educated. The schoolmaster was not abroad on the Mountain, and neither John Shore nor Willy could read or write; but they knew many other things that they felt to be of far more importance than the doubtful glory of being "a scholard," and were far from finding their ignorance oppressive.

John, indeed, was not as conservative in his view of this question as Daddy Culbert, who always told a story in this connection of a man who insisted on being educated, and forged, and was finally hanged, and deduced from it: "This here's what comes of readin' and writin'." He had even determined to learn a great deal, that he might teach Willy something that might lead to his "betterment," and with this in view had taken to studying carefully the circus posters at the black-smith's shop. But this was a tentative process, into which he could not throw himself with the heartiness and sense of mastery that characterized his efforts to impart accomplishments to "Burygyard." He had heard a bird in Texas whistle Dixie "right off," and fol-low it up with the Star-Spangled Banner, changing its note and coat with as little scruple as the Vicar of Bray. And that had fired his ambition, and he and Willy had agreed that their bird could, would, and should do the same thing, and thought it of the first importance that he should have a lesson every day, no matter what be-sides was done or left undone. So every night Pap would get out his violin, tune it carefully, and play the first five notes of Dixie over and over again for about an hour, encouraging, rebuking, admonishing his pupil the while with untiring zeal and faith in the ultimate result. And "Burygyard," his cage on Willy's stool, would indulge in a series of hoppings, and shirkings, and perverse lurkings in corners that aggravated his master the more because he would sometimes sing the strain as well as Mario could have done it, three or four times in succession, though he showed generally an in-veterate tendency to stop after the third note, and burst into a brilliant improvisation of his own, which, as he doubtless knew, was much better worth hearing. And Willy would clap his hands for joy, and praise, and scold, and laugh, and shout, assisting at all the sessions of Burygyard's night-school with an interest that never flagged, and an enthusiasm that was perfectly infectious. And then Pap would do "a little prac*ty*sin'," and the old house would ring again with the old melodies. And

then he would as like as not play at leap-frog with
Willy, the latter having a surprising fancy for that
particular game rather than some other better adapted
to the lame and halt. Matilda on the other side
of the wall listening to the hum of their voices and
catching bursts of sweet child-laughter would get another wrinkle in her wicked heart and about her thin
lips (finding them so happy in spite of her), and, rising,
she would go to their door, and by merely putting her
head in for a moment, scare away all the contentment
and cheerfulness that, like the firelight, had filled the
room from floor to ceiling. They probably rushed up
the chimney to get out of her way merely, for they
generally came back again as soon as the head was
gone and the door closed again. And at worst in an
hour the fitful radiance of the pine-knots showed Pap's
serene face and Willy nestling close to him—a rosy,
beautiful beatitude,—Blessed are little children and safe
in the arms of God—as it flickered over to the bed in
which both were lying asleep.

VI.

> " The world will not believe a man repents ;
>   And this wise world of ours is mainly right.
>   Full seldom *does* a man repent, or use
>   Both grace and will to pick the vicious quitch
>   Of blood and custom wholly out of him
>   And make all clean, and plant himself afresh."
>
> *Geraint and Enid.*

THE nights were still cold and wintry, but it was bright enough in the shed-room, although Matilda would have scouted the idea of allowing its occupants a candle, and so warm that Willy's cheeks glowed crimson as the apples set to toast before the fire while he clambered up into Pap's lap to " hear stories." He made such a stimulating audience, with his shining eyes (the bluest, brightest, sweetest eyes ever seen, Pap thought) and his eager, excited face, that these narratives, from a nucleus or verbal protoplasm of one dimly-remembered, moss-grown tale about a bear and a bad boy that he had heard in his childhood, developed and extended until the whole field of Pap's life and experience was covered, his memory ransacked, his power of invention severely taxed. There were long-forgotten traditions handed down in his family about " how they used to do in them early times,"—of how the little babies were cradled in logs hollowed out to receive them; of the Indian raids; of how the settlers had been glad to pay a cow and calf for one bushel of salt brought over

16

Braddock's trail from "beyant the country beyant the
Ridge,—'way fur off yonder, Willy boy."
"How fur?" "Willy boy" would insist on knowing.
"Could you walk there in a day, in two days, in a week,
a year? If you took four horses and harnessed 'em to
a wagon and whipped 'em up all the time, could you
git there by Christmas?" It was only when Pap had
said he "reckoned not" that it seemed useless to Willy
to pursue the inquiry, and the mysterious country immediately became fairy-land,—a region of wonders and
delights, about which he was never tired of thinking.
And then there was "Witch Parsons," an old, old, crooked,
wicked woman, who lived in a cabin in the heart of
a wood, and had a black dog, and a black cat, and the
evil eye. Willy would blanch as he heard how she was
feared and obeyed, and tremble a little, and devour all
the details Pap could give of her terrible powers and
potions and general awfulness. It was almost too fascinating to hear how the witch, when she wanted to spite
certain neighbors, would make their cows go dry by an
infallible process of her own, which consisted in hanging
a *new* towel over her back door with a pin stuck in it for
every cow to be "conjured," and then *in the dark of the
moon* going out at night to finish her work. She had
been seen—"folks had heerd" her, often—muttering her
diabolical incantations and stripping from the pendent
fringe of the towel *buckets* of milk that ought to have
been in the honest udders of ruminant animals miles
away.

Why didn't they kill her? Why didn't folks conjure
her cows? Why was the towel hung on the *back* door
always? And what would have happened if the fringe

had been cut off, say by a sharp boy that had "crep' up unbeknownst" before the witch's time came for milking? Willy wanted to know. He could not get enough of "Mother Parsons," as "folks that was 'feared of her" called her, and was disgusted when Pap, in telling the great cow story for about the seventy-fifth time, got a trifle mechanical in his delivery throughout, and made matters worse by calling the heroine Mother *Brown* forsooth. And then there were Pap's travels, which had really been quite extensive, and seemed to Willy's starved imagination to combine the territorial sweep of Captain Cook's with the remarkably interesting personal adventures of Baron Munchausen or Gulliver. " You've been more miles 'en you can count to save your life, ain't you, Pa-ap? There ain't many places as *you* don't know whur they're at, is there?" he would comment admiringly, more and more convinced of his friend's immeasurable superiority to all the people he had ever known. And then there was "the war," which, although a most thrilling theme, was not as uniformly interesting as any of the others. The benign and gracious face that the old man turned towards him when relating his personal experience of and share in various scenes left so much to be desired in the way of unbridled ferocity that Willy could not but feel that he had never been so disappointing as in the rôle of warrior. There were bits in the raids and skirmishes that were delightful, but the battles were mere sound and fury, with not half the action and gore that he thirsted for. "How many uv the Yankees' heads did you cut off to onst, Pa-ap?" he would ask, turning around eagerly from a fixed and agreeable contemplation of the apples browning and sputtering and wrinkling in a row on the hearth below. And his face would fall when the mild, drawling reply reached him : " Why, none, my son. I fit under old Blue Light yonder fur four year, but——"

" Not *nary* one ?" interrupted Willy.

" No, honey, not none at all. I was precious glad to keep my own on my shoulders, I kin tell you, without troublin' 'bout theirn. *He* was a one fur puttin' his men in tight places and then prayin' 'em out, shore as you are born. Jim Wilkins usened to say, ' The general's on his knees, boys, and that's a sign that some of us will be on our backs soon with no way to turn over; but not sufferin' from cramp, to speak of, from lyin' in one position so long.' Jim was a joker always. Poor Jim."

" Why didn't you jes' run right up to the Yankees and cut 'em in two this er way ?" said Willy, plunging forward and swishing savagely at the rusty andirons, which had lost their legs during the war, if not in consequence of it, and were carefully propped up at the back on two bricks.

" Well, I done some right smart runnin', Willy boy, but it warn't *always that way*," replied the old. soldier, with a hearty " Haw ! haw ! haw !" that was full of enjoyment, and gradually subsided into convulsive chuckles which brought out the natural twinkle in his eye strongly and left it there for some time.

In the fulness of the intimacy that sprang up between them, John Shore laid aside for the first time the reserve that had led him to maintain a sacred silence about everything that related to the supreme joy and grief

of his life. And though he had avoided mentioning so
much as his wife's name ever since her death, and had
never been able to speak of her to her own son even
(still less to hear her spoken of by others), he now got
comfort and pleasure in talking freely of her to this
tender, simple, uncritical confidant who leaned against
his breast, and held his hand, and loved him. Willy
expressed no sympathy, and would only occasionally give
utterance to some of his high, narrow child-thoughts,
extending only a little way on either side, but often
taking in the heaven above him and the depths beneath;
but it was a grateful contrast to the effusive or offensive
speech of others, and beguiled Pap continually into
further confidences. Matilda could be heard scolding
angrily within, and the wind roared without as it seized
and shook the old cottage and swept on to heap the
snow high above the sweet dead wife's grave on the
night that Pap first laid bare his heart and showed the
love there that could not die.

"You see, Willy, this was the way of it. From the
fust moment I seed that girl she was my inthought.
And she's been that ever sence. And I was drawed to
her that powerful that ef I was workin' five miles off
and she wanted me *bad* I knowed it and went to her.
And she was the same. And when I found as how she
felt like I did, I mighty nigh went crazy for joy, and
the world warn't a big enough place to hold me. But
her father, he was opposed to me, and forbid me comin'
'round. En she begged and prayed to him to change
his mind, fitten to melt Masanutton. And he wouldn't
let her have nothin' to do with me. Then I sez to her,
'Ally,'—her name was Alice, but I called her Ally,

16*

mostly,—I sez, 'There's no reason fur him actin' so, it's jes' obstination, and you've got to make a choosement between us.' En she sez, 'John, we'll wait.' En we did wait, and it warn't no use, fur waitin' ain't never yet cured obstination. En she was still fur waitin', and pretty nigh cried her eyes out 'bout it. But I wouldn't; en at last I got her talked 'round, and I got a two-horse fix and we runned away to Harper's Ferry and got married. 'Pears like it was yesterday." (A pause.)

"And then we come back together, and there she set, —the prettiest thing in Virginia, and the sweetest. En her lap was full of oranges I'd buyed fur her at the bridge, and we was both eatin' gingerbread and holdin' hands,—leastways one hand. I had a 'cordion in the other, and was runnin' up and down it, sorter blowin' out my feelin's like, you see. She always did love to hear me play the 'cordion. I was prouder 'n a peacock with two tails that day, and as happy as the Lord makes 'em. 'Pears like it was a thousand years ago."

"Did you come here, to this house?"

"Yes," said Pap, slipping lower in his chair and fixing his eyes on the fire. "This was our home. And I'd fixed up right smart fur her 'bout the house all I could, and made her a beautiful flower-garden. I knowed she loved flowers. I took a power uv trouble (only it warn't no trouble bein' done for her) with that there garden. There was blue-flags from the woods, and white lilies, and sweet pinks, and mournin'-brides, and bleedin'-hearts, and marygolds. I got them 'bout here. And I set out five big bushes of snow-balls, and three of white lilocks. She hadn't never heerd tell of

a *white* lilock till then. And I got some yaller 'stur-
tiums, that comes from the sea, from a gentleman that
keeps a garden in Winston. And I planted her favoright
rose under her winder. It bloomed the day she"——
(Another pause.) "Well, she was as pleased as the next
one when she seed 'em, and there warn't nothin' she
didn't notice, and she sez, 'You've done done all this
fur me, ain't you, John,' and kissed me, and then we
went into the house, and she was better pleased yet
when she seed that, and she took off her bonnet and
hung it up and set down in the new rockin'-chair, and
she looked out of the winder and sez, 'How sweet the
lilocks smells.' I ain't never been able to suffer 'em
since. En then she looks at me smilin' and sez, 'John,
my darlin', we've tied a knot with our tongue this day
we kain't undo with our teeth. Do you know that?'
En then I took her on my lap,—she was a little thing,
Willy, not much bigger 'n you,—'n I sez to her, 'I never
will want to try, Ally.' En she sez to me, 'No more
will I, dear John,' sez she. And we never did." (Another
pause.) "I wuz in the wagon business then, and carried
on at the cross-roads 'bove here a piece. I carried five
men the year 'round, 'n there warn't no better wagons
wuz ever turned out. The axles seemed jes' to come
plum' of theirselves in them days, Willy, and everything
was goin' right with me, when all to onst trouble come
and nothin' ain't gone right sence. Ally she got sick.
It was all the trouble she ever give me. And she
wouldn't never 'low she was more 'n tired. But I
knowed. I knowed! It was a breast-trouble,—some
calls it the consumption. I done all I knowed. I reckon
I got every medicine that's made for it. There was one

splendid one,—' Seven Barks' was the name; it was the grandest thing you ever could want. It cured everything,—the consumption, and scrofily, and pneumony, and all kinds of fevers. You couldn't mention nothin' it didn't cure. The paper that come with every bottle said so. You may know it was good: it cost fifty cents a bottle."

" Who-ee! Every bottle? What a heap of money, Pa-ap! I wish I had fifty cents."

"You're right there, Willy. Well, I give her that and give it to her. There was a closet full of the empty bottles; but it never cured her, someway. I dunno why, 'cept it was the mysterousness uv dealin's. All the comfort I had was working extry to get it, though, and I'd of had it ef I'd had to burn the sto' down where 'twas sold, ef I couldn't of got it no other way."

" Of cose, Pa-ap. You couldn't do no defferent, and her so sick."

" But it warn't no use. She left me." (A long pause.) " This here is a strange, mysterous world of ourn, Willy. I've set and studied and studied over that thing, but I ain't never seed the why nor the wherefore. A body can't understand it. I used to look 'round at my little baby,—Alfred that is now,—sleepin' so peaceful in his cradle (that was at night 'fore I put out the light), and I'd think to myself how strange it was as how he might be blowed out like a candle by death. But I hadn't never no idea 'twould be the mother. It looked like it was on-possible to the last. But it come." (A deep, patient sigh and a silence.) " And everything has went wrong sence she left me. I wuz so weakened down. I couldn't ketch hold of nothin' fur a long while. And then the chances was occupied. And—and I've went wrong, too, Willy. I ain't gone straight,—Lord! no. Don't you think it. You see I los' my linch-pin, 'n I've ben jes' rattlin' 'long fur a break-down ever since. A wagon *kain't* run right without a linch-pin, no way you fix it, now can it? The mysterousness of dealin's,—that's it. I can't git no purchase on it. Her so good, and both of us so happy."

"Whurze she gone to now? Whurze she at right now, this minnit, Pa-ap, say?"

"She went to heaven, my son; shore and certain as there is a heaven, she has went to it."

"How did she git there?"

"The Good Man sent for her," said Pap; and Willy understood; for, strange to say, this is the title universally given to God by the mountaineers, with a perfectly reverent intention. He is rarely called by any other, except when they profane His name.

"Don't you feel bad. Maybe he'll send fur you, too, Pa-ap," said Willy.

"Well, I ain't fitten to go; that's the trouble. And I ain't fitten to stay, neither. I'm no good, noways you fix it. This here life of ourn's a hard, hard job, honey. You've got to have more patience 'n a courtin' man's horse to git through it. En I don't see why I was brung here. I dunno when I'm goin' to be gone. I dunno nothin', 'n nobody don't know no more than me."

After this long talk between them, no further allusion was made to the subject for a long while. Pap probably thought that Willy had forgotten all about it. One lovely spring morning, though, when they had gone together to the wood,—one of those days that seem to draw out tender memories as inevitably as buds, or leaves, or delicious earthy smells that cannot be traced to any one spot,—the child surprised him by referring to it of his own accord. They had come to a halt at a place about which there was a perfect tangle of grape-vines, all in bloom, and breathing out, as it were, their exquisitely delicate and penetrating odor. Pap, after seating himself, had fallen into a reverie, and had paid no attention to Willy. "What's you thinkin' 'bout, Pa-ap? Is you thinkin' 'bout *her?*" said Willy, after amusing himself in various ways for some time, and coming back to find his friend still silent and absorbed.

"Yes, honey, I was. This here's our weddin' day that was," Pap replied. He said no more, and there was another silence ending with a deep sigh.

"Is yer got a misery in yer head? Hainh?" inquired Willy. "I'll rub it for you."

"No, Willy boy. I'm jes' tired, that's all. Don't you worrit 'bout me. I gits beat out sometimes. Ef she— ef Ally had of lived, it don't seem to me like I'd be as tired as I mostly am."

The sunset was a very beautiful one that evening, and Pap and Willy saw it together from the wood-pile where they had been busily engaged for an hour pre-vious providing for the next day's fires. The work was done and the wood arranged in separate heaps to be carried in-doors later. A kite sailing above the next field had fully occupied Willy's attention for some mo-ments, and when his interest in it was exhausted he ran up to Pap, whose axe was at rest, and who was leaning on his crutch.

"Pa-ap," said Willy, calling out to him as he approached, and pointing upward, "Alice is up yonder. Ain't she, now?"

"Yes, my son," said Pap.

"Whurabouts? Whurabouts?"

"I kain't rightly say; but she's there."

"She ain't in that white place," persisted Willy, still pointing. "And she ain't in them black, ugly clouds, is she? She's somewhurs in the blue, ain't she, Pa-ap?" the child added, eagerly, turning his rosy, smiling face up to the solemn sky. Pap looked up into the blue, and then pulled his hat over his eyes and, stooping forward, got another stick of wood. "The ground's too wet for ploughin'," he said, presently. A moment later he took a seat on a log and fixed his eyes on the distant mountains, set along the horizon like great pedestals for silence. The sun was dying like a saint in peaceful glory in the west. The bats were circling above his head. The rosy clouds in the east were fading into gray. He did not know how long he sat there; but Willy played about him for a long while, until, at last, tired of blowing his penny whistle and playing marbles alone, and of getting no answers, above all, from the one person whose companionship and sympathy he felt himself entitled to, he, too, came and perched beside his friend, rammed his hands in his pockets, and cheered himself for a few minutes by rattling their highly miscellaneous contents. Then he leaned against John Shore's arm, which was then slipped gently around him. "I've been a-thinkin' it all over," said the old man, without preamble or explanation,—thinking aloud, as he often did with Willy. "I feel like it was waitin' fur me somewhurs. Don't you reckon that time'll come back to me sometime 'r other, somewhur, Willy? She was always waitin' fur me here. She couldn't never rest, no way you fixed it, 'less I was 'round, onless she knowed what kep' me. I reckon she's waitin' fur me there." They were still sitting there when they heard a voice hailing them. "Pa-ap! Pa-ap! Willy!" called Matilda. "Ain't you brung that wood in yet? Well, of all the lazy, triflin', good-for-nothin'——" He waited to hear no more, but rose with a start and came back to the present, and hastened to avert the wrath that he dreaded doubly,—that is, for himself and for Willy. To keep Willy "out of trouble," to make Willy happy, to see that Willy lacked for nothing, was his constant care, and his efforts to accomplish these objects increased with his increasing love for the child who had now become the one hope, joy, and comfort of his daily life. So now, although Willy drew back at the door, saying, "I don't want to go in there. Matilda's in there, Pa-ap. Lemmy go," he only held his hand the more firmly. "Ssh! Willy boy, you must. We ain't been in there to-day, and supper's 'most ready. Come 'long with your Pa-ap," he said, and drew him into the room. Matilda, out of the tail of her eye, saw them enter, and immediately opened fire on them,—"pouring in grape and canister," Pap called the process, and sometimes "shellin' the woods to drive out the enemy, or get their range," when he talked of her in the shed-room with bolted doors and was in a cheerful mood. She soon saw by his face that she had got *his* range, and, being in one of her most energetic and aggressive moods, she continued for about an hour to move about the room attending to various domestic matters and making offensive remarks. Pap ought to have been, and was, tolerably well used to that sort of thing; but physical fatigue and inward sadness were alike clamoring for peace and rest, and his heart sickened within him as he listened to that harsh voice, and contrasted it mentally with one as soft as a wood-pigeon's. "This here is what my home has come to," he thought, bitterly. "The only house on earth that I love, or that I've got to shelter me. I've got to live here and to die here. And *her* gone. And *her* in her place."

Stung into action of some sort, he got up and sat in the window-seat, looking out into the darkness within and without, and then he slipped as unobtrusively as possible into his own chair and lit his pipe, resolving to be patient and endure what was not to be cured. His silence made Matilda angrier than ever, and she expressed this most characteristically. The room was in admirable order, but, seizing a broom, she began sweeping violently in his immediate neighborhood, making wild dashes all around his chair and under it, and spiteful assaults upon his feet and legs, as if about to send him bodily into the cavernous and flaming depths of the old-fashioned chimney. Without a word he moved back a little, a flush on his face. Stooping down, she seized his felt hat, which he had dropped on the floor, and putting it on his head gave it a slap that jammed it down over his eyes, saying, "Why don't you hang it up? Who's goin' to give you another when that's gone, I'd like to know?" Seeing him thus, and thinking it a funny sight, Willy was imprudent enough to laugh, and instantly got a rousing box on the ears that made him roar instead. "Tildy! Tildy! Stop!" shouted Pap, struggling to his feet. "Let him be! Quit that!" He had often been obliged to see Willy punished and hold his peace, but somehow he quite lost his self-control now. Infuriated by his interference, Matilda caught hold of the child with one hand and of the poker with the other. With one plunge forward of himself and his crutch, Pap rushed to the rescue.

A struggle between them seemed inevitable, but fortunately Alfred walked in upon them that very moment. The gravity of the situation had a curious effect upon him. His manner was bold and his tone positively burly as he seized his wife and put himself between them. "Why, what's all this? What's this?" he demanded. "Tildy! Pa-ap!" He was just in time. Matilda attempted a frenzied explanation. Pap sank back in his chair. "Go along—go right along to the shed," suggested Alfred, in a low voice to his father. "Take Willy." Whimpering and scared, Willy was led away, and when the door of their room was closed and they were secured from all intrusion Pap threw himself upon the bed with his face downwards and lay there for an hour without moving or saying a word. He then got up, and calling Willy to him, undressed him and put him to bed. He was always woman-tender and patient with the child, and having performed these little offices for him quickly and quietly, he caressed and soothed and reassured him. "Go right to sleep, Willy boy, that's what you've got to do," he said. "And love your Pa-ap,—love him always." But Willy could not get to sleep immediately after such an exciting evening, and Pap had to sit by him and hold his hand until he did. Meanwhile they had a little talk.

"Don't you go 'way, now, Pa-ap. Will you? Say?" said the child, afraid of Matilda, but not saying so. "Promise me you'll stay right here."

"No, honey. Pa-ap 'll set here by you and take care of you. Don't you be fearsome. Matilda won't come here. She got her collar off this evenin' and sorter turned herself loose, that's all. She's been rough-like fur a week 'n more. She shan't hurt you, young one. Go to sleep now."

"Stone Newman he says she's a screamer. What's a screamer?"

"Well, a screamer's a bad-tempered person that holds spite. And that's true. I've knowed heaps and cords uv women,—all sorts, pretty much, first and last,—but there wuz never nary one that could hold spite like her. Why, I've knowed her to git wrong side out 'n go right along with it cornstant fur two weeks runnin'. And livin' in the house with that kind uv woman is bad, Willy. 'Tain't the peckin'. You gits used to that, though it's mightily like havin' a hail-storm all the year 'round. Nor it ain't the temper, which you ain't afeared 'ill hurt you, in a manner of speakin', for ef it come to blows a body could soon settle her. But" (earnestly) "don't *you* never, when you're a man, tech a woman fur to hurt her; not so much as her little finger. D'ye hear? Hit's a low-lived, mean skunk that'll strike a woman, and do you remember it. Speak 'em fair, and treat 'em kind, and ef you kain't git along with 'em that er way, you kain't no way at all. Women's like fowls, Willy. They kain't be driv. Ef you tries it they flies up in your face and makes fur your eyes, or goes jes' the way you don't want 'em to. No, as I was a-sayin' 'bout Tildy, it aint the peckin', nor the scoldin', nor the temper. Hit's the *bindingness* uv it. Go which-ever way you will,—it don't make no difference,—you knock agin a stone wall. En it shets you into yourself wuss 'n a coffin, it does."

" Alice warn't like her, wuz she ?" said Willy, to whom the gentle spirit was a " familiar."

" *No, indeed,* and double deed. She warn't a com-menter,—my Ally warn't,—nor a gadder, nor a screamer, nor a scolder, nor a meddler, nor a gammoner. She warn' conversive, though her accostment was better 'n most. She was jes' the sweetest and best woman that ever stepped ; and when a body come in downheartened and plum beat out, she was the comfortinest one the Lord ever made. She was the only one that ever rightly knowed me, Willy."

" You know the cellar, Pa-ap. Under Tildy's room's down there, ain't it ? She'd better look out ! Stone Newman he sez the bad man jes' comes right up through the ground and ketches bad folks by the legs and jerks 'em right down quick to——" Here a knock at the door was heard, and Willy convulsively seized Pap's hand. " Don't go ! Don't let her in !" he cried.

" Oh, 'tain't her. She'd never knock like that," said Pap. And, rising, he went to the door, and found Alfred standing there with a tin plate in his hand, on which were such odds and ends of food as he had been able to collect hastily while Matilda was out of the room.

" Have a bite uv vittles, Pa-ap," he urged, deprecat-ingly. " You ain't had no supper. I'm mighty sorry things has been so onpleasant; but don't you mind

Tildy. Women will be women,—specially Tildy." With this paraphrase of his favorite maxim he thrust the plate into his father's hands, all his honest face full of concern.

"Thanky kindly, my son. I don't want nothin' myself. I couldn't eat nothin'; but I'll give it to the child. Thanky," Pap replied, and the door was shut and bolted again.

"Pa-ap," said Willy, when he had finished the supper thus unexpectedly provided, and had laid himself down in bed again, and been very quiet for full five minutes, —"Pa-ap, had the Good Man and the Bad Man *quar'led* when Alfred married Tildy?" It was a great proof of the perfect confidence that existed between them that all the child's most timid, mouselike fancies and thoughts came out and played fearlessly about this hearth in the warm love-light that Pap diffused about him. But when the old man burst out into a loud laugh over this speech of "Willy boy's" he felt hurt, and shrank blushing into himself, and soon the conversation was rounded with a full stop, for Willy was asleep.

Matilda's capacity for "holding spite" was fully shown for some time after this. Cinderella's sisters were gentle and amiable women compared to her, and weakly indulgent; and Pap got more and more depressed as day after day went by without any softening or brightening in that quarter. She brought a couple of empty meal-bags in on the following Saturday, and, throwing them down near Pap with such force that he was immediately almost covered with the dust, said, acridly, "Now you two be off this minnit to the mill and git both of them filled. Yer ain't goin' to laze around here a passel of triflin' no-'counts, not worth shucks, while I'm workin' my fingers to the bone."

"We'll go, Matildy. We'll go, in course," said Pap, rising as he spoke, and speaking in a tone of mild remonstrance. "But you ain't got no call to git so riffled up. Go slow! Go slow!"

"Oh, I see where goin' slow's brung *you* to!" she retorted. "I've seed enough of it. And you'd be further of I had my way, I can tell you, and——"

Pap had heard enough, and he now slouched out-of-doors. He stood still for a minute, and then walked briskly around the corner of the house. When he got to the irregular, old-fashioned chimney, whose every line and curve he knew by heart, he stopped, and thrusting his long arm up he brought down from its hiding-place a stone jug adorned with a corn-cob stopper. This he set down on the ground, and taking the little tin-cup which was tied to the handle he half filled it, and, throwing back his head, tossed off the contents almost at a gulp. He was wiping his mouth by passing his sleeve across it from right to left and back again, and debating whether he should repeat the operation or not, when he heard a voice near him say, "Is it good, Pa-ap?" and turning suddenly in wrath, saw Willy standing behind him,—Willy, rosy, smiling, sweet-faced as usual, his hands stuffed deep in his pockets, his eyes fixed eagerly on the strange new jug that he had been so surprised to see, juggled, as it were, out of the chimney. "What's in it? Whur do you keep it at?" he asked.

Annoyed by the interruption and the discovery of his secret, Pap spoke roughly to the child. "What are you doin' here? Who called you? Go 'long in the house and mind your own business! Whichever way I turn, there you is, right at my heels." Utterly astonished, Willy fled before him, but was instantly recalled. "Come back, sonny. You kin stay. And, look here, don't you say nothin' 'bout this to nobody,—not to *nobody*. Do you hear?"

His tone was still stern, and Willy was nonplussed, and did not know what to do. Pap to speak to him like that! He couldn't get over it.

"I wasn't doin' nothin'," he finally said. "I jes' asked you——"

"Yes, yes. I know 'bout that," said Pap, replacing the jug. This done, he had leisure to observe that Willy still looked disturbed,—did not understand what his offence had been, evidently,—and was uncertain about the foundations of his world all at once, the roof having just tumbled in on his head when he least expected it. Pap stood still for some moments, looking down and taking out and putting in again the while a couple of long thorns with which he was in the habit of fastening his "galluses" to his trousers. He then patted the child's head, which he drew up against him, saying, in his usual affectionate and pleasant tone, " Well, never mind, honey; never mind. Yer sorter plagued and pestered me a little. That was all. I ain't mad. I didn't never mean to hurt your feelin's. Don't think no more 'bout it. Come along, now, and we'll go fur that meal, we will."

"Wuz it good?" asked Willy again, harking back with childish persistence to the unanswered question, now that he felt that Pap was Pap again and had repented of his harshness.

" Well, no. It ain't to say *good* eggzackly," confessed
Pap, reluctantly compelled to discuss the question. ' "It
ain't what you'd call good. But hit's as searchin' as
a fine-tooth comb, Willy boy. But" (caressing him,
and speaking very emphatically, forgetting also that
the child did not know what he was talking of) " don't
you never tech it, *never*, NEVER, NEVER! You asked
me jes' now ef it was good, didn't you, honey? Good?
Why, it's the wuss stuff ever you could put in your
mouth! Don't you never put none in your dear little
mouth, honey. No. It's black. And it's bad. And it's
bitter as gall. And it's sour. And it ain't well-tasted,—
not a bit. And it smells *awful*,—jes' awful,—Willy boy.
It 'most knocks you down. And it would be the ruination of you, it would. Good? Why, it makes me laugh
jes' to hear you ask that."

" And it's searchin'. Ain't it, Pa-ap? You said jes'
now it was searchin'."

" Oh, yes ; it's that. It—it goes through you—well,
like a knife !"

Pap was leaning with his back against the chimney
and was looking down at Willy, who now looked up at
him with his sweet clear eyes. " Well, what do *you*
take it fur, then?" he asked.

Pap turned his head away. He could not look at the
child.

" I'm 'bleeged to sometimes," he said, in a low voice,
presently, and the color rose with a sudden vivid flush
into his wrinkled cheeks. " Come along, now. We
ain't got a minnit, not a minnit, ef Matildy's to have
that meal, and she'll know why ef she *don't* git it, you
kin bet. Come right along," he added, after another

pause, and hand-in-hand they returned to the front of the house, where the dirty-white meal-bags had been dropped on the steps, which were further ornamented by a row of children all waiting like so many youthful Micawbers for something to turn up. There was some one else there, too,—R. Mintah,—waiting to see Pap, and they went apart from the children as soon as they had exchanged greetings.

"Well, R. Mintah, my dear, you look bore down. What've you got on you this mornin'?" he asked her, when they had turned the corner of the house.

"Hit's Jonah. Hit's all Jonah. And I'm so mis'able, —so mis'able!" said she, with a sudden burst of sobs.

"Why, what's the matter with Jonah?"

"He's took an idee,—the foolishest idee ever was,— and he's mis'able, too; we both are 's sorrowful as kin be, and no need to be. Oh! what's folks born fur anyways? I wish I didn't feel nothin'. I wish I didn't kyur fur nobody. And after all that's been between us! Oh, Jonah, what does make you so blind and deef? Oh, me! Oh! me! Hit's too much. And all an idee," lamented R. Mintah. "Jes' all an idee."

She could not go on, and Pap said, reflectively, "Idees is bad to handle, R. Mintah. You kain't ketch hold of 'em. You kain't git at 'em well, nor git no purchase on 'em to move 'em. Sometimes with luck you kin git one by the tail and jerk it out, but you mostly makes bad worse. They're mighty bad things, idees, and breeds more trouble than death 'll cure. But what's Jonah thinkin'?"

"He's thinkin' that I—that him and me—that Marsh Culbert—oh, hit's too much! He's got a persuasion on him. He thinks that me and Marsh—oh, he's crazy!" She stopped again to sob, and Pap, who never could bear to see a woman cry, stood by and administered such consolation as "Don't yer, now. Don't yer! Hold yerself up. Don't you cry."

"I didn't never think," said she, "when the time come fur him to come out of the horspital, and I went down to Winston and fetched him back, with him laid out in the bottom of the cart with his head in my lap, and him so good and kind, and tellin' me how glad he was to see me, and me tellin' him how I'd done my outmost to git to him,—I never thought nothin' could trouble me no more in this world, seein' Jonah was 'live and well, and I was 'live and well, and we'd both lived to see soch a home-bringin' of my dear darlin'. And now it 'pears like it's too much trouble to breathe, and there ain't no use in nothin'. Oh! why did he go and do like he's done here lately?"

"What's his notion?" asked Pap, again trying to get at the root of the matter. "Is it a changement of his feelin's? Say, honey? Men 'speriences a changement of feelin's sometimes, you know, and——"

"Oh, don't you go and say it's *that!*" she exclaimed, starting back as if he had struck her. "Don't you, now. You don't reckon, sho' 'nough, hit's *that?*"

"Well, no. I ain't said so, R. Mintah. Don't you go picking up my words before I fairly gets 'em out. I sez men does 'sperience a changement of feelin's,—leastways, some men does,—so folks *says.* But not many, honey. Mighty few. Hardly any. I ain't never knowed—Hum! Well, *I* warn't the sort that changes. Maybe 'twould ef been better fur me ef I had of been.

And I don't believe Jonah ain't, neither," replied Pap, saying exactly the thing he did not mean. "But tell me 'bout it."

"He's got a persuasion, Pa-ap, that Marsh Culbert and me is—I'll *never* say the word. You see, Mother Newman she kep' on writin' him while he was in the horspital 'bout Marsh hangin' 'round and stickin' like a cockleburr, and he got the notion that Marsh was goin' to set me. And he warn't, no sech thing. 'Twas Mandy he was settin' all the time. And then Jonah come home. And Mandy got out and off with him, and took to carryin' on with Bill Mathers 'cause he was a preacher's son, and more genteel, she 'lowed. And Marsh hadn't never went to be genteel, and loved her jes' the same, and more, and come 'round cornstant, hopin', I reckon, she'd change back agin. And Jonah set around, and watched, and suspicioned, and now he says I love Marsh, not him, and has give me his advisement to marry him, and not *him*, and he says—he says I've made too free with him. *Me!* ME!! Jonah said *that!* Them was his words." The thought of these terrible words, and who had spoken them, brought the loudest wail of all from the unhappy girl, and a small river of tears had flowed down her round cheeks and been wiped away with her apron before her tumultuous emotions were sufficiently under control for her to say more. "He won't see nothin' like it is. He won't hear nothin' like it's said. He don' believe nothin' I tell him. Oh, I'm so mis'able! I don' know what's got into him that was so defferent."

"Hum!" began Pap, judicially. "R. Mintah, this here's one of the ideas that can be ketched and pulled

out. I kin ketch it, I reckon. But you must pull it
out,—you are the only one that kin. Jonah's done gone
and got jealous. That's how it is. He's got his eyes
crossed· in love, and he kaint see straight, no matter
which er way he looks. He's jealous. And he's got
obstinated, and bent, and set, and determinated, and
ornless his eyes gits put right he kain't do no defferent,
and he won't. He's a—Hum! Well, now, I tell you
what, you go 'long home, child, and leave him to me,
and don't you werrit no more 'bout it at all. It 'll all
come right. Them that changes once can change
twict, and maybe that 'll be the way of it; anyways, it
'll all come right. Go 'long back of the lane. Your
eyes is all swol' up not fit to be seed, my dear, and you
won't meet nobody, skasely, ef you go back a piece
and then turn to your right. Goo'-by."

A good deal consoled, R. Mintah put on her sun-
bonnet and turned away. Pap got a glimpse of her
tearful face down the long rosy tunnel that the eye had
to traverse before it was reached, hidden away under an
immense calico crown, as uneasy a head as ever wore a
royal one. He was moving off, also, when she came
back. " I hope you ain't thinkin' hard of Jonah," she
said. " He ain't never went to act wrong by me. Hit's
jes' a possessment. That's what it is. Hit's mighty
distressful, and has made me onhappy and mis'able in
my mind. But I didn't go to say nothin' agin Jonah.
Not a word. No, indeed. I know he's onhappy, too,
jes' like I was that day he kissed poor Belle, that's
dead and gone whur there ain't no trouble. I don't
blame him. No. Hit's a possessment. But what does
that freckle-faced fool boy keep on comin' 'round fur?

I hate the sight of him. I wish he was dead. No, I
don't, neither. But Marsh Culbert, Pa-ap,—one of them
mean, stinty Culberts! They're all no 'count; but they
ain't had no chance; and they don't git no better off
for all their pinchin', and them close as onion-skins.
Hit's might curious. And none of 'em a-patchin' to him.
Him! Jonah's crazy! Plum' crazy! I've studied over
it when I've been by myself, and I ain't done nothin'
never that I'd feel bad to think about, or nothin' to set
Jonah agin me, and I don't know how it is this thing
has growed like a gode. Oh, Pa-ap, talk to him! *Make*
him see! To think he'd think I'd care as much as my
old shoe fur Marsh Culbert of all, and make free with
any man. Oh, hit jes' kills me! My head burns like
fire."

"Poor child! poor child! I never heerd the like.
Don't you, now. *You!* Jonah's a born—Hum! He's
done jumped clean out of hisself this time."

"Don't you think hard of my dear Jonah, Pa-ap!
Hit's jes' a possessment, is what I sez to myself all the
time, and I ain't told nobody. But hit's the possesstest
possessment that ever was. Look at the defference
'tween him,—'tween Bill Mathers and my Jonah! But
long as he's s'picioned me I've jes' got to bear it. And
don't you think hard of him. I'll never, fur what he's
done been to me ever sence I was knee-high to a duck,
as the sayin' goes,—so good, bringin' in my wood, and
—oh, boo-hoo! hoo! hoo! hoo!"

"Jonah's a fool, a nateral-born fool!" exclaimed
Pap, unable longer to restrain his real sentiments.
Such a look of dignified, unutterable displeasure spread
over R. Mintah's face, such horror came into it when

she heard that offensive combination of letters four applied to her peerless, if misguided, Jonah, that Pap immediately added, hurriedly, "Askin' your pardon, R. Mintah, and meanin' he's foolish 'long of bein' in love."

"Hit's my fault. I ain't oughter to said what I've said 'bout my darlin' Jonah," she replied, remorsefully.

"No offence, my dear; no offence," said he. But even so, confidence was not immediately restored between them. When Pap, however, had fully recognized his mistake, and praised Jonah as warmly as he had cried out upon him, matters improved. "Leave it be," said he, finally. "I'll fix it up all right and tight fur you, I reckon. Hit's chancey, but we'll resk it."

Again they parted, and again R. Mintah ran back to him. "I can't be easy tell you *promise* me you won't think hard of Jonah," she said, with a sweet, appealing look at him. "Hit's on my mind that I've spoke agin him and set you agin him, and it's not his deservings, and it's a shame to me that knows what he is, and was chose to be his wife onst. I'd better have bit my tongue off."

"I don't, and I won't, I vows and declares and swears," said Pap, with all the seriousness the occasion demanded, and R. Mintah, content with this, gave him a bright glance and hurried home.

When left alone, Pap stood still a moment. He thrust his hands deep in his pockets after buttoning up his coat. He walked a few steps slowly, paused, retraced his steps, paused again, then suddenly looked sharply around and about him, and dashed off to the spot where his evil treasure was concealed, and, with the greatest haste, poured out and drank off another cupful from the stone jug, replaced it, and sauntered back to the front porch. ˙Matilda, who waged war against the whole tribe of little Mountainites, was just driving the children away when he got there, and they were looking and lingering in the hope that he would appear.

"Come 'long to the mill with me, children. Fall in," said he, picking up the meal-bags. And nothing loath about a dozen representatives of the Brown, Logan, and Simmons families fell in behind him, and they were soon trooping down the lane together,—the girls lank, petticoatless, carefully bonneted, obliged to run in order to keep up with the party; the boys with their trousers rolled high above their naked knees (in order to be ready for such agreeable incidents as brooks and liquid mud), and all of them talking, questioning, laughing, without the least constraint, and only a chastened, repressed consciousness that there were Matildas or parents in the world and a hereafter. They all looked at and appealed to "Pa-ap" (as they called John Shore with a long drawl as like the bleat of a sheep as it was possible for human lungs to emit) every other moment. All the children for miles around knew him. They were all fond of him. They all owed him far more than they ever knew, much less paid. But it was curious how the smallest and least shrewd youngster among them knew before he was six years old that this paragon of a friend, benefactor, protector, champion,— who was all things to all children,—was for some mysterious reason not held in the high consideration that ought to have been reserved for a being so gifted, fascinating, lovable. Why should Matilda, who was hateful and hated them, be spoken of with respect? and Mr.

Carver, who preserved towards them an attitude of
armed neutrality, and was so cross, so dull, so ugly,
almost with reverence, while "Pa-ap," the delightful,
accomplished friend, who could do anything that he
was asked to do, and knew everything one could want
to know, and never failed to give help, comfort, pleasure, to all who approached him, was invariably talked
of in a way that showed deep, dark disapproval? It
was most enigmatical and disagreeable to know that
such an estimate was set upon a creature of such special
and valuable endowments, and to be actually reproached
with being "in cahoot" with him, their kindest, best
friend. They could not, and would not, give him up,
though, and so it came about that everybody agreed that
"Johnny Shore was jes' the ruination of them children,"—a few women excepted,—notably Mrs. Logan,
who had one of those families in which there were
always three children who were too young to wipe
their own noses or shut the door or get out of the way,
and who, noticing his tender treatment of these helpless twigs among her olive-branches, always contended
that he was not "near as black as he was painted by
other pots and kittles, and a good friend to the children,
she would say." A good friend he was to them, and
they found no fault in him, perhaps because he found
so little with them. A good guide, too, for could
he not go to the birds'-nests, and persimmons, and nuts
in the woods as straight as a crow could fly? And he
was their philosopher,—a philosopher whose wit and
wisdom left many a mark as it played around them and
over their heads, say while digging bait preparatory to
setting a row of sun-bonnets and baggy-backed, bullet-

headed youngsters to fish with the willow-rod and pin-hook substitutes for tackle, which he was always being importuned to make for "Bill's brother," or "Nancy's cousin," or "Betty's sister," and that pleased them so much, nor deceived the smallest, most unworldly blue-bottle fly or trout when presented to their notice. And he was their historian, finally, his method being unconsciously that of Herodotus as he related to an open-mouthed, eager-eyed audience: "The general's orderly come to me and shook me as I was layin' asleep in a fence-corner, and he sez to me, sez he, 'John, git up, for we've got to skedaddle like lightnin'. The Yanks is piled up as high as the Ridge over yonder, and they'll be down on us like a flail in another minute,'" etc., etc.

VII.

"Every one is as God made him, and oftentimes a great deal worse."—CERVANTES.

PAP saw a good deal of the children in the course of the next two weeks, for Matilda's spite like the weather held, and to escape the sound of her voice he would have done almost anything. The only thing that he could do was to go off on expeditions that consumed the greater part of the day, and so get out of her way. This he did as often as he dared, and start when he would, before he could settle his torn old sugar-loaf felt on his head and seize his crutch, his purpose had

not only gone abroad, but his followers (the "Trundle-
bed Tigers," as he facetiously called them when he
drilled them) had mysteriously sprung up about the
door and waited there to join him. Sometimes he
would go over to Mrs. Logan's, put the trio on his long
lap, declare "There's too many people in this world,
shore. I'll have to drown some of you, certain," en-
circle as many more, perhaps, with his long arms, and
blow soap-bubbles or play cat's-cradle for an hour, and
occasionally accept her invitation to "stop and take
a bite," with secret thankfulness at escaping "a meal
of vittles" at home with its inevitable accompaniment
of "Tildy's talk." And at night he would bolt himself into the shed-room with Willy and try to interest
himself and Burygyard the querulous in the higher
education which that very conservative southern bird
despised, and received only under protest,—a scornful
sparkle in his eye, his manner irrelevantly, flippantly
vivacious, his interpolations and interruptions grossly
rude, and his tail cocked contemptuously in a dozen
different ways. Pap could not but be amused by his
pupil's conduct, especially by his way of suddenly con-
verting himself into a ball, rolling into the furthest
corner of his cage (as an intimation that he had retired
from public life), closing his eyes, and affecting to be
deaf, when bored by hearing his lesson repeated *ad nau-
seam* on the violin. And then, not caring to play, he
would put away the instrument, and, having the evening before him, would put Willy through the manual of
arms. This was always done in the same fashion.
"Fall in Company C," Pap would say, and Willy would
eagerly seize the footless andirons and place them in the

middle of the room, side by side. "Now git Jim Wilkins." (Willy had heard all about Pap's comrade, and
they had gradually got into a habit of calling the leg
bought with his last gift by his name.) "He never
would turn out without the long roll was beat, skasely,
at night." Willy would add Jim Wilkins and himself
to the row. It was Pap's habit to lay aside his wooden
leg in the evening, and prop his own stump up on a
chair in front of him, and from this position he would
give the most extensive orders for the execution of
various military manœuvres. "Dress your line," would
be the next command, and Willy would try to get himself and his comrades as nearly as possible on a line,—
a task not without difficulties, as he complained to Pap,
seeing that, unlike the Household regiments, the men
of Company C were not strikingly alike in size and
build. "Shur! that don't matter, Willy boy. There's
fat and lean, and big and puny, and all sorts in the
army. You kain't pick and choose. And yours is all
cornscripts, 'ceptin' Jim. He warn't never the sort to
wait to be cornscripted into a fight. No, indeed! They
don't hardly know the right hand from the left foot."

"They ain't got no feet. They ain't got no hands,
neither," objected Willy.

"Well, that ain't no matter, neither," said Pap. "Ef
they'd of had 'em, they'd of been shot off, don't yer see,
so what's the use? Go on, why don't yer? Harm
harm! Hound harm! Present harm! Groun' harm!
Corporal Brass has done got turned 'round the wrong
way, honey. He ain't facin' the enemy. Hain harm!
Right about! Tech Jim Wilkins up a little. Right
face! Forward! March!"

When it came to marching, of course Willy distanced
all the other members of "Company C, First Virginia
Foot," and being complimented by Pap upon his sol-
dierly bearing, was as much gratified as though his com-
petitors had not been a little handicapped in this race
for distinction. Over and over again would this per-
formance be repeated, with such variations in Pap's
inarticulate but resonant commands as suggested themselves to the old soldier. Sometimes Corporal Brass
would be thrown out on the skirmish-line and pick off
staff officers and even generals ("Bang!" "Bang!") by
the score. Sometimes Sergeant Iron would be entrenched
in a rifle-pit (disguised as an empty water-bucket), and
dodged shells, whenever he put his head out, in the
most skilful way. Sometimes Jim Wilkins, with "eyes
right," and "little fingers to the seam of the pants, and
palms of the hands turned outward," would drill for
half an hour at a time with a wisp of straw wrapped
about his foot, as one of the awkward squad, while Willy,
in raptures, would shriek out his delight, and when the
mistakes were very glaring and ridiculous, would turn
a somersault or two, as he was rather fond of doing.
And generally drill closed with Willy's galloping madly
around the room in a double-quick several times and
bounding finally into Pap's lap, where, you may be
sure, he was embraced and made welcome as the only
survivor of Company C, all the other members of that
unfortunate organization being invariably knocked
down—I mean shot dead—by one awful blast from
Willy's imaginary cannon at the foot of the old stove
(a deadly tomato-can, more fatal far than if it had been
full of nitro-glycerine), or perhaps cut down in the

prime of life by one sweep from his wooden sword. They lent themselves to this act more readily than any other, and were much more satisfactory in it, Willy thought, thanks to certain constitutional peculiarities and fatalities. They scored in it every evening their only success, and Willy, who was Federal or Confederate, as the exigencies of the moment might demand, was never tired of falling upon them and battering them with all his might.

"What! puttin' a wounded man to the sword?" said Pap one evening, tired of the din. "Shame on you! Look at old Blue Light yonder. He's *pintin'* straight at yer fur a coward."

Willy stopped, looked, was impressed, and after this the quality of Willy's mercy was very much strained, for he grew so intensely sentimental in his feelings about wounded soldiers that for a week he was a perfect nuisance with his lint and bandages and potions for "po' Corporal Brass" or "po' old Sergeant Iron," and was all pity and generosity, prattling very prettily of the new sentiments that had been temporarily aroused in his youthful bosom. Only temporarily, for this Nightingale view of war, as a great opportunity for the exercise of Christian charity, soon palled upon him. He said he was "tired of nussin'," and added that "it warn't no fun," and fell upon the corporal and the sergeant with more fury than ever when the reaction from all this fine feeling suddenly set in. Corporal Brass, so called because of a dented metal knob that still remained to him from that distant period in which he had known better days, lost his head in this onslaught, and was now scarcely to be distinguished from his fellow-soldier, the sergeant; but like true veterans both of them might be slain but could not be conquered, and fought their battles o'er and o'er every evening regularly.

Pap would look on, all smiling placidity, while they were being demolished, but when Willy would have assaulted "Jim Wilkins" in the same way he would interfere. "You let him alone," he would say. "I ain't goin' to have you kickin' Jim 'round the place, nor nobody else. He's defferent. I won't suffer it;" then with an appeal to Willy's ever lively imagination, "You'd better keep out of his way, or he'll git you down and stawmp you." Sometimes—generally, indeed—Willy was the *deus ex machinâ* of these engagements; sometimes Pap got down on the floor as commander-in-chief of all the forces, and conducted a particularly brilliant campaign with his crutch, forgetting, for the moment, his own sad fortunes in the fortunes of the mimic war he had in charge, and surprising himself into many a laugh. But the next moment, perhaps, he would sigh and get up and hobble back to his chair, telling Willy to "put away them things and ondress." And he was sad enough, Heaven knows,—bitterly miserable,—during the long, wakeful nights that followed, and got up in the morning gloomy and dejected every day for a week,—an unusual mood with him and one that Willy could not understand. Finally, one day he disappeared, and Willy wondered still more, and went about asking impatiently, " Whur's Pa-ap? Whur's Pa-ap at?" No one knew; and at dinner Matilda said sharply to her husband, "Your Pa-ap's gone to town, ain't he?" and Alfred said, " Y-e-s.

I sent him," which was a pure fiction, as no one knew better than his wife.

"More fool you, ef you done it, which I ain't took in," she said. "No indeed."

"Pertaters ain't nowhur this year. It's mighty curous 'bout pertaters. Ef the eyes ain't cut jes' *egg-zackly* like they ought to be——" began Alfred.

"Oh, shet up, simpleton!" exclaimed Matilda. "It ain't only pertaters that's got eyes, I kin tell you. What did you send him fur? Tell me that. Hainh?"

"'Hurts and meddlers goes hand-in-hand,'" quoted Alfred, with a timid roll of his eyes, and a thrust of his knife down his throat that gave him the air of attempting his life. This silenced Matilda for the moment; but all that afternoon at short intervals Willy was asking, "Whur's Pa-ap at? Whur's he done gone to?" and, getting evasive or contemptuous replies, was more sensible than ever that something was wrong. He went off, at last, to have a play with the Newman boys, and when he came in Pap's crutch was the first thing he saw, set against the wall. He was about to burst into the shed-room and relieve his heart and mind of the day's experience and of a great plan for the morrow, when he met Alfred coming out of it with an unusual look of resolve and reserve on his face. "Come 'long 'way from there, Willy," he said, and took the child by the shoulders.

"Why? What fur? Ain't Pa-ap in there?" said Willy, pulling away from him impatiently. "Lemmy in!"

"You kain't go in there to-night, child," said Alfred, and his firm tone struck Willy at once and carried a conviction that the mysterious something was in the air again and that he must yield. "You'll sleep in our room to-night, I reckon. Pa-ap he's got a—a sorter of indisposement. He's got to be quiet. Come 'way."

Matilda at supper was silent, and sat up very straight, indeed, with a red face, and her lips pinched in and focused to a remarkably fine point, while Alfred followed her every glance and movement, and Willy tried to make out what "it" was. At bedtime it was Alfred who fumblingly attended to his buttons and strings, seeing which Matilda announced, "That brat ain't to stay here." And Alfred, after making an excursion into the shed-room, came out and said, "I reckon he'll do in there," and cautioning the child to be "mighty still and not talk nor move" took him in and put him into the cotbed, where Pap was already lying. The day had been a tiring one, and after a little more wondering and a good deal of staring at the, for some reason, strange figure beside him he fell asleep and knew nothing more until he heard Matilda's shrill call, "You Pa-ap! You Willy! Darthuly Mely! Git up! Day's a-breakin'." He scrambled up and looked about him. Pap was no longer beside him. He dressed himself as best he could. And then came breakfast, with Alfred looking troubled, and Matilda warlike in the extreme and very emphatic in her way of handling dishes and kettles and pails, and Darthulia Amelia Bradd (a pale young person had in to help with the quilts to be put in), half timid, half simpering, as if she would like to be amused if she dared.

To Willy's "Whur's Pa-ap, anyways?" of desperate inquiry all three looked unutterable response, but

Alfred only said, "He'll not be home jes' yet. You can go 'long and play with Stone and Pete to-day."

"But whur's——" he began again.

"Ssh!" said Alfred, significantly, and kicked his bare foot under the table, bidding him hold his tongue. All that day passed, and he was "'lowed" to stay all night with the boys, his friends, which was a thing he had vainly begged for many a time, yet which now that it had come made him seriously uneasy somehow. The next day it was the same thing. Still no Pap, more mystery, and an atmosphere of repressed sulphur and brimstone about the cottage. Willy could not understand it, and wondered most of all that night, when he could actually hear Pap's voice as he talked and laughed uproariously in the shed-room, yet was still forbidden to go to him. It was very late that night before he was allowed to go in, and then Alfred put him to bed with the same counsels and cautions, and Pap was lying there like a log, still dressed and with his boots on. There was no light except the faint one from the window. He could hear Bunny whisking briskly about his cage in the dark. Burygyard gave out a few low, melancholy notes. The child got nervous and excited. He sat up in bed. He called "Pa-ap! Pa-ap! Oh, Pa-ap!" at first in a whisper, and then louder as his distress increased. Getting no answer, he beat roughly with his little fists on Pap's breast, who still lay there in that unnatural, awful quiet and silence that said so much. At last he could bear it no longer, and springing out of bed he ran into Alfred's room and arms. "What's the matter with Pa-ap?" he demanded. "Is it a breast-trouble? Is he goin' to die, and be put in a

K   19

hole in the ground, whur he can't never come back no
mo'?" Matilda was out of the room, and Alfred was
very kind. "It's jes' a indisposement," he said. "Don't
you werrit 'bout it, child. He'll be hisself agin, all
right to-morrow. Here! come along!" and taking his
hand he opened a door and said, meaningly, "Darthuly
Meely, this here child's afeerd. Let him stay in here
with you, won't yer, to-night?" It was so arranged,
and the pale young person was very kind, too; but
Willy's innocent thoughts were still of the "breast-
trouble,"—the serpent coiled in the breast against which
he had leaned his little head so confidently and happily,
hitherto, with no sort of misgiving.

He saw Pap—the Pap that he knew and loved—next
morning, but he was not himself as Alfred had promised he would be. There was no laughter to be heard
from him. He was gloomier than Willy had ever seen
him. He was wretched in body and mind, and humil-
itated into the dust. What Willy saw was that he
looked white and sick, and he felt surprised that he
should be so irritable. When he would have embraced
him in the fulness of his relief and content at finding
what he had lost and missed, Pap repulsed him, and
would have none of his caresses, saying, "Go 'way,
child. Go 'way from me. I ain't fitten' for you to
kiss, nor keer for, nor nobody else." When breakfast-
time came, he wouldn't stir. Willy was called to the
meal by Matilda, and when Alfred would have gone for
his father she said, "I'll not equalize myself with no
sech. Let him *starve*. He's not a-goin' to set down
with *me*," and it was Alfred who, after breakfast, sent
Willy in with some bread and coffee. He might have

spared himself the trouble, for it was not touched. Pap lay on his bed all day and ate nothing, and said as little as possible, and puzzled Willy more than ever. He got up when evening came, and Willy, when he came in, found him taking down his pictures of Lee and Jackson, and the chromo-advertisement, and putting them away out of sight on a shelf in the corner.

"What you doin', Pa-ap?" he asked.

"You see what I'm doin'. I'm a-takin' these here down."

. "Whyfor, Pa-ap? Hainh?" said Willy.

"I ain't fitten to have no sech 'round. I don't want 'em here," he said, and went on with the work of removal. "I've done hung that Burygyard outside, too. I ain't goin' to have him starin' like he'd never see a person befo'."

"Yer don't feel good, does yer, Pa-ap? Yer feels bad 'bout somethin', don't yer?" said Willy.

"Well, ef I does, it's what I oughter. I kain't feel as bad as I am; that's certain," he replied, with forlorn emphasis.

"Yer *ain't* bad, no sech thing! You're *good.* The best sort, that's what. Po' Pa-ap, I'm mighty sorry you've been sick," said Willy, and left the chair on which he had been hitching about, with his hands in his pockets, for some moments, and would have put an arm caressingly around his old friend's neck, but he got up suddenly, crying out, "Oh, honey, *don't!* Don't!" and throwing himself back on the bed gave smothered vent to several sobs, while Willy looked on aghast.

If Matilda had been hard and bitter and scornful before, she was now as terrible to Pap as the "light-

ning-looker Lamachos," and as " gorgon-crested" as ever
Medusa was, although her hair was red and short and
generally done up in curl-papers twisted up viciously at
the ends and further secured with large brass pins.
She railed, she scolded, she sneered, insinuated, snubbed,
until one would have supposed that the veriest worm
of humanity could not but turn upon her. But Pap
sat through meal after meal, singularly submissive and
silent, never resenting anything that she might say,
and never attempting to defend himself, no matter of
what he was accused. She " wouldn't have trouble took
for no sech," she said ; so he was admitted to the table
again, after the first day, and was obliged to avail himself of the doubtful privilege. Alfred's round face got
a chronic pallor during these weeks, except when his
nervousness found a fresh and singular vent. When the
domestic barometer stood at "stormy," he would suddenly
inflate his cheeks, apparently to the point of bursting,
and smite upon them with his clinched fists, and would
then puff and snort and chuckle in an elaborate effort
to be gay and playful and perfectly at his ease that
was really pathetic. He reefed every yard of conversational canvas that he carried, and scudded under the
barest proverbial poles, yet was invariably caught in
one of the spiral whirls in which Matilda's wrath, following the law of storms, circled about and seized upon
those who were far and those who were near alike.
He tried feebly to befriend his father in some such
fashion as " Bad might be wuss, Tildy," or " Fly high
and fall low was wrote fur men and birds," but with
the first angry word of her reply he succumbed, out
would go his cheeks, his face would get scarlet, his eyes

almost start from their sockets. A blow from his fists, the consequent explosion, and then puff, snort, and chuckle would follow again in ludicrous and invariable succession. Pap's meek acceptance of the treatment he received both puzzled and angered Willy, who did not understand that this miserable sinner was getting from it the curious satisfaction that a fanatical saint might from flagellation.

"Don't yer do that, sonny," he said to the child when he found him making faces at Matilda behind her back, which was one of the secret satisfactions of his partisanship, if a rather ineffectual one, so far as any benefit to his friend was concerned. "I deserves what I gits, and a big sight more. You let her be."

It was not until one of the Landon men fell ill of scarlet fever, and Pap had nursed him through it, that he seemed to recover his old cheerfulness and equanimity. People on the Mountain had a good many forms of pride, and as many distinctions of their own as the great world can show. The Stubbs, for instance, "had starved, but hadn't never begged." The Browns "had always had a horse, leastways a steer." The Snoodgrass family always "got their religion hard, and lost it easy." The Newmans—if Mother Newman was to be believed—"hadn't never been ones to crawl, but walked right off." The peculiar glory and characteristic of the Landons was that "they warn't people that went to bed for nothin': they dropped where they stood."

So when Jackson Landon, in accordance with the family tradition, "dropped" at a neighbor's into scarlet fever, Pap volunteered to take care of him, and did so most kindly and faithfully for three weeks, and came

19*

home whistling the day his patient went home, and went straight to a certain shelf, where he got down his pictures, brushed the dust from them, still whistling, and tacked them up gravely in their old places.

"Pa-ap," said Willy, who was looking on, "you done put old Blue Light back agin whur he belongs at, ain't yer?"

"Yes, honey. You see I've done nailed him back. Hit's more 'n some could do, I tell you, to nail him to any one spot. He warn't never to be found whur folks looked fur him, no more 'n a flea, he warn't. No indeed. Go where they would and when they would, he was always in the other place, miles away. Yes. Hit's good to have him 'round agin, ain't it, Willy boy?"

"Was he a-pintin' at *you*, Pa-ap, when you took him down?" said Willy. "Don't you know? Like he was at me that time. You know."

"He was, honey, *straight*," confessed Pap. "That was it. He seed me. I knowed what he thought of sech as me, and I couldn't suffer it. Turnin' my back done no good. I had to take him plum' down."

"But he ain't pintin' at you *now*, is he, Pa-ap?" said Willy.

"Well, no, child. He's sorter shut his eyes. You see, I was a good soldier, and he wouldn't like to be hard on an old soldier ef he could help it. He was a merciful man,—good and kind to the worst of us always. Yes, a merciful man; but we'd sooner have seed Old Nick than him when we'd been stealin' and burnin' and sich. He was turrible then as thunder and lightnin', he was."

"Was Ally a-pintin' at you, too, Pa-ap?" asked Willy, when the chromo's turn to be replaced came. "*You* didn't do no stealin' nor burnin' like the others, did you?"

"Well, I've took chickens and sich, and I've slipped many a rail off the fork, and—and there was other things, but that warn't nothin'. I wish I hadn't never done no worse. Chickens don't *look* to die natural deaths. They ain't usened to it, and maybe they wouldn't like it. A low lingerment ain't to my mind, neither, when it comes time to break camp and surrender. And as for rails, when a man's marched all day, honey, and toted a heavy musket, and has had precious little to eat, and has got a snowbank to sleep in, with maybe not a blanket to kiver him, he's *bound* to git warm ef he's got to set the world on fire to do it and roast hisself in the ashes. No, Ally, she warn't a-pintin' nor so much as a-lookin' at me. You see her eyes is down in the picture, and she was that sort that she wouldn't of looked at me fur nothin' ef she'd of knowed I didn't want to be looked at. But I knowed what she was a-thinkin' with her eyes throwed down to keep me from seein', and—(hammer, hammer, hammer) I ain't never see no eyes as blue as hern. Your'n puts me in mind of 'em now and agin, Willy boy, but they ain't to be compared."

It was not long after this that Pap undertook a bit of delicate and difficult negotiation in the interests of R. Mintah. Jonah's imagination, like that of most jealous lovers, was that of "common sense turned upside down." He had indicted and arraigned his gentle little sweetheart before a private packed jury of his own, and got a verdict that ought to have suited him entirely, but that, as a matter of fact, made him wretched, and he laid his case before Pap at great length. The reasonable and consistent lover who had kissed Belle Podley objected to young Culbert's " taking the hand witch was belonging to another,"—that is, shaking hands with R. Mintah. He had a dozen other grievances equally serious and well founded. She had walked home from church with "that cuss." Her engagement ring had gone,—been lost she said, given away to Culbert he was sure. She " warn't the same," —which was remarkable under the circumstances,—and so on, for two good hours that ought to have been given to the family wood-pile. He " warn't fooled," he said, nor was he, except by himself. " *She's mine,*" he said, in conclusion. " And I've got the privilege of her, and she shan't have nothin' to do with nary man livin', not so much as talkin' with 'em, nor settin' in the same room with 'em, nor *lookin'* at em, if so be as I don't choose to have it so. And I won't have that Culbert 'bout. I'll chase him off the Mountain ef he comes to the house agin. And ef that don't do I'll quieten him."

In short, this shock-headed and sore-hearted rustic was as jealous as a Turk, and would have liked to shut his perfectly innocent and devoted little R. Mintah up behind the highest walls that could have been built; and not alone to have shut her in, but to have shut out every other member of his own too dangerous sex, and set up the domestic system of the Bosphorus along the banks of the Shenandoah. It is not necessary to go into Pap's arguments and remonstrances. Only a sincere desire to straighten out this tangled skein of sentiment in which the heart of a sweet girl was wrapped and suffocated induced him to say a word. He would have greatly preferred to "shake the young ijit," as he told Willy, to whom he said that Jonah and R. Mintah had "got wrong." "But the mind,—the right mind 'll come," he added, feeling that when a woman cannot be happy without a particular prize booby it is the duty of society to satisfy her if it can.

The result of his intercession was shown by R. Mintah's rushing into the shed-room one day with a radiant face, her tears still shining on her cheeks, and her pink sun-bonnet dangling by its strings about her neck,—R. Mintah as tremulously joyous and bright as a sunbeam, —saying, "Oh, Pa-ap! It's all done come right! Jonah's forgive me! Jonah's took me back!" Her fearful crimes and misdemeanors had been condoned, and she, the tender and true-hearted and injured, was overjoyed at being "forgiven,"—"took back." Pap took the hand "witch"was belonging to another," and the tears were in his own eyes as he said, "That's right, R. Mintah. I'm glad fur you, my dear, seein' you've got a setment of your heart on him. Won't you take a cheer? It's raight blustery to-day, ain't it?" But R. Mintah poured out her joy and gratitude standing, and was much too restless to settle down anywhere. She pulled a huge apple out of her pocket with difficulty and gave it to Willy with a kiss.

"Be sure and give your Pa-ap some," she said. "I'd like to give him a whole orchard, fur he's done *everything* fur me," she said, and with a bright look and "good-by!" scudded home to tell Mother Newman all about it. Jinny White, going over there that afternoon with some ginger-cakes of her own baking, heard of it, too.

p

Mrs. Newman went over the whole affair,—indeed, from beginning to end.

"I was set agin' it at first," she said. "It laid me on a care-bed fur a long while, through Matildy bein' so opposed, mostly. But I'd had the child sence she wus a baby. And she set there and sewed day upon day, and never said a word, but the tears drapped and drapped. At last I jes' had to give in, after that there picnic, when she come back to me scared out of her senses 'bout him, and me thinkin' him killed. I never could deny that Jonah nothin'. And she ain't never give me an answer back sence I took her out of that Lane yonder, nor a bit uv trouble. Matildy, she was tearin', ragin' mad 'bout it, and me givin' in. She says R. Mintah don' know nothin', and ain't got nothin', and don' belong to nobody. And that's so. We ain't to say *rich* exactly" (looking around complacently on her miserable surroundings), "but we're in what I call comfortable circumstances, and has always been thought well of. 'Tain't so bad to me, her not being edgercated. I ain't no scholard myself. Matildy, she can read right off, and spell 'most any word I give her, and write pretty near anything she puts her mind on. She's powerful smart. And she's always talkin' 'bout R. Mintah havin' no edgercation. But I don't mind, not havin' one myself. I laid off to git edgercated onst; but I knowed it would take three months, and up to that the children had come so fast and the work was piled so high I hadn't got it. And that time there come a hard winter, and all the children took and got the measles among 'em, and their father laid down with the lumbago and pine-knots skase, and no books, nor money to buy 'em, nor nobody to rightly know what they said ef I'd of had 'em, so I clean give up the idee. And I don't see but what R. Mintah 'll do well ef she acts right by Jonah and all. Do you?"

"No, indeed," Jinny agreed. "She's got enough to do, or will have, without wastin' her time gittin' *edger-cated.* Give me my health, and a good stove, and a broom, and a bucket, and a dish-pan, and some flat-irons, and anybody can take *books* that likes, and get along with 'em, I sez. I ain't got no use fur 'em, and never will have, nor nobody else that's got to work fur a livin', is what I sez. Them poor, foolish, rich folks that couldn't milk a cow or bake a loaf of bread ef they died fur it has got to have *somethin'* in their heads, and so they gits edgercated, and sets around in fine clothes, and does nothin' all day, and looks down on sech as you and me. But I reckon ef they had their livin' to make they'd find out what their edgercation was wuth mighty quick to lean on. Hit's a poor thing to my thinkin', that there edgercation."

"Well, you and me's agreed," said Mrs. Newman, "and I'll never hanker fur it agin, let Matildy say what she likes. And I'm glad Jonah and R. Mintah's made up together. It was his fault. Though he's my son, and knowed to be my son always, I sez agin it was all his foolishness, along of that Culbert boy bein' here all the time sparkin' A. Mander. His father felt mighty bad 'bout his quar'l with Marsh's father, him bein' killed that way, and he was sorter glad for him to come here lately as a make-peace, and wouldn't send him off to please Jonah. And I knowed how it was fur all, but I couldn't move 'em, father nor son. Fur though he's my

husband, and I ain't never said but what he was my
husband whenever asked, he certainly is the setest man
in his own way that ever was 'ceptin Jonah, his son,
and my son likewise, but specially his'n, through bein'
a mule sometimes fur movin' on, both of 'em, and a
mountain fur stoppin' still right in their tracks. And
that A. Mander, she's 'most as bad. But it's all come
right, and I reckon it'll stay right now. But marriage-
makin's is powerful queer when you come to think, ain't
they, now? I never 'lowed to see a Culbert in my family,
nor my Jonah takin' R. Mintah fur a partner, shore and
certain. And I reckon I'll see queerer things than them
before I die, ef I live long enough, and all I've got to do,
I tells myself, is to be a mother to one and all and treat
'em kind.   Jonah 'll not deny but what I've been a
mother to him, and A. Mander's done said she was
'shamed of how she's acted. And that R. Mintah 'll be
a daughter to me as long as she breathes the breath of
life. Bless her little heart! It ain't only Jonah that
loves her, but pretty nigh everybody. Reach me that
rollin'-pin, Jinny, and I'll do the children some figger-
biscuits."

In this pleasant way was the long fever of disquiet
that had been the portion of all the elder members of
the Newman family for many months replaced by a
healthier and happier state of affairs.   And all went
well for some time with Pap, to whom it was due, and
with his household in the shed. Burygyard took a
start suddenly and whistled off a whole strain over
which he had been halting and pouting and boggling
for months. Bunny had never been brisker or more
lively, sharper of tooth and brighter of eye. Willy, as

Pap remarked, "growed like a weed," and got about an inch of bare leg between his little brogans and his ridiculously big but woefully short trousers. And Pap was very busy collecting "kindlin'" in his spare time which he meant to sell that he might get Willy clothes and send him to school when winter should come. The jug in the old chimney was empty, had tumbled over on its side, had lost its cork, was covered with dust. And the serpent in Pap's bosom was coiled, motionless.

"I'm gittin' on fur an old man, Willy boy, but I'm feelin' peart as Bunny here lately, and I'll git you fixed up and started right on the road you've got to travel befo' my head gits cold. Yes, indeed. See ef I don't. I thinks a heap of my little boy, that's my inthought all the time, and my darlin' comfort; and ef I could, I'd give him a gold world with silver fixin's to live in, and never let trouble nor nothin' hurtful come nigh him," he said to the child one day when they were together in the woods and he was binding withes about the little bundles of pine, five in a bundle, laid out before him. "Lemmy see. Twenty-five a bundle. One, two, three, four, five, —that's a dollar and a quarter. We are layin' it up, honey! Just a-pilin' it up, sure as you are born! Hit's splendid, this. Jes' tech a light to it, and it'll flame right up in your face like ile, hit's so rich. The fat's all there; only the light's wantin' fur a blaze. That's it. Whur they'se *made* like this,—things, that is,—I ain't talkin' 'bout nothin' pertikiler, you see,—you've got not to have no lights 'roun'; you've got to be mighty keerful to keep 'em away from each other, or you're gone, fur it's all ready and waitin' and wantin' to ketch fire. That's the trouble with—some. Don't

20

you try to fetch in morc'n one bundle; you ain't big enough yit to carry more, honey. Pa-ap 'll hobble along some way or other with the rest, ef he *is* gittin' on fur an old man and crippled 'bout the legs like all Company C is."

He did not look a very old man, but a gaunt and grizzled one, as he stood beside Willy leaning on his crutch, the bundles gathered up under his arm,—over six feet, with a patient slope to his shoulders that seemed to tell of grievous burdens long and meekly borne. The attraction of gravitation had visibly affected everything about him. His long, delicately-distinct brows, and the corners of his sensitive mouth, ran down. So did the heels of his shoes. His coat, of as many colors as Joseph's, yet of none (predominant that is and universal), swagged in the back in a series of ripples like a lake into which Pap, a stone, had been thrown. The very wrinkles in his trousers, seen from the back, swept in a low-spirited way below his calves. But the deep crow's-feet about his eyes showed that nature had done what she could to make honorable amends for the depressing turn given to the whole outer man by destiny. A constitutionally cheerful temper had been bestowed upon him—a philosophic calm, and capacity for meditation, as opposed to exertion—that would have made him a happy man but for the " but" that in some form or other always mars such gracious designs; but for all that made him what he was, instead of somebody else. A happy man he was, in spite of everything, for some months, during which the " heap of kindlin' " grew larger and larger and Pap's hopes and plans had swelled to match until he actually had

Willy grown, educated, and—pardon so much to his ignorance—in Congress.

And then—I hate to write it—there was another disappearance, more mystery, wrath, grief.

The serpent had waked to life. The poor pine had been there all along, and the devil had supplied a light; the consuming flame raged high again, and Matilda, with a fiend's laugh of exultation, said, "Pa-ap's drunk! I knowed it would come." It was the same experience over again, —the same temptation, fall, remorse. The "kindlin'" had been sold; but Willy had gained nothing by the transaction, and Pap had lost much. The pictures in the shed-room were all taken down again by a pair of trembling hands, and an unhappy creature took up his life again, having bound a heavier burden than ever upon his back.

"Johnny Shore never was no 'count noway. He's goin' the way of his father," said the Mountain, which respected Mr. Carver, who, if he was rarely sober, did his drinking in a large stone farm-house set on a fine, large unencumbered farm, and said of him, with positive pride in the possession of such a financial magnate, that "he had been found drunk with as much as a hundred dollars about his clothes."

But "Johnny Shore," who had given away his cottage and every acre of his patrimony, and could rarely afford to indulge a vice at all,—"Johnny Shore" was utterly contemptible, and "no 'count," of course.

VIII.

" Keep thy purse and thou shalt keep thy friend also."—Moujik Proverb.

THE view from the old cottage porch was one that might have been coveted for a palace, so fine was the distant magnificence of the three chains of mountains to the right, rising one behind the other, with purple shadows and transparent mists folded and floating between; so fair the wide, sunlit plain in the foreground; so nobly protecting and encompassing the Ridge standing sturdily up in defence of Virginia and Virginians away to the left. Nothing was wanting except the eyes to see and appropriate all this beauty; but these had been denied Matilda, who came out, indeed, and looked about her with frowning impatience one morning during the " ingathering" (as harvest time is prettily called on the Mountain), but saw nothing of it.

" Whur's that good-for-nothin' old Lawrence* gone to now ?" she demanded, angrily, of nobody in particular. " Willy ! Willy !"

In response to this call Willy came forward reluctantly from around the corner of the house, concealing instinctively as he got within view the top with which he had been playing.

---

* " Lawrence" is doubtless a term of English origin. It was applied in early days in Virginia to a shirk at " house-raisings," " log-rollings," and " ingatherings" (of harvests), but is now used in a broadly contemptuous sense.

"Here! here! What you been doin' 'round there?" she asked, sharply. "Nothin' good, I'll be bound." Willy flushed guiltily and tried to thrust the criminating top still farther behind his back.

"You go find your Pa-ap, and tell him ef he 'spects to git a bite of vittles in my house this mornin' he'd better be quick about it, do you hear?"

"Ya—m," assented Willy, and she went in-doors again, banging the door after her.

Thus commissioned, he limped about the place a bit in search of Pap, but soon made up his mind that that was useless, and started out into the Red Lane. He left that presently, and, climbing the fence, struck across a field. Arrived at its farthest point, he put his hands on his hips and struck an attitude, with his haystack hat pushed off his sweet face, the little-big breeches girded high up under his shoulder-blades and armpits, and his wonderful waistcoat dropping to his calves.

"Pa-ap! Pa-ap! Oh, Pa-ap!" he shrieked in his highest treble pipe. "Pa-ap!" But he got no answer. He tried another "Pa-ap! Come to breakfast," and still getting no response, turned away.

Once out of sight of home, his pace had slackened, and he was in no hurry to go on now. The sun was lighting up brilliantly a delightful world. The air was sweet with a thousand woodland scents. Swarms of yellow butterflies were challenging him for a chase. Birds were flying about overhead, and lighting in this or that tree. The last daisies of the season were begging to have their heads switched off by his whip,—his new whip that Pap had given him, and that he had been cracking ever since. Surely that was a minnow

20*

that flashed in the light, as he came to the brook that, if followed, would lead through the lower meadows straight into the Landons' spring-house. And now a snake-hole this. What bliss to drag a serpent out by the tail as Jonah did last week! How good "the feel" of the wet grass.

It was not in boy-nature to be in frantic haste to carry other people's messages and neglect all these invitations to idleness, but after a while Willy did go on, reluctantly, across two meadows and a stubble-field, and as he approached some haystacks set on the edge of a wood he heard sounds that set him off into a painful, dragging movement which was his nearest approach to a run. This soon brought him flushed and smiling to a certain fence-corner in which Pap was seated, with his violin tucked under his chin, playing away in the most absorbed enjoyment of his own music, the day, the view, and his surroundings generally.

"I knowed you'd be here!" exclaimed the child, rushing against and violently arresting the ecstatic swing of the arm that held the bow, and then, dropping down beside him on the grass, he turned a frolicsome somersault that ended in his coming up *vis-a-vis* to his companion with straws sticking in his hair and his waistcoat very much hitched up in the back.

"Git up, my son. That ain't pretty. Look at your close, all every-which-er-way!" The tone was one of remonstrance, but was neutralized by the tenderness that literally suffused Pap's face whenever he looked at the child,—a beautiful look of deep love that seemed to take away all that was harsh in the prominent features and worn lines of the face.

.He had laid his instrument down on the grass, and now took it up gently, saying, " I'll play you a chune, Willy boy. You'd like the ' Fisher's Hornpipe,' now, wouldn't you ?"

" Not now, Pa-ap. There ain't no time. Breakfast's ready, and you'd better hurry, *I tell you!*" advised Willy, sagely.

" Ready, is it ? I hadn't no idee it was so late," Pap replied, an anxious light coming into his eyes, the ready smile that had carved such deep " crow's-foot" around them dying out. Rising to his feet, he carefully wrapped his violin in its bit of faded shawl, and, glancing over his shoulder at the child, said, " Is she very— hainh ?"

Willy understood, and nodded emphatically and gravely.

" Very well, sonny, then we *will* hurry. It didn't seem to me like the sun was that high. When I gits to fiddlin' I don't take no 'count uv the shadows, though, and that's the truth. I reckon I'll ketch it hot and heavy this time. 'Tain't the first time, either," said the old man, the twinkle coming back to his eye as he spoke. " Well, I've been under fire before now; I reckon I kin stand and take it. She's always sour at best. Jim—poor Jim !—usened to say she'd been weaned on pickles. I lost a friend when I lost him, I tell you, Willy. We was like hemlocks and spruces in the war. When you seed one, you hadn't far to look for t'other, and there never was a day he wouldn't share his tobacco with me. You're sorter blowed with runnin', ain't you, honey ? Will I carry you a piece ? I kin, I reckon, till we git over to that ploughed field yonder. Come 'long."

Nothing loath, Willy climbed up and up, and finally perched on his shoulder, and slipped his little walnut-stained hand around Pap's neck.

" You take the fiddle and I'll pack you both. Hold on tight," cautioned the old man, and off they started, but at a leisurely pace, for the rhythm of Pap's being was such that even in his youth and prime he had been constitutionally incapable of haste.

Knowing quite well the necessity for speed, he stopped twice on the way: once to let Willy gather some leaves from a maple-bough that drooped temptingly overhead, and another time when a rabbit darted past and stopped at a little distance in front of them.

" Thar he is! Notice how he sweeps them ears of his'n 'round. The cunnin' little cotton-tail! He looks like—folks, now, don't he ?" commented Pap, and Willy drummed delightedly on the old man's chest with his heels, and was for jumping down and going after it, but was not allowed.

Arrived at the steps of their house, the child was put down and given the violin. " Here, honey, you jes' run around with this and put it in the box under my bed whur it always stays. En don't you knock it 'gin nothin', or I'll give you a laced jacket."

Unterrified by this threat, to which he was quite used and took at its exact value, Willy only said, " Will yer wait fur me, Pa-ap? Wait fur me."

" Course I will. Don't you be afeard, my son. I ain't. I don't kyur." At this moment the front-door opened, and involuntarily Pap dropped back three steps on the path.

It was only his son Alfred. " I heerd you, Pa-ap. Come

in. Mr. Carver's happened in to breakfast with us," he said, in a low voice, made more indistinct by the food in his mouth. He winked knowingly and reassuringly as he spoke, and Willy having returned they all walked together into the dining-room, where Matilda and Mr. Carver were seated at table.

"Howdy! I hope you see yourself well," said Pap, ducking his head in greeting to the latter from the door. Getting a half nod in return, he went forward, took his usual seat, and put his feet up on the rounds of his chair when he had seen Willy comfortably settled next to himself.

Mr. Carver, an enormously stout man, with a small, cautious, elephantine eye sunk well in the back of his head, now availed himself of the opportunity to indulge in one of his most prolonged bovine stares.

"'Tildy, your coffee's powerful good," said Alfred, after about five minutes had passed without her taking the least notice of his father. "I ain't never poured better down my throat. I've done had two cups. Give Pa-ap a cup, ef it ain't all done been drunk up."

"You talk like there warn't always plenty,—like we had to count noses, like some,"—she snapped, "when I've got more on the fire, and ten pounds in the house. What 'll Mr. Carver be sayin'?"

"Well, give Pa-ap a good cup," said Alfred. "He's waitin' here fur it."

Now Pap's pictures, alas! had been down again a few weeks before, and he was in the worst possible favor with his shrewish daughter-in-law, who gave him a spiteful look as she dashed a liberal supply of hot water into a cup, colored it faintly with an odious decoction of chicory, omitted the sugar altogether, and passed the delightful mixture up to its destination, saying, contemptuously, " Well, what of that? *Let* him wait and welcome."

Alfred felt that he had made a mistake. He passed his hands instantly across his mouth, rubbed his nose upward very briskly a few times, and got off a glittering generality to restore the impersonal tone of the conversation.

" 'Pears like folks ain't a-goin' to be able to meat tharselves this year. Mast is mighty skase," he said, averting his eyes from his spouse.

" *I* don't jedge so. Nothin' of the sort. Whur did you git that foolishness?" said Mr. Carver, who, as one of the large farmers of the neighborhood,—a representative one, he considered,—felt it to be at once his duty and privilege to contradict every statement about agriculture that did not emanate from what he believed to be the proper source. With thirty hogs waiting to be killed, Mr. Carver was not going to be told that any scarcity existed.   .

" En what if it is?" he added, turning his huge body around towards Alfred, and looking at him with severe disapproval. " What ef it it is? *Feed 'em on corn*, I say." With a large barn in his mental background bursting with that cereal, Mr. Carver could afford liberal views.

" Pass up your cup, Mr. Carver," said Matilda, affably, much impressed by the insolence of his prosperity, and his condescension in consenting to breakfast at the cottage. " Don't be bashful. And take another biscuit. Take two."

Nothing had been offered Pap all this time, and Willy noticed it.

"You ain't got nothin' to eat, Pa-ap," he whispered, anxiously. "What 'll you do?"

"Take a bite of shoat?" said Alfred, who heard this; and, without waiting for a response, he took advantage of Matilda's being occupied to furtively convey a spare-rib to his father's plate and hastily add a biscuit.

He had barely accomplished this when he caught Matilda's eye, sat up suddenly in his chair, transfixed a potato with his fork, and said, "Days is begun to close in," as if uttering a solemn verity,—very much, indeed, as though he were giving out a text.

"Is that all what you're goin' to git, Pa-ap? Won't she give you no more?" whispered Willy again.

"Ssh! Don't you werrit 'bout Pa-ap, honey," the old man whispered back. "I'll take some pertaters. They sticks by the ribs, and are mighty fillin'. Don't you want some?"

He did a little private foraging on his own account, accordingly, sub Rosa-Matilda (Mrs. Alfred Shore's full name), and, coming to the surface of polite society again, waxed conversational.

"I seed Mat Childers, yesterday," he said, "from down 'bout the Ridge, and he says the corn do look pitiful down there this summer,—pitiful. Farmin's a powerful sight of trouble, anyways. Seasons is got so, what's good fur corn is bad fur wheat; likewise con-trarywise; and pasture is givin' out, I can see. I'll thank you fur a biscuit, Alfred. Yes, ef I was a young man, and had my time to go over agin, I'd turn my back on ole Virginny mighty quick, and go whur you kin git out your two crops every year as shore as summer comes 'round."

Mr. Carver, who was scraping off the gravy and potato from his knife on the edge of his plate, now stopped, and as he looked at Pap his heavy lower jaw seemed to settle down in his throat with a movement of angry remonstrance.

"That's all blamed taradiddle foolishness you're talkin'," he said. "That's what it is. There *ain't* no such country. No land that God ever made 'll give no two crops in one year. No, sir. The best field I've got wouldn't do it ef it was kivered knee-deep with these here new phosphites that some uses; and there ain't better fields on the face of the yearth. As fur farmin', the land sticks by them that sticks by her. Now you've heerd my horn."

With an emphatic nod he went back to his knife-cleaning, feeling that he had been final, put half a biscuit into his right cheek, and devoted himself in ponderous silence to the business before him again.

"You see, Pa-ap, he's a mover," put in Matilda, personifying a peculiarity after the fashion so noticeable in the homespun English of the Valley. "You can't keep him in no one place no more 'n the sun. He's been out to Californy, and Texis, and I don't know whur. Virginny ain't good enough fur *him*. He's been all 'round. But *I* don't see what he's got by it."

She gave an insulting laugh. The color rose to Pap's face, and the wrinkled, toil-worn hand that held his coffee-cup to his lips trembled violently, but he said nothing.

"'Tildy! 'Tildy!" exclaimed Alfred, with feeble-for-

cible indignation. And then in alarm he coughed ostentatiously, made a lunge forward upon the butter-
dish with his knife, and, having helped himself to about
a quarter of a pound, gave out another text solemnly:
" Hum! Turnips is feelin' the wet."

" What's the use of goin' a-ramblin' and a-scramblin'
over the world, anyways?" demanded Mr. Carver, ener-
getically. " What do I want to go to Agy and to Spagy
and 'way off yonder beyant Milltown fur?" (A village
twelve miles distant.) " I ain't been fifty mile from home
fur sixty year. No, sir! And that time was when my
father moved up here from Albemarle, and brought me
'long with him. That's all the travellin' ever *I* did or
means to do. What's the gain of travellin'? Whar's
any better place 'n ole Virginny? Tell me that. Hit's
the best place that's been made at all, and I've got the
best farm in the State."

Mr. Carver shared the general and natural delusion
of farmers, and of course he was not contradicted in a
company composed of his social inferiors.

" Well, we've been put here——" began Pap.

"That's what I say. Let folks stay whur they're
put, and there won't be no travellin' but what's needful
right 'round you. What's the use of havin' places ef
folks won't stay in 'em? What's the use of havin' places
at all? Counties,—this here county? You might as
well be in Clarke or Loudon to onst!" said Mr. Carver,
and looked about him wildly and angrily as he pounded
the table with his huge fist, as if the foundations of
society were being broken up, and the idea of an illim-
itable waste of territory, in which a Carver might be
anywhere, was insupportable and not to be borne for a

moment. "I don't want to go nowhur at all, and I
don't want no furriners comin' in here. Furriners is
bein' the ruin of this country now. They're comin' in
from Deer Crik" (six miles off) "and Winston and Milltown and 'way beyant Caton, and they're just bein' the
ruination of business and the handlin' of crops and
everything," he concluded, with temper. "Folks was
made fur places, places was made fur folks, and it spiles
both to separate them; hit's the ruination of both.
Stay whur you're put is what I sez all the time, and
does, moreover."

The places Mr. Carver had mentioned were all in his
immediate neighborhood, and his "furriners" were all
native Virginians; but when he talked of "this country" he meant to use the word not in the broad sense
of the United States, or even his own State, but in the
restricted one of his own county. Every county was a
country to Mr. Carver, and his own county was *the*
country.

Poor Pap was too abashed to attempt to defend his
views, and Alfred never had any views to defend; but
Matilda came shrilling in with: "You're 'bout right
there, I reckon, Mr. Carver. I'm fur folks stayin' at
home, and mindin' their own business too. Only some
of 'em's so triflin' they ain't got no business to mind."

"That's so," said Pap, who had made the expected
application of an apparently abstract statement. "Nor
no homes, neither. More fools they."

"Oh, ef bein' a *fool* was all, it could be stood; but
when there's wuss behind——" said Matilda, who,
being an incarnate nutmeg-grater, was now quite in her
element.

"Ahum! ahum!" broke in Alfred, in mortal dread of a collision. And then shooting out his eyes at the inoffensive milk-pitcher on his right, he announced, gravely, "Patridges has been seen 'round," a remark that elicited no reply whatever.

Having finished his breakfast, and being anxious to efface himself, Pap now pushed back his chair a little and tilted it, and crossed his hands above his head. He sat there for some moments, silent, while Mr. Carver and Alfred talked of sport; but, being very social in his instincts, he presently joined in their conversation, saying, "I've often heerd my father talk 'bout old times in this country time and time agin. These hills was just choke-full uv bar, and deer, and all sorts of game then, and now you're mighty lucky ef you git a few wild turkeys."

"Venison certainly *is* a well-tasted dish," remarked Mr. Carver to Matilda, with an impressive stare at each of the company in turn, and the air of a man of liberal views making a dangerously novel statement, which, however unpopular it may be, he is prepared to stand by and uphold at any cost.

"Take another egg ef you don't mislike 'em biled," said Matilda, obsequiously. "Don't you be backward, now, in comin' forrard. 'Vittles' praise is said by stays.' But I forgit. He! he! he! You don't wear 'em!"

"No, I'm 'bleeged to you, marm," replied Mr. Carver, alluding to the proffered egg and not smiling at all at the witticism. Mr. Carver was not aware that in saying "marm" he was only following the most fashionable precedent,—that of the court set of long ago, whose languishing pronunciation of madam has filtered down through English nobles to English commoners, and finally to Virginian mountaineers. Nor did he know when he turned his cup bottom upward in the saucer, and balanced the spoon carefully on top, as an act of final renunciation and intimation that he was superior to any and every temptation, that he was perpetuating a fashion that used to obtain in the finest companies,— a signal mark of high breeding in the great ladies and silken gallants of a past period,—now the "manners" of a rustic Virginian whom they would have called "a varlet."

"I reckon there 'll be a chance fur some of us to taste the feast-pot soon. You've heerd 'bout the weddin' that's comin' off in the neighborhood, ain't yer?" said Alfred, presenting a new topic of conversation respectfully to the notice of the great man. "Pa-ap here plays in the musical line, and he's goin' to do the fiddlin'. He can make right smart noise when he gits started. He jerks an uncommon lively bow." Alfred was proud of his father's reputation as the best musician in the country-side, and was divided between a desire to seem dispassionate and a wish to do him justice.

The remark, however, was unfortunate. Mr. Carver did not attempt to conceal the profound contempt that filled his whole mind at the mere mention of such a frivolous pursuit. He knew that Pap had another weakness, which in a rich man, and especially in himself, wore the aspect of a venial foible, not a sin that need interfere with a well-to-do farmer's being saved in the least. But the man who "fiddled" was hardly worth the damning, according to Mr. Carver's creed. He looked across the table at Pap with a grim disapprobation that bordered on dislike, and thought that he " 'peared like a man that ' fiddled.' "

"Peter Robinson !" he exclaimed, when the feathered idea had fully made its way through his thick skull. "You play the fiddle, do you? In the name of goodness, is that all you've got to do? Can't you *find* nothin' better to do ?"

Pap unclasped his hands, stopped tilting his chair, and colored again ; but being thoroughly accustomed to hearing music ranked among the vicious puerilities of life, he said nothing in defence of it, and Mr. Carver went on : "Who's this here a-gittin' married ?"

"Hit's my wife's brother, Jonah," replied Alfred.

"Who's he a-weddin' ?" asked Mr. Carver, still disapprovingly, as if all marrying and giving in marriage were distasteful to him.

"That girl,—that orphelin'—— Hello! Simon Peter and Stonewell Jackson! Come in! Come here!" interrupted Pap.

This last was a combination hardly to be expected in this world, though presumably not an unnatural one in the next, where the sturdy soldier and simple fisherman may be on very good terms, for all we know. The salutation was meant for two barefooted, frowsy boys, who had come in and were hanging irresolutely around the door, staring as only the youthful rustic can. Stonewall Jackson, unlike his distinguished namesake, was not prepared to advance even when thus encouraged, but took up a strong position in the rear and would not budge.

His twin brother, rounding his eyes a little more than usual, advanced as if under some mesmeric spell, or as if he were walking in his sleep, and when he got quite close to Pap fell to twirling his hat, which for a wonder he had doffed. He looked up, he looked down, he looked around at "Stone" for inspiration, perhaps, to see if there was any way of escape open to him, and then in a loud voice and in a disjointed, mechanical fashion delivered the message with which he was charged—under fire: "Pa-ap, mother says to come there to onst to go to town to git the fixin's that's wanted fur Jonah's weddin'."

"All right. Indeed and double deed I will, sonny. Go back and tell your ma certainly, I'll be there te-reckly," replied Pap, promptly, and his kind smile played lambently on the boys as he filched a biscuit apiece for them from under the very nose of the enemy.

The boys got a little more human under this application, and now fell into the background with Willy, and even smiled and fell to comparing their knives with his presently. The interruption broke up the party, and Mr. Carver rose and said he had "'lowed to be further before then," and made his farewells.

"This here's a tol'able old house, ain't it?" he asked, as he was mounting his horse.

"Over a hundred year. And there never was a better builded. It ain't had no work much done on it sence. I love ev'y stone in it," said Pap, glancing up at it affectionately.

"Oh, then this here is your house?" said Mr. Carver, settling his foot in the stirrup.

' "Yes. That is, hit's my *son's*," he explained. "But I reckon it'll outlast us both, and a good many more like us. I've done give it to my son." Poor Pap was not unwilling that Mr. Carver should know that he had not always been as he was,—homeless and penniless. But this was worse than "fiddlin'": it was lunacy to Mr. Carver's mind; and Pap did not even get a word of farewell by way of recognition of his past respectability. He felt wounded and humiliated when Mr. Carver rode away on his handsome horse with only a " Good-day, marm," and a " Come over, Alfred, and we'll see 'bout that there colt." And he was still standing at the gate, wrapped in unpleasant revery, when he felt some one tugging at his coat. It was "Stone" Newman, holding a rabbit in his hand which he was shyly proffering. " I caught this fur you this mornin', Pa-ap. I've been layin' fur it fur a week. Here, take it," he said, and was surprised by the warmth of Pap's thanks.

" Why, bless your little heart! Did you now? Caught it fur Pa-ap, that ain't got nothin' to give you back. Well, that was the kindest! Thanky, my son. Lord, what a world 'twould be without children and dogs and sech like animals that's got hearts and feelin's and ain't—folks! I'm jes't as 'bleeged as I kin be, honey. I've been jes' a-pinin' fur a taste of rabbit fur the longest. Yes, indeed. Pa-ap 'll not furgit this. Now, run along home,—skedaddle, and tell your ma I'll be there right off."

That was a day in the Newman family. From the moment that love and grief had carried the day, Mother Newman had privately determined to give Jonah and R. Mintah such a " send-off" as was rarely seen on the Mountain. As a woman, she dearly loved a wedding,

even when she had no special or personal interest in it.
As a mother, she had every reason to concern herself
with this one. " I'm a-standin' double in this here thing,
father, and you're a-standin' double, moreover. Fur I'm
Jonah's mother, and knowed to be, through showin'
him from three days old, and him as red a child as I ever
see, or had, to come out fair-complected, and me not
pretendin' not to be his mother even when took up by
some about measles and sech, through him catchin' of
'em not bein' liked by neighbors that *their* children has
give everything to mine. And you're his father, and
behind none in actin' up as sich, which all wouldn't of
walked their legs off to keep a baby quiet, and taught
him to work better than a grown man when he warn't
hardly able to hold a axe and spade, and him favorin'
you so you *can't* say he ain't your son ef it was in a cote
where folks 'll swear black's white, as I've often heerd
you say. And R. Mintah's a poor, lost, and left child
that'll witness agin the one that brought her into this
world some day and 'lowed to be my own by a good
many, and me her mother, in a manner of speakin'.
And so are you, leastways, her father, or standin' for a
father, which she was 'bleeged to have one, and has,
ef he ain't gone to a worse place, which, ef he has,
it ain't no more 'n what he deserves, though I hate
to think of any bein' lost, even them that's left their
child 'round for us to find and bring up. Me standin'
double, then, fur mothers, and you standin' double fur
fathers, I sez we'll give them two the biggest weddin'
we kin make out, and bless 'em fur good, kind children
that's been a blessin' to us, and send 'em away to theirselves."

"I don't want to see you standin' fur no sech woman as R. Mintah's——" began Mr. Newman.

"I've *done* been standin' fur her, now, fur nineteen years, and I ain't goin' to fail the child, no matter what sort of woman goes and calls herself a mother," objected Mrs. Newman.

"Well, I ain't a-goin' to stand-fur sech as *him*,—that's flat. Ef he was here this minnit I'd maul him like a meal-bag!" exclaimed Mr. Newman, testily. "I ain't never bin no sich, and I ain't a-goin' to be to please nobody."

"You've got to be. You've got to give R. Mintah a chance. You've got to be a double father to them two, and you know you ain't the man not to. But it won't be fur long," persisted Mrs. Newman.

"Well, I won't say no more. But you've missed the pints. Law is law, and hit don't take no 'count of double fathers and double mothers. No, indeed. But there's another pint. Onst they're *wed* they're *one*. And *them* bein' one theirselves makes us single fathers and mothers, too, and there needn't never be no more talk 'bout no others," said Mr. Newman, who had kept the legal mind.

"Now, father, this I sez, and sez agin to you, and don't you forgit it. Ef anybody—that Sally Hearn—comes pryin' and pokin' 'round you 'bout R. Mintah, don't you tell her *nothin'*, and talk like she didn't belong to nobody, and was jest a orpheline, fur it would be a shame, and her standin' up to git married that minnit, poor thing!"

"I won't, mother," promised Mr. Newman. "I won't open my mind to her; not a crack. And you kin take that five dollars Don Miller give me fur that black and white heifer, and spend every red cent of it on that weddin'. But we can't be doubles; it ain't law nor it ain't gospel, neither."

These delicate and important "pints" having been settled, Mrs. Newman gave herself up to and fairly revelled in the preparations for the great event that was to double nothing except Jonah's joys and expenses.

The cooking-stove and the beds came down, causing as much excitement among the children as though the roof had fallen in. A grand house-cleaning set in, revealing the fact that it had long been hideously needed. Then such a making, baking, beating, such boiling, frying, roasting, such hurrying, and scurrying, and worrying set in as had never been seen in that house, or, rather, outhouse, before (the stove had been set up there), and could scarcely be contained even by "the yard," as the back premises were called. R. Mintah was out of the way of much of it, being up-stairs at her needle-work. And Jonah avoided it, saying he'd "as lieve be chased by a mad bull 'most." And his father went away for two whole days and was scarcely missed. But Mrs. Newman, broad and placid, directed the whirlwind and rode upon the storm. Jinny White and relays of other women were there, notably "Darthuly Meely," whose cakes were quite equal to her comfortables. Even Matilda condescended to look in and find fault with what had been done every day. And Pap was there, cutting wood, drawing water, lifting off kettles, picking chickens, "drawing" ducks, whittling skewers, doing a thousand things with all his own fatal good-nature. As for the twins, they were everywhere.

They were nearly wild with delight over the situation, and drove every one else quite daft by their behavior. They had Willy and a long train of other children at their heels, and no comet was ever followed by more disastrous consequences. Simon Peter fished steadily, and most successfully, in troubled waters for "goodies" of various kinds all day, and had a series of miraculous escapes from the avenging wrath of his elders. Stonewall Jackson tarnished his fair fame over and over again in the same field of action with no success at all, and attempting to filch the icing from the wedding-cake after dinner got his deserts in a different shape, and was much battered about the head by Darthuly Meely, no longer pale and much outraged. Something was borrowed from every neighbor within a radius of three miles. More was offered by every woman who had a heart in her bosom, the memory of a wedding past, the hope of a wedding to come. Friends of the family were sending in such dainties as they could spare or make up to the last moment of grace,—that is, while "the blessin'" was being asked. Distant acquaintances, even, showed their sympathy and interest in various ways, from volunteering the loan of "a *real silver* teaspoon" to roasting a sucking-pig, with the traditional apple in his mouth and his tail curled tight as any sensitive-plant before the approach of the carver. Pap trudged all the way to Winston, went *around* the fatal street that contained the irresistible "sto'" with the screen in front of the door, and hams and vegetables and what not in front of it. He made Mrs. Newman's purchases of peppermint-candy, oranges, and the like. He would have trudged all the way home again, and Heaven knows what he would have done with his parcels, had he not been offered "a lift," which he thankfully accepted. He rode home radiant with the sense of the good he had done and the evil he had avoided, to find Mrs. Newman dreadfully "put about" by the discovery that there "warn't no seats," and spend the afternoon borrowing chairs in the neighborhood, and limping back with them to the house, now in a gala state of cleanliness, almost destitute of incommoding furniture, and adorned as it had never been even for a "buryin'," with green boughs put everywhere, about twenty candles in as many bottles, and a white sheet gracefully festooned about the very flour-barrel in the corner. This done, Pap went home. There he sat himself down to rest a bit, and eat something and smoke his pipe, after which he got out his pictures and put them up, placing a little sprig of fir above the chromo in a tender impulse that moved him to connect his Alice with "little R. Mintah's weddin'." He it was who had been decorating the Newmans' house, and his thoughts had been as busy as his fingers all day. His mind was very full now of a puzzling question. What should he give R. Mintah? He could not reconcile himself to giving nothing, yet he had nothing to give. Suddenly his eyes rested on Burygyard, whisking about in his cage high on the wall. "Why, *of course.* There's *him!*" he thought. "She's always said he hadn't his match, and though I hadn't never 'lowed to part with him——" Down came Burygyard at once, a good deal frightened and flustered, and was borne off to the cottage. Arrived there, the first person that Pap came upon was R. Mintah,—R. Mintah peeping in at the door to see for herself the wonderful and beautiful transformation-scene of which she had heard, and crying, " Oh, ain't it elligint! Ain't it too splendid ! Whur's Jonah at? Has he seed it ?" She fled from before Pap's face on being discovered. "Here, Willy boy, you run along with this to her," said Pap, putting the cage in the child's hands, " and tell her it's all I've got, but give with all my heart, and welcome."

Willy shuffled off, and presently R. Mintah, half-way up the dark stairs, called out, "Oh, Mr. Shore! Thanky, thanky. You oughtn't to a-went and give me him! Sech a bird! Thanky kindly. It's *mighty* kind of you, and jes' a splendid present! Don't you disappint to-night. D'ye hear?" Even in her short print gown and curl-papers R. Mintah was not the fright she felt herself to be, and need not have scampered away; but that " Mr. Shore" was as fine a bit of feminine tact as ever issued from high-born dame in brocade. It sent Pap home with a shining face of content, to spend an hour in the shed-room in trying to make a wedding-garment of his one every-day and all-the-year-round suit, which melted into the red earth, the green leaves, the brown dust, the yellow harvest-fields of the mountain as perfectly as though nature had given it to him as she does the coat of the chameleon for a defence against his natural enemies as well as wind and weather, but which obstinately refused to take on that spruce newness and slop-shop splendor befitting the occasion. "I'm cleanin' myself fur the weddin'," he remarked to Willy, who was looking on and had heard all that the day had brought forth for him. "I've had a *pertikiler* invite, and R. Mintah 'll be expectin' of me."

22

He spoke with pride. Mrs. Newman had indeed confessed that he had "helped mightily," but, having a good many things on her mind, had forgotten to ask him to come back, although she had counted on him for "the fiddlin'."

But that "Don't you disappint" rang sweetly in his ears and warmed his heart.

"R. Mintah was tickled to death with Burygyard. I seed her feedin' him and playin' with him up-stairs, and she said you certainly had been kind to her always, and she hadn't never had nothin' agin you. She said you was a good man," remarked Willy.

"But I ain't, no. Bless her heart! That's to say, goodness is streaky, honey. That sorter streak's always been easy to me; but there's others—— Well, never mind. I *ain't* good. Folks is got the right of it, there. But I might have been wuss 'n what I am, I reckon. And folks don't 'pear to take no 'count of that at all. Gimmy that brush and I'll black my shoes. She said I warn't to fail to come, and I want to look right. Do I look right, Willy?"

When sundown came Mrs. Newman mounted to the room in which R. Mintah sat, and shut the door after her. "I'm a-goin' to dress you up fur this thing myself, R. Mintah," she said, "seein' you're my child, or as good as one, and better 'n some. And I ain't goin' to let nobody else come nigh you, fur this here is my place. I've done got shut of all of 'em, and all's ready, and waitin', and here's your Mother Newman willin' to do all that's to be done fur her daughter that's to be, and has been, always, ever since she was fetched in by me out of the Red Lane nigh twenty years gone by. And

you a drulin' with your first tooth then, and a cooin' like
Pete's pigeon, as sweet a baby as ever was, and no more
'feard of me than of you'd been then what you've done
been ever sence, my own dear child. Is yer things laid
out? No, indeed. The twins even didn't want to have
nothin' to do with me at fust, and 'Tildy's give me a
heap of werritting, and A. Mander's too free often with
that tongue of hers, but you've *never* done nothin' nor
been nothin' that's give trouble to me and your double
father. Hit's mighty curious. I reckon the Lord sont
peace and a blessin' along with you. You and Jonah's
been the two that's give us most back for what we've
done fur you, and though there's richer and edgerca-
teder, I reckon, I tells you now that I hadn't my right
mind when I give in to and took part with 'Tildy and
made you onhappy, and I ask your pardon fur all, and
has meant to before you married my son."

It can be imagined with what heartiness this forgiveness was accorded; with what meekness R. Mintah
abased herself before "Jonah's mother," and proclaimed
herself utterly unworthy of the exalted future before
her; with what tears and kisses the two women sealed
a new bond of love and relationship, and then devoted
themselves to the function of "dressin' the bride fur
to go to meet the bridegroom."

At last the hour came. All the friends of the family
had been assembled for two hours before it came, down-
stairs, and had been ranged in rows around the walls
on the "cheers" of Pap's borrowing, some of which
were recognized by the guests and criticised as "this
blamed old thing of mine that the back won't never
stay on no way I fix it;" or "this here three-legged

stool of your'n 's mighty shaky and I misdoubt it holdin'
a person like me." Outside there was quite a little
gathering of people, women chiefly, who were either
strangers to the family or had been thought "too low-
down" to receive an invitation. They had arranged
themselves in small and extremely critical groups near
the windows, lounged on the sills in comfortable and
unabashed abandon, and made themselves merry,—far
more so, indeed, than the regularly invited, whose demeanor was very much what it would have been if
they had assembled to see Jonah and R. Mintah buried
instead of married, and who had the air of waiting
patiently to see the two bodies brought in. The position of the uninvited was a strong one,—that of the
opposition always is,—and they showed themselves a
formidable minority, or "remnant." They could see
and hear everything, and felt themselves at liberty to
say whatever they pleased. They pleased to make a
number of very telling and unpleasant remarks. The
manufacture of polite nothings being a conversational
art either not understood or scorned in rural entertain-
ments, there was a good background of silence within
the room against which such speeches as "Law sakes!
Ef there ain't Sally Lewis, dressed up in her sister
Marthy's things! And they're miles too big fur her;"
or "Jes' look at Al Peters struttin' 'round like a little
Bantam rooster in that linen duster;" "Don't it take
the rag offen the bush, that dress of A. Mander's?"
together with such exclamations as "Hi, ain't we fine!"
or "My! here's the whole family in yaller. Pumpkins
is cheap, I do reckon!" on the part of the Adullamites
stood out in bold relief. The intimate knowledge that

the critics had of the position, circumstances, and characters of the company enabled them to hit the bull's-eye every time, and they scored so many successes that the least sensitive and conscious of the guests grew wretched under the ordeal, while others grew red, and retorted angrily enough upon their persecutors, and still others only waxed more shy and silent every moment. It was not until Mr. Newman rose in his wrath and drove the enemy off the place altogether that anything like confidence was restored, or the exchange of greetings and country civilities resumed. And even then the company was not wildly hilarious by any means. It was divided into little groups, by a principle of natural rejection, rather than selection. In one corner was a dozen or more of stubby, knotty old men, a good deal bent as to their backs and knees, but good for many a day's hard work yet. Pap was seated with, or, rather, near, them. Their talk was of politics and local matters generally. It was: "Was you at the cote-house Saturday night to hear Bob Duffy speak? You oughter bin. It was elligint, I tell you. He kin holler louder 'n any man on the stump, they do say. And it ain't you nor me as 'll understand what he's drivin' at. No, sir. He's powerful smart and *deep*." Or it was: "There ain't a drop of water in Deer Crik, skasely. I never knowed it to run dry in all my born days," a remark that brought out a scornful "*You* never knowed! What you ain't knowed comes to more 'n you'll ever have the head to figger up. Deer Crik's been two two years runnin' *twict* sence I've been a man," from Daddy Culbert, who was strong in recollections.

The conversation then turned on cows, and Mr. Alfred Laudon was complimented on this score by Mr. Newman: "That there cow of your'n is a deep milker, Al. What breed is she, and whur did you git her at, anyways?" which begot a discussion about "breeds" that was almost animated for a few minutes, after which silence fell upon the group again. Pap felt it to be an oppressive silence, and began to talk of trees. In the course of his remarks he asserted that "any tree kin be grafted on another tree ef the barks is alike," and tried to maintain his theory; but his statements were all received with incredulity, solemnity, and contempt-uous superiority. Sensitively alive to the estimation in which he was held by them, this treatment only made him the more anxious to make an agreeable impression upon them, and he accordingly related a stirring ex-perience of Western life that had come under his notice in "Californy," in which one man had "stabbed another to his vittals." Pap meant vitals, but was taken at his word, and it was made clear to him that his companions only listened under protest, were not minded to go through the farce of pretending to believe him, and considered that he was showing an offensive familiarity with social conditions that never had and never could come in the way of respectable, home-staying Virgin-ians. The matrons meanwhile were ranged opposite and discoursed of the proper way to "set milk," the dyeing of yarns, and making of quilts, the difficulties of rearing children, of managing perversely-pipped chickens, and of other domestic matters. They also gossiped a bit of the high contracting parties to the wedding, Jonah and R. Mintah, and of what folks said and what was "true" and what "warn't so at all." The

maids, arrayed in the cheap glories of gay calicoes and
muslins only, had yet contrived, with feminine art, to
look as pretty and attractive as some of their more
fashionable sisters, and discussed with equal interest
the fashions,—the best way to " loop a polonay" and do
the hair. Near them, of course, grouped around the
door, where instant flight was possible at any moment,
were the sturdy, bronzed young farmers, in their Sunday worst, and a state of unconquerable, dreadful embarrassment. They were profoundly conscious of their
abnormal splendor, and felt all elbows and knees, turned
crimson when hailed by some audacious "piece" of a
girl, and had a general uneasy sense that they looked
like fools, were being ridiculed in precisely the quarter
where they most wished to be admired, and were only
safe as long as they took the national motto, *"E pluribus
unum,"* for their own. A. Mander and Marsh Culbert
sat apart from everybody, holding each other's hands in
the most obviously and obtrusively sentimental fashion,
and chewing sweet gum as well as the cud of delightful
anticipation. A dank and grewsome female, panoplied
in shining black calico, and wearing a black sun-bonnet
which she resolutely refused to remove, had come early
and settled herself in the chimney corner like a huge
black spider. Once established there, she leaned forward, crossed her long black arms on a lank black lap,
gave the company transient glimpses of a cadaverous
countenance and glittering eye, and conversed in a
deeply-melancholy and carefully-subdued voice of funerals, of "a noble-lookin' corpse," and "beautiful
buryin's" to her next neighbor. She had got as far as
the gallows, in a description of the execution of a noted

murderer which she had attended with evident enjoyment, when the door opened and the bridal party entered.

IX.

"Then was our maid a wife, and hung
Upon a joyful bridegroom's bosom."
UHLAND.

THE dank and grewsome was a person of importance on the Mountain. She was a "measurer," and perhaps was as justly entitled to be lugubrious in bearing and apparel as undertakers are elsewhere. Not that her function was that ghastly one. It was a mysterious and solemn one enough, but it was connected with the living, not the dead. If any child had what was known variously as the "ondergrowth" or the "take-off,"— was puny and sickly, that is, and appeared to waste away,—the very first thing that an anxious mother did when her fears were aroused was to send for Mrs. Uriah Hopper; such was the title of the D. and G. And Mrs. Hopper would come (a black-calico priestess of Mountain mysteries), and would be welcomed with the respect due her office, and be propitiated and consulted with as much touching deference and simple faith as though she had been a Delphic instead of a nineteenth-century oracle. After due consultation and deliberation, she would take the ailing child into a dark room, strip it, measure it from the crown of its head down to the tip of its big toe, rub it off with oil, wrap it in a blanket, and put it to bed. She would then take a string, tie a knot in it for every month of the child's life, and show it to the mother. She then tied the string to the gate-post, making a peculiar knot of her own. If the string wore away, the child recovered and throve proportionately. If the string did not wear out, the child was measured again, and this time the string was burnt. If that did no good, and the child died, it was clear that not even Mrs. Hopper could save it. There was not a mother on the Mountain who did not defer to Mrs. Hopper as she would not have done to any one else in the world, and they talked of her with bated breath of how she had "learnt how to measure from her aunt who knowed;" of the children she had snatched from death when they were almost at their last gasp; and of the cases in which "they was too strong for her." But though they bowed the knee in the house of Rimmon, they did not serve a tyrannous mistress. Mrs. Hopper was a benevolent edition of Witch Parsons, and was not feared. And she exacted no payments for her services, though she was pleased to accept such voluntary offerings as came to her.

This being her position, it was natural that she should have sat alone and apart from the others even on this purely festive occasion. A priestess cannot be genial and make herself agreeable when it is her mission to be awful. The dank and grewsome was not there for laughter and small talk. When the great moment came, she fixed her glittering eye upon the principal offenders in the bridal procession, uncrossed her long arms, rose to her feet, whipped out a black calico handkerchief, and swayed backward and forward all during the ceremony, uttering from time to time subdued groans of sympathy and interest in the awful act.

A wild clatter of children's feet had heralded the approach of the party, and the twins, who brought up the rear, rushed promptly to the front and secured a position favorable to unlimited goggling,—one of them, indeed, being on Jonah's very feet, which were almost big enough to have accommodated both. The sight of Mrs. Newman in a bright green dress with a well-defined waist, and an overskirt and *flounces*,—Mrs. Newman, who had never been seen in anything except drab calicoes of no fit at all, and about as much cut as her own stocking-bag,—was almost as impressive as that of Mr. Newman in a new butternut suit of his wife's making, and the most fashionable accessories, such as a paper collar and a cravat. The appearance of the Newman children—whole, clean, quiet, the boys with suits that were pocket-editions of their father's, the girls flounced, aproned, be-curled as " no Newmans" had ever been before—could not but strike the company as a miraculous achievement without a parallel, until their attention was drawn to " Darthuly Meely," whose hair was exquisitely arranged in seven distinct tiers of the tightest, reddest curls that ever depended from a single scalp, or repaid the torture of a week's papillotes by the glory of one moment's dazzling display; whose blue gown was carefully cut to betray a bony neck of a porcelain hue (such as city milk is apt to take on) finished off with a string of Roman pearls.

But all these paled before the splendor and glory of the bride and bridegroom. Jonah had apparently varnished his head as well as his shoes. His honest face

not only shone from recent and vigorous applications of
yellow soap and a crash towel, but radiated sheepish
delight and self-consciousness from every pore. He wore
a new black suit of funereal hue, with delicate sugges-
tions of a more festive occasion in the white cotton
gloves, the yellow cotton cravat with a ruby pin thrust
in it, the red handkerchief stuck in the most *dégagé* way
in the world in the breast-pocket. His large red ears
stood out above a high collar such as Bones, the min-
strel, witches the world with, as if determined to hear
for themselves what was going on. His shoes creaked
out a warning to him to pause ere it was too late, and
reflect that he was about to take a step that could not
be retraced, and might be "putting his foot into it."
A perfect cloud of mingled musk, bergamot, pepper-
mint, rose before, about, behind him. He was magnificent, irresistible!

Little R. Mintah in her stiff skirts might almost have
been taken for a reticule hanging on his arm at the
first glance, so inconspicuous was she comparatively in
the matter of inches, though with her pretty, delicate
features, and air of refinement, she was much more like
a lovely wild-flower about to be nipped off by an over-
grown calf. She wore her red dress (the dress that had
been given her for the picnic) to please Jonah. She
had made certain modifications and alterations in it to
please herself. This lily of the field had toiled, if not
spun, in order to do this. She had made thirty-six pairs
of gloves the week before, and forty-six the week before
that, for the Winston factories, and had walked twenty-
four miles to deliver them. With the money she had
bought—tell it not to Worth, or Pingat, or Miss Flora

McFlimsey—some yards of white mosquito netting, and being a clever little womankin with her needle, she had evolved a toilette that was as becoming as though it had been composed of satin and Brussels lace. The netting boiled up frothily about the bottom of the skirt in an indescribable way, and was fastened around the neck and sleeves and fell all about her as a wedding-veil, and made a charming background for her small, dark head and sweet pale face, with the rapt eyes,—the large, tender eyes that had first attracted the royal notice of the heir of the house of Newman.

Jonah on entering had ducked his head at the company in his embarrassment with a circular motion intended to convey a general salutation,—a greeting to which no one responded except old Daddy Culbert, who belonged in his degree to "the period of manners," and bowed low in his chair in return, saying, "How are you, sir, and your lady? How do you find yourself?" but was immediately hushed up and corrected by his grandson. Seeing this, Jonah fell back upon his collar and ruby pin, which he "settled" repeatedly, his face growing redder each time as he heard Darthuly Meely and the other maids tittering behind him. R. Mintah just clasped her hands over Jonah's arm, and cast down her sweet eyes and thought of no one about her, so full was her heart of an unspeakable joy and rapture with which none could intermeddle; and so they stood and waited. The couple had not been long in the middle of the room, although, petrified as they were with fright, it doubtless seemed an age, when the outer door opened and "the preacher" walked in, and after depositing his hat on a chair, placed himself in front of them, and without any affectations or delays made them man and wife. This done, the Rev. John Mathers delivered a homely, earnest address that was full of good sense and good feeling, and that lasted about ten minutes, and the deed was done. He then retired into the background, where room was respectfully made for him, and where Mr. Newman joined him. " We're obleeged to you, sir. Mightily obleeged, all of us," he said. "I hope it's done been done all right,—*accordin' to law*. You don't think it can be broke up, nor split up, nor set aside, nor nisi-priused, nor habeas-corpused, nor no sich, now, do you? I've had a deal to do with cotes, and I know ef a thing ain't *accordin' to law* it 'll just pester the life out of a person. No offence to you, sir." Mr. Newman was not unwilling to let it be seen that he knew the legal bearings of things, and was not the man to walk into the snares and pitfalls that were set for more ignorant folk.

" They're married as hard and sure and fast as any couple ever was in the State of Virginia, sir," affirmed Mr. Mathers, not without heat, to which Mr. Newman replied carelessly as he tugged at the hair in the centre of his favorite mole:

." Well, I didn't know, you see. I thought maybe they *might* git mandamused, or mittimused, or quo warranted, without all was done *accordin' to law;* fur that law's a one fur gittin' folks down and werryin' of 'em to rags, and givin' of 'em wuss and wuss agin every time they opes their lips to complain, ef I knows anything about it. En I made up my mind long ago that I'd sooner fight a cirkiler saw, and that ef I or mine fooled with it we might look to end on the gallows, ef we hadn't done no more 'n kill a cat. I knows the law. And I didn't want them two that don't know it like me—and there's few that does, or has had reason to—to git into no trouble. No offence to you, sir, at all."

R. Mintah, meanwhile, was receiving the congratulations of her friends, after a tremendous amount of "saluting the bride" had been done, in which Jonah led the way with a resounding kiss that went off like a pocket-pistol, and brought a rush of color to R. Mintah's cheeks and caused her to stoop forward in confusion, the better to wipe her lips with a handkerchief which was sewed to her side to prevent its being lost,— a very grand *hemstitched* handkerchief given her to use on the great occasion by Jinny White. The compliments and good wishes of the friends who now pressed forward were expressed in very different ways. With the dank and grewsome they took the shape of a polite assurance that she "hadn't never see two that bore up better in the hour of trial;" with Jinny White some praise of the wedding-dress "as mighty tasty," and a plaintive appeal to R. Mintah to take care of it, as she "might come to need it to be buried in." With Alfred it was: "Well, R. Mintah, you two's done hitched up together. You can't help nothin' now. Weddin's like dyin': you feels that all's too late. You can't help nothin'. And folks doin' it ev'y day with no more notion of it.—Oh, hit's turrible! Jes' turrible! Turrible!" Here Matilda gave him a scowl and a nudge that he was far from expecting, he being under the impression that she was in the next room. She also called him an "ijit," and he hastily added, with a complete change of tone, " But *you'll* like it, in course, R. Mintah; in course! Certainly! Hit's fine!" With this he swelled out his cheeks to their utmost capacity, smote upon them with more than ordinary force, and fell into an uncommonly prolonged and acute attack of chuckles, in which he laughed and gasped and gurgled all at once in a really alarming way, suggestive of hysteria, and almost calling for burnt feathers, or sal volatile. An angry " Be quiet. Quit your foolishness, simpleton," from Matilda, failed to take effect for some time, and so far from growing quiet he wandered about the house for the remainder of the evening, and even drifted outside, and sat aimlessly on the fence for quite an hour, not twenty yards away from the spot where the Newman turkeys were roosting,—happy birds!—with no thought of the hot water, roastings, bastings, in store for *them.*

Pap had been sitting silent and mortified ever since his rebuff from the elders, who had let him severely alone, except when they looked at him over or under their horn spectacles with a glance indifferent, vacant, cold, or a " What kind of a sort of a fellow *is* this we've got here?" of puzzled inquiry from some " furriner," who lived some miles away, and only half divined that he was " no 'count" and had best be left to his own company and devices. He felt shy about going up to R. Mintah. To cross the room and set himself up to be stared at, as it were, seemed impossible. Such bold proceedings were not for Pariahs, he felt; so he sat still, with Willy leaning against him and trying already to wink the sleep out of his round eyes, and with other companions, in the shape of his own thoughts, that he would have gladly shaken off, they were so bad. Only yesterday, as it seemed, he had been a bridegroom, too, and had stood in just such an assembly, feeling immortal in youth and love and joy. And he remembered another bride, the best and fairest among women. "Then" and "now," the twin vultures, were tearing at his heart,—that bright "then" when he had been so rich that all the tribute and treasures of the world could have added nothing to his wealth; this dark "now" of bankruptcy in which there were none so poor as to do him reverence, and in which only one thing— the little child that his arm encircled—stood between him and the utter darkness and despair of unloved, unhonored old age. His eyes, in roaming around the room, fell upon his violin, wrapped in the dead wife's shawl. The poor, faded, threadbare thing was as familiar to him as any sight in the world; but he got a heartstab from it now, it was eloquent of so much besides his lost happiness. He withdrew his arm hastily from about Willy, and, leaning forward, rested his head on his hands with his fingers shielding his eyes.

"Old Johnny's gittin' tired. Look yonder at him a-noddin' and ready to fall off the bench. Ha! ha! He's had enough of this," said one of the youthful rustics to Darthuly Meely, who "He! he! he'd" with a sympathetic snigger over the amusing spectacle.

"He's done bin to town to-day, maybe," remarked rustic the second, not to be outdone in wit. "'Tain't the first time he's crookt his elbow sence daybreak. That's why he's so peart and lively to-night. I reckon he'll roll plum' off on the floor in a minnit."

R. Mintah noticed him, too, and came tripping towards him, saying, "Pa-ap! Pa-ap! Ain't you got no words fur me? Ain't you goin' to shake hands and wish me joyful?"

Pap started up and looked bewildered. "R. Mintah, my dear! Is that you? God bless you!" he said, brokenly, and then released her hand suddenly, seized his crutch, and made his way rapidly out of a side-door into the darkness. He was still sitting on the door-step when one of the rustic youths already mentioned came in search of him, saying, "They're minded to have a merry-bout in there, and is askin' fur the fiddler. That's you, ain't it?"

"No, it ain't," said Pap. "I can't play to-night. I ain't a-goin' to play." He was very sorehearted, and the manner of the request had not been soothing. R. Mintah came running to him, though, the next minute, saying, "What's this? What's this 'bout you not playin' fur my weddin'? Oh, Pa-ap! You ain't never meant it. Jonah's and me's weddin'! Hit's never ain't possible! Why, it's you that has brought us to this. Ef you hadn't of holpen me and talked to him like you did we wouldn't have had no weddin', and I'd have gone single to my grave. Not play? And him sech a beau-tiful dancer! And me ready to jump over the house! And you playin' so eligunt! Come 'long in this minnit, which you've always been a good friend to me,—always."

Of course Pap relented. There never was a creature more susceptible to kindness; and for affection, or affec-tion's sake, what would he not have done or been? "Well, R. Mintah, to pleasure you, I can't say you nay, seein' it's your weddin'-night,—me that have knowed you sence you warn't as big as my Willy."

As he entered with her, a general murmur of satis-faction filled the room, entirely selfish in its origin, but helping to put the old man in tune. "Now we'll git somethin' that's wuth the listenin'," said old Jacob Potter to his neighbor, Tim White. "I always did like a tune, and Johnny Shore kin play the fiddle first-rate. Hit's about the only thing he's good fur."

"I never cared fur no noises myself," said Tim, and ran his hand through his hair several times, as he had a way of doing.

"Well, tunes is like roads; when I kin git a tune of the right sort that I kin git a holt on, and travel straight on with slow and sure without its forkin' off every minnit a fresh way, and yet that's got pretty turnin's onst in a while to it, I will say it's pleasant,—that's to say, when you know the turnin's and are fixed fur to take 'em right," said Mr. Potter, as if apologizing for a weakness.

"I like the jews-harp, myself, 'bout as well as anything," said Jim Wilkins's father. "My son usened to hit a sight of lively jigs out of his'n, poor fellow!"

"Old Hunderd is what *I* call a tune," said Daddy Culbert. "There's a heap in Old Hunderd, and there ain't no hurry 'bout it. You kin hold on to it as long as you like, and you always knows whur you've done got to, and what's comin' next. My father could er been heard a mile, I do reckon, when he put hisself on it. But save me from them slippery, skippery things that folks calls tunes nowadays, that's in one ear and out the other befo' you knows what's the matter, and has runned off and is 'way yonder out of sight before you've well got the taste of the cheese in your mouth, —maggoty things, always on the move."

"Yes, sir; you're right there. I says so, too," agreed Mr. Wilkins, gravely, and Mr. Potter nodded sagely.

" And as for me, I likes ' Hail Columbia,' when pinted out, better 'n any of 'em. There's a power of music in ' Hail Columbia.' I can't rightly say as I knows it from other tunes,—there's such a many of 'm I can't be wer-rited with 'em,—but *when pinted out* I always says, ' There's a power of music in that there hime,' " said another of the group, the grandfather of innumerable Browns.

" It takes a deal of hearkenin'," said Mr. Wilkins, looking towards Pap, who was screwing up his pegs very carefully and tum-tumming at the strings to see that they were in proper accord. " I wouldn't of thought it."

" Oh, yes. Hit ain't so easy, fiddlin'. Hit beats most. There's worse done," remarked Mr. Potter.

Pap heard this, and brightened under it, and felt himself included with music and all musicians in a kind of general amnesty.

" Why, yes, there is," admitted Mr. Peters, senior. " I don't kyur ef a fiddle's 'round myself at Christmas and ingatherin's and weddin's and sich. There ain't no great harm as I kin see in fiddles, 'ceptin fur fiddlers, who are mostly no 'count. And there's no-'counts that ain't fiddlers." Such a concession was a thing that could never have been expected from Mr. Peters, who was granitic in formation and of the Silurian period in point of prejudices. Pap heard and smiled, and tucked his beloved violin under his chin where he stood, and gave a long scrape from tip to end of bow and looked about him with positive assurance.

" Run, git me a stool, Willy boy, to rest Jim Wilkins on," he said, to his little shadow ; and, going across the room, he turned an empty water-bucket upside-down in the low window-seat, and having enthroned himself, with Willy's help, gave a second scrape of his bow to say that he was ready. Willy hopped off with his crutch, and it was lucky that both were got out of the way in time, for the effect of Pap's signal was almost electrical, and in a moment the bashful youths, who had been clinging together all evening so desperately, parted company by one impulse, and, as bold as lions, advanced, seized a maiden apiece by her elbow or hand, and marched with her into the middle of the room. Gone was all stiffness and embarrassment from that moment. A babel of talk burst forth. Podge Brown, who had been the envy of his own sex and the delight, apparently, of the opposite one, was suddenly completely eclipsed and altogether deserted. Podge could not dance.

Not being afflicted with the faintest trace of shyness, he had been talking to the girls all evening and making himself irresistible in his own fascinating way, showing his easy feeling about society and familiarity with its usages in a variety of ways. He had begun by seating himself on the same bench with the maidens,—between A. Mander and Darthuly Meely indeed,—and had brilliantly excused the boldness of the intrusion by saying that "merlasses must look to catch flies." He had continued to get off a great number of equally original and lively sallies, to the great amusement and satisfaction of his audience, and the disgust of his companions near the door. He went so far as to make a mock declaration of affection, which he called "a pop," to two young ladies seated some distance below him. He ended by tickling them all, which threw them into the greatest possible state of arch confusion, and produced such protestations, affectations, profuse giggles, and threats that, naturally, he was driven in self-defence to make fresh demonstrations, whereupon all the timid darlings took refuge in each other's laps, where they embraced and kissed each other most fondly, and quite by accident looked over at the now furious masculine majority who suffered and were strong. But with the very first bars of "Zip Coon" the conquering Brown found himself no better off than Napoleon at Elba, and in a flash about twenty couples were hard at it, jigging, and hopping, and spinning, and twirling, and not caring a pin what became of him. Away they went, in pairs, and faced each other, and set to, and capered, and bounded, swung half around a circle, fell to their "steps," swung back into place again, seized each other around the waist and spun madly around for a moment, faced each other again, set to, and so on *da capo* with fresh energy and other "steps" until not a breath was left in a single body. Such coquetting and pirouetting, such bright eyes and flushed cheeks, such freedom of movement and native grace among the girls! Such swing and fling, such rampings and stampings, such shouts of delight from the men! Such perfect, unrestrained enjoyment for all! "Zip Coon" melted into "Miss McLeod," "Miss McLeod" was merged in "Money Musk," "Money Musk" slipped into "Gray Eagle," "Gray Eagle" ran into "Yellow Stockings," "Yellow Stockings" was skilfully pinned without a break to "Fisher's Hornpipe."

On they all went, Pap playing with a fire and enthu-

s

siasm that worked the dancers up to the highest pitch
of excitement, playing as if there wasn't a heartache in
the world and never had been, his eyes half shut, a
smile on his face, beating time regularly with his left
foot, the dancers dancing to match with all their might
and main, and heart and soul, and with every muscle
of their bodies. The old floor sent up clouds of dust.
The walls trembled and swayed. The windows rattled.
The candle-sticks clattered. The broom fell in a fright
against the disguised flour-barrel. The twins shrieked
for joy, and danced, too, about the door after their
own fashion. The elders leaned eagerly forward, and
beamed, and oscillated on their seats, and nodded to
the music, and exclaimed, and patted the floor with
their sticks. And still the reels and reelers went thundering on. Pap grew paler and paler, the dancers were
all aflame, but still there was no pause nor break. And
now came a loud roar and a mighty tramp. It was a
mercy that the shell of a tenement did not collapse like
a card-house as all the couples bounded off in the
" grand cirkit" all around the room, doing the long
glide and hop of " the Irish trot," which, being well
named for wildness and fury, would have been trying
to the constitution of the most substantial structure.
Utterly exhausted when this highly characteristic outburst of Milesian mirth was over, the dancers fell into
the first seats they could find. The first frenzy of movement was over, and Pap could and did stop, too, and
proceeded to mop his face with his handkerchief, which
he then rolled into a tight ball and returned to his
pocket. Nobody thanked him, nobody joined him, except Willy, whom he sent off again to bring him " a

gode of water," but nevertheless he felt that he had his reward. "The folks is had a good fling, ain't they, honey?" he said to the child when he returned. "It was as much as I could do to keep Jim Wilkins here from jinin' in. He pooty nigh stepped off when it come to 'Yellow Stockings,' he did. It was always a favoright of his'n. Many's the time I've played it fur him when my fingers was so stiff with the cold I couldn't hardly hold my bow. Poor Jim! I wish he'd of been here to-night. He would of enjoyed hisself, and pleasured others too. He was a one fur weddin's. He was always jokin' about sich things. I remember him sayin' when he come back from bein' took prisoner that when he seed the street-cars in Baltimore,—sorter carts they is, honey, thut runs constant on rails to carry folks about their business,—he said they remembered him of the married state. All the folks that was in was always wantin' to git out; and all the folks that was out 'peared like *they* couldn't be satisfied without they got in. He was that way. He was a joker; but he looked behind things, too, so to speak." Some little time passed before any more dancing was done, and then a sensation was created by Jonah's challenging Alf Peters to "a break-down." Jonah was considered by many people the "handsomest dancer on the Mountain." Alf Peters had won "the endurance prize" for break-downs the week before at the fair. Great interest was naturally felt in such a contest. Both men began by removing their coats, and after a few preliminary stamps and steps each threw back his head, shoulders, and arms, and settled to his shuffling and double-shuffling with a will, "the folks" gathering about them in a circle, Tim

White "patting Juber," Pap fiddling for his life, and R.
Mintah shrieking out in her feminine treble squeak,
"Don't you stop, Jonah! Go on! Don't git beat, Jonah!
That's you!" the opposition petticoated element encouraging Alf in much the same fashion. A more exciting struggle for supremacy was never seen on the
Mountain, and how R. Mintah's eyes did shine with
gratified pride when Alf Peters, pumped into an exhausted air-receiver, suddenly stopped, sank on the
floor, and thereby confessed himself vanquished. "He's
give in! I *knowed* it would be so! Stop, Jonah," she
cried. But Jonah went on for some moments to show
that he could do so, not that there was the least danger
of any dispute or altercation, everybody having seen
for some moments that Alf had lost his steadiness and
was reeling as a top does before it comes to a stand-still.
When Alf rose and sulkily resumed his linen "duster,"
with ill-concealed disgust, Jonah cocked his hat very
much on the back of his head, stuck his thumbs in his
suspenders, and made the tour of the room with R.
Mintah hanging on his arm and looking up to him with
fondest admiration. He then lit a five-cent cigar, and,
in the fulness of his satisfaction, he actually went up
to his late deadly enemy, young Culbert, and offered
him one, adding a hearty clap on his back that was
almost enough to produce a hemorrhage, on the spot.
"Ain't you 'most dead, my dear?" asked R. Mintah of
her giant, anxiously.

"*No*," he replied, with great scorn. "I ain't teched.
Git out there and show me what you kin do."

Out they got on the floor. Jonah stuck his arms
akimbo. Pap, who had exhausted his repertoire, went

back to "Zip Coon." R. Mintah caught up her skirts, turned out her elbows squarely, stuck her pretty head roguishly on one side. Jonah, with a wild "Whoop-ee!" jumped fully two feet into the air, clapped his heels swiftly three times together before he alighted, whirled to the right, whirled to the left, advanced, retreated, gyrated.

R. Mintah teetered forward prettily on her toes, flew right, flew left, with a little fluttering motion like that of a butterfly with wings outspread, retreated when he advanced, advanced when he retreated, glanced archly now over the right shoulder, now over the left, her cheeks like damask roses, her eyes like stars.

Jonah darted towards her with his arms extended; R. Mintah slipped under them and floated away. Jonah danced all around her; R. Mintah kept well out of his reach. Jonah pretended that he was exhausted, and let his steps die away to a faint shuffle, intended to convey the impression that he was quite spent; R. Mintah relaxed her vigilance. Jonah immediately darted forward again, and this time seized the little wife around the waist, and, lifting her up in his strong arms, deposited her bodily on the mantel-shelf, and left her there,—a sweet novelty in chimney ornaments. The shouts of the delighted audience had not died away, when Mr. Newman appeared at the door, very tall and straight, very solemn and formal. "Suppur-r, ladies and gentlemen !" he said in loud, mechanical voice, with a whirr in it as of a clock running down. "Suppur-r-r ! And please to form yourselves in couples of two and walk out."

This was a welcome sound to Pap, whose head had

24

dropped lower and lower over his violin, and who had been playing for some time with intermittent vigor. And to the elders, all of whom were drooping, too, and some of them dozing. And to Podge Brown, who had been threatening to go home for hours, but somehow had not gone. And to Matilda, who had sat bolt upright all the evening, looking almost as sour and odious as she was. And to Willy, who had rolled off and under a bench, and was "sound," as Pap remarked when he waked him. And to Stone and Pete, who had not been able to close an eye for thinking of it. And to the dank and grewsome, who rose with alacrity to respond to the summons, but, with all the others, was stopped by Mr. Newman, who gave out: "The bride and the bridegroom will form theirselves as the fust pair of two, and lead forth before all, which will follow on." This plan of Mr. Newman's for ensuring due and proper precedence necessitated R. Mintah's being taken down from her exalted position, and Jonah effected this in a twinkling, whereupon R. Mintah, by dint of standing on tiptoe, managed to administer a mock-violent box on his ear. Peace being restored between them, both suddenly became very dignified and grave. R. Mintah put on her white cotton gloves, which she had taken off. Jonah did the same, and pulled up his collar, moreover, and held his head as high as he could get it. R. Mintah took his arm, and, having "formed theirselves," they waited a moment for the other "couples of two" to do the same, and then marched out of the room, solemnly, with measured steps, at the slowest possible rate of speed consistent with moving at all, to "Bonaparte crossing the Rhine," from Pap. To have laughed or talked during this progress would have been a gross indecorum. But when they had arrived at the supper table and taken their places, when Mr. Mathers had asked a blessin' at great length, and been blessed for not making it shorter, and when Mr. Newman had called out warningly, "Ladies to get their fill *fust*, gentlemen, and don't you disremember it. *Guzzlers* to wait *till the last.* Begin to commence to wait on your ladies, gentlemen, and don't spare the vittles pervided and made and set out before you for the same,"—then, I say, there was noise enough. A vague reminiscence of various legal documents had been floating through Mr. Newman's mind all evening, and an anxiety that everything should be done according to the law written in his own mind for such occasions. And Mother Newman, who had been beaming promiscuously and most contentedly upon everybody all evening, felt that she had never seen him appear to such advantage, and rejoiced to see him "actin' the double father" to perfection. A bountiful supper, that, and certainly a merry company. Podge Brown was again in a position to show the superiority of head over heels, and became every moment more fatally fascinating. Before Mr. Mathers had well got out his "Amen," he was sportively pouring coffee in the custard, and daubing the poundcake with mustard, by way of showing the tricksy quality of his wit, and from this he went on to other delightful and genial antics that completely enslaved all the young ladies about him, whom he tickled impartially and persistently, causing them to "think they'd die," and to assure him that they "would split their sides," to say nothing of spilling their coffee, dropping their plates, and choking over and over again. But although thus devoted to the sex at large, Mr. Brown was a man, and an unmarried one, and so it came about that he gradually and very artfully narrowed the circle of his charming attentions until Darthuly Meely was the object of most of them, and before the banquet was consumed he had contrived to give her the most signal marks of his preference, such as pulling down her hair, breaking most of her pearls, and repeatedly pulling her chair from under her. Something, however, must be allowed for the expansion of stocks and stones even under certain favorable conditions, and Mr. Brown was but mortal man, Darthuly Meely the dynamic force surging within him and seeking expression in playful fancies. Even Timothy White made three remarks in the course of that supper, and looked almost animated when fruit-cake was handed. And Jinny's tongue wagged freely in spite of such apparently insuperable obstacles to conversation as biscuits, and apples, and cakes, and pickles, of which her mouth was full. "You did jerk the liveliest to-night," she said to Pap. "When I knowed you was dead and in your grave, I usened to tell Alfred often that fur fiddlin' his Pa-ap beat all. And so you do, John, no matter who's the next one, fur it's jes' *livin'* music ef ever I heerd any, and you with *a leg* buried, anyways, to my certain knowing. Hit's jes' a wonderment how you kin."

One lady present certainly got what Mr. Newman wished all to have, and that was the dank and grewsome, who, considering that the meats were not cold baked, nor served on or out of a coffin, contrived to dispose of enough and to spare. She was still sitting over in a corner with a plate in her lank lap heaped high with a miscellaneous collection of eatables, with which she was apparently making close connection as far as could be seen (which was not far, the black sunbonnet being cast down within an inch of the same, and mysterious sounds of chumping, and cracking, and gulping, and gurgling going on under its immediate protection as behind a screen), when the company trooped back to the living-room, leaving Simon Peter and Stonewall Jackson still skirmishing in the rear,—perhaps to cover their retreat and bring off the D. and G.

The evening was now over, as soon appeared. Mothers began to think of their babies and of their bread. Fathers "reckoned it was 'bout time to be gittin'." Grandfathers yawned dolorously, and were no longer to be kept up even by their sticks. Seeing this, Mr. Newman made his last official declaration: "Them that goes with the bride to her home-bringin' will git ready to start right away, and ef they've got any saddlin' and bridlin' to do they'd better be mighty quick about it, as aforesaid." A general commotion of preparation now ensued. Children were sought for, shawls and bonnets resumed, farewells made, and the heads of families, the elders, and the little ones made their way outside, unhitched their " teams," clambered into their carts, and then waited, as etiquette demanded, for the departure of the bride and groom. Out came R. Mintah the next moment, followed by Jonah, and all cloaked and hooded. The night was black and starless, and it had been difficult to distinguish anything or anybody, but now fully fifty pine-knots were lit in rapid succession, and flamed and smoked in the fresh breeze that blew from the direction of the Ridge. And now R. Mintah was swept up on a white pony, with a beautiful flowing tail and mane, by Jonah. And now Jonah mounted a big bony chestnut, and laid his hand on his wife's bridle-rein. And now the young men and maidens mounted their respective steeds, and fell into line behind the first pair who were to be like another first pair, of whom it is said that "Adam delved and Eve span." And now Stone and Pete rush out and whisk up behind two of the cavaliers, and cling there like a couple of limpets. And now R. Mintah cries out, "Good-by! Good-by!" over and over again. "Good-night, Pa-ap. Good-by, dear Mother Newman. Good-by, Father Newman. Come over soon. Good-by all." And Jonah gives two short "good-nights," too, and the procession starts. The gleam of R. Mintah's red dress and hood is seen for some time, and then is to be seen no longer. The carts and wagons all go creaking, rattling away. The procession turns into the Red Lane now, and the young men and maidens burst into a song full of joy and triumph. Mother Newman turns away in tears. The dank and grewsome flits out into the darkness like Poe's raven. Matilda stalks off towards home in a temper because Alfred has lingered so long. Little Willy is fretting, too, and appears to be trying to gouge out one of his blue eyes with his fist. The procession is winding around the Mountain now, and they can see the torches still flaming, still smoking, still borne aloft. And now they have suddenly disappeared. Father Newman goes in and shuts the door. Jonah and R Mintah are married. Pap, Alfred, and the child stumble home in silence,—the old leaning, moss-roofed home, with the tottering porch and the wavy chimney, into which a bride as young and fair as R. Mintah walked so long, long ago. As they enter the gates, the clouds part a little and show a brilliant stretch of stars. And Pap looking up at them thinks of one who has passed beyond them.

X.

" How long be crying, ' Mercy on them, God !'
  Why, who art thou to teach, and He to learn ?"

OMAR KHAYAM.

" And a Voice spoke : ' Come unto judgment,
  Ye who called Allah too merciful.' "

EDWIN ARNOLD.

THE wedding seemed to have had an unsettling effect upon Pap, whose condition, morally and mentally, was always one of fluidity, and who consequently was subject to high tides and low tides and a thousand changes of feeling and purpose that more solid and stolid folk escape altogether. He said, when Willy asked, "What ails you, Pa-ap? Yer don't want to play nor to go nowhurs, nor to do nothin'," that he was " downhearted," and that was it. R. Mintah had been happily settled for a week in the cottage that Jonah had built for her on the other side of the Mountain, and was almost as much in love with her new cooking-stove as with her husband, and had received and entertained every friend she had with the most effusive hospitality, yet Pap had not kept his promise to stop by and see how she was "gittin' on." "It don't matter; she'll not miss me," he thought. "I reckon I'd of been in the way ef I had of went. I mostly am, anyway. Hit's a big world, but I 'pears to take up too much room in it. I have saw that mighty clear fur a long while, and maybe 'twas so before I seed it. Ef it wasn't fur Willy——" It was not until he had been hard at work for ten days, and had got a third supply of "kindlin'" ready for market,—a much larger, richer store of fagots, sure to bring a good deal more than he had ever got,—that his spirits began to revive at all. "Hit's every red cent of it goin' into the bank fur you, Willy boy," he said to his little confidant; "but don't you let on I've got it, fur she'll take it away. I'm going to put it whur nobody can't get it, so they tells me ; not even me, fur it's goin' in as William Elbert's, don't you see ? That's you, honey. Ain't that a smart way to fix it ? I'm goin' to walk right in, and I'm goin' to say to the man in the coop that they've got there, 'Here, mister, here's five dollars. Hit's a big sum of money, and it's been sawnt here fur you to keep by Mr. William Elbert, that's a friend of mine' (that's you, Willy boy), 'and nobody ain't to have the handlin' of it but him.' I won't hitch my horse till that's fixed right and I've got shut of it. I won't look beyant my nose. And I'm goin' to git the money all in a chunk. I ain't goin' to take no dimes,— dimes is bad, Willy. Don't you never keep 'em about your clothes. They—gits lost."

"That money you had was all dimes, wasn't it, Pa-ap, last time ?"

"Well, yes ; it got *turned* to dimes. And it got—lost —in a manner of speakin'."

" You was mighty sorry, wasn't you, Pa-ap?"

" Yes, indeed, *I was*, honey. And this here ain't agoin' into no dimes. I'll give the whole chunk to him, and he won't lose none of it. He's usened to takin' care of jes' heaps and cords of money. Why, I shouldn't wonder ef he had a dollar fur every day in the year behind them bars! Yes, money and time's things you kin keep in a chunk; but ef you once split 'em up they're gone. I wish I had some more of both. I'd do a good part by you, my son. But I reckon you'll do as good as most. And when you git big and is growed a man, and has got a fine business, me and you is goin' to live along together all pleasant, and pleasure around mightily, ain't we? Me, and you, and Bunny, and Jim Wilkins, and Corporal Brass, and Sergeant Iron? What a heap of us! Hit's lucky some of us don't take much room: there wouldn't be no place to hold us. Lord! I wish it was now."

" I'm goin' to have a farm, and cows, and horses, and dogs, and sheep, and all kinds of stock, and a bunch of shoats, and Rowan ducks, and turkeys, and chickens, and a red waggin, and a cart, and a buggy, and pea-cocks,—I forgot peacocks,—and a orchard, and a garden, and all the rabbits and pigeons I kin ketch and raise, and a snake in a bottle, and a rattin' purp, and a saddle like Alfred's got, and a pair of boots that comes way up, and——" Willy had not nearly finished his inventory, but was interrupted,—

" You ain't said nothin' 'bout me. Ain't I goin' to be there?"

" I'm *comin'* to you," said Willy.

"Oh! you was, was you?"

"When I'm done growed up like you, Pa-ap——"
He was interrupted again.

"You ain't to go and grow up like me, honey. Like
me! Don't you never talk that way agin, my son. It's
hurtful to hear you. No indeed. There can't no two
grow up the same way. And you ain't *no kin* to me,
my darlin'! You'll grow up mighty defferent to me,—to
all,—and be better, and more respecteder, and richer,
and luckier, and every way less misfortunate than some,
—Billy Jones, that there Billy Jones that's knowed as
Crazy Billy, I'm thinkin' of."

"But I *will* be like you," said Willy, who was not
used to contradiction from Pap, and indeed was very
much spoiled by him.

"You shan't! Ef you say it agin I'll whop yer!
And ef you was to do it you'd kill me,—that's what.
Do you want to go and kill your poor old Pa-ap?
Say? And you can't, neither. Folks is like eggs. The
hatchin's one in a dozen, and the raisin' counts fur
another, but the egg is all the rest. You ain't my sort
of egg, and you ain't 'bleeged nor obligated to be no sech
bird. I'm a black old crow, honey, but hit's a rejoice-
ment to me to think as you are a little white pigeon
that can't never be a crow. No, you ain't to be like
your Pa-ap, nor to want to be, fur I'm one of them that
was spoilt in the makin' or the bakin', and I tells you
so before you find it out, so you can't never go and say
as Pa-ap set hisself up before you to be patterned after.
You'll be tole by some as Pa-ap's a bad man, honey.
Well, we won't talk 'bout that. But I've been good to
you, ain't I? You won't never go from me, Willy?

You love your old Pa-ap, don't you? Pa-ap would give his life fur you; and not be givin' much, neither."

"Yes, I does," affirmed Willy, who had been standing in one of his graceful attitudes with his legs crossed and his hands rammed deep in his trousers pockets.

"Come here, my darlin' little boy!" exclaimed Pap, and Willy complying he pressed him against his side and stroked his soft cheek for some moments in silence. "Do you love Pa-ap or boots the best? Hainh?"

"I loves *you* the *best*," said Willy, after a severe mental conflict, "but I jes' *hanker* after them boots. Jonah's comes up to his knee-jints and he kin go through snow up to his waist in em, and ketch horses, or kill pigs or anything."

"Oh, and that's what *you* want with 'em. Ha! ha! ha! Oh, you are a man, you are,—Pa-ap's own little man! Bless yer! I'd jes' love to give you them boots, honey, shore. I'm well acquainted with a man in Winston that's got 'em to sell: the prettiest, all fixed off with red 'round the tops. I could jes' see your little legs workin' in 'em and you hobbin' about in 'em as big as the next one. But I reckon we'll have to wait fur 'em; times is got so bad fur Pa-ap. I ain't got nothin' I could sell. There used to be a right smart chance of stock 'bout the place when I was a child; but my father—— That's a good whip of your'n yet, Willy, or will be when it gits a new handle and another cracker. Some folks would steal the money; but it would be a big sin fur a little gain, and I ain't never teched nothin' all my life long that was belongin' to no person. And I wouldn't fur the world. I'd starve first. I ain't the man to do sech a low thing. No, indeed."

Pap's visit to the bank was delayed for ten days after this. The more he thought of the red-topped boots and of what Willy's joy would be in possessing them, the more he felt that he must make or find a way to get them. So he increased his store of wood, counted his bundles, reckoned up what he would have, shook his head, and was for the moment baffled. Next day he sold his one gray hen, and a lame duck to Darthuly Meely, who was "fixin' to git married," and meant to feather the nest of the future with some poultry of "her own bringin' and raisin'." Then he counted again, and again shook his head. "The weather's warm; I don't want no coat. That'll be it!" he argued, and sold the coat, counted again very carefully on his fingers, and smiled, this time, and thought, "I'll go to-morrow. Won't my boy go plum' crazy 'most when he sees 'em."

He rose at daylight next morning, accordingly, and going out to the hillside pasture, brought in the family horse, who was nosing about among the stones there looking for something to eat. The result was so disheartening that he would, as a colt, have made no resistance to having the bridle slipped over his head, and, as it was, actually came slowly to meet Pap, and wearily regarded him as if he had hoped for something in that quarter, too, and had been disappointed.

"Po' old fellow!" said Pa-ap. "I hain't got a bite fur you,—not a bite. This here's a hard world me and you's got into, Billy, ain't it now?" and so took him by the forelock and led him in. Billy's whole appearance was a confirmation of this fact, and nothing that he could have said, if he had been endowed, like Balaam's ass, with the gift of speech, could have been as mournfully eloquent. No horse, except a towel-horse, was ever more angular about the hips and well defined about the ribs. He had only one eye. He was string-halted. He was broken-winded. His back had not been entirely well for ten years, and it is doubtful whether he had ever had enough to eat in his whole miserable life. His coat had once been black,—a thousand years before, in that dim period in which he had gone frisking about a world of green grass that he believed would develop into abundant pastures, but which never did yield more than the scantiest nibblings; in which he had laughed at the stones on the hillside, not knowing how they were destined to break his teeth; and had galloped about with the most foolish notions in the world of what it was to be a civilized horse, tossing his mane in the faces of those who would have enlightened him. It was now whitey-brown, like a certain kind of wrapping-paper, and wrinkled about him as if it were paper, badly put on.

Such as he was, he was invaluable to the Shores, and Pap had nothing but praise for him, as he invested him with a set of harness which was certainly more original than ornamental, composed, as it was, of rope, odd bits of leather, a shuck-collar, and grape-vine traces.

"Good Billy! Good old fellow! Cheer up now. It ain't fur to whur you're goin'. No. Me and you's goin' on a good errand this day, if you did but know it, —to put money by fur little Willy to git edgercated and take a front place with. Not like you and me, Billy. Back, sir!"

Thus accoutred, Billy was attached to an extremely

primitive vehicle, with scarcely any iron about it,—a sort of elongated hen-coop swung on poles, having wheels of the most solid description, sawed out of the section of a tree, and a tar-bucket ˙pendent in the rear. Having inspected the harmonious whole, and spent a good deal of time in tying up, strengthening, splicing the dubious places in the gear, Pap shut his knife and put it with the ball of twine back in his pocket, and leading Billy on a bit, hitched him to the fence to wait until breakfast should be over.

" Is that you, Pa-ap? Is you done hitched up? Can't I go, too? Let me go, too, won't you? Say?" exclaimed Willy, running out to join him.

" No, honey. I can't take you this time. I can't, indeed. Alfred and me's goin' two together *pertikeler.* But when I comes home you jes' look back there by that there tar-bucket and see what you'll see! That's all. Come 'long in to breakfast." When Pap came out again, he had his own quota of bread intact in his hand and proceeded to feed old Billy with it, who turned his head mournfully towards him when hailed with " Here you are! You poor old critter, you! Put this down. Maybe it'll help you a leetle, lackin' the right fillin," and feebly disposed of it, with a kind of low-spirited satisfaction that was suggestive of a long course of depressingly inadequate " feeds," tempered by unsubstantial windfalls like the present one. He then looked around again at Pap with the peculiar roll of the eyes so expressive of a lingering faith triumphing over much painful experience, and Pap, answering it, said, " No more, Billy. Not a crumb. You don't want to *bust,* do yer?" and climbed up into the hen-coop to wait there

for Alfred. At this moment Mr. Carver came riding up
on a stout cob, looking as solemn and severe as when
he had ridden away, and roared out Alfred's name at
the top of his voice. Alfred came out hurriedly, and
Mr. Carver entered upon a matter of business,—something relating to a cow he had bought of him, which
had developed a post-sale tendency to hollow horn.
After some talk between them, meekly apologetic on
Alfred's part, deeply disapproving, not to say surly,
on Mr. Carver's, the former concluded that it would be
necessary for him to go and have a look at the interesting invalid. So he got out a large leathern bag that
would have held the small change of the Rothschilds
and gave it to his father, saying in an impressive whisper
to his father, "'Twas fur this I was goin' to town.
Matildy's savin's fur pooty nigh two years. *Twenty-five
dollars!* That's money, now, hain't it? I 'lowed to
put it in bank myself, and it's what I ought to do, I
do reckon. But this here cow, now; throwed back on
my hands,—couldn't *you* do it? Jes' hand it in, and
bring back the showin' fur it they'll give yer. Kain't
you, now?"

"Why, certainly, and surely, my son," said Pap.

"Hit's *money.* Don't you forgit that you've got a big
pile, and——" Alfred stopped. "Go do nothin' with it,"
was what he thought, but he substituted "disremember
to take it; and git the showin', mind! I do reckon
I oughter to go. But Mr. Carver says she's shakin'
her head backards and furrards constant and——"

"What are you fearin'?" asked Pap, testily. "I ain't
never stole nothin' as you knows on, nothin' of your'n,
is I?"

"No. No. Well, go 'long. But bar in mind hit's *money*,
Pa-ap," said Alfred ; and his father shook the rope reins,
and old Billy made an effort, and the hen-coop went winding on its creaky way down the lane. It did not get
very far, though, for, as invariably happened when Pap
started to town, somebody came running out of every
other cottage with "arrants" (errands) for him to do,
and he had, of course, to stop and get his instructions.
Grandma Williams sent out in hot haste to beg that he
would take her "eye specs" in and have them mended.
"Both par's broke and she can't do nothin'," said her
messenger. Mrs. Williams's spectacles were as well
known on the Mountain as Mrs. Crœsus's diamonds in
New York, and the fact of her having two pair represented as much opulence. Then there were Mrs. Newman's turkeys to leave at "a sto'." And Jinny Hodges
wanted a spool of cotton "bad." And Mrs. Landon
had some butter "waitin' a week to be kerried." And
Mrs. Culbert couldn't "git along another minnit 'thout
some terbacker." Altogether, by the time the Red
Lane had been traversed, old Billy was quite worn out
with the strain of so many false starts, and the hen-
coop was full of baskets and bundles, piled high above
the wood, and Pap's mind burdened with a dozen com-
missions, although he had cheerfully agreed to everything proposed. Once on the turnpike, however, he
laid aside all care, and, with cheerful cries to his equine
Cyclops, set himself to enjoy the drive. His bosom's
lord sat lightly on his throne. He turned more than
once to look at the little load of kindling behind him,
as if to assure himself that it was there. He had already in his own mind deposited the money he was to

get for it, and laid the foundation-stone of Willy's future fortune. He was at peace with himself and all the world. The day, too, was very beautiful, and Pap, ever susceptible to such influences, enjoyed that, too,—enjoyed the autumnal glory of the woods, the greening wheat-fields, the fir plantations; noted the hawk's reposeful movement overhead, the intense blue of the sky, cloudless, except where a long chain of cloud-Alps stretched behind the actual mountains more than halfway around the horizon. "This here's *a country*," he thought, meaning that at its worst the Valley is so rich in color and gracious of curve, so full of noble effects of outline and delicately-beautiful silhouettes in foliage (as of gigantic bits of seaweed set against its clear skies), that the ugly skeleton of a world revealed farther north by falling leaves, and the desolate swamps that show such gloomy depths and wastes farther South, were by comparison odious. His thoughts were as bright as the crowds of yellow butterflies that started up all along the road as old Billy jogged past them. Ah, yes! He would work and save more money for Willy. Willy should be "high-learnt" and "notable" and "go ahead." Willy should be "a man to brag on;" and he shouldn't have to be ashamed of his Pap, either. All that was behind him,—put away for good and all. The warmth of the sun was not more grateful on his coatless back than these genial and inspiring beliefs. Willy was "gittin' a leetle too high some ways, and would have to be brung down," if he could bring himself to discipline him, but what after all were such childish faults? What a dear little fellow he was! How he would delight in "them boots!" He turned now into the Winston road.

The Mountain was now on his right, and the particular
deity whom the Indians believed to inhabit it seemed a
friendly and benignant spirit, with a care for poor old
men and helpless children, as he glanced back at its
blue bulk of familiar outline. It was still " twelve mile"
to Winston. Old Billy walked for the most part, and
seemed to be doing a great deal in doing that, as Pap
noticed, and so forbore to urge him to greater speed.
The sun waxed extraordinarily hot with the heat of a
last day of summer. The dust made Pap nearly as
white as a miller, and old Billy several shades more forlorn than ever, although that had seemed impossible.
The drive had grown monotonous, as the freshness of
the morning had worn away, and Pap looked behind
him with interest when he heard the rattling of wheels.
A wagon was close upon him. He recognized the driver,
but pretended that he had not seen him, and looked
straight ahead for some moments. The wagon gained
upon him, and finally came alongside. " Howdy,
Johnny! Howdy. Goin' to town ?" said a voice that
Pap knew. Pap affected not to hear. " Goin' to taown,
ain't yer ?" reiterated the man, and now Pap was obliged
to reply. " 'Twould 'pear so, Lem'l," he said, shortly,—
very shortly for him.

" So am I," said the man.

" I don't reckon,—I ain't got no notion as we'er goin'
the same way," said Pap, very decidedly, with a feeling
of strong irritation. Why had Lem'l Harding come to
blot all the fair prospect when he was feeling good, and
doing good, and had cast in his lot with the faithful and
peaceable in Israel? It cast a shadow over him merely
to look at his companion ; and impatient to be rid of

him, he whipped up old Billy into the mournful sem-
blance of a trot, and left him behind, hearing, "Hum!
What's the matter with *you*, Johnny? You ain't always
so high and fur off," as he moved away.

Lem'l Harding was a man of evil reputation on the
Mountain. He was known to be "a horse-trader," and
suspected of being a horse-thief. He was accounted so
hard and shrewd in his bargains that it was said of him
that "the devil buttered couldn't slip through Lem'l's
fingers." He was known to be so unscrupulous that it
was constantly supposed that he would be "jailed."
Yet, somehow, he contrived to keep on the right side of
the prison-doors, and gained a half-respectful consideration, even, by his clever avoidance of all the punishments due his dubious dealings. A tremendous poli-
tician was Lem'l. His vote was always to be had for
the bidding, and he would have helped to put Beelzebub
in office for a consideration, but none the less he prated
eloquently of all the issues at stake in every election in
a tone of the most lofty public morality and private de-
votion to all noble ends, and would stop for three hours
on the high road to "argy the rights of it" (with the
price of his own wrong-doing in his pocket), *en route* to
the polls, dazing, confusing, and quite overwhelming
some muddle-minded mountaineer of limited views and
incorruptible character, whose whole political creed was
embraced in "old Virginia forever," and a fond belief
that taxes would be "took off" by the right party if the
right party could ever get in. When Mr. Lem'l Harding was not pulling at a long weedy beard and discussing some vexed political problem, he was talking about
the war; and although he was known to have "hid out"

in the mountains all during that struggle he was so eloquent in his description of the battles in which he had *not* been engaged (when no old soldiers were around) that he passed for a veteran often with a younger generation, and represented himself as having distinguished himself on a thousand fields, and saved the day over and over again, with such a wealth of inaccurate accuracies as to time, place, weather, contending forces, commanders, strategic movements, and results that he sometimes deceived even the elect. But John Shore was not one of those who thought him as terrible in war as in peace, and whenever a Shenandoah scout was in the audience it was observed that Lem'l was straightway transformed from a lion to a lamb, and though he could no more have got up a blush than his wife's brass "perservin'-kittle," he had the grace in such companies to eliminate himself from his reminiscences of the war, and content himself with pointing out Lee's mistake in not "marchin' spang on Washington," and proving that Grant could have taken Richmond any day he wanted it.

Pap had no sort of respect or liking for him, "knew him fur a skulker," believed that he "beat his wife, as folks said,—'twas like the coward,"—vowed that he was "the meanest white man in the whole country-side." But the fellow's glib tongue and a certain surface good-fellowship had made it difficult to decline the pleasure of his acquaintance altogether; and the acquaintance once made, Lem'l had found it easy to enforce rather than cement it, for they had this much in common,— the same vice,—and while there was the width of the world between the weakness of one and the wickedness

of the other, and though Pap sober would have preferred any companionship to that of "Shifty Lem'l," as
Mr. Harding was called on the Mountain, there had
been other times in which a community of evil-doing
had established a relation that Pap at once hated and
submitted to. Mr. Harding was not easily rebuffed, as
may readily be imagined, and in a little while his wagon
was on a level with Pap's again, and he had reopened
the conversation.

"That's a fine big load of your'n," he said. "You'll
have money to spend."

"Not a dime," said Pap. "This here is to be put by
fur Willy in bank to git edgercated with."

"Oh, pshur! that won't go fur," observed Mr. Harding. "You might's well spend it,—withouten you've
got mo' 'n that."

"That's as I think, I reckon," said Pap, and turned
away his head.

Nothing more was said for a while, and then Mr.
Harding began again,—

"Got in your fodder yit? We all's had our'n in a
week, and better you never seed."

"I don't have nothin' to do with farmin'," said Pap,
and tried to get old Billy into another trot, seeing which
Mr. Harding jerked up his team and fell in behind, saying, "Yer mighty onsociable to-day. You must er put
your clothes on wrong side out when you dressed yerself, ain't yer? I've *knowed* you more speakable before
now," with much significance.

On they went for a mile and more, and then came
upon Darthuly Meely, who had started to town at daylight, and was walking along with her shoes in her hand

and a basket on her arm. She hailed them and asked Pap for a lift, which, after a moment's reflection, he granted. With much mincing coquetry of mien she came up over the side of the hen-coop and seated herself among the bundles, saying, "I ain't never been seed with *my* foot to the ground befo' in all my born days. But my! but these shoes pinch. They oughtn't to hurt. I give a dollar fur 'em. But hit's jes' seemed like I couldn't take another step in 'em. And there warn't no use in wearin out the *stockin's* jes' so fur foolishness. I didn't 'low to meet nobody. My! I certainly am 'shamed befo' your face. I'm goin' to put 'em right straight on this minnit." Darthuly Meely had her little affectations like some other maidens, and fluttered about considerably before she got settled to her satisfaction. Pap only smiled and said, "Pshur! whur's the shame?" Shoes were not made for "folks" to walk in for miles and miles, but were an ornamental finish to such expeditions, it was thought, on the Mountain. And stockings were will-o'-the-wisps to be longed for, and seen afar in shop-windows, very occasionally secured, and still more rarely worn. Darthuly Meely's had red stripes and she was very vain of them, and cast many a glance at the only persons who were near enough to be dazzled by her splendor as she invested herself with the order of the garter and its accessories. Mr. Harding took advantage of this much encouragement to draw near again. Old Billy had looked around with a plaintive "Oh, Lord, how long!" glance when he became aware that his burden had been increased by a hundred and thirty pounds of rustic loveliness, and had then struggled nobly on. It was not difficult for

Mr. Harding with his four horses to keep pace with him. A lively conversation began between Darthuly Meely and himself. Pap not wishing to join in it kept silent. Then, noticing after a bit what a pull poor old Billy was having of it, he got out, and taking his crutch walked for two miles beside his four-footed friend, not sorry to have the hen-coop between himself and Mr. Harding's restless black eyes. Mr. Harding hailed him, and offered him a seat in his wagon, which he declined. Darthuly Meely waxed arch, and declared that she was "loadin' that waggin' up fur a bad breakdown," and started to get out. Mr. Harding, to her great surprise, of course, offered her a seat, which she accepted. Darthuly Meely would have flirted with Mephisto, and Mr. Harding was the only available substitute for the Prince of Darkness at hand. Pap begged her to stay where she was, but she insisted that it would be "onmerciful, and onmerciful was a thing she wasn't and wouldn't be." So Pap got back into his place, and on they went again. "He's keepin' hisself to hisself, and is mighty fur and cogitive," said Mr. Harding, *sotto voce*, "but I've *knowed him* sociable. Oh, yes, I've knowed him sociable."

It became more difficult every moment for a man of Pap's kindly nature to reject the conversational advances of Mr. Lem'l Harding. "Let's halt a bit. That critter of your'n, Johnny, is blowed,—regular blowed." Pap did not wish to stop, but it was evident that old Billy did, so they halted awhile. It was now impossible for Pap to "keep hisself to hisself" any longer, and what he would have called "a stiff conversement" followed. "Johnny, he's goin' to *bank*;

he's proud," said Mr. Harding. " I shouldn't wonder
ef he'd got fifty cents to lay by."

" I've got thirty dollars, or will have when my wood's
sold," said Pap, quickly, not insensible to the sneer,
and then added, " but hit's all Matilda's 'most. She's a
savin' woman."

A glint of light sprang into Mr. Harding's black eyes.
He gave Pap a long, attentive glance. " That poor
critter of your'n needs a feed. Look at him. Got any
corn to feed to him ?" he said.

Pap looked at old Billy, whose uncertain forelegs
were a good deal hooped, and whose long neck was
stretched up the bank in search of a tuft of anything
that a miserable horse could eat. " No. I'm mighty
sorry. But I hain't got nothin' fur him," confessed
Pap.

Down got Mr. Harding, or, rather, off, from the stout
horse he was riding postilion-fashion and into his
wagon, where he sought and found a bag of corn. This
he brought forth, and, scattering about half a bushel
down before old Billy's incredulous eyes, said, " Thar,
let him take all he wants."

Pap was astonished. Lem'l was not supposed to be
of the prodigal sort, except in the first person singular.
Pap was softened, more so than by any favor that
could have been shown himself. " Thanky," he said.
" Thanky kindly, Lem'l," and loosed old Billy's bit and
bridle that he might thoroughly enjoy the treat, saying, " Now, Billy, boy, do you jes' *stuff*. It's what I'd
give you every day ef I had my way or my own.
Don't you let up on it till yer can't swaller." Billy did
not need this injunction, it is certain. Stuff he did,

swelling visibly before their eyes, snuffing greedily at every ear, as it rolled here and there, in an agony lest it should get away from him before he could make all this bliss his own, and leave him a prey to the bitterest memories of what might have been.

His face was softened and mild when he again looked at Pap and asked him to let his girth out two holes, which was done, Pap saying, "You feel like a egg, don't yer, Billy?" and patting his neck as he slipped back the bridle, "I wish I was a critter. I wish that much corn 'd fill me, leastways, not bein' a critter," he thought, and the satisfaction he had in mind was not a gastronomic one.

By the time Winston was reached, Mr. Harding had contrived to get on reasonably good terms with Pap. Darthuly Meely alighted on the edge of town, thinking that she avoided thereby being taken for a country-girl, and took her way down one of the side-streets, where, to her great mortification, she was stopped not five minutes later by a lady who wished to know whether that was butter in her basket and what she asked for it.

"This here is your way cf you're goin' to any bank," said Mr. Harding to Pap. Pap made no answer.

"I said this here was your way," repeated Mr. Harding.

"Yes. I heerd you," said Pap.

"I'm goin' 'round that way," said Mr. Harding.

"*I'm* goin' this here road," replied Pap, and was about to turn off in the opposite direction, when Mr. Harding said, "That road don't lead nowhur. This here is your road, Johnny."

"I reckon I kin diges' my mind 'thout you chewin' it

fust to make it easy fur me, Lem'l. G'long, Billy," said Pap, dryly, and off he went, leaving Mr. Harding checkmated for the time being.

It was about this hour that Matilda, going out into the Red Lane, found an old gypsy seated near her gate on the remains of a wooden rocking-chair, with a heap of bundles tumbled down at her feet. She was the most ghastly old hag that one could see in a lifetime. She would have been burnt for a witch on sight anywhere in England or America a hundred years ago. The witch of Endor could never have been more wrinkled, yellow, toothless, forbidding, nor the Fates or Furies more haglike and full of sinister suggestion. She looked a thousand years old, and as though she had spent every day of the time in purgatory. Her dress was torn open in front, that she might breathe more freely. Her one wisp of gray hair fell over her shoulders from beneath what had once been a hat. Her poor old feet were bare and covered with dust. Altogether she was such a terrible incarnation of the misery and poverty that exists in the world, that one would have supposed that the veriest Pharisee, seeing her, would smite upon his breast, and cry, "God forgive me my share of the sufferings of my fellow-creatures," and long to tear off his costly robes and broad phylacteries, "go, sell all." She had been sitting there for some time weeping in the mechanical fashion of the very old, crooning and complaining to herself: "Oh, here we are! But we'll not be let to stay. They drive us off everywhere,— everywhere. They tell us to git out of the road, even, and won't let us cook the little we've got by the roadside, 'cause it frightens the horses, they say. Oh, they don't know what we suffer! They don't know what we suffer! Some few of 'em's kind; not many. They're mostly hard and mean and wicked. And they call themselves Christians. Oh, they don't know what we suffer! Them that would help us can't. Them that can't, won't. That's the way of it. On the tramp since the 1st of March, and my feet all cut up with the stones. I want a house and a bed and some butter. I don't have anything I can eat. I ain't tasted butter I don't know the day when. I can't eat everything. My teeth's all gone. Oh, ef I had a bed to lie down on!"

Matilda caught part of this lament as she advanced, but was not in the least touched by it. The old womam went over it all again, poor soul! as if it were out of the bitterness of her soul that her mouth spake, adding that her son had gone to get some wood and water to make a fire and cook what they had, if they were not "driv off." But driven off they were. Matilda hated gypsies, and was merciless. When the son came up she abused the pair roundly as tramps, and vagabonds, and worse, and obliged them to move on. The man grew impudent in return, but gathered together his bundles and prepared to obey. The old woman's skinny claws tightened upon her shawl, and if she had been terrible before, she was more so now, as, trembling with passion, she rose and, coming close to Matilda, glared upon her in ghastly hideousness. "Curse you! Curse you! Curse you for a flint!" she shrieked out. "You drive me away,—an old woman, past seventy, that's dropped down at your gate. *Your* turn 'll come. *I can wait.* You are born, but you are not dead yet. Curse you for a *Christian!*" The hate, the fury, the scorn of her glance and voice, was enough to appall the stoutest heart, and as she hobbled away a chill ran through Matilda's veins.

She was not a good woman, but she was a superstitious one, and there was horror for her in the prophecy and menace of the gypsy. She would have run after her and tried to soothe and propitiate her by offering her food, fire, all that she lacked. But she felt that it was too late. The two figures were still in sight,—the son bent double almost by his burdens, the mother by heavier ones,—her years and sorrows,—weeping again, and again crooning out, " It's always the same. They drive us away. They won't let us stay nowhere." But Matilda was right: it was too late. She went into the house and sank on a chair, her thoughts full of what had happened. She was still sitting there, all alone, when she suddenly felt as though an unseen hand had clutched her heart and released it only to drive a knife into it. In short, she had a violent spasm of the heart, the result of an organic defect that she knew nothing of, and of the excitement she had undergone. Willy found her there an hour later when he came in, and was as much surprised as she had been when she called him to her and said, in a voice that he had never heard before, " Willy, you don't hate me, do you? I ain't been kind to you, but I will. Don't bear no grudge agin me, will you?" Matilda a saint would be. She had got an awful fright, and was as eager as any Hindoo to propitiate Shiva, the destroyer.

Since the days of the grand old prophet who cried, " I, the Lord God of recompenses, will surely requite, saith the Lord," no human voice had ever carried greater

panic into a human breast than the gypsy's had done
into hers. And the incident, irrelevant as it seems, had
a direct and important bearing on the events of the
day. The sky was overcast now, and the chill and
darkness consequent upon the sun's withdrawal still
further affected Matilda's mind. As soon as she could
do so, she lit a fire in the stove. She put a chair near
it for Willy. She got him first a large slice of bread
covered with preserves (opening a bottle that she kept
for the greatest occasions), and then one of cake. She
promised him fifty cents. She told him she would get
him a pony. That she would send him to school. That
his father had been her favorite cousin. That he should
benefit by her savings. She called him "dear" and
"darling Willy." She made him sit on her lap, though
he did not covet the honor. It was no wonder that
Willy stared and stared, and stared again, and could
scarcely believe that it was Matilda. He sat on the
edge of his chair at first. He was afraid to swing his
feet. He was scared when he let some crumbs drop on
the floor. But the new Matilda swept them up without a word,—indeed, actually with pleasure, it seemed.
She got more and more friendly, indulgent, confidential.
She told him that his Pap was a good-for-nothing, and
a vagabond who was "po' and wuthless," and could
never do anything for him. She vowed that she would
do everything, and more too. It was a most curious
spectacle to see them together,—Matilda insistently,
persistently benevolent, Willy half flattered, half frightened, wholly amazed. As the supreme authority of the
house, he had always respected her with the respect
that all children have for authority, and to see the

u   26*

sceptre laid at his feet, and this pride abased before him, made him in the course of an hour fully aware of the change in his position. He presumed upon it, even, but was not checked or restrained, much less scolded.

Meanwhile, Pap had sold all his kindling for more than he had ever got before, and had all his money in "the chunk,"—not as large a pyramid as those put up to show the yield of gold in California for a year, but as imposing and dazzling to his mind. He stopped at the store where the red-topped boots were hung out, and bought them with greedy haste, snatching them down from the nail before the clerk could serve him, paying for them with pride, and suspending them carefully back of the tar-bucket. He then started down a side-street that intersected the main one *en route* to the bank. He had gone about a square, when he heard himself loudly hailed. "Johnny! Johnny Shore. Here!" He pulled up, and saw Mr. Newman beckoning to him from a blacksmith's shop. "Come here! Come here a minnit," said Mr. Newman.

"What's it? I kaint," replied Pap.

"Jest a minnit," said Mr. Newman, imperatively. "I'm buyin' a critter off Lem'l, here, and we ain't agreed. You was in the cavalry; you ought to know a critter, and what it's wuth."

Pap was mortal, and what merely mortal man could resist such an appeal?

"Well, I oughter," he said, and smiled and complied, dismounting, and leading old Billy to a rack in an open space back of the court-house, where he hitched him, and where Billy instantly drooped, wilted, collapsed all over, as only the poor horse of a poor farmer can.

When he joined Mr. Newman with a "Well!" he found him as exercised about the "pints" of this case as he had ever been over those of his memorable lawsuits. He said that he and Lem'l had had a defference of opinion 'bout that critter, and Lem'l had said, "There's Johnny Shore. He was in the cavalry. Jest you ask him." It was some time before the matter was settled. It was settled in Mr. Newman's favor in accordance with Pap's decision. Mr. Newman was triumphant. Pap was naturally pleased. Lem'l seemed low-spirited and defeated.

"You've got the better of me; but to show I don't set it agin you, why, I'll treat all 'round; leastways, I don't want it said as I'm leadin' Johnny off. Here's the money. *You* treat," said Mr. Harding to Mr. Newman, aside, putting a dollar in his hand.

Mr. Newman instantly agreed. "All right! Come along. We'll take a drink on this," he said. And Pap went. Just one, and with Mr. Newman, not with Lem'l, was his reckoning.

That afternoon a great storm fell upon the Valley and swept summer away with it on the wings of the wind full a thousand miles. The reverberations of the "live thunder" among the mountains as it "leapt from crag to crag" were magnificent and prolonged. The lightning bayoneted the blackness above them, pulsed all through the heavens, lit up all the wide, wet plain with its dread flashes. And as for rain, it was as if Lake Superior had been poured through a sieve down upon the earth.

Along the road that had once been a trail—a road no longer gleaming white with dust and dazzling in the sunshine, but beaten into a gray, glistening rivulet—came a very different Pap from the one who had passed over it so blithely in the morning,—a wild, wretched-looking creature drenched to the skin, chilled to the soul, mud-splashed, most miserable. About an hour before he had waked as in another world to a confused sense of many things having happened as in a dream. Where was he, and what had happened, he wondered? He soon found out that he was in the vacant square in which he had left his wagon, which was not ten feet away. The storm, and what he was doing exposed to it, had next to be accounted for. The next thought was of Willy's boots. He hurried to the back of the wagon, and there they were, just where he had put them. Still much dazed, he started to unhitch the horse, when suddenly he thought of Matilda's money, and felt with agonized haste for the bag containing it. It was gone! Frantic, he climbed into the wagon to look for it. It was not there. More frantic still, he got out and looked all about him. It was not to be found. Sobered by the shock, but half maddened by it, he rushed down to the main street as fast as his crutch could take him, and ran in a frenzied way up and down the street, and in and out of the stores, raving excitedly of his loss and meeting only with repulse and contempt. At last, in utter despair, he gave up the search, made up his mind to go home, returned to the square, took another look there, the rain beating upon him all the while, and finally, cursing his folly, got into the wagon. It was poor, patient old Billy who started off, of his own accord, and took the right road at the right turning. Pap was the merest automaton of a driver. It is doubtful whether in the deep distress and agitation of his mind, the acute torment inflicted by his thoughts, he was conscious of the fact that another storm was raging about him, though his nervous terrors may have been insensibly increased by it. He could scarcely see where he was going for some miles, the rain continuing to pelt down with scarcely abated violence. But he knew that he would be *there* very soon, only too soon, and would have to face Matilda.· Twenty-five dollars! Oh, it was monstrous, hideous! A fine lady gives that much for a vinaigrette, a bonbonnière, a thousand trifles. But on the Mountain it was equivalent to twenty-five hundred, and with Matilda to twenty-five thousand. It was no wonder that his soul sickened within him when he thought of it.

The rain ceased. The Mountain came in view looking like a huge whale disporting itself in a sea of mist. The wretched man's teeth chattered and his knees trembled in a nervous chill of apprehension when he saw it. It was not the Mountain, it was Matilda, and he saw his own figure projected like a Brocken spectre against the white clouds that still hung about it. When he got home, he hitched his horse near the gate, walked up the path, waited at the door fully ten minutes, and then opened it in sheer desperation. Matilda was not there, but Alfred was, and to Alfred he blurted out the terrible truth. Alfred was profoundly moved. He raced up and down the room with his hands in his pockets as white as the wall for a moment. And then he swore freely, but he was not brutally furious. Matilda came in, and at sight of her Pap's heart stood still. He stood before her in abject woe, pale, trembling, his head bowed with unutterable grief and shame. He could not utter

a word.   It was Alfred at last who said, pleadingly,
" 'Tildy, don't take it hard. Don't now. He's lost all
your money." Matilda's was not a white or speechless
wrath.   It was a blue fury.   She was terrible as she
stood there and poured out upon Pap every drop of all
the vials of wrath stored up in her coarse and cruel
nature.   He dropped into a chair and covered his face.
When she accused him of having stolen the money, he
looked up and cried, " That's a misthought.   I didn't
tech it, not a cent of it."   When she continued to rail,
he called, " Oh, don't.   Don't, Matilda.   Don't be so
wreakful.   I'll work forever but I'll make it up to
you."
    This roused all her scorn.   " *You* make it up.   How ?"
she began, and railed worse than ever.   " I'll do anything.   I'll sell my fiddle !" moaned Pap.   The mention
of this instrument seemed to put Matilda utterly beside
herself.   She swept like a whirlwind into the shed-room,
dragged it out from under his bed, brought it in, dashed
its brains out, as it were, against the door-post, and
threw what remained, with the little shawl that had so
long been wrapped tenderly about it, into the fire.   Pap
started up, but only looked on spell-bound.   Alfred cried
out, " 'Tildy !   'Tildy !"   Willy, who had witnessed the
whole scene, burst out crying in his fright.   Her rage
not yet sated, she seized Pap by the arms and pushed
him out of the door and down the steps, shrieking, " Git
out of my house, you drunken old thief!   Never set foot
in it again,—never !"   She banged to the door.   Alfred
and she had some high words, but Pap heard nothing.
He was stunned, for he had fallen headlong.   It was
some little time before he at all recovered his senses,

and he was passing his hand across his forehead in a dazed way when Alfred came to the door with his crutch in his hand. Not waiting to hear a word, he seized it and rushed away, leaving his son standing there gazing blankly after him.

It was about half an hour after this that Pap slunk into the shed-room. Willy was there, down on the floor with his back to the door and his playthings scattered around him. He was so intently engaged that he did not hear Pap enter. Pap looked down at the dear, familiar little back and the curly head. His expression changed, and grew more natural. " Willy! Willy, my darlin'!" he said, and dropped on the floor near him. He was about to gather him in a passionate embrace, and had his arms about him, when he discovered that Willy was shaving himself with Alfred's razor. "My darlin'!" he cried, in horror, and, seizing it, wrenched it from his grasp.

Willy's whole heart was set on shaving himself "like Alfred," and it angered him to see the razor for which he had so vainly longed, and had just secured, spirited away from him by force. He turned upon Pap, gave him a rough little push, and said, angrily, " Go 'way. You're a drunken old thief!" The child was only repeating with unconscious cruelty what he had just heard, but in Pap's morbid state of diseased suscepti- bility no allowance was made for this.

There was the weight of the world in that little hand,—a black, loveless, pitiless, unbearable world it seemed to the old man. His little " Willy boy," whom he had so loved, more than his own soul,—his child, his darling, for whom he had sold the coat off his back,

for whom he would have laid down his life, and a
thousand happier ones,—to call him *that!* He gave the
child a look,—a strange look, Willy thought it. He rose
slowly from the floor, took his crutch again, opened the
door, and went out. It was no longer raining. The sun
was setting behind the distant mountains on his right.
Above them stretched a sea of golden calm framed in
black clouds that parted farther on showing a strip of
exquisitely translucent blue, and a smaller space flecked
with the green the sea shows above coral reefs. On his
left, Massanutton's spur stood out in high relief, darkly,
brightly blue, against a rosy background. Except for
these, there was no color to be seen. The whole heavens
were hung in black, tinged in the east with amethyst
by the dying lord of day. All the landscape was sombre
and sodden. The surf-wind of the mountains had
sprung up and was breaking and roaring on its distant
shore, and sweeping moaningly over the plain below, as
Pap skirted the side of the hill and disappeared in the
hollow on the other side. There was a large, turbid
pool at the bottom of it, encircled by unsightly ghosts
of dead grasses and weeds at this season, but with one
lovely late-blooming bush of wild aster flowering whitely
near the brink. When Pap saw it, he stooped and picked
a bit, looked at it for a moment, threw it away, looked all
about him. His eyes rested on the strip of blue, and
Willy's speech about his dead wife came back to him.
"Ay, *she's* there!" he thought.

*   *   *   *   *   *   *   *   *

A little later some tattered, frightened clouds that
had overhung the pool hurried away to the north.
The evening star sprang laughing out into the blue.

In the cottage, Jinny White, who had dropped in, was trying to light the lamp.

"Why, what's the matter with it?" she said, after the fourth failure. "Hit's got water in it. That's a sign,—a sign of a drowndin'."

When she finally succeeded in her self-imposed task, she set the lamp in the window, through which its long yellow rays shone friendly and far,—the window of the house in which John Shore had lived, loved, suffered.

But a life, like the light of the world, had sunk in night.

THE END.